MIRROR, MIRROR

I stiffened as I saw a figure appear behind me. It materialized out of thin air, and its arrival was so abrupt it took me an instant to realize what it had to be. I whirled around, needing to face it rather than have it at my back, but that did no good at all. I couldn't use my magic to defend myself— and the thing laughed when it saw I had remembered that.

Suddenly it began to walk toward me, shuffling along the bare wooden floor on bare white feet. I yanked the candle from its holder, took aim and threw hard. The candle flew straight for the thing's face, smacked into it . . . and kept on going. It sank into the face. And when it was gone it left behind nothing but a dirty smirk and a laugh . . .

Other Avon Books by
Sharon Green

Dawn Song
Silver Princess, Golden Knight

THE HIDDEN REALMS

SHARON GREEN

AVON BOOKS • NEW YORK

THE HIDDEN REALMS is an original publication of Avon Books. This work has never before appeared in book form. This work is a novel. Any similarity to actual persons or events is purely coincidental.

AVON BOOKS
A division of
The Hearst Corporation
1350 Avenue of the Americas
New York, New York 10019

Copyright © 1993 by Sharon Green
Cover illustration by Daniel Horne
Published by arrangement with the author
Library of Congress Catalog Card Number: 93-90227
ISBN: 0-380-76626-4

First AvoNova Printing: September 1993

AVONOVA TRADEMARK REG. U.S. PAT. OFF. AND IN OTHER COUNTRIES, MARCA REGISTRADA, HECHO EN U.S.A.

Printed in the U.S.A.

RA   10 9 8 7 6 5 4 3 2 1

For Ricia Mainhardt
More than an agent; a damn good friend

CHAPTER ONE

It wasn't my fault. I'll be the first to admit it usually *is* my fault, but not that time. It was a simple accident, and Master Haddil shouldn't have—But maybe I ought to start from the beginning.

At first it was a perfectly ordinary day. I'd dressed to go riding right after breakfast, but the heavy gray clouds that had been threatening since the day before finally let loose. It wasn't exactly rain that came down, not with the air as cold as it was. Half sleet and half snow, likely to become all one or the other before very long, and nothing any sane person would deliberately go out in. I'd stared at it through the diamond-paned window of my kitchen, not very pleased.

And then I'd gotten curious. Water fell from the skies in different forms, but it was still water. We drank it, bathed in it, washed things with it, cooked with it—but how much experimentation had been done? If memory served there wasn't very much, and what better day to correct that? There were all sorts of things to try with water, so I headed for my workshop to get started.

All right, so I *didn't* change out of the heavy riding clothes and boots. I tend to keep my house on that world on the cool side; when I'm in the mood for cold weather, I want to know it's there. Staying in those clothes shouldn't have made any difference . . .

Well, I gestured a bucket of water into being, then thought about what I wanted to try first. A sorceress at my level is

1

capable of quite a lot, but I didn't want to use magic to make water do things. I wanted to *investigate* water, with magic just another tool. But what was there to try . . . ?

And then I saw the single drop, shimmering at the rim of the bucket. What *was* a single drop, and how much water had to be present before it became two drops, or three, or a dozen? Some drops were smaller or bigger than others, so where did the cutoff point come? Was it possible to extend the cutoff point, using magic only lightly? How far beyond was it practical to go?

The questions increased to a dozen, then began multiplying. On top of that I'd gotten an idea, which in turn suggested a test to answer the questions. Wording my spell carefully, I used the water in the bucket to make a sphere a foot and a half in diameter. I was able to hold the sphere in my hands without bursting it like the soap bubble it resembled, which was one of the things the spell had specified. I had to be careful, but I *could* hold it.

Once that was done, I brought into being nine more gallon buckets of water. The first question to be answered was how many gallons the one-gallon sphere would be able to hold without rupturing or leaking. That meant filling it slowly and watching for the natural stress point, not forcing it to hold what *I* wanted it to. A wizard could have gathered the waters of an ocean into a ball; that wasn't what I was trying to accomplish.

I had just finished adding the contents of the fourth bucket when the Summons came. The sphere was very full but not yet leaking, and then my attention was taken by the entry that chimed into existence not two feet away. It looked like a perfectly ordinary doorway, except that the name Haddil sat in large block letters on its top. A quick spell matched the master's true resonance with the work, which meant it really was him doing the Summoning. Come *now*, was the message, one Master Haddil had never sent before. There had to be some kind of trouble . . .

Without wasting another moment, I stepped through the entry. Moving from world to world like that is effortless, so much so that you sometimes forget to watch where you're walking. One step, after all, and not even across a raised threshold. It let me out just short of a real doorway, one that *did*, unfortunately, have a raised threshold . . .

So it *wasn't* my fault. Maybe I did forget I was still holding the sphere of water, but that wouldn't have mattered if the entry had been put *beyond* the raised door sill. All my attention was on the room I approached, trying to see who was in it. It seemed to be a conference room in the Palace of Ease at Yellow Rivers, and the master wasn't alone. People came in by ones and twos through other doorways that must also have had entries behind them, and Master Haddil was in the midst of creating even more. I heard part of one spell as I approached, and then—

And then my heavy riding boots made me trip over the sill. My reflexes were good enough to keep me from falling, which was the major part of the problem. As my arms flew up to reestablish balance, my hands *threw* the sphere of water I'd forgotten I was holding. I recovered my footing in time to see the sphere go sailing toward Master Haddil, and immediately felt relieved. Master Haddil, after all, was warded against magic with his own wizard's strength, so my sphere couldn't possibly reach him.

And it didn't. But his warding also didn't destroy the sphere, as I'd thought it would. Instead, the sphere *bounced*—straight toward the man who stood beside Master Haddil on his right. Again, since the man was Sighted, it shouldn't have mattered; his own warding should have protected him. What's that saying about "should" and "would" and "could"? To make a long story even longer, he wasn't warded. The sphere hit him head-on, burst the way it was supposed to, and drowned him in five gallons of water.

"Chalaine!" Master Haddil screamed, staring in horror at the man who was drenched from head to foot. "What have you done this time? Have you any idea? Even a hint?"

Chalaine, that's me. Master Haddil pronounces it as though it should be Abysmal or Catastrophe, but he's always done that. Things tend to go badly for me, especially when he's around.

So I was used to being accused, and that's why I didn't say anything as I watched the big drowned man use one hand to wipe water out of his eyes. His long, golden blond hair hung in strings, his dark tunic and leather

breeches sagged, and his boots must have been full.
Even his swordbelt was wet, and I had just enough time
to wonder why a magic user would be wearing a swordbelt
before he moved his hand in a banishing gesture. All the
water and wetness disappeared immediately, of course,
leading me to also wonder why no one else had thought
to do that.

Like Master Haddil. "Forgive me, Your Highness, but I
should have done that," he apologized, tugging at his bright
yellow robes. "It's just that girl—when she appears, my
mind ceases to function. Are you all right?"

"I'm not so delicate that I dissolve in water, Master
Haddil," the big man returned, annoyance in his deep voice.
They were both trying to ignore the hysterical laughter
coming from the other new arrivals, all of whom were
Sighted. "If the girl's that bad, why did you include her
in the Summoning?"

"She isn't *bad*, Your Highness, merely a catalyst for
chaos," Master Haddil answered with a sigh. "If we simply
avoid her close proximity, we should survive with only
minor damage. If you'll excuse me now, I'll finish creating
the rest of the entries."

The big man nodded sourly, and Master Haddil went back
to work. By then I'd crossed over to a deep leather chair,
hoping that sitting quietly in one place for a while would
calm the upheaval I'd caused. It was almost as though cause
and effect were two halves of a piece of rope that sometimes
folded back on itself. Normally each effect needed a separate
cause, but the folding brought about effect after effect after
effect . . .

And I was always in the middle of that folding. I sighed
as I leaned back in the chair, noticing that the big blond
man hadn't even given me a second glare, let alone a second
look. Well, there was nothing unusual in that, not once I'd
"caused." People don't enjoy being in the middle of chaos,
not even if they're Prince Bariden of Melen. Which was
who he had to be. Third son of King Agilar of Melen, and
unexpectedly born Sighted.

Two more entries were created, one after the other beyond
adjacent doorways, and Master Haddil still wasn't finished.
The conference room had been built especially for the

use of a wizard, with more than two dozen doorways spaced around its circumference. Normally those doorways led only to various corridors or halls in the Palace of Ease, specifically the corridors and halls just outside the room. If an emergency happened and the king needed to meet with his nobles quickly, his wizard could establish entries through the doorways and bring them right to him.

But this time it was Sighted who were being brought through, and not just any Sighted. From the few I recognized, Master Haddil seemed to be Summoning everyone he'd ever taught who hadn't yet reached wizard strength. Since it wasn't likely he was simply holding a reunion, something important had to be going on. Once the Summoning was over, we'd all find out about it together.

In the meanwhile, those who had already arrived were finding places to wait. Small groups had begun to form, using couches, chairs, and the small tables they surrounded, for the purpose. The furnishings in that room were all brightly colored silks and brocades, reds and yellows and blues and greens, all bound around with the royal maroon and gold. Some parts of it looked like an autumn tree had exploded, but that was the way the king liked it. Lots of bright colors all thrown together, and never mind if some people had to squint against the glare.

Aside from the colors, the room itself was magnificent. Round and high-ceilinged, it gave the impression of large sunshiny windows bright with the warmth of summer, the beautifully made furniture gleaming in reflection of that. The effect came from magic, of course, since the room had no windows at all. And it was warm despite its size, reminding me about the heavy clothes I wore. I thought about changing entirely, but wasn't in the mood for dress-up. A short spell simply changed my white tunic, brown breeches, and brown boots to lightweight form, and that served the purpose.

I wasn't the only one who sat alone in the room, but I *was* the only one pointed out to newcomers by whatever group they joined. After that the story was retold, and then came the inevitable laughter. But most of the laughter seemed to be aimed at Prince Bariden, as though he'd had some hand in what had happened to him. It occurred to me that in a way he had, by not being warded, and that made me curious. Why would a magic user *not* be warded, especially if he was also a prince? Even I wasn't that blasé or absentminded . . .

I had some time to consider the question, but before I came to any conclusions, Master Haddil finished the Summoning. Almost two dozen people had come through the entries, and every one of us looked at him when he raised his arms for attention.

"It pleases me that all of you honored your obligation so promptly," he began, looking around at the group. "As the one who taught each of you his or her craft, I have the right to call on you for assistance should the need arise. It's my unfortunate duty to inform you that more than simple need has arisen."

Soft murmurs of surprised comment came from a few places around the room, and not only because of what had been said. Now that I looked directly at Master Haddil, I could see what certainly must be worry lines creasing his face. His gray-touched brown hair was less neatly combed than usual, his light eyes were bleak, and he seemed not to have slept in much too long. For someone who was Court Wizard to King Agilar of Melen, he looked pretty awful.

"In the last month a . . . situation has developed that I— haven't been able to get to the bottom of," he continued. "Before I go into details, you're entitled to know that there will be a good deal of danger for anyone who assists me. I . . . have already lost four of you, those I Summoned more than a week ago. I had no idea—I certainly wouldn't have— without warning them—"

His voice broke completely then, and he stood in the middle of the room looking down at his folded, robe-covered arms, silently trying to pull himself together. It occurred to me that yellow was an odd color for a wizard's robe, but it probably had been the king's idea. Master Haddil's grief and guilt were so clear he might as well have been projecting them, giving us the feeling that black would have been more appropriate. A new round of murmurs arose, accompanied by stirring, and a man from one of the small groups stepped forward.

"Master Haddil, are you saying you're giving us the choice about whether or not to become involved?" he asked, his brows knit with disturbance. "Four of us have already been ended, and there's a good chance more will go the same way?"

"They haven't precisely been ended, but the rest of what you said is accurate," Haddil agreed after taking a deep breath. "I cannot in all good conscience demand your assistance, not with something like this. I ask for your help, but will understand any refusal to give it. Take a moment to consider, and those who decline may then leave."

Everyone stared at Haddii for the first moment, and then those in groups began to murmur among themselves. Those who sat alone simply looked thoughtful, but none of the deliberation took very long. Without glancing at Master Haddil again people began to leave, presumably to go back to safer and more important pursuits. Since I didn't have anything more important—or at least nothing that wouldn't keep—I stayed to become one of thirteen with similar opinions. That number wasn't the best of omens for most, but for me it had always been lucky.

"Well, we're left with a larger number than I had anticipated," Master Haddil observed once the last back had disappeared through a doorway. "You all have my thanks, of course, but I must repeat that I want you to be very certain. If anything happens to one of you . . ."

He didn't want it weighing on his conscience any more than it already did. The problem was actually Master Haddil's, which was why he felt like that, but we already knew that. The man who had spoken earlier had been one of the first to leave, so we sat without commenting until the wizard was ready to go on.

"All right, let's get down to details," he conceded with a sigh when no one else moved. "The problem began about a month ago, when the king guested a deputation of merchants from the city. Business had been going so well for them that they were ready to branch out, and they came to discuss possible trade treaties with the king. Trading with people you won't be able to collect from isn't very good

business, nor do you want to get involved with potential
enemies. Not that this realm has many enemies . . ."

His voice trailed off again as though his mind had become
distracted, and some of us exchanged glances. This wasn't
the Master Haddil we knew, and the difference was disturbing. He was badly shaken by the—situation, and in another
moment we found out why.

"At any rate, the king held a feast the night they arrived,
and the next day the first of the discussions was scheduled
to begin. Everyone showed up in the conference chamber at
the appointed time—except for the head of the deputation.
Thinking he'd overslept, they sent a servant to his rooms
to wake him. The servant came back on the run, reporting
that the man *hadn't* overslept. There was something wrong
with him, and a healer had already been sent for. The healer
arrived promptly, spent a few minutes with the man, then
immediately called me.

"When I first walked into his bedchamber, I was startled," Master Haddil continued with a sigh. "The man sat
in a chair at his breakfast table, the remnants of his meal
spread out before him. To the casual glance he was about
to take a last swallow of coffee before going to dress, and
I nearly apologized for intruding. Then I realized that he
wasn't moving, and in fact was breathing only shallowly.
The healer had tried rousing and neutralizing spells, thinking he might be drugged, but nothing had worked. It was
almost as though someone had stolen his soul . . ."

If Master Haddil didn't shiver, some of the rest of us
weren't far from it. Death, being natural, is acceptable,
even if it's caused by unnatural means. What had happened to the merchant didn't come under the same heading,
and a sudden chill insinuated itself into the warmth of
the room.

"And that was only the first of it," Master Haddil said
into the deep silence. "Two more merchants were taken the
same way before the rest packed up and left on the run,
and then two of the king's advisers were stricken, one right
after the other. By then I'd Summoned your predecessors,
but they weren't able to discover any more than I had.
Ilainna, Saydra, Hannar and Gadran—one night they were
fine, the next morning they'd become a group of living

statues. Maybe they did discover something, and paid the price for forbidden knowledge. Do you see now why I told you to be very, very sure?"

The haunted look in his eyes touched each of us in turn, an odd sort of pleading that was only partially for help. The rest of it seemed to be begging us to get out of that mess as fast as possible, for his sake as well as our own. After hearing the details I'd almost decided to do just that, but then he'd mentioned which Sighted had been taken . . .

I shifted in my chair in the midst of the new silence, fighting to keep from demanding that he get on with it. I knew Ilainna, Saydra and Gadran only slightly, but Hannar—He and I had been lovers, and after that, friends. Finding a lover isn't hard even for someone like me, but a friend . . . who wasn't ashamed to have others know . . . who had been there for me that time I'd needed someone so *badly* . . . now he was the one in need and, chilled or not, I'd be there to do everything possible.

But glancing up showed not everyone felt the same. Of the thirteen who had been left after the first culling, another eight were in the process of leaving. That left four others besides me, but they looked as determined as I felt. They must have had similar personal reasons, and Master Haddil seemed to accept that once the others were gone.

"So we have five who have made up their minds to experiment with the unknown," he said with a sigh. "And, of course, Prince Bariden, who is involved on behalf of his father. I wish it were possible to thank you for coming and then send you home, but I need you too badly. Right now I'd like each of you to make a small tile with your name on it, half inch by one inch, in white. Then place it facedown on this table over here."

He walked to the table he meant, a round thing of gold and red enamel, and waited for us to do as he'd asked. It took no more than a moment to speak the very brief spell that produced the tile, and then I joined the others in placing it on the table. Each tile had its maker's resonance as well as his or her name, which had to be why Master Haddil hadn't simply produced them himself. He wanted something with our individual traces, and now he had them.

"Rather than assign working partners, I've constructed a spell that will choose the best possible working pairs from among you," he said, glancing around at us. "We'll need all the help we can get in this affair, so I'm sure you'll all cooperate."

We nodded to show that we would, but the nods of the other four, two men and two women, were a bit on the reluctant side. I had no idea who they were, but they, apparently, knew me. None of them said a word, but their glances informed me their cooperation would be minimal at best if one of them was named *my* partner. Well, that was all right. I was used to working alone.

Master Haddil waited until Prince Bariden put his tile down with the rest, and then he muttered a single sound I didn't catch. The tiles immediately began to spin around, as though each one was trying itself against the others. That told me Master Haddil had prepared his best-match spell in advance, and then had keyed it to a single sound. The language of spells may be a verbal shorthand, but you'll never find a complex spell described with no more than one sound.

It didn't take very long for the combinations to sort themselves out. The six tiles separated into three pairs, and the pairs formed an almost circular triangle in the middle of the table. Master Haddil reached for the pair of tiles at the right of the base, and turned them over.

"Vaminda and Regel," he said, smiling at the two. Vaminda was a couple of years older than me, with blond hair, green eyes, a slender build, and a sweet, understanding smile. Regel was her age but not as sweet, with brown hair, brown eyes, and a short, neatly trimmed beard. The two glanced at each other, looking a good deal happier than the other man and woman. Master Haddil reached out again for the left side of the base, and the unnamed two watched with bated breath.

"Nolar and Jilla," the wizard announced, possibly proving bated breath adds to the strength of fervent prayers. Jilla was very close to my age with black hair and dark eyes, but seemed to have the self-assurance of a woman two or three times older. Or that of an absolute monarch. Nolar was clean-shaven with the same black hair and dark eyes, but there the similarity ended. Despite being a year or so older, he seemed less assured than his new partner.

And then it came to me who *my* new partner had to be. Without looking at him, I reached out and turned over the two remaining tiles. Yup. None other than the now-dry Prince Bariden.

"That means, of course, that the final pair is Prince Bariden and Chalaine," Master Haddil said, rubbing it in. "With that settled, I'll now be giving you initial assignments. After that, you'll follow whatever trails and clues you come across on your own."

"Did our predecessors work in pairs?" Jilla asked, interrupting smoothly. "If they did, it might be a better idea for us to work separately. We can't show we're better than them if we repeat their mistakes."

"Your predecessors worked singly," Master Haddil informed her evenly, obviously working to keep from saying anything else—less friendly. "That was one of the reasons I decided on pairs this time. Now—"

"And we aren't here to make other people look bad," Regel said to Jilla, his new partner Vaminda smiling sweetly and nodding in agreement. "We're here simply to let others know how selfless we are, how dedicated to what's right, and how supportive of Master Haddil. Nothing else matters."

"Not even all the accolades that will come to whoever figures this puzzle out?" Nolar asked him, coming to the aid of his own partner Jilla. "I don't believe in modest anonymity. When I finally prove just how good I am, I want everyone to know about it."

"When you really are good, the only one who has to know it is yourself," Prince Bariden put in suddenly, his deep voice cutting across comments from the other three. "If *you* don't know it, what others think is useless. Just as it is about most things. Now how about letting Master Haddil get on with it."

All four of them muttered to themselves, two resentfully, two piously, but that was as far as it went. Master Haddil paused another moment to be sure of that, then continued.

"There are certain lines of investigation that haven't yet been looked into," he said, gray eyes moving among the four who had spoken. "For instance, it's certain that magic is involved in this mess, but we still don't know *why* magic was used against the victims. Very often when you discover motive, the one responsible suddenly becomes obvious. Jilla and Nolar, I'd like you to interview the families and business associates of the three merchant victims, especially the first. Find out about any enemies or people with grudges, and whether anyone involved has had recent dealings with magic users."

He then turned to the other pair. "Regel and Vaminda, I want you to do the same with the two stricken advisers. And while you're about it, see if there are any ties between them and one or more of the merchants. Did the merchants want the king to make a treaty with someone those advisers were set against? Did the advisers suggest a realm the merchants would have had minimal profit from at best? What about personal grudges, things that had nothing to do with the talks? Is there anyone who had something against *all* of the victims? The four of you should compare notes often, to see if there are any common links."

The four of them nodded dutifully, but from the way they avoided even glancing at each other, I had doubts about how much comparing would be done. And they looked bored already, as if they'd thought investigating a mystery like that would be more exciting.

"And last but not least, Prince Bariden and Chalaine," Master Haddil said, looking only at the male half of the team. "I'd like you to go over the places each of the victims was found, inch by inch if necessary, to see if you can pick up any trace of the one responsible. Was the deed done from a distance, or do you believe an entry was used? Are there similarities between the locations, some one point that makes them identical? Some one point that makes them totally different? *Anything*, especially if it supplies a clue as to who or how."

The Prince took his turn at nodding dutifully, but since I hadn't even been glanced at, I didn't find it necessary to do the same. Instead I asked, "And what assignment have you given yourself, Master Haddil? Something with a chance for more definite results, I hope."

He finally turned to look at me thoughtfully, and then he nodded. "You and Hannar were rather close, weren't you, Chalaine? I'd forgotten, but I remember now. And yes, my own assignment has a chance to generate more definite results. I'm working to break through whatever spell is holding the victims living but lifeless. My one most fervent hope is that their essences weren't taken for some twisted purpose. If that proves true, we'll never get any of them back."

That chill wind blew through the room again, but this time I wasn't the only one riffled. Regel paled somewhat under his beard, Nolar looked briefly frightened, Vaminda's smile turned from sweet to sympathetic, and Jilla shrugged. All of us were reacting in our own separate ways, including my own new partner.

"Then we'd better get started as quickly as possible," he said, the words more of an order than a suggestion. "If those essences *are* going to be used for something, our only hope of stopping it is to find the one responsible. Let's go."

It was fairly obvious he was talking to the other four, and they responded by immediately heading for a door that would take them through the palace to the locations of their assignments. Each pair was engaged in low-voiced discussion even before they were out of sight, probably deciding on how to begin. Master Haddil banished all the entries he'd created with a single gesture, then also headed out of the room, unconsciously brushing at his robes to straighten them.

Even before that, my partner had disappeared completely in yet another direction. He'd given his orders and then had left with a broad stride, supremely confident that any unimportant details would follow along behind. Without his needing to even glance at the detail. I paused to get a few thoughts in order, then chose my own way out into the corridors.

The Palace of Ease was what all palaces should be like: opulence on a gigantic scale with an equal amount of comfort. Melen was a wealthy kingdom filled with satisfied, wealthy people, and rather than resent the riches their king displayed, his palace made them proud. It also employed a large number of the kingdom's less affluent citizenry, which added to everyone's happiness. Too many poor, jobless people were bad for a kingdom, not to mention unsightly.

I used the conference room to orient myself, then headed for the main kitchens. I'd learned my way around while I was studying with Master Haddil, even though it had been necessary to stay out of the royal family's way. The king didn't mind his Court Wizard spending time training those who also wanted to be higher level magic users, but Master Haddil felt it would be an imposition if his students were visibly there. The kingdom was too safe and secure for him to have much else to do besides teach, but he was still firm on the point.

Rather than use invisibility to satisfy the requirement I'd used the deep night, wandering the corridors and halls while most people slept. I've always been a creature of the night, so doing it that way hadn't been much of a hardship. I'd also gotten to know some of my fellow night creatures, those who preferred working late hours and those who, being new, had been assigned to them. It had been more than a year since I'd left, but there should still be those around who remembered me.

The main kitchens were staffed at all times, fully staffed between the hours of dawn and midnight. The king wasn't much of an early riser, but the queen tended to start things moving at first light. She expected the day's baking to be done, all meals planned and more than started, all cleaning well under way. At the other end of the scale was the Princess Efria, who slept till noon then invited people to late night suppers. The staff had to cope with all of that, or they would have gotten another staff.

Right then it was the middle of the day, just past lunchtime according to the position of the sun. I stopped just inside one of the kitchen entrances, the only spot immediately available for keeping out of the way of the rush. There were enough people hurrying around to fill a small town, which the kitchens were almost large enough to be. It had only been a short time past breakfast on the world where my cold weather house was, but watching all that activity started to make me hungry.

"Chalaine, is that you skulking in that corner?" a boom-ing voice demanded. "It *is* you, and not a word for an old friend. Whatever is this world coming to?"

By that time the speaker was about eight feet away, standing with wide fists on wider hips and forcing everyone to go around her. She also wore the sort of devilish grin that didn't usually go with a woman her size, a grin that said she liked fun more than authority. Not that she didn't also have the authority. Benatha Aylie ruled completely in the royal kitchens, either personally or by proxy. She watched me try three times to cross the eight feet between us, laughed at the measly foot-and-a-half's worth of progress I made, then finally took pity on me.

"What you need is the sort of size *I* carry," she informed me after simply walking forward and letting everyone else get out of *her* way. "With the queen holding a reception for the ladies of the city this afternoon, that traffic won't slow down until bedtime. Let's get you some place where we can sit down and talk."

She put a giant arm around my shoulders, then led the way left toward her alcove. The area was furnished like a very small sitting room a short distance away from a chop-ping and skinning table, two of the roasting hearths, three of the freestanding soup cauldrons, and a minor storeroom. The area was also no one's but hers, and anyone trying to use it uninvited would be lucky if they were able to leave again on their own.

"I had a feeling you'd be showing up about now," Bena said as she deposited me in a chair before moving to take her much larger one. "Everyone in the palace knew Haddil was going to be Summoning help today, which was prob-ably why he took an early lunch. Are you sure it's smart to get involved in this? The first four who came to help were supposed to be the best, and now look at *them*."

For once her face wore nothing of a grin, and the short amount of time she'd teased me showed how upset she was. I knew she wanted to be reassured, but not if I had to lie.

"One of those four is a special friend of mine," I told her with a shrug. "Would *you* be able to simply turn around and walk away?"

"For a freak, you make an awfully good decent person,"

she grumbled, not very happy to get an answer she couldn't argue. "Most of those other freaks don't give a damn about anybody but themselves, especially not if giving a damn means they have to put themselves out. I've always wondered what makes you so different."

"How many freaks do you know as well as you know me?" I countered, feeling no real insult at what she called me. A lot of people considered the Sighted to be freaks rather than gifted, but most weren't as honest about it as Bena. Or as fair. My being a freak didn't stop her from being my friend.

"I've run across a lot of freaks in my time," she assured me, her wide face still unusually serious. "Even the ones who didn't treat me like dirt acted like they were doing me a favor eating what my kitchens produced. What none of 'em have is good manners, but you do. *That's* what makes you so different."

"You didn't think so the first time we met," I reminded her with a badly swallowed grin. "You called me a clumsy sneak thief, and an underfed one at that."

"And you told me to keep my night-cook opinions to myself," she came back, finally recapturing a grin of her own. "You hadn't come to steal food, only to look around, and you weren't underfed, you were fashionably slender. I always wondered why you didn't zap me when I laughed."

"Not because I wasn't tempted," I assured her, feeling myself relax as I always did around Bena. "But if I had the king would have put a bounty on my head, and that would have been the end of my studies. I had no idea who you were, or that someone in your position would be a night rover like me."

"I didn't know who you were either, or why you would study with someone like Haddil." Her light brown eyes were on my face again, not as grim but certainly serious. "He's one I'd watch starve with a smile, and you have no reason to like him any better. All he ever did was criticize you, but not in a useful way. If I treated my chefs half that bad, they'd pick up and walk out."

"Not the ones who were determined to study with you," I disagreed. "There are a lot of people in the worlds who have an incredible amount to teach, even though they have little or no personality. You don't have to like them to learn from them, and Master Haddil had one really big attraction for me. I knew he'd never let me be sloppy in my lessons because of my reputation. For some reason, I generate a lot of supposed toleration from a lot of people."

"For some reason," she echoed, back to studying me. "And for the same reason you generate panic in others. They don't know how to deal with that—special talent you sometimes show, so they react according to their natures. I never saw it for myself so I can't say if it's true or not, but you tell me you cause problems at times for the people around you. Things happen, and those things aren't pleasant, so people get rattled. Even if it never happened to them, most don't know how to treat you, so either they pretend they're tolerant, or they panic."

"Which doesn't change the fact that they do react like that," I said with a sigh. "Master Haddil became impatient instead—which usually made *me* nervous—but that didn't keep me from learning. It did cause some spectacular 'accidents,' though . . ."

She chuckled when I let the words trail off, finding more amusement in most of those few but incredible incidents than I ever had. Complex accidents as opposed to the simple sort, more involved than any of the situations could possibly have called for. Like that first time it had happened directly to Master Haddil . . . I'd rolled on the floor when I'd heard about it, even though laughing wasn't the usual way I handled hearing about it . . . As a facet of talent, that sort of thing leaves a lot to be desired . . .

"Bena, tell me what you know about what happened," I said, shifting to another unpleasant topic. "All those people who were left as empty shells—doesn't anyone have an idea about why it was done, if not by who?"

"One's as good a question as the other," she replied with a shrug. "Some are saying the merchants and the king's men were planning something that would hurt everyone in the kingdom but them, and the EverNameless stepped in to stop them. Others think it has to be an enemy of Haddil's, trying to make him look bad. The king's worried that it might be someone testing a new spell, one that they'll use later on their real target. The queen thinks it's someone getting even for not being invited to one of her parties. If you happen to have a favorite theory, just ask around a little and you'll find five or ten other people who think the same thing."

"And what do *you* think?" I asked instead, unsurprised at the way people were taking it. "You always know what's going on in this place, and more importantly you know rumor from fact. Give me something I can work with."

"I wish I could," she said, sympathy in those light-dark eyes. "And not just because you bring out the mother in me. Whatever took those people like that could take one of us next, like me, for instance. The idea scares me worse than being invited to a new bride's first meal, but there's nothing to build a real theory on. Nobody *knows* anything, everybody's just guessing. And everybody's worried about who'll be next."

"Why are people expecting more victims?" I asked, tripping over the oddness of that. "The merchants and king's men could have had a common enemy, and the Sighted were done because they came close to finding him. The king's theory is as silly as the queen's, and both match the thought that the EverNameless would bother. But everybody, including you, expects more victims. Why is that?"

"That's another good question," she allowed, brows raised in surprised thought. "I hadn't looked at it like that before, but—You're right, we do expect more people to be taken. Why don't you have something to eat while I try to figure out why that is."

"Bena, I ate only a couple of hours ago," I said with a sigh, suddenly finding myself in a too-familiar position. "I really don't think you can call me underfed any longer, and on top of that I haven't much time. Right now I'm supposed to be somewhere else, and if I don't get there soon, we'll probably be able to hear the explosion from here. Is there anything at all you can tell me, no matter how silly or useless you consider the information? Take a minute to think, but don't try to force it. I may have to leave now, but I'll be back later some time."

"Right now I can't think of anything," she admitted, her wide brow creased into a frown. "Something just might come to me later, so don't forget about coming back. If you're still in one piece, that is."

Her last words were accompanied by a sudden, mischievous grin, making it my turn to raise brows questioningly. Bena would never joke about my staying unhurt, even if she *didn't* know how much it would take to harm me. And then I noticed that she was looking past me, and the answer became perfectly clear.

"What the hell are you doing in *here*?" a deep, angry voice demanded from behind me, confirming a guess that had been a virtual certainty. "Chatting with friends over tea wasn't part of our schedule."

"You're right, Your Highness, she does deserve a good scolding," Bena promptly put in, that look in her eyes increasing. "If you're the one she was supposed to be someplace else with, she has no business visiting with an old woman instead. Give it to her good."

"Bena," I muttered warningly, but that did as much good as you would expect. I was ignored completely—but only by her.

"Well?" my new partner demanded again, coming around to my left. "Answer my question."

"I'd say you've already answered it yourself," I responded, not quite looking at him. "But it doesn't matter, because I'm through here anyway. Let's get to that schedule you mentioned."

"Just a minute," he said as I stood, one big hand coming to my left shoulder. "What do you mean, I've already answered the question myself? I don't ask questions I already have the answer to."

"I'm sure you don't," I said with a nod, glancing around the kitchen. "I must have been mistaken, the way I often am. Let's just forget about it and get on with what we're supposed to be doing."

"Don't accept that, Bariden," Bena said suddenly as the hand finally began to leave my shoulder. "She has a nasty habit of holding people at arm's length by refusing to argue with anything they say, even if it's wrong. You two seem to have gotten off on the wrong foot, and if you continue to let her push you away it can only get worse."

"I'm sorry, Bena, but you've somehow gotten the wrong impression," the man answered, most of his impatience gone. "She and I don't have a personal relationship, only a working one. She can push me as far away as she likes, and I won't mind a bit. But you really do have to excuse us now. Let's go, girl, and this time try not to lose me."

Once again he strode away, leaving me to wonder if that was the only method of walking he knew. Bena, now looking upset, started to say something, but I took off after my partner before she could get the words out. She deserved to be upset for practicing out-of-the-blue matchmaking, and hopefully whatever embarrassment she felt would keep her from doing it again very soon. Expecting it to stop her for good would be living in a dream world.

I had to use a minor repulsion spell to get out of the kitchens without getting run over, but Prince Bariden didn't have the same problem. He had more size than Bena, but distributed it differently. Rather than being fat he was just plain big, broad shoulders above a massive chest, thick arms, wide, flat waist, muscled legs. He also had big feet, but I suppose he would have looked funny with small ones. What he looked was dangerous, something most magic users took pains to avoid. Maybe it was the sword.

His broad stride led the way from one corridor to the next, and although he never looked back I was sure he knew I was following about ten feet behind. Mostly he seemed to be involved in his thoughts, as though something were bothering him. I wondered if it had anything to do with the problem, and if he knew something I didn't. He finally turned into a corridor in the guest wing, and stopped in front of one set of double doors.

"This is the apartment where the first merchant was found," I was informed as soon as I reached him. "It's as good a place to start as any, even though too many people trampled through it before Master Haddil closed it off. If we don't get anything here, we'll go on to the others in turn."

"Don't step in yet," I said as he reached toward one of the doors. "I'd like to try to get a body count first, and the setting of Master Haddil's exclusion spell will be more than the tail end of it. It will also let me know if anyone's been in here since the spell was set."

"I can see where that last would be useful, but why a body count?" he asked with the usual frown in his voice.

"What good will it do knowing there were fifty people rather than forty?"

"If fifty people went through that doorway and we can find the traces of fifty-one inside, we then check the windows," I said, thinking about how to word the spell. "If *they* weren't used instead of the door, we'll *know* an entry or something else magical was used to get in. Finding traces of something is easier when you know that that something was definitely there."

"I hadn't thought of that," he responded, the admission ungrudged and actually almost neutral. "It's a good idea, so I'm glad *you* thought of it. Why don't you look at me when you talk to me?"

The question seemed to hold nothing but curiosity, but I have to admit I was surprised he'd noticed. Right then I was still studying the double doors, so I shrugged.

"You can consider it a bad habit, if you like," I suggested, continuing on with that habit. "You'd be best off ignoring it. Now let's see how effective my spell is."

I raised my hands and spoke the spell, causing the doors to do something they were capable of but not usually required to do. All doors "know" how many people pass through them, it just takes more than a simple request to get the information. There was an instant of recollection during the time period specified, and then the right-hand door began to open and close. It did it seventeen times, hesitated a full five heartbeats, then closed more fully with a click.

"Seventeen people went in and out, but no one after the exclusion spell was set," I reported. "Now we can check that against the number of people who were actually in the rooms."

He made a vague sound of agreement and led the way in, using the key phrase Master Haddil had given him to exempt us from the exclusion spell. It would have been possible to enter even without the key, but it wouldn't have been easy to start with and eventually we would have found it impossible to stay. Even some unSighted could have managed to get in, but their stay would have been a lot shorter.

The apartment's reception room was a good size, large enough to accommodate at least two dozen people comfortably, more if it happened to be necessary. The wall lamps had come on when Prince Bariden had snapped his fingers, but they were the only source of light. There was a closed door to the left and one to the right, lots of chairs and couches and tables and wall paintings and knickknacks—but no windows.

"The merchant was found in his bedchamber, through that door," my partner said, nodding to the left. "Let's count and separate the traces in here, and then we'll have something to compare the ones from in there to."

"First let's see what's behind there," I answered, heading toward the door to the right. "It's probably nothing but a guest lavatory, but it won't hurt to take a look . . ."

Looking inside showed exactly that, a full lavatory including a porcelain bathtub. Why there would be a bathtub I had no idea, but walking closer showed it had even been used at some time. A grayish residue partially circled the drain hole, but the rest of the tub was clean. The sink was closer to being spotless, as was the commode, both of which were emptied by magic rather than piping. I could feel the trace of similar cleaning spells around each of them, a trace the tub didn't have. Pipes carried *that* water away . . .

The lamp I'd turned on suddenly went dark, which shouldn't have happened. When you light a lamp with magic, it doesn't go out again for no reason. Realizing that made me turn toward the doorway, and sure enough, the reason stood there with folded arms.

"When I spoke to you, you didn't seem to hear me," he said, faint annoyance back in his tone. "Don't you think we have better things to do than stand in small rooms staring off into space?"

"Sometimes I get distracted," I half-apologized, feeling my cheeks grow warm. I *had* been wasting time, wondering about cleanser residue while nine people lay helpless and half-alive. I can be a real imbecile at times, and it was just my luck that this particular time had had an audience. I quickly headed out of the room, and my audience stepped back to let me through the doorway.

"I'd appreciate it if you could save being distracted for when you're alone," he said as I passed him, doing a good job of making me feel worse. "Do you know a spell for separating and identifying traces, or do we have to construct one ourselves?"

"I know a spell," I answered, forcing myself to concentrate on what was at hand. "It was developed by forensic wizards, so you don't have to worry that I constructed it myself. It goes like this."

I spoke the spell I'd learned just for the fun of it, adding the proper gestures at the proper time. A rush of wind came, as though we stood outdoors, and then the traces began separating under glowing numbers. Traces are like delicate scents or light touches are to the physical, indistinct but definitely there. I could sense the traces with my abilities as a Sighted, and even tell one from another; what I couldn't do was get a firm grip on them.

"But the numbers only go up to eleven," Prince Bariden objected. "I thought you said there were seventeen people involved."

"There were seventeen instances of people going through the doors," I corrected, carefully studying the traces under the glowing numbers. "That could be seventeen individuals, or one person going in and out seventeen times. I used this spell once just to see how it worked, and I noticed that it was really efficient. Multiple traces are shown under a single number, but they're separated by tiny black dots. Like that one, under '1'."

"Two dots, which means three traces," he murmured, now understanding what he was seeing. "The next four numbers have one dot apiece, which means two traces each. The last six have no dots, which means those people came in only once."

"And the first, with three traces, probably stands for the victim," I agreed. "You'd expect the man who lives here to be in and out the most. There are only three, because he wasn't here that long. The ones with two traces are probably the servant who found the merchant, the healer who sent for Master Haddil, and someone else, maybe another servant. The fourth is definitely Master Haddil, since I happen to know his trace well enough to recognize it. The rest—servants, most likely, and maybe a couple of curiosity seekers."

"If it becomes necessary, we can find out," he said, and then I felt the weight of his stare on *me*. "You said you'd used this spell once before, but I've never even heard of it. What could you possibly have used it *for*?"

"I—used it because I was curious," I admitted, feeling the return of the heat to my cheeks. "It wasn't *for* anything, only to see how it worked. Now let's do the same thing in the bedchamber, and see what we get from there."

I strode off toward the bedchamber without waiting for any sort of answer, fervently hoping there wouldn't *be* one. I was beginning to feel downright gawky rather than simply awkward, and I hated it. As soon as I found the guilty party we were looking for, I'd get out of there as fast as possible.

The bedchamber wasn't quite as large as the reception room, but it didn't miss by much. Silk hangings decorated the walls, the furniture and the bed curtains were color-coordinated, and the private meal-nook had armchairs at the table. Like the first room, what it didn't have was windows, which might or might not be helpful. That depended on what we found in the way of traces, and there was no sense in not getting right to it.

I spoke the spell a second time, and after the wind had blown through got the sort of results I'd been hoping I wouldn't. One person had three separate traces, again probably the victim, Master Haddil had been in there twice, and one other person twice. The remaining five had come in one time each, but none of them looked very promising.

"We'll have to do some deliberate comparisons, but I think we have a problem," I told my partner. He'd followed me into the bedchamber, but hadn't said anything. "Unless I'm mistaken, every one of these traces has a match in the next room."

"If that's true, then no one came through an entry," he responded, once again sounding thoughtful. "That should mean the guilty party walked in through the door, and is therefore someone whose trace we found."

"Not necessarily," I disagreed with a sigh. "If the culprit was sneaky enough, he or she could have used a delayed spell. You speak it after you pass someone in the hall, say, and it's designed not to work for another three or four hours.

Or, if the Sighted was strong enough, he or she could have stood out in the hall and still reached the victim. Since we don't know what was done, we also don't know how close you have to be."

"Then what was the point in counting traces?" he demanded, frustration thick in his tone. "I thought you expected to learn something from it."

"I did learn something," I answered with a shrug. "I learned that no one used an entry to get into this room. If I can eliminate enough other possibilities, whatever I have left will be the answer."

"I just noticed something," he said, and suddenly his hand was on my arm, pulling me around to face him. "Not only don't you ever look at me when you speak, if you're not paying attention you say 'I' rather than 'we.' I take it that means you see yourself working alone, rather than as part of a team. Is there some particular reason I'm being dismissed like that, or is it just that you don't happen to like me?"

Frustrated anger carried him all the way through the speech, but surprise at having his hands on me made me look up directly at him. Obviously it wasn't his intention to harm me, otherwise my warding would have flared blue and thrown him back. My warding didn't flare at all, but suddenly he looked thrown anyway. Light brows rose over pale blue eyes, and the scowl that often twisted his broad, handsome face disappeared completely.

"Hey, I'm sorry," he said at once, both hands releasing me immediately. "This insanity has been getting to me, making me almost as crazy as whoever is doing it. I didn't mean to frighten you."

"You didn't," I answered with my own furious anger, having more trouble than usual in keeping it from showing. He was staring down at me in the way I'd seen so many times before, the way I hated more than almost anything else. Abruptly I turned away and said, "Let's finish the comparisons, and then we can get on to the next place."

He made a faint sound of agreement, but that was all he said. Big, tough Prince Bariden of Melen, folding up as quickly and easily as anyone else. I spoke a spell to bring the bedchamber traces out into the reception room, and once there began comparing. But most of me was running on automatic, my mind being too busy with other things to cooperate.

Other things! I wanted to scream and stamp my feet and break fragile glass items, but I'd indulged the urge at other times and it hadn't done any good. I happen to have been born with very large, very dark eyes, and if I'd been even a little less stubborn I would have changed my appearance a long time ago. Someone had once said I resemble a frightened, wounded doe when I look straight at people, and that throws them off completely. Most, to their credit, I suppose, if they don't know about my talent for causing catastrophe, immediately turn kindly and concerned and anxious to help make things better.

There's another reaction, of course, and I definitely prefer that one. I took a deep breath as the last of the traces searched for their matches, knowing that definite preference said a lot about my nature. Some people took one look at me and immediately tried to take advantage, picturing me as the shy, helpless sort who could be walked over in complete safety. I usually had fun with that kind, kicking their feet out from under them even before they realized their mistake. What I *didn't* have fun with was the first reaction, especially from people who felt bad about "frightening" me . . .

"Well, it looks like you were right," my partner said with a sigh. "There are no unaccounted-for traces, so we know an entry wasn't used. That doesn't leave us much to work with, even if it does eliminate a possibility. Eliminating the rest won't be as easy if we can't figure out what they are."

"We can make a list later, after we've seen the other locations," I replied, waving a hand to get rid of the traces. "If the second and third victims were also merchants, their apartments shouldn't be far."

"No, you're right, they're just down the hall," he said, his tone gentle and reassuring. "Follow me, and I'll show you."

I followed him as requested, but would have preferred doing it while pronouncing the list of all those words you aren't supposed to use in mixed company. Prince Bariden was being very careful not to frighten me again, and wasn't *that* comforting. I'd tried hard to avoid the circumstance, but the Fates were still against me. And we still had so much time we'd need to be in each other's company . . .

CHAPTER TWO

We checked traces in the two merchants' apartments and then in those of the king's advisers, but might as well have skipped it. Only two traces were to be found in all five places, Master Haddil's and what turned out to be the healer's. We finished with the sitting room all four of the Sighted had been found in, and finished was the proper word. Nothing in the way of a clue or suggestion came jumping up to present itself.

"That seems to be that," Prince Bariden said after a long period of silence, looking around the tan, brown, and gold sitting room. "We're out of locations and out of ideas."

"Not yet," I disagreed, wishing I had more hope for the success of what looked like our last few chances. "I don't know about you, but I still haven't seen the victims themselves. Since we know the guilty one touched them in some way, maybe we can pick up part of a trace from *them*. There are also one or two other things to be done, but first I need to take a break and get something to eat. I'll meet you back here in about an hour, and we can see the victims together."

The idea of having to look at an unliving Hannar upset me, so I headed out of there even faster than I normally would have. I was almost to the door when a big hand wrapped gently around my arm, pulling me to a halt.

"Why are you always in such a hurry?" my partner asked, the lighthearted look pasted on his face almost making me flinch. "I was going to suggest getting something to eat

before we continued, but you beat me to it. Why don't
we have the meal together, and at the same time get to
know one another? I know you must have studied here in
the palace, but I don't remember ever meeting you before.
I hope you're not going to tell me we did meet?"

By then his expression had relaxed, and the charming
grin he showed looked almost natural. He really was handsome when he wasn't frowning, but his newest reaction was
also one I'd run into before.

"No, we never met," I reassured him—unnecessarily, I
would have bet. For one reason or another, people don't
often forget meeting me. "But before we do all this
getting-to-know-each-other, I have one question. What's
my name?"

His charming grin faltered and he said, "I don't understand," but he sure as Hellfire did. "You have to know
your own name," he tried next, obviously working to keep
it light. "I'm sure you'll remember once we get some food
into you."

"I can remember without the food," I told him, ruthlessly
demolishing his new grin. "What I'm trying to find out is
if *you* remember, which I don't think you do. You heard
my name at least two or three times, so come on. Tell me
what it is."

"What makes you think I don't remember your name?"
he asked, now trying to play it cool. "Have I been referring
to you as 'Hey, you' without realizing it? And what has
your name got to do with our taking a meal together?
If we're going to be partners in this, we'll certainly eat
together more than once."

"I have this rule about never breaking bread with people
who can't remember who I am," I said, folding my arms as I
looked up at him. "What tells me you don't know my name
is the fact that you took my arm to stop me, rather than
speaking to me as most people would. For all you knew I
could have hiked up the gain on my personal warding, but
that still didn't stop you from touching me. Would you like
to claim now that you didn't know I was a sorceress?"

"Is this the reason you were so quiet for so long?" he
countered, his face darkening a bit under its tan. "Because
when you finally do open up, you do it like a steel bear

trap? Why are you acting as if I tried to assault you? All I did was invite you to share a meal."

"And all I did was ask you my name," I pointed out, refusing to let him argue a safer topic. "Show me I'm wrong in my beliefs, and I'll certainly apologize."

"You don't give an inch, do you?" he said, and the observation wasn't a compliment. "Most men hate being put on the spot like that, and most princes refuse to allow it. Are you so used to dealing with princes that getting one mad is nothing new? Or do you just like hearing me say you're right? Which, I'm once again forced to admit, you are. I know I heard your name more than once, but for some reason it didn't stay with me. So what happens now? Execution for the heinous crime of being distracted by what we're working on? If so, go ahead and do it."

The look in those blue eyes was completely steady, not even a corner of the charm showing. He hadn't enjoyed admitting the truth but had done it anyway, and now waited for what would come because of it. I usually make a habit of encouraging honesty, but not to the point of stupidity.

"What happens now is what I said before," I told him, ignoring the dramatics of his speech. "I'm going to get something to eat, and I'll meet you back here in an hour. Do enjoy your own meal."

I heard what sounded like a growl as I turned away, which was just fine with me. His sudden interest in sharing a meal with me was certainly an extension of his initial reaction, that of a strong man wanting to protect a poor little female. After the urge to protect seems to come physical desire, but I'll be double-dyed in purple and pink if I know why. Enough men had reacted that way to make me certain of it, so it must have been a male thing. As if that was supposed to make me feel happier about it.

I gloomed my way through the halls and down a flight of stairs, then took the corridor that led to my favorite hide-away. Not far from the kitchens is a small, walled-in garden, one that no one from the royal family had ever used while I studied with Master Haddil. I knew that because I'd used it so often, and just then I needed its quiet beauty to help me out of the deeps. I know men can't help acting like men, but having it happen again and again is completely depressing.

If, just once, I could find a different reaction . . .

I sat on one of the stone benches with a sigh, then spoke the spell that created the food I wanted. It all appeared on an oblong tray beside me, and the first thing I reached for was the coffee. The last couple of hours hadn't been particularly strenuous, but they *had* been wearying.

"I knew I'd find you here," a voice said, and then Bena Aylie moved around from the left toward the bench opposite mine. She still wore her long-skirted brown dress and gray apron, and she stopped by the bench without sitting. "I thought you were going to come back to talk to me again? And what are you doing eating out here, when you could be eating decent food in my kitchens?"

"One of the nice things about this garden is that I don't have to fight my way in and out of it," I said as I reached for the sandwich on the tray. "And although this *is* later, it isn't the later I had in mind for talking. This later is for eating excellent food and relaxing. How did you know I was here?"

"Maybe I found you the way Prince Bariden did earlier," she said, walking a few steps closer to me as she frowned at what was on the tray. "How excellent can that stuff be, if it wasn't made by one of *my* chefs? And it wasn't, was it?"

"No, it wasn't," I agreed around a mouthful of sandwich, then chewed and swallowed before adding, "Prince Bariden found me with magic, probably by using a tracking spell. Since you aren't Sighted, I doubt very much that you did the same. Don't tell me you had someone watching for me?"

"All right, I won't tell you," she agreed in turn, still giving cold disapproval to my food. "I'd love to know how you can sit there calmly poisoning yourself, when it would have been just as easy to get something decent. That soup even *looks* funny."

"That's just the distortion from the protective spell keeping it hot," I told her after the next bite. "Why don't you taste it before telling me how bad it is."

I banished the insulating spell with a flick of my finger, then produced another spoon which I held out to her. She sniffed in disdain, thinking about refusing, then realized she had to put up or shut up. She accepted the spoon, stirred the contents of the bowl twice, then brought the coated spoon to her mouth.

"So, you've taken to lying," she pronounced once the spoon was out of her mouth again. "I should have known you'd never settle for seconds when firsts are so easily available. That's Lidiar's best vegetable soup, which means it's the best anywhere. There are one or two chefs who can almost match him, but no one anywhere is better. What about that mousse?"

She bent again to take a very small bit of my dessert pudding, then nodded with satisfaction after tasting it.

"Even through the residue of soup I know that taste," she said. "Nida's mousse is famous on every civilized world in this sector, and the only dessert chef better than her died ten years ago. Why did you say you weren't eating from my kitchens when you were?"

"Bena, what soups was Lidiar supposed to make today?" I asked without looking at her. "And didn't I hear some place that Nida was supposed to be married and away on her honeymoon around this time? Did something happen to make her change her plans?"

There was heavy silence from the woman standing over me, enough of it to let a bird in the trees trill its pleasure and then be answered. It really was a beautiful day, reminding me that I hadn't eaten picnic-style in much too long.

"All right, I'm asking for an explanation," she said at last, putting down the spoon before returning to the opposite bench to sit. "Lidiar made potato soup, barley soup, and beet soup today, and only those three. Nida left on her honeymoon two days ago, and her assistants wouldn't dare try mousse on their own—at least not yet. Where did you get that food?"

"I got it where I get most everything else," I told her, finishing the last of the sandwich and reaching for the soup. "The last time someone tried discussing this with you, you went for them with a rolling pin. Talking about magic seems to give you indigestion."

"Nothing gives me indigestion, and I don't happen to *have* a rolling pin right now," she gritted out, her annoyance with me growing. "You're right about me not liking talk about magic, but we're also talking about what *my* kitchens produce. Since you couldn't have simply taken the food, I want to know how you got it."

"I got it by being a magic user," I said, finally meeting that light-dark stare. "In order to do magic, you have to describe something in the language of spells. The more detailed a description you can give, the better the hold you have over the object and the more strength you can bring to bear.

"If I described that stone bench you're sitting on as just a stone bench, I couldn't affect it much because there's not enough description. If I described it instead by saying it was Rangri marble and Tansan wood, five feet long, three feet wide, and three feet high, I'd have a better grip on it and could do more. But if I really wanted my spell to work, I'd add that the marble came from the north side of the quarry, had a fifth level density, had a blue-veined pattern two millimeters wide, and so on, doing the same for the wood. Then I could make that bench sprout wings and fly away if I liked. Do you understand that?"

"I understand that you'd damned well better leave this bench alone," she stated, glaring at me harder. "And if you have to put so much into those spells of yours, why doesn't it take an hour to do each one?"

"Because the language of spells is a verbal shorthand, one sound or gesture able to stand for strings of words or phrases. Like tsp for teaspoon, only more so. I don't know the abbreviations for pinch and dash."

"That isn't funny," she grated into my grin. "Only amateurs follow a recipe exactly, and that's what this freak stuff sounds like to me. This first and then that, and don't ever change it."

"Some of the stronger wizards change it," I disagreed, reflecting that she knew more about magic than she was willing to admit. It was true that spells had to be spoken precisely the same to get the same results, but I hadn't told her that. "Half of the ones who fiddle with changes make big names for themselves, almost as big as those famous chefs of yours."

"What about the other half?" she asked, trying not to feel pleased at the thought of all those artists under her wing. "Do they give it up and get married and have children?"

"Most of them spend the rest of their lives as three-foot, orange frogs," I said, exaggerating only a little. "Or they disappear in a puff of smoke one day, and no one ever sees them again. Changing spells without knowing exactly what the change will produce is dangerous, a lot more dangerous than changing a recipe. The worst a mishandled recipe can do is make you throw up. A mishandled spell can literally turn you inside out, or freeze you in one position for the rest of eternity."

"And playing with that sort of thing is what *you* do," she stated, suddenly pale and indignant. "I knew I should have tried talking you out of learning it, knew it that first night we met. You have a lot less sense than *my* kids had, so I never should have just let you go your own way. I should have said something and kept on saying it—"

"Bena, please," I interrupted, refraining from reminding her that she *had* said something, more than once. "Sighted who try to deny what they are end up insane, and I do *not* do the sort of thing you mean. I'm just a harmless sorceress who has no intentions of *ever* getting involved with the dangerous stuff. I may be curious, but I'm not crazy."

"That's a matter of opinion," she returned, still not happy with me. "You don't have to tramp through an entire mud puddle to get splattered; stepping in one corner of it is usually enough. And you still haven't said how you got that food. Did you say a spell that caused Lidiar and Nida to cook for you?"

"I don't do zombie spells, even when using one would be practical," I responded, making no effort to keep the stiffness out of my voice. "As a matter of fact, I wouldn't use one even if they were legal. Have I ever told you how much I appreciate your high opinion of me?"

"Okay, okay, you can unbottle that tail," she grumbled, shifting her bulk on the bench. "I didn't mean to insult you, and I apologize. So how *did* you do it?"

"I Saw the ingredients the first time I ate the various dishes, and have been able to copy them ever since," I told her with a shrug. "Any Sighted above magician and witch level can do that, and many probably have. That's why the king's chamberlain tried to suggest that you have the dishes protected by magic. Unless and until you do, every magic user coming by can afterward eat as well as the king. Or sell the recipes to anyone who wants them."

"Sell *my* chefs' recipes?" she demanded in horror, finally getting the big picture. "To every shopkeeper and fishwife in the city? In every city? Chalaine, I thought we were friends. Why didn't you tell me this sooner?"

"I try not to tell people things they don't want to hear," I pronounced, for the second time holding her stare. "Not long after we met, you asked me not to discuss 'freak stuff' with you. As a friend, I respected that request. Are you saying I was wrong to do it?"

"No," she grudged after a short hesitation, shaking her head with a sigh. "No, obviously I asked for it. Can you fix it so that this kind of thing can't happen again? I don't mind *you* having the dishes, but a stranger who would sell them—!"

"Ask the chamberlain to have Master Haddil do it," I recommended. "Not only will he do a better job, he has to have another wizard in this world who maintains his spells when he leaves for a while. I don't, which means the protection would disappear the minute I stepped through an entry or a gate."

"I thought you planned to be around for a while," she said, and somehow I got the feeling the subject had been changed. "I mean, now that you've met Prince Bariden and all . . . Didn't you like seeing how attracted he was?"

"Attracted?" I asked with a short laugh. "How can you say that with a straight face? He told you himself he couldn't care less about me, and he stuck to that until he got a really—fullface—look at me. After that he wanted me to eat with him."

"I swear, I never know how to take the things you say," she complained, looking at me with brows raised. "Of course he was attracted, why else would he bother to say he wasn't? Somebody would think you knew nothing at all about men. So what are you doing out here instead of being somewhere cozy with him?"

"Bena, how much time do you spend with people who think there's something wrong with you?" I demanded, suddenly all out of patience. "I don't mean people who are concerned about you in general, but those who think of you as crippled? And I don't mean handicapped, because that's not the same thing at all. How much time do you give people like that? An hour, half a day, two or three days at a clip? I'd really like to know."

"Chalaine, I don't understand why you're angry at me," she said slowly and seriously, no longer playing the archetypal matchmaker. "The last thing in the world I want to do is upset you, but sometimes the teasing gets out of hand. You've—never been this bothered before."

"That's because I've never been through so many disasters before." Her soothing apology hadn't made me feel better, and I couldn't imagine what would. "He started out by apologizing for frightening me, and didn't even hear it when I said he hadn't. That was after he'd gotten a good look at me, of course, and from then on there wasn't a harsh word out of him. When we finished the first stage of our investigation and he asked me to eat with him, *I* asked *him* what my name was."

"Oh, don't tell me," she said, looking appalled. "He didn't know your *name*? No wonder you're so out of sorts. Even being a prince doesn't excuse something like that."

"He didn't think it was a hanging offense, but I disagreed," I grumbled, putting the soup bowl aside in favor of the coffee. My spell had specified that the cup continually refill itself, so I didn't have to nurse it. "Aren't there *any* men in the worlds who judge on something other than looks? His eyes told him I was a wounded, helpless little thing that needed to be looked after and protected, and he didn't enjoy it when I refused to act that way. If I'd whimpered and limped a little, he probably would have done handsprings."

"You know, that doesn't sound like the Prince Bariden *I* know," she mused, staring at my tray without seeing it. "When he was a boy, he started to play at slipping into my kitchens without me seeing him. If I caught him I would make him sit down and tell me about his day, and then I noticed I was catching him more and more often. He didn't seem to get on well with his brothers and sisters, but not because there was anything wrong with *him*. He's a full-grown man now with a reputation or two he'd be better off without, but he's never stopped treating me decent."

"Maybe that's because you're almost as big as he is," I muttered, then looked at her curiously. "What did you mean about a reputation or two? Has he made himself notorious?"

"Only in a way," she hedged, then glanced at me and sighed. "Well, you can see part of it for yourself, in that sword he wears. They had him learning weapons from the time he was really small, but I don't think they expected him to be as good with them as he is. He's been challenged three times to serious fights, and answered all the challenges personally. As a prince of this kingdom he could have used a champion, but instead chose not to."

"That's stranger than you know," I said, my brows way up there. "Those who are Sighted don't usually get involved in physical fights, not when using magic is so automatic to them. It would be like—oh, an ordinary man trying to fight a duel while hopping around on one leg. If his other leg wasn't tied to keep him from using it, sooner or later he would forget and stand on it. Did the Prince forget and end up doing something he shouldn't have?"

"He most certainly did not," Bena huffed indignantly. "Bariden is an honorable man, and he killed those three fair and square. He would *never* cheat, not even if it meant losing. But he didn't lose, and that's what has people talking. His oldest brother Trayden is heir to the throne, but even though he's good with a sword, he isn't as good as Bariden. People are afraid Bariden intends to challenge his brother once their father is gone."

"And with him being Sighted, they're also afraid they'll have an unopposable tyrant for centuries rather than for a single lifetime," I summed up, finally seeing the point. "None of them will consider the possibility that he'd make a *better* king than his brother, because a freak couldn't possibly be. What's the other crime he's accused of?"

"It's—not exactly a crime," she grudged, and I had the feeling she'd hoped I would forget about that second part. "Or maybe it is, I don't think I know any more. He—has something of a reputation with—women, like where they're always after him, you know? He—usually lets himself be caught, but—not for long. *I* say he's looking for the *right* woman, and when he finds her he'll stop looking."

"But in the meantime he's forcing himself to have fun," I summed up a second time, ignoring her gallant interpretation of not-so-gallant actions. Bena tends to think the best of the strays she adopts, even if they happen to be freaks. Or fast-living princes.

"Chalaine, he's a man," she said with an exasperated sigh. "Men do things like that, but not because they mean harm. Would you be happier if he was a prim and proper virgin? Men tend to think virgins are special, but women know better."

"Bena, I wouldn't care if he also had bad breath, flat feet, and writer's cramp," I told her as clearly as possible. "He may be a man, but he's one I don't care to know any better than I already do. If you're looking for someone to pair him up with, look somewhere else. It would eventually get to be annoying to have to remind him what my name is."

She winced as though she'd forgotten about that, but didn't get the chance to make any more excuses. Just as she parted her lips a servant came rushing out into the garden, and he looked frightened sick. Since I was the one he headed toward, I knew something else had happened. I didn't yet know what, but had the definite feeling I'd regret what I'd eaten . . .

Bariden, third prince of Melen, cursed himself silently as he watched the girl walk out of the room and disappear up the hall. He hadn't been that clumsy with a woman since the age of fifteen, when an older woman of nineteen had let him know she was interested. He'd been nervous with his first older woman, but only to begin with. As soon as he realized that all women, young or old, responded the same, he'd been just fine.

Until about five minutes ago. He ran a hand over his face, possibly in an effort to wipe away invisible boot prints. She'd stomped him up one side and down the other, and to say he hadn't expected it would be vast understatement. Women just didn't talk to him like that, even if they *weren't* very happy.

"And how the hell did she know?" he growled, still finding it incredible that he'd actually forgotten her name. He didn't believe the explanation she'd given him, about his touching her rather than speaking. That was the sort of thing you thought of after you already knew, and she hadn't been guessing. For a shy and quiet girl, she was unbelievably sharp . . .

He felt the urge to go and *do* something, but instead went to a comfortable chair, sat, and spoke a spell for the meal he wanted. He'd been too busy to stop for lunch, and then he'd been too distracted. Never in a million years had he expected that old spell of his to work *now*, in the middle of chaos, and certainly not with a girl who had almost drowned him the first time they met . . .

Bariden shifted his sword into the chair's slot, then reached for the wine he'd specified with the food. What he needed right then was someone to talk to, but not just any someone. Bena, for instance, would listen sympathetically and then give him advice, but chances were good that the advice would be wrong. She didn't understand magic, and therefore tended to dismiss it—along with most Sighted. The unSighted didn't usually have his kind of problem . . .

He sighed when he realized he had only one choice of whom to talk to, even though the conversation wasn't likely to be pleasant. ReSayne was one of the strangest entities he'd ever come across, and that was saying a lot when you considered some of those he'd met during occasional trips. ReSayne's people were somehow related to demons, but not in any way a human would understand, he'd been assured. They called themselves fiends and considered themselves better than demons, but again refused to discuss in what way. There was a lot they refused to talk about, but ever since he'd helped ReSayne—in some way he still didn't understand—his problems weren't part of the refusal.

Bariden took a sip of wine before replacing the glass on the tray floating in front of him, then reached to his left hand with his right. Using his right little finger, he pressed his left hand just below the wrist bone, an action he wasn't likely to perform by accident. At the same time he said, "ReSayne . . . ReSayne . . . ReSayne . . ." as though sending out some sort of message. After three repetitions, he stopped and went back to his meal. The fiend would have heard him, and would come as soon as possible.

He was just about finished with his duck à l'orange with stuffing and honeyed yams, when the air in front of him began to ripple. Fiends didn't use entries any more than demons did, although they both used gates on a regular basis. The rippling air began to swirl, and as it did, very bright rainbow colors appeared. The colors grew bright enough to dazzle, and then they settled down to simply float.

"Bariden, how could you?" a smooth, light voice asked from the middle of the colors. "Stuffing and yams with duck à l'orange? A prince is supposed to have style, not a lumberman's appetite. And how do you like my new look? Isn't this nicer than thick blue smoke?"

"Absolutely," Bariden agreed, ignoring the comments about his taste in food. "Flashy and gaudy are *you*, ReSayne. Do you by any chance have some time to listen?"

"Bariden, dear boy, why else would I have responded to your summons?" it said, and then its voice went morose. "Although I dislike admitting it, you're probably right about the gaudiness. I'll just have to think of something else, but that's for later. Where are we, by the way? I can feel the strangest spell on this room."

"That's an exclusion spell, to keep people out," Bariden explained as ReSayne settled down to a solid form. The form it chose, though, was that of a fancy straight-backed chair, with cushioned seat in orange and two eyes in the polished-wood backrest. The eyes were a bright leaf green, and Bariden couldn't help thinking that his father would probably love ReSayne.

"We have something of a problem around here, but that's not what I need your help for," he continued. "There's this girl, and that spell I told you about a couple of years ago, and the fact that things have been going from bad to worse with every move I make. I never went through the awkward teenager stage, but I'm beginning to think that's because the experience was saving itself for now."

"That does sound serious," the ReSayne chair said, bright green eyes blinking thoughtfully. "Why don't you tell me about the girl and the spell, and then we can get into what's been going wrong."

"I suppose I should start from when she drowned me," Bariden mused, reaching again for his wineglass. "She was one of those Summoned to help with this problem we have, and she and I ended up being paired as partners."

"She drowned you," ReSayne stated, and this time the eyes looked impressed. "She must be a good deal more formidable than the females you usually associate with. I hadn't thought it would be possible to find one larger and stronger than you, but—"

"No, no, no, she's *not* bigger than me," Bariden interrupted. "You can see how well I'm doing even with explanations. She's about average height for a woman, I suppose, and seems to be built fairly well. Her hair is—auburn, I suppose you would call it, brown with a lot of dark red, and it's long enough to reach her behind. She wears it braided, to keep it out of the way, I guess, but I'd love to see it loose. And her eyes, the biggest, darkest eyes I've ever fallen into . . ."

"Bariden, if you want to daydream, you'd be best off doing it alone," ReSayne's voice came after a moment, bringing him back to the present. "If you want to talk instead, it's more effective when you use words."

"Words, right," he agreed after clearing his throat. "You can see what kind of shape I'm in . . . At any rate, what she did was bring this big—bubble, I thought—through the entry with her, and somehow it got away from her. It went straight for Master Haddil, but he uses personal warding. It bounced off his warding straight at me, but why would I bother trying to avoid what looked like a giant soap bubble? Only it wasn't a simple soap bubble. When it hit me it burst, and gallons of water poured out of it all over me."

"I would have enjoyed being there to see that," ReSayne chortled, its green eyes narrowed with amusement. "And to have seen that very interesting bubble. Was that when you discovered your bottomless fascination for the girl?"

"What I discovered was the urge to mutilate," he answered, finding ReSayne's reaction the expected one. "After I banished the sogginess I ignored her, otherwise I might have been tempted to commit mayhem. I'd parted company with my latest—female companion just the night before, and as unpleasant as it had been, I was somewhat down on women just then. When I ended up paired with this one to work on our problem with no possible way to refuse associating with her, my mood turned even sweeter."

"But that obviously changed," ReSayne commented, probably to hurry the story. "When and where, not to mention why?"

"When we began working together, I couldn't help noticing how sharp she was despite also being very quiet. She knew what had to be done, and went ahead and did it. But she hadn't once looked straight at me, not even when she spoke to me, and that quickly became very annoying. After a while I grabbed her, and forced her to look directly at me."

"And ended up being thrown across the room by her warding," ReSayne concluded, the green eyes all but nodding. "I could have told you *that* would happen. How many times have I pointed out how foolish you're being when you refuse to use warding of your own? Haven't I—"

"ReSayne!" Bariden interrupted again, in no mood to be lectured. "Let's save that argument for another time. The point here is that I *didn't* set off her warding. It must be keyed to intent, and it wasn't my intent to harm her. Instead, I got my first good look at her—and that set off the spell with a vengeance."

"Now's the time to refresh my memory about that spell," ReSayne cued him, not in the least insulted over having been interrupted. That meant it intended to return to the interrupted subject later, a realization that made Bariden groan on the inside. The fiend never forgot anything that involved lecturing, leading Bariden to wonder if it took invisible notes . . .

"Only a few years after I began to study magic, a wizard came from another realm to speak to my father." Bariden remembered the episode clearly, more clearly than most things from that time in his life. "Master Haddil was off doing something or other on one of the planes he frequents, so the wizard, Tramfeor, felt it would be impolite to visit long. But while he was here he spent some time talking to me, asking about my life and my studies and such. I remember getting the feeling he already knew the answers to the questions he put, but that had to be my imagination. If he already knew the answers, why would he have bothered to ask?"

"Some wizards are like that," ReSayne assured him, the green eyes moving three inches higher in the chair back. "They like to pretend that they know everything, just to impress the people around them. If they did know everything, they'd be fiends rather than wizards."

"Yes, of course," Bariden murmured diplomatically. "Well, his questioning got around to how well I liked girls, so I told him. He didn't think it was unusual that I'd already had more offers than I'd been able to take advantage of, or that a lot of the girls had been encouraged in their interest by their mothers. I was a prince, after all, and one who was Sighted. Either of those things alone would have made me a 'catch,' but both together guaranteed that I would do exceptionally well in life. When he said that, it made me feel very strange. It hadn't occurred to me that the girls were more interested in *what* I was than in what sort of person I was becoming."

"But weren't you all barely more than children?" ReSayne asked gently, almost as though it could feel the pain he'd experienced. "Children are usually self-centered and shallow, or so I've been led to believe."

"No one past puberty is still a child," Bariden stated, reaching again for his wineglass. "Your basic personality is formed and set even before then, and once your body changes you're fully adult. If you've decided by then that what a person has is more important than what he is, nothing short of getting kicked in the teeth two or three times will change your mind. If anything can change your mind. Tramfeor noticed how disturbed I was, and that was when he offered to teach me the spell."

"Your dramatic pause is very effective," ReSayne said as though it were complimenting a toddler. "Now that I've noticed, do feel free to go on."

"It was a Spell of Affinity aimed at the opposite sex," Bariden answered, almost in a growl. ReSayne could be so damned *annoying* ... "It's meant to tell me just how well a particular woman will match with me, just how seriously committed she's capable of being. Until now I've had glimmers, small bursts of light when I looked into women's eyes. Some were stronger than others, like the one with Miralia, the girl I just broke up with. At first I thought she was the best match for me, the glimmer was so strong. But there were certain things about her—Well, let's just say she and I disagreed over a few matters I consider important."

"Am I correct in assuming the burst of light was stronger with the new girl than it was with this Miralia?" ReSayne asked. "If so, I fail to see your problem. As you felt it necessary to pursue the former woman, now you must pursue the newcomer. You bipolar entities always make things so difficult when they're really quite—"

"ReSayne," Bariden interrupted, knowing the fiend was getting ready to leave again. "Whether or not to—'pursue' the girl isn't my problem. The burst of light I got from her was so strong it almost blinded me. Of *course* I want to get to know her better, but—I did something really stupid, and now she doesn't want to know *me*. Considering the fact that she's a Sighted, I thought you might be able to help me figure out a way to—to get her to change her mind."

Bariden all but muttered the last of his words, which immediately put vast amusement into the leaf green eyes studying him. ReSayne was enjoying itself, and wasn't *that* outcome surprising.

"My dear boy, you must really be desperate," the light voice purred while the green eyes shifted leftward along the chair back. "For a human of your experience to be asking help from a fiend—? Whatever you did to annoy her must be of monumental proportions. I can't wait to hear what it was."

"I—had to admit I didn't know her name after hearing it three separate times," Bariden grudged. "Don't ask me *why* I didn't remember, maybe it's the way women usually repeat their names for me over and over, to be sure I don't forget. Somehow she knew all about it, and even admitting she was right didn't help."

"Oh, Bariden," ReSayne said in shock, the green eyes wide. "Even a life-form such as myself can appreciate a blunder like that. And with a female Sighted? The woman must be truly remarkable if she didn't reduce you to a pile of ashes on the spot. You'll certainly need every bit of charm you possess to even begin to make headway against *that*."

"I've already tried charm, and it didn't work," Bariden said morosely. "If I didn't know better, I'd think she was warded against it. For such a pretty little thing, she's— well, like a meat grinder. Completely quiet and harmless until you start to turn her handle. And I sure as Hellfire turned her handle, but now it seems to be going on by itself. What I need is a suggestion on how to get it to stop."

"Is that all?" ReSayne said in a pooh-poohing tone. "Nothing easier, my boy. Just do something *for* her that will outweigh the insult you gave. And now that *that's* settled—"

"No," Bariden interrupted immediately, before the fiend could change the subject. "That *isn't* settled. Generalities I've been able to come up with on my own. It's specifics I need some help with, like suggestions on what I could possibly do for her. What is there *to* do for a woman who's also a sorceress?"

"Bariden, the time has come to speak plainly." ReSayne's green eyes stared unblinkingly at him. "I'm aware of the fact that you have very little experience in the actual pursuit of females. For most of your adult life *they've* pursued *you*, which must certainly have had its pleasant moments. Now, however, the effort has become yours to make, and the first thing you do is ask someone else to solve the problem for you. Is that what being a prince does to a human male? Turns him incapable and dependent?"

Bariden was about to heatedly deny the charge, but the quietly sober way the fiend had spoken made him pause. ReSayne wasn't usually *that* serious, not unless the point it discussed was more than somewhat important. And now that he'd stopped to think about it, the charge was uncomfortably true. When it came to—fighting his own battles with a sword, say, he would have considered it cowardly to go running to others to ask for their help. His current situation was harder and more dangerous than a sword fight, but still . . .

"All right, I'm forced to admit you've made a very good point." The words weren't easy, but Bariden said them anyway. "If this is important enough to be a problem, it's one I have to solve for myself. I just wish you weren't also right about how little experience I have with pursuit. Even Miralia came to *me*, although she did make me work for the privilege of sharing her bed. One problem was that it never stopped being a privilege, never grew into something we both looked forward to . . ."

Bariden let the thought trail off, at the same time gesturing away the tray with the remnants of his meal. She'd accused him of being spoiled by all the female attention he'd had, unable to appreciate the real, true gesture she always made. He was nothing but an ungrateful boor, telling her she ought to be behaving like his legion of trollops. If he didn't know what a real lady of quality was like, he ought to find out before accusing her of improper behavior . . .

He hadn't been accusing Miralia of anything, but her attitude had made him wonder if he *was* being a boor. She'd walked away from him with her head high and her body stiffly offended, and two hours later his mother had sent for him. Somehow she'd heard about the exchange, and had lost no time in telling him again what a disappointment he was to her. He'd listened with jaw clamped shut to her usual lecture about how she'd never dreamed she'd give life to such a sorry excuse for a man and a prince, and then he'd left. Later, when Miralia had announced that she was ready to listen to his apology, he'd told her he was still trying to figure out what he'd done that needed to be apologized for. She'd then informed him he needn't come back until he did figure it out, and he'd agreed that that might be best . . .

"Was there anything else you needed to discuss with me?" ReSayne interrupted his thoughts, for once in a gentle way. "I *am* somewhat involved with a project of my own at the moment, but since I'm already here, you might as well take advantage of the fact."

"No, no, there's nothing else," Bariden decided aloud with a sigh. "There are some things I'd love to palm off on others, but I don't know anyone stupid enough to willingly accept them. The one thing I might eventually need your expertise for is this mystery I'm helping to investigate. The lives and well-being of a lot of people are at stake, and if we can't figure it out ourselves I'll need everything you can offer. Hopefully your own project will be finished by then."

"Even if it isn't, I'll probably be willing to be distracted," ReSayne answered, and then the chair melted into a blue-gray cloud that had the same leaf green eyes. "Your mystery sounds intriguing, and the moment I have time I want to hear all about it. If my project is completed sooner than anticipated, I'll come right back rather than wait to be summoned. And I may even have a new look by then that will satisfy us both. Good hunting with your problems."

Bariden nodded his thanks as the fiend faded from view, deliberately making no comment about the next possible new look. He had enough to worry about without that; trying to anticipate what ReSayne might come up with would drive him even crazier than he was right then. What he needed was some solitary time filled with serious thought—

"Your Highness, excuse me," a voice came from the hall. He looked up to see the anxious face of a messenger peering in through the open door, but the man didn't enter. For a moment Bariden wondered why, and then he remembered about the exclusion spell.

"What is it, Stollen?" he asked as he stood. Since there was nothing left to do in that room, he might as well find someplace else for his thinking. But when he walked out and pulled the door closed behind him, Stollen looked only faintly relieved.

"Your Highness, it's happened again," the messenger said in a strained whisper, obviously trying to keep the word from spreading too quickly. Which had to be why he'd waited for Bariden to reach him before speaking. "Since you're one of those working on the problem, I've been sent to bring you there. Master Haddil is unavailable at the moment, but the healer has been sent for as well."

"Who is it this time?" Bariden asked as he gestured for the other man to lead the way. "And what about— my working partner. Has *she* been sent for?"

"Yes, sir," Stollen answered even as he started off. "The sorceress Chalaine was expected by Benatha Aylie, so another messenger is checking with Bena first. If she isn't there, he'll have to search. And the victim this time is Diri, one of the maids who usually works in this part of the house."

Bariden was surprised to hear that, but speculation would be more profitable when he reached the scene of the occurrence. In the meantime, he took a moment to really appreciate the messenger system his father had put into effect. There were messengers scattered all over the palace, and their job was to know the whereabouts of those people in the palace who mattered. In normal times one of their number made the rounds every couple of hours, gathering information from individual messengers and collating it for a complete picture. If someone needed someone else, it rarely took more than a few moments to locate that person . . .

And just then they'd done him more of a service than simply locating him. He smiled as his mind repeated the name Chalaine, a name he really should have remembered. He still didn't know why he hadn't, but he wasn't about to forget it again. The investigation they were working on had to come first, but after that . . .

By the time Stollen showed him to the maid Diri's rooms, Bariden had lost a lot of his satisfaction. Diri had worked her way up to a quasi-supervisory position, and for that reason had earned a small apartment of her own. The two rooms were tiny compared to the major apartments, but they were worlds better than the dormitory slots or shared cells many of the other maids lived in. Diri worked along with the girls she also supervised, which meant it was hard to understand why she'd become a victim. Could she have learned something important, and been silenced before she was able to tell anyone?

"The healer is already here, and so is the sorceress," Stollen told him in a soft voice. The man undoubtedly knew that from the other messengers standing outside the room, both of whom looked frightened. From inside came the sound of sobbing, and when Bariden reached the doorway he found out who was producing it. "That's the girl who found her," Stollen supplied. "It wasn't like Diri not to get back to work on time after lunch, but her girls thought she might have needed to do something. When hours went by and they still hadn't heard from her, one of the girls came looking. The messenger in this section heard her screaming, and immediately sent for the circulating supervisor."

Bariden thanked Stollen, then left him outside and went in alone. The tiny sitting room had only a single easy chair, positioned opposite the doorway in the far right-hand corner of the room. The crying girl sat huddled in it, her face buried in her hands, clearly wanting to be as far from the unmoving body to the left as possible.

Diri sat in one of the four chairs around the small table to the left, an almost-empty cup of something on the table in front of her. Her left hand rested on a book and she seemed to be reading, but no book ever written could absorb someone to *that* extent. The woman was barely breathing, and when the healer, who was crouched in front of her, touched her arm, it was as though he touched a statue.

It was then that Chalaine appeared, from the doorway to the right that must lead to Diri's bedroom. She glanced at him as she passed in front of the crying girl, but she didn't speak to either of them. Instead she walked to the center of the room and began to study the walls. For someone who had wanted to see a victim, she was paying more attention to the interior decorating than to Diri.

"Was there anything out of place in the bedroom?" he asked, just to be saying *something*. The paneled design the walls had been painted with was intricate and more attractive than one would expect in a place like that. Still, Bariden didn't enjoy the idea that Chalaine preferred looking at *it* to looking at him.

"The bedroom is neater than any pin ever made," the girl muttered, still staring around. "It also has a design on its walls, but not separated into panels like in here. Do you see anything . . . unbalanced in any of these sections? There's something wrong, but I can't put my finger on what."

Bariden started to demand what a painted wall could possibly have to do with the mystery, but that was the whole point. They hadn't been able to find *anything* to do with the mystery, and for all he knew the answer *was* on the wall. With that in mind he began to look more closely at the panels, trying to compare each section with the ones to either side of it. He also moved farther into the room, but hadn't taken more than two steps before Chalaine made a sound of satisfaction.

"That's the one," she said, pointing to the first panel beyond the far left-hand corner of the room. "That section there is the one that doesn't match. Can you see it?"

Bariden's view was blocked by the stricken Diri and the now-standing healer who continued to try to reach through to her. On top of that, Chalaine was moving toward the panel she'd singled out. In order to see what she was talking about, he had to swing right before circling in behind Chalaine to the left. At that point there was nothing in the way—and that was when it happened.

Like a giant, invisible hand, the compulsion reached out and grabbed him. He *had* to get to that section of wall, and as fast as possible! Nothing could stop him, nothing *would* stop him! Clouded by vast confusion and unyielding determination, Bariden broke into a run. Having no real idea what he was doing, he also failed to understand when Chalaine stepped directly into his path. Her back was to him as she examined the wall panel, but she didn't reblock the compulsion. It continued to pull him, and he just kept running—even when he crashed into her, sending her forward ahead of him—up to the wall—and then through it—

CHAPTER THREE

I fell into something soft when I went down, and it took a moment to realize it was also cold. I was too dazed to understand immediately what had happened; I heard the cursing from my right, and then a hand touched my shoulder.

"Are you all right?" Prince Bariden's voice demanded, and then he was trying to help me to my feet. "Come on, you can't just lie there in that, you'll get frostbite. We've got to find our way back."

"Frostbite?" I echoed, getting up only because he was doing the lifting. "Back? What are you talking about? What happened?"

"I must have hit you harder than I thought," he said, sounding savage. "Damn that setter of traps. Here, take a quick look around and then we have to get moving."

He helped me turn away from him, and what I saw then made no sense. We stood in an open wood at dusk, thick white snow covering the ground, new flakes falling silently all around to add to them. It was also cold, very cold despite the lack of wind. How could we possibly have gotten to a winter wood . . . ?

"I think it's safe to guess what bothered you about the walls in Diri's sitting room," he said from behind me. "There was an entry hidden just at the surface at one point, and it distorted the pattern of painting just a little. But it was also primed with a compulsion aimed at *me*, demanding that I get to it as fast as possible. I remember starting to run, and didn't stop even when you got in the way."

"Which made you knock me through ahead of you," I added, finally remembering getting shoved hard toward the wall. "I expected to be flattened, but ended up flying through the air instead. But if we came through an entry, where is it? I'm starting to freeze solid."

"I hope it's masked rather than one way," he answered as I brushed snow off the front of my tunic and breeches. "If it isn't, we'll have to call up an entry of our own. Or you'll have to. I've never called up an entry, and I understand you need certain coordinates."

"You do, but it isn't a problem," I assured him. "I have the coordinates to a lot of places, so you aren't as trapped here as you were obviously supposed to be. But first I'm going to do something about these clothes I'm wearing. It's too cold for summer lightweights."

I could see my breath as I spoke, so I hurriedly added a warm-clothes spell to the speaking. It was short and simple, which means the reaction came very quickly. The spell carved itself into the air in glowing letters, overbright in the dusk, and then the letters began to crumble from the bottom. Tiny pieces fell the way the snow fell, and in no time at all the letters were completely gone.

"Fantastic," the prince muttered from behind me, his tone full of disgust. "This place is sealed by someone with wizard strength, and no one's spells will work but his. Apparently he wasn't taking any chances about my knowing an entry spell after all. We'd better get to shelter before we try to figure out what to do next."

"What kind of shelter is there around *here*?" I asked, my teeth already beginning to chatter. I'd also wrapped my arms around me, trying to remember I *liked* the cold.

"That way, through the woods," he said, putting his hands to my arms to turn me. Behind where he'd been standing I could see something that looked like a house a short distance off. It was dark and looming rather than well-lit and cheery, but we weren't in a position to be choosy.

"Then let's go," I said, pulling away from the delightfully warm hands that had been touching me. I needed something warm just then, but Prince Bariden's hands weren't it. He could save that for when he got back to his horde of girlfriends.

It wasn't possible to run through the deepening snow, but the hurried shuffle I adopted brought a small amount of warmth. My companion drag-trotted beside me to the right, his left palm against his sword hilt, his eyes moving around the woods we passed through. There couldn't be many beasts out hunting in a snowstorm, but even one would be one too many. With that in mind I added my own looking around, at the same time hoping snow wasn't what that world always had. If it turned out to be the norm, we could run into any number of hunting beasts who considered it a lovely day . . .

Whatever the true situation was, we finally reached the house without anything attacking us. The thing was larger than it had looked at first, but wasn't any lighter. Dark stone blocks made up what we could see of it, with a heavy wooden door closing off access to the inside. I was so cold by then that I didn't *care* what was inside. Even if it was something dangerous that preyed on visitors, it would still have to fight to keep from being kicked out of its lair.

Prince Bariden, his grim expression saying he felt the same, gripped the metal knocker and pounded on the door with it. The metal must have been cold to the point of pain, but he pounded away as if he didn't care *what* he held. But he used his left hand rather than his right, which said he knew he might be leaving some skin behind.

I could almost hear the sound of his knocking reverberating inside, a demanding boom-boom-boom-boom that echoed around in emptiness. If no one came to answer the door we'd have to try to break in, and I didn't even want to think about that. There were no windows in view from where we stood at the front door, and—

"Watch it," Prince Bariden said softly, at the same time stepping in front of me. The large wooden door was beginning to open, with nothing to show who or what was doing the opening. The hinges groaned rather than screeched, and then—

"Come on in fast, before you freeze," a light, friendly voice urged. "And before *I* freeze, from standing near this open door."

I couldn't quite look over the prince's shoulder, so I

moved to the right to look around him. Standing in the doorway was a pretty blond girl about my age, her smile matching the friendliness we'd heard in her voice. Not exactly what we'd been expecting, but . . .

"Thanks," my companion told her, then reached around to push me through the doorway first. "We really appreciate this."

"For a minute I thought you were alone," the girl said to him with a laugh, stepping aside to let me pass. "It's been all pairs so far, but you never know. I'm Janissa."

"Nice to meet you, Janissa," he acknowledged with a smile, then helped her push closed the door. "I'm Bariden, and my companion is Chalaine. What did you mean when you said it's been all pairs so far? Where are we, and what's going on?"

"We have no idea where we are," Janissa answered, diverting me from marveling over the fact that Prince Bariden had managed to learn my name. "We also don't know what's going on, but we've found a theory most of us like. As pure guesswork, it tends to give us *something* that makes sense. Come on into our gathering room, and we'll tell you about it after you've met the others."

She turned and led the way toward the right, through a wide, dark hall that was lit by a single torch. Everything around us, floor, walls, and ceiling, seemed to be made of the same dark stone, without anything in the way of adornment. It was a lot warmer inside than it had been out in the snow, but that's not to say it was *warm*.

Janissa, wearing a long dress of pale green and what seemed to be matching slippers, ignored a shadowy doorway to the left in favor of the one beyond it. Soft light came through that second doorway, and when we reached it I could see there was a fireplace which added to the light and warmth. Around the fireplace was an austere room of rigid comfort, a place for someone to relax who didn't really enjoy relaxing. Stiffly rather than deeply upholstered chairs, couches that encouraged sitting up straight, small, sturdy-looking tables, nothing on the walls but mostly empty torch sconces. No decorations, no frills, not even carpeting on the stone floor. And five people sitting loosely together, watching us walk in.

"Everyone, this is Bariden and Chalaine," Janissa said, stepping aside to gesture at us. "It looks like our friend is at it again, and maybe this time we'll get a usable clue."

"I certainly hope so," one of the men said as he stood. "We haven't been here all that long and the company is certainly congenial, but I'll be happier if I'm free to go about my business. I'm Vadran, and this is Wellia."

He was tall, brown-haired and blue-eyed, and his very attractive smile seemed aimed mostly at me. The woman beside him, introduced as Wellia, had the same brown hair and blue eyes, but wasn't as tall. Her smile and nod seemed intended more for Prince Bariden, which balanced the greeting. Vadran wore black boots and trousers and a blue tunic, while Wellia was in a dress and slippers like Janissa's, only in a blue like Vadran's tunic.

"We were the newcomers until you two arrived," a second man said, also standing now. "That doesn't mean we're not just as anxious to get out of here, an attitude you'll unfortunately be finding out about for yourselves. This is Idara, and I'm Halad."

Once again Halad's smile was for me, Idara's for Prince Bariden. These two were redheads with dark eyes, and they were dressed like the others except that Halad's tunic and Idara's dress and slippers were a reddish brown. The pattern was absolutely clear, and then the last man stepped forward to clinch it.

"I'm Kamen," he said with a smile all for me. He was tall, blond, and green-eyed, wearing a light green tunic that matched Janissa's dress. "Janissa and I have been here the longest, so we tend to feel like the host and hostess of the place. Why don't we take you two upstairs to find the clothes that will have been provided for you? After you've gotten past being cold and wet, we can exchange information over a meal."

"I think we'd rather do some drying out by that fire," Prince Bariden said, all but taking the words out of my mouth. "That way we can exchange information right now, without having to wait. Kamen, you said you and Janissa have been here the longest. Just how long is that, and how did you get here?"

By then we were already on our way to the fireplace, but

Kamen didn't seem to be bothered by having his suggestion ignored. He glanced at Janissa, and then shrugged.

"By the day-and-night cycle of this world, it's been about four weeks," he answered. "As for how we got here, we're still not quite sure. Janissa was simply walking from one of her houses to another by entry, and I was on my way to Conclave. I'd called up an entry to take me there, but when I stepped through I was ankle-deep in snow with Janissa only a few steps away. When we spotted this place we headed for it, and found the door open and inviting."

"*Not* inviting, but better than the snow," Janissa amended. "About a week later Vadran and Wellia came knocking, and a week after that Halad and Idara. This week it seems to be your turn."

"We were all going elsewhere and ended up here," the brown-haired Vadran said. "Not only are we all Sighted, we each became one of a matched set. But you two don't fit into that, and I wonder why. Is the game almost over, or has the player simply decided to change the rules?"

"The game he means is what goes on in this house," red-haired Idara said with a small shiver. "I'm sure you've already discovered that your spells don't work here, and that because of the wizard strength of whoever set this up. He or she seems to want to watch us cope without the help of magic, and that hasn't been easy. The player feeds and clothes us and keeps us warm, but for everything else we're on our own."

"Everything else means the—things—this house is haunted with," brown-haired Wellia said with her own shiver. "They appear mostly when you're alone, occasionally when you're with someone who can't do much better than you. Then you have to drive the thing off somehow, or else it will—disgust and nauseate you."

"But only if you're female," Halad said, taking his turn. "If you're male the thing will be out for blood or broken bones, which may or may not be worse. The only real weapon in this house is that sword you're wearing, Bariden, but even if the rest of us had the same it would make no difference. I can't use a sword, and I doubt if Kamen or Vadran can either."

"He's right about me," Kamen admitted while Vadran

simply shrugged and nodded. "I never thought I'd need any weapon beyond magic, which proves how shortSighted it's possible to be. But now that you know about us, what about you two? As Vadran pointed out, you two aren't matched. Did you know each other before you got here?"

"It so happens we did," Prince Bariden answered, turning partially away from the fire I was still drying myself at. "Chalaine and I were working on a serious problem our realm has, and apparently the guilty party was afraid we would get to the bottom of it. A new victim was made for us to go look at, and the room was booby-trapped with an entry and a compulsion. The compulsion forced me through the entry, and Chalaine was accidently swept along."

"Which means one of two things," I contributed, only glancing over my shoulder. "Either our guilty party and your game player are one and the same, or our guilty party simply happens to know about what's going on here, and took advantage of it to get rid of us. At this point it's a matter of pick the one you like best."

"But maybe we can figure out which one it is," Kamen said, his green eyes suddenly bright. "If two more rooms and sets of clothes have been prepared, then you're expected rather than just tossed in. If they're not, you weren't meant to be here."

"That only works one way," I disagreed while everyone else commented or exclaimed. "If no rooms are prepared, that means we were tossed in. If rooms *are* prepared, that could mean the original spell on this place allows for new-comers automatically. It doesn't have to mean our guilty party is your game player."

"I hadn't thought of that," Kamen said as he blinked, and then he produced a grin. "But the thought occurring to me now is that we finally have a real thinker among us. I have a feeling you're the one who will find us a way out, Chalaine."

"Isn't that funny," Idara said, toying with a strand of her red hair. "I was just thinking that about Bariden. I hope at least one of us is psychic."

"As long as it's not psychotic," Halad said from beside her, looking amused. "This place is enough to do that to anyone. Why don't we go upstairs and check out the room situation? If they *have* been provided for, they'll at least be able to change for dinner."

"And it *is* getting close to that time," Janissa put in. "if there isn't any provision for them, we'll have to share what *we* get. Let's get started now."

All six of them made sounds of agreement as they began to move, drawing the prince and me along with them. I would have preferred staying by the fire, and not just because my clothes were still wet. That whole situation felt really strange, even beyond the strangeness it was supposed to be. Six magic users trapped in an unpleasant situation, and all they'd done was settle in? Granted they couldn't use their magic, but still . . .

The group led the way left out of the room, and only a short distance away was a wide staircase. The steps were some sort of polished stone, hard to see in the dimness of the single torch burning nearby. It was also colder away from the fire, but that wasn't the only thing trying to make me shiver. That house insisted on feeling deserted even with eight people walking through it . . .

The staircase led to a second floor that somehow gave the impression of being larger than the ground floor. Corridors stretched left, right, and straight ahead, and we were directed left. This corridor had occasional candles burning in sconces on the walls, while the others had been dark.

"The first two bedrooms, to left and right, were given to Janissa and me," Kamen said with appropriate gestures. "The next two belong to Vadran and Wellia, and the third set to Halad and Idara. If you two have been provided for, the fourth pair will be lit."

The doors to the indicated rooms were open, and I could see what was probably the light from only one or two candles in each. I wondered if it was our fellow captives who were so frugal with the candles, or if that was our host's doing. And then I forgot the point as we reached the fourth pair of doors.

"Well, so much for us getting a useful clue," Kamen sighed. "These rooms were dark, and now they're lit. One way or another you two have been included in, so we might as well get you settled. This way, Bariden."

He and the other men took the prince to the left, and Janissa touched my arm before heading right. I followed her into a fairly large chamber that was as formally stiff as the gathering room downstairs, and just as spartan. Against the far wall to the right was a large bed without canopy or curtains, and farther right was a plain wooden wardrobe. A couple of small tables held unlit candles in plain silver holders, utility uncombined with any sort of beauty. To the left of the door was a fireplace complete with fire, two uncomfortable-looking chairs set a few feet away in front of it. Closer to the door on the right was a washstand with basin and pitcher, and that was it as far as interior decoration went.

"The inside door of the wardrobe has a mirror," Janissa told me, walking over to open it and prove the point. "You'll notice there's only one dress and pair of slippers in here at any one time, but that's all you'll need. When you take your worn clothes off put them in here, and the wardrobe will take care of them."

"But *you* have to take care to change as quickly as possible," Wellia added. "The longer you're alone, the better the chance that one of those—things—will come after you. You can't avoid them entirely, but there's no sense in making things worse."

"Easiest is being with one of the men when it happens," Idara put in, checking herself quickly in the mirror. "The thing always turns out to be one that goes after *them*, so you don't have to put up with the awfulness more than once in a while."

"Don't the men mind if you take advantage of them like that?" I asked. "I know they're supposed to be big and strong and all, but dumping the whole load on them doesn't seem fair. Even if they know all about it and insist on doing it like that—"

"They do insist," Janissa interrupted with a smile. "They get their own benefit out of the arrangement, so they don't mind at all. But dinner should be ready soon, so you ought to get changed now. We'll be waiting downstairs."

The other two added their smiles to hers, and then all three left. The last one out closed the door, but I just stood there for a moment wondering what *hadn't* been said. I would have bet gold on the fact that there was *something*, and maybe even two or three somethings. For people who had been dragged unwillingly into some unspecified experiment, they'd adjusted to the situation awfully fast and awfully well . . .

The clamminess of my clothes reminded me rather quickly that I was there to change, so I gave up on speculation for the moment and turned back to the wardrobe. The dress hanging in it was dark brown trimmed with red, not exactly my favorite color combination, but predictable. The slippers matched perfectly, of course, so I took them and the dress over to one of the chairs near the fire.

Once I was out of my own things and into dry, I spread my wet clothes as close to the fire as was safe for them. The wardrobe could have back anything it gave me, but I didn't care for the idea of losing what I'd worn to that world. When you have a choice, even in what clothes you'll wear, it's easier to keep from going along with the demands of others. The six previous victims of that trap might have settled in, but I had no intention of doing the same.

With my wet clothes taken care of, I went back to the wardrobe to check my new finery in the mirror. The fit was perfect, of course, and even the colors didn't look as bad as I'd thought. The dress was long enough to brush the top of my slippers, was long-sleeved, and closed with buttons up the front of the bodice. The material was very soft and rich-feeling, like silk but without the slipperiness of silk. Most of the red trim was lace, and—

I stiffened as I saw, in the mirror, the figure appear behind me. It materialized out of thin air, and its arrival was so abrupt it took me an instant to realize what it had to be. I whirled around, needing to face it rather than have it behind my back, but that did no good at all. I couldn't use magic to get rid of it or defend myself, and the thing laughed when it saw I'd remembered that.

The thing. Actually, it was supposed to be a man, but not your ordinary, everyday type. He was fairly tall but stood round-shouldered, as though preferring to blend into the crowd rather than stand out. He was long-faced and dull-eyed, but wore a smirk as though he thought no one else was as good. He also had long-fingered hands, the sort that are constantly on the move and just itching to touch you. He was dressed in a long and belted maroon robe that was too dirty to look anything but repulsive, and his very light-skinned feet were bare. All of him was light-skinned, fish-belly dead rather than simply untanned.

And then the look in his flat, dull eyes changed, showing sly and crafty eagerness rather than plain stupidity. I'd seen that look before, the one that said he'd just realized I could be taken advantage of, and I hated it as much as the rest. He was virtually made of what I detested most in a man, and the thought of his coming closer made my skin crawl. If he ever touched me it would be sickening . . .

The thing laughed again and suddenly began to walk toward me, shuffling along the bare wooden floor in bare white feet. It was almost as though he'd waited to let me get a good look before doing it, just to make it all worse. Everything I hated in a man, looks and attitudes both . . . he knew what I was thinking and feeling, and intended to use that against me . . .

Anger flared beside disgust, but even as I turned and ran toward one of the small tables on my left, I couldn't help wondering what the point was. The gameplayer's spell had created and sent the sort of man I'd never be able to stomach, but according to what I'd been told it wouldn't harm me. I had no interest in waiting to find out what it *would* do, but that question was answered just as I reached the table.

"Where you goin', pretty?" the thing asked in a thin, high-pitched voice, condescendingly amused. "You can't get away from me, you oughta know that, and I'm not gonna hurt you. Just a little snugglin' and touchin' and a few kisses, and then I'll be gone. Until the next time. Come on, be a good girl and stand still. The sooner we start, the sooner I'll be done."

"You're done right now," I muttered, reaching hastily for the heavy candle standing unlit in one of the sticks. I noticed that when you mix anger with disgust your hands shake, but I wasn't about to let that stop me. I yanked the candle from its holder, accidently knocking the holder off the table, but that didn't matter. If I had to throw *it* after the candle, I'd just pick it up again.

The candle was heavy enough to make a good impression

on anyone, so I took aim for the composite man's head and threw hard. I was usually good at hitting what I aimed at, and that time was no different. The candle flew straight for the thing's face, smacked into it—and kept on going! It—*sank*—into the face, and when it was gone it left behind nothing but a dirty smirk and a laugh.

"Nice try, pretty," he said in a greasy way. "But now that you know you can't stop me, why make trouble? Come on over here and let's get acquainted."

He'd paused a moment earlier, probably to let me learn how useless throwing things was, but now he'd started walking again. Rather than waiting for me to come to him, he was doing the approaching. I wasn't afraid, exactly, not when it wasn't something deadly coming at me, but being sickeningly repelled was almost worse. And the worst of it was that I couldn't think of anything to *do*, nothing that would let me defend myself . . .

And then I saw the thing pause, his smirk wavering for just an instant. A peculiar expression flickered on his face, and then he took a longer step before resuming his shuffle and amusement. It was so odd I couldn't help but notice, but for a moment I didn't understand. Why in the worlds would he do that . . . ?

As soon as I looked down, everything became clear. The silver candlestick, the one that had been a victim of my clumsiness and had ended up on the floor—*that* was what the thing had so carefully avoided! Good old silver, a magic user's best friend! I wasted no time in reaching for the second candlestick, got rid of the candle, then turned to the thing with my newly found weapon in hand.

"What do you expect *that* to do for you?" he tried to bluff, now forcing smirking amusement even though he'd stopped again. "You feel the urge to try another throw? Go ahead then, throw it and see what happens."

"I already know what would happen," I answered, looking straight at him. "You would avoid the throw rather than letting it hit you, and then I would be without a weapon. If you're so eager to show you're not afraid of it, just keep coming."

Frustration flashed through those flat, dull eyes, an emotion he tried to hide, but then he realized the game was up.

I wasn't guessing about the silver, and I wasn't warning him to keep away. If he tried to come near me I'd bash him with the candlestick, and smile while I did it. When you're not afraid to hurt someone they know it, even if they're constructs.

"You think you're so smart," the thing said sullenly, his good time ruined. "Well, it so happens I didn't want to have anything to do with you anyway. I don't like life-forms that *cheat*."

With that he disappeared back to the nothingness he'd come from, possibly thinking he'd left me feeling guilty. If the day ever came that I felt guilty about defending myself . . . I shook my head with a sigh, wondering how even a construct could be that thick-skulled. I also wondered what the gameplayer would try next, now that the first attempt hadn't worked. There were any number of unpleasant things to be considered, but luckily I was diverted by a knock at the door. Hastily pushing aside thoughts of true horror, still clutching the candlestick, I went to the door and opened it.

"I thought I'd see if you were ready to go down to dinner yet," Prince Bariden said from where he leaned against the doorpost with folded arms. "Are you expecting to need a candle, or are you just still mad at me?"

"It so happens you're my second visitor," I said, stepping back to let him come in. "The first was a walking collection of everything I dislike in a man, who announced that we were going to kiss and touch and cuddle. Now we know what the operating spell sends after female Sighted in this place."

"Is it still here?" he demanded, losing the casual air as he strode into the room and looked around. "What did it do to you before it left?"

"I doubt if he was going to do more than he said he would, but he didn't even get to do that." I followed more slowly, wondering how much of his agitation was on *my* behalf. A man who targets a girl wants to get to her first, without someone else cutting in front. "I accidently discovered that the construct didn't get along with silver, and used this candlestick to convince him to be on his way."

"Convinced him," Prince Bariden echoed with a snort

of amusement, turning to grin at me. "Saying that, you probably smashed him flat with it. And you look like such a sweet, gentle little thing. As long as you're sure he didn't hurt you."

"I told you, I don't think hurting is part of what it's *supposed* to do," I said, ignoring the fact that he looked genuinely concerned again. "Being pawed and mauled by someone you can't stand may be nauseating, but it doesn't qualify as traumatic for many girls above the age of fifteen. No, that thing had another purpose, but I'm damned if I know what. You didn't have a visitor of your own?"

"Not even a suggestion of one," he said with a headshake, now looking thoughtful. He'd changed clothes too, and his tunic was a blue to match his eyes. "Maybe the fact that I'm armed kept anything from trying."

"Unless your sword is silver, which I doubt, I don't see that happening," I disagreed. "The first thing I did was throw a heavy candle at my guest, and his face simply swallowed it up. Cutting him into slices probably wouldn't have worked either, not when he wasn't truly human. It's possible he or something like him will try again, so I intend to hang onto this candlestick."

"That you should have to really bothers me," he said, the concern sliding toward self-condemnation. "You ended up here because of me, and even though I didn't do it deliberately, that doesn't stop it from being my fault. I'd like you to know that I'm really sorry."

"Excuse me, but I don't understand what you're apologizing for," I said, watching as he turned away. "The compulsion on the entry was so strong it dragged you to it and through, and it was my own bad luck I got in the way. Or my own thickheadedness, for not being suspicious about an entry being present when there was no sign of one at any of the other scenes. How does any of that make it *your* fault?"

"The fact that I didn't realize being partners with you would put you in danger, that's what makes it my fault." He'd turned back to look at me, to show just how unhappy he really was. "I should have anticipated an attempt to get rid of me before I learned something important, and kept you well in the background. The arrow can't hit you if you aren't standing between it and its true target."

"Ah, so *you're* the only one they wanted to get rid of," I said with a nod, finally understanding. "They weren't counting on my being drawn along with you, or even following after if you went through alone. They knew I would simply stay in the palace and putter around, getting nowhere with the mystery once my invaluable partner was gone. Now I see."

"Why are you taking my attempt to apologize as a major personal insult?" he demanded as this time I did the turning away. "It's hardly likely our enemy knows you, but he's certain to know me. If a trap was set, and it was, logic would say it was set for me. And not just logic, since you didn't set off the compulsion and I did. Would you be happier if this was all aimed at you, and *I* was the one accidently dragged along?"

"You're absolutely right, I was just being foolish," I said, brushing at the skirt of my dress. "Now that that's settled, we ought to get downstairs. If they're holding dinner for us, they could be as hungry as I am."

I headed out into the hall and after a brief hesitation Prince Bariden followed. He didn't say anything else, but it felt as if he wanted to. Personally, I was sorry I hadn't just accepted his apology and let it go at that. He was a prince, after all, so it was natural for him to consider himself the most important person around. If our enemy didn't know me our enemy wasn't as clever as we thought, but that was beside the point. In the prince's eyes I wasn't important enough to be lured into a trap, so why argue?

At the bottom of the stairs I turned right, and a few doors down, also on the right, was the dining room where our fellow victims waited. They sat at a table set for eight, but one that could easily have held twelve. Again the room was mostly dim, but two candelabra on the table would keep the coming meal from being a mystery. What I could see of the room itself said we were still going with stiff and formal, utility first, comfort second, decorative a long way beyond third. When we entered, the low conversation broke off and Kamen rose to his feet.

"Glad to see you two are all right," he greeted us with a smile. "Chalaine, your place is here to my right, and

Bariden, yours is to Janissa's right at the other end. Once we get settled, the food will start coming."

Without hesitation I moved left toward his end of the table, and the prince did almost as well going right. His very short pause might have meant he saw all the women he would be in the middle of, and was savoring the largesse to come. I silently wished him a hearty appetite, and took my place without comment. Kamen, to my left, remained standing until I sat, joined by Halad to my right and Vadran to Kamen's left, directly across from me. Once I was settled, they resumed their own seats. Prince Bariden had Janissa to his left, Idara to his right, and Wellia directly across from him.

"Is there some special reason you're carrying that candlestick?" Kamen asked me. I noticed that his tunic was a darker blue than Prince Bariden's, and so were his eyes. "Did you think you'd need to fetch your own light in order to see what you were eating?"

"Not at all," I answered, partially distracted by the platters of food that were appearing along the center of the table. "This candlestick is my weapon against any future unwelcome visitors, so you can expect it to be my constant companion. Dragging it around is a lot more pleasant than what almost happened."

"*Almost* happened?" Vadran echoed from across the table, exchanging surprised glances with Halad and Kamen. "You mean one of the sendings came at you, but you were able to stop it? How? Idara hit one with a chair, and that did nothing but make it laugh."

"I discovered by accident that it can't abide coming in contact with silver," I told him, noticing peripherally that the three women were also listening. "That sort of an aversion is too basic to change, so I'd say it will continue to work against any construct sent."

Peculiar expressions moved across the faces of the men as they glanced at each other again, but when it came to speaking one of the women beat them to it.

"What about the thing sent at you, Bariden?" Idara asked from his right. "Were you also able to chase it away with silver?"

"Since nothing was sent at me, I didn't have the chance

to try," the prince answered, aware that all eyes were now on him. "If something *had* been sent, I probably would have first tried to—"

"Nothing sent?" "How can that be?" "What's going on *now*?" "I don't understand."

The protests all came at once, running together and almost drowning each other out. Some of them even sounded indignant, so I decided it was a good time to ask a few pointed questions.

"That wasn't the way it was supposed to go, was it?" I asked all of them, drawing their eyes. "We were supposed to have come down here shaken from our first brushes with the moves of this—game. You were all certain it would happen."

"What makes you say that?" Kamen countered, looking at me in a very neutral way. "It's true all the rest of us had almost immediate encounters, but what makes you think we were all that certain it would happen to you two?"

"One reason is the fact that you left to *let* it happen," I obliged with a humorless smile. "You just said you all had almost immediate encounters, and yet the girls left me to dress alone, and you boys left my partner. That means you *wanted* us to run into our respective attackers, and were all ready with your own first move. Would you like to claim there's no significance in this seating arrangement?"

The glances flickered back and forth again, and this time the women were included. With them ranged around Prince Bariden and the men around me, we were obviously expected to involve ourselves in *something* having to do with the opposite sex. Just what, though, was the next question to be answered.

"Just what is it that you think we're trying to force you into?" Janissa put from her end of the table, a faint flush to her cheeks. "You sound as if you suspect some—devious plot on our part, aimed at luring you into our clutches. What are we supposed to be guilty of?"

"I'd say bad judgment, if nothing else," I answered with a shrug, reaching for a wineglass that was now filled. "You know you were all brought here for a purpose, to do something whoever set this up wanted you to do. With that in mind you should have noticed what you were being forced to do, and understood that doing it was just plain cooperating with your capture. How fast do you expect to be released if you behave the way the gameplayer wants you to?"

"A lot faster than if we resist," Idara stated, her own cheeks reddened. "And resisting could have made things worse, so what good would it have done? Those things could have been sent to do more than touch and kiss us, and then what would we have done?"

"Maybe found out sooner that silver will stop them?" I suggested, then watched as all three women flushed darker. "Those constructs are stomach turning, but they're not so bad that they'd make you desperate to find something that would stop them. By cooperating with the desires of the gameplayer, you denied yourselves the sort of state of mind that lets you find a way out of an unbearable situation. It *wasn't* unbearable, merely unpleasant, so you avoided it by accepting an arrangement that wasn't all that bad. What I still don't know, though, is what the men get out of it besides the obvious."

"I seem to be the only one who doesn't understand what's going on," Prince Bariden said when the silence descended. No one was looking at anyone else any longer, and the air of discomfort was thick enough to feel. "What sort of arrangements are we talking about?"

"I was told that the constructs don't bother the women if they happen to be with the men," I answered, looking around as I spoke. "That would indicate they usually sleep in pairs, since your time of greatest vulnerability is when you're asleep. This seating was probably arranged to let us choose our first partners, but it's unlikely nothing more than sleep is involved. Of course, if I'm wrong I'll certainly apologize."

None of them spoke up to say that I *was* wrong, and no one even seemed to remember there was food on the table. They all appeared to feel horribly embarrassed, which was perfectly ridiculous.

"All right, so you all take turns sleeping together," I said, letting them hear the annoyance I felt. "I realize no one ever does that sort of thing anywhere else, but that's no reason not to talk about other subjects. Like what additional benefit the arrangement has for the men. Since *they* can still be attacked, what is there that adds the urge to cooperate?"

"Don't you think the easy sex is enough?" Kamen asked, now sounding and looking angrily defensive. "That's all men think about, isn't it? What other reason do we need?"

"Give me a break," I responded with a groan, aware of the same stares from the other two men. "Even teenage boys think about more than sex. And what kind of an experiment would this be, if half the subjects were going to react in a completely predictable way? You do understand this is an experiment, don't you?"

This time all the looks exchanged were filled with surprise, which answered my question. They hadn't even gotten that far in figuring things out, and suddenly they were filled with actual interest.

"What sort of an experiment could this possibly be?" Vadran asked from across the table. "To see how quickly strangers will take to one another? I'll admit I didn't like being forced to cooperate, but the choice was between a painful beating from something I couldn't defend myself against, or making love to one of three attractive women. I couldn't see what playing stubborn would get me, so I went along with it."

"There's a part you still don't know about," Halad said from my right, obviously agreeing with Vadran. "Those things would still appear if there was a woman with us, but seemed to be incapable of striking at that woman. If we put her in the middle neither of us was hurt, and then the thing would disappear. Could the experiment be to find out how well we would learn to cooperate?"

"I doubt it," I said with a headshake, finding that too simple an answer. "If that was the aim, you would have discovered somehow that cooperation was the key to getting out of here. Chances are the point is more involved, like just how far you could be pushed before you stopped being cooperative. Vadran mentioned that one of your choices was an 'attractive' woman. What would have happened if the next pair showing up were a very handsome man and a rather plain-looking woman?"

"That's easy," Wellia said with a laugh from the other side of Halad. "We three would have each done our best to be the one who welcomed the man, which would have left one of our current companions with the woman."

"And whichever one of us was left with her would have a different choice to make," Kamen pounced, looking excited. "Making love to a plain woman is still worlds better than getting kicked around, so we would probably cooperate again. But what about the couples after that? What if eventually the woman was not only physically ugly, but also had one of those poisonous personalities? Would we be so used to compromising by then that we would accept her without hesitation, having decided that anything was better than getting hurt? If not, at what point would we dig in our heels?"

"That possibility would work for us as well," Janissa said, glancing at the other two women. "If the new arrivals were a gorgeous woman and a plain man, how long would any of us refuse plain when the only other choice was nauseating? But the game would probably get more involved after that, since nauseating would quickly be balanced by repulsive. Maybe the constructs would start hitting *us*, too."

"None of which tells us how we're supposed to climb out of this," Wellia said, looking seriously disturbed. "I started out making the best of an unpleasant situation, but this will get worse than unpleasant before it's over. Once people get used to giving in to small tyrannies, they find themselves giving in to large ones as well. If the gameplayer is trying to find out the point I'll say no, then he has what he wants. I'm now saying no, and I won't change my mind again."

"Not even to keep one of those—*things*—away from you?" Idara asked, her face pale. "I don't like this any better than the rest of you, but I'll take an ordinary man any day rather than a—a—Damn it, we're still trapped here!"

"But maybe not for long," Prince Bariden said soothingly, reaching to his right to pat her hand. "Something someone mentioned gave me an idea, but there's still one unanswered question. If everyone including Chalaine had one of these constructs sent after them, why was I the only exception? If a sharp edge was likely to stop them, there would hardly be knives on this table as part of the settings. That means my sword had nothing to do with it, so what did?"

Everyone considered that in silence, diverted from the first thing he'd said. I wasn't diverted, but a possibility still occurred to me.

"Since all of you are Sighted, does that mean all of you used normal warding before finding yourselves here?" I asked. "No, the question isn't silly, so please answer it."

"The question *is* silly," Idara contradicted. "When ordinary people pay good silver to have themselves warded, why would one of us do without when the cost would be nothing? Weren't *you* warded?"

"Yes, I was," I replied, seeing that every one of them agreed with her. "The point here is that my partner wasn't, and that could be the answer. The constructs are made to key on our warding, nauseating to female, and attacking to male. Since we each warded ourselves, the work would have our own individual trace."

"If you're serious about his being unwarded, that must be it," Kamen said, once again looking around at the others. "But wait a minute. How can something created by magic get through our warding? The girls were touched and we were hit and kicked, but that shouldn't have been possible."

"You're confusing a magical creature and the use of magic," Prince Bariden said before I could respond. "Most warding protects you only from the direct use of magic or an *effect* caused by magic. It won't stop a physical attack from anything including a magical creature, not unless you're so proddish you have it set specifically to do that. If you do you won't be touched by anything including a heavy wind without setting it off, and will probably leave a trail of unconscious bodies every time you move through a crowd. Anything less is just about useless, which is why I don't bother. Most people assume I'm warded, which is just as good as actually having it."

"That makes a strange kind of sense," Halad said as he blinked at the prince. "I'll have to think about it once I'm home again, but right now I'd rather discuss your earlier comment. Did you say you have an idea about how we might get out of here?"

"I did, but before we try it I suggest we have dinner," Prince Bariden responded, reaching for one of the platters near him. "There's no guarantee my idea will work, and if this food disappears again before we eat it, we'll end up going hungry. We'll take care of this first, and then see about escape."

Once again there were a lot of glances exchanged and this time I joined in the effort, but there was nothing to be done. Prince Bariden was giving all his attention to the food, and unless we wanted to try to force him into talking, our only option was to do the same. A general movement toward the bowls and platters told me which option the others were going with, which was hardly surprising. Muttering under my breath about the high-handedness of those with titles, I reluctantly did the same.

Dinner was topped off with coffee all around, the cups having a standard refilling spell that any good Sighted host or hostess would provide. By that time the prince was chatting lightly with the attentive women around him, and the men at my end were talking desultorily among themselves. Not being interested in conversation, I wasn't speaking to anyone. I'd fallen into a dark mood over all the time we were wasting, and couldn't seem to climb out of it again. What if Prince Bariden's idea didn't work, and we were trapped there? How long would the stricken left behind us be able to survive in the pale shadows they now lived in . . . ?

"Now that we're comfortably filled, I think it's time for an experiment of our own," Prince Bariden suddenly announced, beginning to rise from the table. "If you'll all come with me, I'll explain what's needed."

Everyone hurried to follow after as he headed for the hall, but I took a final swallow of coffee before making my own way out. If Prince Bariden's idea didn't work, what would there be left to try . . . ?

"Okay, now that we're all here, we can give it a try," the prince said when I joined the group in the hall. "What we want is an entry out of here, but, as Chalaine knows, I'm not familiar with entry spells. The rest of you will have to pick a destination, and that's where we'll try to go."

"I'd say our best destination would be Conclave," Kamen offered above the comments of some of the others. "That way we can report what was done to us, and get some wizard strength on *our* side. It won't help if we just go home, and then wake up tomorrow to find we've been taken again."

"But how are we supposed to go anywhere at all?" Idara asked with a worried expression that was becoming familiar. "With the gameplayer's blanket spell still working, none of *our* spells will do the same."

"None of our *individual* spells," Prince Bariden corrected before anyone else could add to the protest. "No single one of us is strong enough to counter the gameplayer, but what about all of us together? If the gameplayer had the strength of eight trained Sighted, would he still be involved with silliness like this? Aren't there better things to do with your time once you develop that much strength?"

The only proper answer to his question was maybe, but none of us wanted to be the one to say the word. Doubt can negate the strongest effort when it comes to spells, and what we needed then was the greatest push we could generate. Punching through a wizard's already-cast spell could be tricky no matter what our combined strength, but that was hardly the time to mention that point either.

"Well, all we can do is try," Halad said, shaking his red-haired head. "If it doesn't work we won't be any worse off, and if it does we're out of here. Is there anyone besides Bariden who doesn't know the spell for an entry to Conclave?"

There was a lot of looking around, but no one spoke up to say they shared the lack. It was odd to think that any Sighted could reach sorcerer strength without visiting Conclave at least once in a while, but there was no real time to think about that. The others were beginning to link hands, the most effective way to increase the strength of a shared spell.

"Let's put the entry into the doorway to the dining room," Prince Bariden suggested as he took the hands of Janissa and Idara. "That way if it doesn't work, we can all go back for dessert. Is everyone ready?"

A variety of nods answered him, none of them as lighthearted as his comment about dessert was supposed to make them. His linking in would add a portion of his strength to the effort even if he wasn't speaking the spell, so there was no sense in waiting for some nebulous better time. He glanced around one last time, then said, "Begin," the way a wizard instructor would have. That gave us our benchmark and suggested rhythm, and we began to speak the spell. The first thing you learn when you start to study magic is the standardized way of speaking a spell. In later years you develop your own personal style, but no one ever forgets what they learned first.

The spell wasn't very involved, and as we began together we finished together. There had been something of a drag on the words as I spoke them and I suspected the others had felt the same, but with the last syllable out there was a—popping—of sorts. It was very much like your ears adjusting to a change of altitude, and when we looked at the dining room doorway there was a faintly glowing outline that hadn't been there before.

"It's really there!" Vadran shouted, turning to Wellia, picking her up, and spinning her in a circle. The others were also laughing and jumping around, but Prince Bariden was simply grinning. Idara paused to throw her arms around his neck and kiss him, but for some reason that didn't ruin his mood. As soon as she turned away to find someone else to kiss, he chuckled his way over to me.

"Looks like we did it," he commented over the yelling and whooping. "And I do mean 'we.' You said something about this not being an experiment about cooperation, because then it would take cooperation to escape. Hearing that made me wonder if you'd touched on something we weren't supposed to see, and from that came the idea about combining strength. Do you want to lead the way through the entry, or let everyone else go first?"

"I think it's going to be a matter of first come, first gone," I answered, nodding toward the activity I'd been watching. "Kamen is about to lead Janissa through, Vadran is right behind them with Wellia, and Halad is bringing up the rear with Idara. If we don't get a move on, they'll leave us behind."

I headed for the end of the line with that, and after a brief hesitation the prince followed me. Once again I had the feeling he wanted to say something, but that wasn't the time for anything but the briefest conversation. Kamen and

Janissa stepped through the entry, Vadran and Wellia right on their heels, Idara alone turning to gesture us after them before following with Halad. The prince was beside me as I began to step through, but suddenly there was a—crackling blur—and then—and then—

CHAPTER FOUR

And then Bariden found himself outdoors again, Chalaine beside him. Wherever they were it was midafternoon, and although the air was cool there wasn't a trace of snow. There also wasn't a trace of the six people who had gone through the entry before them, which was definitely not an encouraging sign.

"If this is Conclave, it's changed a lot since the one time I visited there," he commented, looking around at the very ordinary countryside. Grass, trees, sky, and sunlight, nothing threatening or even vaguely sinister. A short distance away from where they stood was a dirt road, fairly wide and looking fairly well traveled.

"I'd like to know whose idea of a joke this is," the girl said in annoyance, also looking around. "That crackling blur, just as we stepped through the entry—it didn't happen for any of the others, or I would have noticed. They ended up at Conclave, and we ended up—where?"

"Someplace there's no immediate way back from," Bariden told her, having already turned to examine the entry they'd come through. The thing was gone, not the least hint of where it had been, nothing but a stretch of meadow to be seen with woods just beyond.

"Great," Chalaine muttered, having turned herself to see that the entry was gone. "Now we don't even have the choice of jumping back into the frying pan if this turns out to be the fire. And I'm cold again."

Almost by reflex she spoke a spell to replace her dress

with the boots, breeches, and tunic she'd left behind, only in slightly heavier material. Bariden understood the spell perfectly—and then blinked when the clothing flickered into being. He'd enjoyed seeing her in a dress, but that had nothing to do with his reaction.

"Hey, we can do magic again," he said, then proved it by providing himself with his own original clothing. "Now all we have to decide is whether or not to try for Conclave again."

"You think we ought to go straight back to the palace?" the girl asked, big, dark eyes just brushing past him. "I thought the stop at Conclave could be used for getting wizard-strength warding against future compulsions, but I suppose Master Haddil could do that for us. But first I'm going to get rid of my own warding. I didn't like what it brought to me in that house trap, and I don't care to have the same again."

"Wait," Bariden said before she spoke the words and used a banishing gesture. "That might not be the best idea right now. Why don't we wait to see what happens next."

"What will happen next is my creating an entry to take us out of here," she said, looking around at the landscape. "What do you think will jump us before I can do that?"

"I wasn't thinking about something happening before," he answered, finding it impossible not to stiffen against the faint impatience in her tone. As though she were dealing with someone very young and not too bright . . . "It was *afterward* I was considering. If the enemy was prepared to stop us from reaching a destination decided on almost randomly and what should have been unexpectedly, what will happen the next time we try?"

She hesitated a moment, obviously thinking, and then said, "Let's try it and see," before raising one hand and speaking a spell. Logic told Bariden she was calling an entry into existence, but logic was the only one who knew that. Nothing else seemed to notice, and all faintly glowing doorways were conspicuous by their absence.

"I don't believe that," she stated, glaring at a volume of air that should obviously have contained more. "This *has* to be someone's idea of a joke. How can magic work for everything but the calling up of an entry?"

"A better question would be, why is the enemy so determined to keep us away from the palace?" Bariden suggested. "First we're forced out, and now we're being kept from going back. Is there something scheduled that we might stop if we were there?"

" 'We'?" she said, for a moment looking straight at him. "I thought you were the only important one in all this. Why has that suddenly changed to we?"

"What would be the sense in disallowing entries if I was the only one who was supposed to be here?" Bariden was trying to keep his voice mild as he explained his thinking, but the girl wasn't making it easy. Every time she spoke to him, he felt like—"And why did that compulsion have to be so strong? Instead of making me run, it could have simply caused me to walk through the entry without fuss. That way no one would have noticed until I was through and taken, and that would have been the end of it. Not to mention the fact that the *two* of us were diverted here by that last entry. Am I supposed to believe it couldn't have been me alone just as easily?"

"We still don't know what you're supposed to believe," she pointed out, a hint of her favorite lecturing tone behind the words. "First you thought you were the only one who counted, but now I've gained equal prominence. Or almost equal. Never let it be said that I'd presume to think of myself as being on equal footing with a prince. But I do feel honored that I'm not being dismissed out of hand any longer."

"All right, that's the last of it I'm going to take," Bariden growled, finally fed up. "If you think you have any complaints against me, get them said so we can clear the air. I don't like getting sniped at without having the chance to strike back."

"You're right, I've been unforgivably rude," she responded immediately in that neutrally dismissive tone he was beginning to hate. "Just chalk it up to my being a commoner, and try to overlook it. I'll make the effort not to presume again."

"Not this time," he denied, grabbing her arm as she began to turn away. "You've already had your last time of getting in the final word by insisting on dropping the subject. You've been snapping at me almost from the first minute we met, and I want to know why that is. What have I ever done to you?"

"Shall I start with the way you couldn't be bothered with remembering my name?" she asked, those dark eyes now flaring at him. "Or is that a point I'm supposed to have forgotten? Maybe I ought to go with the way I was supposed to be so very flattered when you finally did notice me and turned on the charm. Was I supposed to chuckle and enjoy the attention, feel special because I'd soon be able to number myself among your hordes of—female acquaintances? Imagine, *me* drawing the attention of a prince! How lucky can you get?"

"So that's what's wrong with you," Bariden said, finally letting her arm go. "You're one of those reverse snobs. You should have told me, and then I never would have bothered you."

"How dare you?" she demanded as this time *he* began to turn away. "I am *not* a snob, and you have no right to call me one. If there's anyone—"

"You're just like all the rest!" he returned harshly, turning back to look at her with memory of that other time. "All those oh-so-special Sighted I met the one time I went to Conclave. 'Dear boy, a *prince*? How quaint and utterly amusing. Imagine, the boy's a *prince*. We'll have to try not to let that make a difference.' You claim to be outraged over the fact that I didn't remember your name, but isn't that only because I'm a prince? If an ordinary man had done it, wouldn't you have forgiven him by now?"

"Why—I—no, I don't—" She stumbled over the words, her eyes wide and confused, but Bariden wasn't finished.

"I think the answer to that is, of course you would have. You would have understood it wasn't done on purpose, and accepted an offered apology. And as for my second crime, the one where I found myself attracted to you—that was obviously a mistake. You see, some years ago I spoke a Spell of Affinity aimed at women. I wanted to be sure that the woman I eventually ended up with was someone who wanted *me*, not just a prince. When I looked into your eyes and the glow of the spell flared brighter than ever before, I let it make me forget the fact that you're one of *them*. Now that you've reminded me, you can be sure I won't forget again. The first Sighted woman I tried to get to know will also be my last. Right now I'm going to follow that road to see if it leads any place useful."

Once again Bariden turned away from the now silent girl, but not to walk to the road. As angry as he was a little exercise would have helped to calm him, but just then he preferred to retain his anger. He spoke a spell to create a copy of his favorite horse, then walked over to the construct when it appeared. It was less than the living original would have been, limited to form and behavior only, but as a mount it was more than adequate.

He climbed into the saddle and headed for the road, making no effort to look back to see if the girl would follow. She wasn't an ordinary girl, after all, she was Sighted. If a sorceress wasn't capable of taking care of herself in a place where her magic worked, no one was. There was nothing Bariden could do for her that she couldn't do for herself, a circumstance she'd managed to make very clear. And he'd been so worried about pursuing her in the right way. For him there *was* no right way, not even with the help of an Affinity spell. She looked at him the way those other Sighted had, as if he were a freak, and that was worse than anything unSighted women did. At least with them his being a prince meant something positive, and his also being Sighted was nothing more than unusual.

Bariden brooded for a while as he rode along, and then he became aware of being followed. The sound of another set of hooves came behind his mount's along the road, which undoubtedly meant the girl had called up a horse of her own. But she rode a few feet back, pacing him rather than trying to catch up. Well, that was fine, probably even for the best. The less they had to do with each other, the happier she would undoubtedly be.

When he'd left the meadow he'd turned left up the road, as far as he could tell heading roughly west. There had been no real reason to choose that direction rather than the other, it was just better than standing still while thinking about it. The landscape hadn't changed from ordinary woods around the occasional ordinary meadow, but after a couple of miles there was suddenly a meadow with grazing cattle. Along with the herd were three boys with sticks and two dogs, all of whom were busy watching their charges.

"There's no fencing, and that herd looks too big to belong to a single farm or even two farms," a quiet voice said from behind him to his right. He'd stopped to look at the cattle, which had obviously given the girl a chance to move closer. "I'd say we probably aren't far from a town or city, and that's probably who the herd belongs to. Maybe someone there will be able to direct us to a gate."

"That would be useful," he commented without looking at her, then touched his heel to his mount to start it moving again. The sooner he got back to where he'd come from, the sooner he'd also be able to get back to important concerns.

As they continued along the road the girl dropped back to the position she'd been in earlier, which meant the ride for the next few miles was a silent one. After a while Bariden wondered if he should have responded a little more warmly to her attempt to start a neutral conversation, but eventually decided it hadn't been called for. He didn't want *any* kind of conversation from the girl, and as soon as he got back he would tell Master Haddil he intended to work on the mystery alone. He didn't need any more Sighted partners to—

"What in the name of chaos—!" he exclaimed. The road had led around a tight and heavily treed curve, and finally rounding that curve brought a surprise. The trees ended abruptly no more than fifty yards ahead, and after that the road ran between two grazing meadows directly to a large town about a mile away. That part was normal enough, but the rest—! Crowds of what looked like every man, woman, and child from the town filled the two meadows, each group standing behind a solitary figure on a small, raised platform. The two figures wore long, dark gowns, and beyond the fact that they seemed to be looking at him and the girl, Bariden could make out no other details.

"Can that welcoming committee be for us?" Chalaine asked as she moved up again to ride to his right. "If so, I'm not happy about the only way they could have known we were coming."

"The enemy," Bariden agreed with a nod, watching carefully as they rode nearer to those two gowned figures. "The only one who could have known we were coming is the one who caused us to be here. But maybe this has nothing to do with that."

"Then I'd love to know what it does have to do with," she muttered before falling silent again. Bariden echoed that wish silently, but not with the hope that they'd be able to ride on and never find out. They were being watched too closely for that, and as they got within ten feet of the two platform figures, the crowds behind those figures briefly applauded. For all the worlds as if they were being welcomed to something . . .

"We greet two travelers on the road to Lovaire," the figure to Bariden's left suddenly intoned. "Do you come this way with a purpose?"

"Yes, as a matter of fact we do have a purpose," Bariden allowed, trying to be cautious. The figure who had spoken was male, with a long white beard and matching hair, worn above a dark blue gown decorated with moons and stars and other supposedly mystical symbols. Across the way to the right was a woman, and although she wore the same sort of gown, she had black hair with no more than two narrow streaks of white. Both figures stood very still and tall, and the sternness of their expressions reminded him of stock characters in a bad play about magic users.

"And you, girl," the woman intoned next, her voice only slightly higher than the man's. "Do you also ride the road to Lovaire with purpose?"

"Actually, we both have the same purpose," Chalaine answered, looking the woman up and down. "Don't you have anything better to do with your time than stand around asking silly questions? Even if we were just wandering, our purpose in riding this road would be to continue wandering. Strange you should miss that, when even a—'girl'—didn't."

Her tone had been so even and easy, Bariden was taken completely by surprise. Obviously Chalaine didn't like to be called 'girl,' and didn't mind showing her displeasure when it happened. Only—damn it, didn't she have enough sense not to do something like that until they knew what they were in the middle of? He had the very strong urge to shake her hard, especially since the two people were drawing themselves up even straighter.

"It would seem, then, that a challenge has been given and accepted," the man said, annoyance now heavy in his voice. "It matters not who challenged and who accepted. Only the outcome will be of concern, and that is a foregone conclusion. Now we begin."

"Hold on a minute," Bariden said with one hand up, trying to keep trouble from starting. He was a firm believer in defending himself if attacked, but things got complicated when the person he was with instigated that attack. "Wouldn't it be better if we talked about this first?"

Rather than answering in words, the male figure raised both arms and muttered into his beard. Bariden had enough time to see that the woman was doing the same without the beard, and then he was covered with all sorts of insects and worms, flying, crawling, slimy, and trying to sting or bite. Surprise and disgust made him immediately start to brush and slap at the things, but that did no good at all. In desperation he tried a banishing gesture, but that was just as useless. By then the things were attacking his eyes, and trying to crawl into his nose and mouth. He had no idea what he could possibly do next, short of destroying the man in the white beard—

And then Chalaine spoke a brief spell, and the things were gone as quickly as they'd appeared. Bariden coughed while he tried to calm his mount; the horse construct hadn't been bothered, but his rider's thrashing around in the saddle had turned the beast skittish. A glance at the bearded man showed him looking annoyed, but before any words came Chalaine spoke up.

"Now he and I are both warded," she said, apparently addressing the woman as well as the man. "Since your illusions will be useless from here on, you ought to consider giving it up. If we have to suggest that again, it won't be in words."

"That, young woman, was magic, not illusion," the man returned coldly. "If you don't know the difference, we'll soon teach it to you. Whatever trickery you used to avoid the first lesson won't continue to protect you for long."

He raised his arms for the second time, and again the woman across the road did the same. The people in the crowds were watching almost breathlessly, some of them pointing and whispering to each other. Bariden could see food and drink sellers moving here and there, their trays of wares suspended by straps over their shoulders. If there had been tents, he would have sworn it was a fair . . .

"You warded me?" he said low to the girl. "What made you think that would do it?"

"This time the attack worked against you, but not against me." Her voice was just as low, and for some reason she looked almost embarrassed. "When I saw you trying to banish those things and not being able to do it, I was sure they were illusions that warding would block. I'll remove it again as soon as they finish with their—lessons."

Bariden nodded without saying anything else, most of his attention on the robed and gesturing two. They were still muttering what should have been spells, but nothing was happening. Considering everything it was possible to do even if someone was warded, he didn't understand that. He waited another pair of moments, and when there was still nothing happening he decided to ask the question out loud.

"Excuse me, but my companion and I would like to know what you think you're doing," he said, turning his head briefly to include the woman in on the question. "We didn't come here to sit and watch you wave your arms in the air."

Everyone in hearing drew in their breath in shock, a vocal reflection of the fury the man showed. The woman, on the other hand, looked frustrated and faintly frightened, which still told him nothing.

"Whatever it is you hide behind guards your puny selves well," the man spat, his anger all but regal. "But as we cannot touch you, so will you find it impossible to touch us. In this instance, a draw is a victory for *our* side."

"That doesn't necessarily follow," Chalaine said mildly into the man's sudden smirk. "And if this is a contest of some sort, *we* should be getting a turn. Do we have to wait for some kind of signal, or are we just supposed to go ahead and do it?"

"Chalaine," Bariden began, trying to keep her from starting something again, but the attempt was too late.

"Ignorant girl!" the bearded man laughed. "Those who can, do without let. Those who cannot, pretend to await permission. Need we ask which *you* are?"

"No need to ask," Chalaine responded immediately with a smile. "I'll be more than happy to show you."

"Chalaine, wait," Bariden tried, but once again he might as well have been talking to himself. She raised her right hand to point as she spoke a short spell, and the wooden platform the man stood on obligingly disappeared. He went down the four feet to the ground with a thump and a yell, sprawling like a bearded sack of oats. The crowd immediately erupted into laughter and cheering, and when Bariden glanced to the other platform, it was to find it already abandoned.

"The woman took off before I could make it her turn," Chalaine said over the crowd noise when she saw the direction of his glance. "I love the bully-follower mentality even more than that of the actual bully. She's lucky she did leave."

"I wonder how lucky *we'll* be," Bariden said, abruptly seeing the group of official-looking people making their way through the crowd around the bearded man. Some of them were richly dressed, but the larger number wore what had to be guardsmen's uniforms. "If we get out of this without being lynched, remind me to have a good long talk with you. The topic of conversation will be, 'The better part of valor.' "

Bariden was sure she could see how annoyed he was, but she didn't get the chance to argue or protest or even to apologize. That group of people had reached the roadside to his left, and it was them he had to pay attention to. Of the four men who were well dressed, one stood alone in front while the other three bowed.

"We offer the greetings of Her Majesty Queen Lova, ruler of the city and realm of Lovaire," the first man said with a polite bow of his own. "The queen sends her congratulations on having won the yearly contest for magicians, and bids the winners feast with her in the palace. The privilege of leading you there is ours."

"Just a moment," Bariden said as the man turned to signal that horses be brought up. "We didn't know this was a contest for magicians, and we aren't legitimate entrants. We happened along by accident, and simply defended ourselves. We're looking for directions to the nearest gate."

"Gate?" the man echoed, while those behind him glanced at each other blankly. "Do you mean the gate to the city? There are other, smaller gates inside, of course, but—I can see that *isn't* what you mean. Can you describe what you're looking for?"

"No," Bariden said with a sigh. "At least not to anyone who isn't Sighted. What about—" He looked immediately toward the bearded man Chalaine had dropped to the ground, but he wasn't there any longer. Like the woman, he'd disappeared into the crowd. Great. "What about the man with the long white beard? If we could speak to him for a couple of minutes, or anyone else who's a—magician . . ."

"I'm afraid Arnwell won't be appearing in public for a while," the spokesman said with the headshake that had made Bariden's words trail off. "This is the first time in five years he hasn't won the contest, and humiliation will certainly keep him out of people's sight for a time. He hasn't been very popular, you understand, not like the previous holder of the office. I'm sure the lovely young lady will do much better along those lines."

"The lovely young lady doesn't qualify for this contest any more than I do," Bariden said as the man beamed at a startled Chalaine. "We haven't been at magician level for years, so you'll just have to hold your contest again. We offer our apologies for intruding, but we really can't stay. There are extremely important matters waiting for us back home."

"I'm sure there are, but none of us can direct you to this—gate—you're seeking," the man replied smoothly, tugging at the sleeve of his brocade coat. "If you'll accept the queen's hospitality for just a short while, we'll make every attempt to locate someone who can help you. Arnwell's apprentice, for instance, might be less difficult to find . . ."

This time it was the man who let his words trail off, giving Bariden the chance to understand he had no choice. It would be easier finding someone Sighted in the city than at random in the countryside, and if they refused the queen's invitation they might be barred from the city. He didn't like the idea of having to go along with even part of that game they'd stepped into, but there really was no other choice.

"We thank you for the offer of hospitality," he said at last, giving in as graciously as possible. "And also for whatever assistance you can give to help us on our way. The lives of innocent people could well depend on our speedy return."

"The pleasure will be ours, sir," the man answered with another bow. "I'm Nalkin, the queen's Privy Aide. If you'll both follow me?"

This time the horses were gestured over and mounted, and they began to make a procession toward the city. The people in the crowds applauded and shouted and waved things, but Bariden's glance at Chalaine said she wasn't seeing any of it. The girl seemed lost in disturbing thought, possibly realizing at last the full extent of what she might have gotten them into. If she didn't, he'd certainly point it out when they had their little talk . . .

The ride to the city and through it to the palace didn't take very long, and then we were shown to guest quarters. Two of Nalkin's people took Prince Bariden one way, while Nalkin and the fourth took me another. The guard escort was left mostly outside the palace altogether, but there were enough like them inside to keep the halls from looking empty. Nalkin told me to ring for a servant if I wanted anything at all, and he would be back to let me know what time I would be presented to the queen. Then he and his friend bowed and left, finally giving me a chance to be alone with my thoughts.

The apartment I'd been given was a large one with other rooms leading off through arches from the first, but I did no more than glance around before sitting in a large, comfortable chair done in thick-napped white velvet. I'd been doing a lot of thinking lately, but that wasn't to say I had everything nicely worked out. I'd really put my foot in it, and this time there was no one but myself to blame, not even bad luck.

I spoke a spell that gave me a large cup of coffee, the refilling sort, then sat back with a sigh. The argument Prince

Bariden and I had had after coming through to that world—I could still hear him calling me a snob, one of *them*, making me feel as though I'd helped to beat up on someone who couldn't fight back. I now knew why he never went to Conclave, or had bothered to learn the spells for entries. Since he lived in the world he'd been born into, he didn't feel the need to search for one of his own. Or one where he'd be likely to find other Sighted. The Sighted had hurt him badly, and he had no desire to go looking for more of the same.

But he'd broken that rule for me, and I'd responded by treating him just as badly as those overblown idiots he'd met on his one visit to Conclave. He *had* been wrong, though, in thinking I would have been understanding about his forgetting my name if he hadn't been a prince. That sort of thing had happened to me too many times with other men for me to laugh lightly and dismiss it, but there had been no need to be *that* nasty.

I sipped at the coffee as I crossed my booted ankles, determined not to get up and pace. I'd spent the entire ride from the entry feeling horribly guilty, and my one lame attempt to start a normal conversation hadn't worked. With all that weighing on me it hadn't been hard to jump down the throat of the first person to say the wrong thing, and that first person had been the female magician-apprentice. Naturally, the jumping had just made things worse, but before I could regret what I'd said, that fool with the beard had sent his illusions after Bariden . . .

"Which, of course, made me jump immediately to Bariden's defense," I muttered to the coffee. "It's ridiculous to think the man needs *me* to protect him, but I couldn't stand hearing him insulted. He just sat there taking nonsense and abuse from the bearded fool, and I couldn't stand it. I had to do *something*, so I made the fool look ridiculous."

But Bariden hadn't appreciated that any more than anything else I'd done, not if his promise about "having a long talk" meant what that sort of thing usually did. I'd obviously put my foot in it yet again, but then he'd done something that had distracted me from the guilt. In the conversation with Nalkin *he'd* done all the talking and made all the decisions, just as though I wasn't there—or wasn't bright enough to be consulted.

I took another swallow of coffee, aware of how strange annoyance on top of guilt felt. Or maybe it was anger instead, I couldn't quite decide. Another memory that kept bothering me and interfering was the one about the spell Bariden had mentioned, the Spell of Affinity. Those things were supposed to be really reliable when used properly, but that was also the problem with them. Being told there's an affinity between you and the person you're looking at only helps to increase your interest, not the affinity itself. If you've gotten no more than a minimal glow, chances are that's all you'll get. And telling minimal from best possible is a matter of comparison. If most of the people you meet show only a faint flicker, the first one to show up who could be a fairly good friend looks in comparison like a sun flare . . .

Which had to be what had happened in my case. The man saw a stronger glow, one that said we could conceivably become friends, and immediately jumped to the wrong conclusion. He was looking for a woman he could trust enough to love, but that wasn't likely to be me. I'd always considered the idea of royalty silly, the custom of royal offspring even sillier. I mean, if all you have to do to gain a title is be born, how important can that title really be considered? Not to mention the fact that no one like that could possibly find someone like me of interest . . .

"So there you are." I looked up at the words to see Bariden coming in, through the door left open by Nalkin. "Since we have the privacy here, we can use it on that talk I mentioned earlier. You *do* remember what I said?"

"I remember," I conceded quietly, hating that all-business distance in his voice. From what he'd said we could have been friends, but I'd ruined the chance of that. So much for reacting by reflex instead of with thought. Chalaine, you're a real winner. Action and reaction and reaction and reaction.

"Good," he said, taking a blue velvet chair near mine. "Then let's get right to it. Do you have any idea what kind of trouble we might have now, and all because you let your temper get the best of you? What do we do if the queen

decides you now have to take the place of that Arnwell?
You did defeat him, so you might be required to take up
his duties. Do you think we can spend a year here and not
have it matter?"

"It would be more than a year," I muttered to the coffee
in my cup. "Arnwell went undefeated for five years, which
has to mean he was the strongest around. I don't understand
how that can be, but not understanding doesn't change the
fact that it *is*. Even if they held a competition daily, it
isn't likely someone better than magician level would ever
show up."

"That makes it even better," he said, the anger in his tone
gaining strength. "I'm delighted to see that you're back to
being analytical, but that doesn't solve the problem. Since
we aren't likely to find a gate very soon *without* the help of
these people, what do you suggest we do next? Refuse to
cooperate and forget about the gate, or agree to cooperate,
find out where a gate is, and then ignore it? Since you're
the one who got us into this, the choice ought to be yours
as well."

I couldn't help noticing that he hadn't listed lying and
then running out as one of our options, but that wasn't
surprising. I had a feeling his word was important to him,
just as mine was to me. He was right about the possibility of
there being a problem, but the solution wasn't as involved
as he thought.

"Since I'm the one who got us into this, I'm the one
who'll get us out," I said to the coffee. "If I have to give
my word about staying here I'll do it, and that will leave *you*
free to use the gate. No sense in both of us paying for what
only one of us did, and I'm not likely to be missed. And it
isn't as if we were going to continue being partners."

"No, it isn't," he agreed after a very short pause, some of
the edge gone from his words. "But that has nothing to do
with the fact that I'm not about to leave you here. I don't
believe in running out on people, not even ones who don't
think much of me. When we leave we'll be leaving together,
just the way we arrived." There was another pause, this time
a longer one, and then he said, "What did you mean, that
no one would miss you? Everyone has *someone* who would
miss them."

"It isn't important," I answered with a shrug, shifting a little in the chair. "I spend so much time alone, I suppose I've gotten into the habit of thinking—Well, it really isn't important."

"I see," he said after another moment, and then there was nothing. I felt so terrible I wished he would leave, but couldn't manage to make the request vocal. It seemed I was destined to do something wrong no matter what I was involved in, and destiny isn't often comfortable or easy to endure. There had been such hostility in his voice, and I'd earned every bit of it.

"Look, I may have been a bit too—intense—during those words we exchanged after coming through the gate," he said at last. "I didn't mean to make it seem like the end of the worlds, so there's no sense in taking it like that. We got into this together, and we'll get out of it the same way. All I ask is that you give me the chance to smooth things over, without getting upset and doing something to make them worse. I have a lot of experience in dealing with the people around my father's court. There's not much sense in wasting it, is there?"

I shook my head to agree there wasn't, which was the best I could do. So he hadn't been ignoring me during his conversation with Nalkin, he'd just been trying to smooth things over before I could make them worse. That wasn't hard to understand, in fact it was downright easy. If there was one thing I could be counted on for, it was to make things worse.

"You know, it's just come to me that we've been on the go for quite a while," he said, now trying to sound encouraging. "The problem with moving from world to world is that you think you should still be going strong if evening hasn't come yet. We left evening behind when we came through the entry, but we couldn't do the same with tiredness. Why don't you get some rest while I do the same in my own apartment, and we'll talk again later, after the feast."

This time I nodded, but I still couldn't bring myself to look at him. For once his hesitation didn't last very long; after a very brief moment he got up, and then his footsteps were taking him out of the apartment. I waited until the door was closed, then banished my coffee cup and went to look for a bed to lie down on. Anything to keep from having to live with my thoughts any longer . . .

Bariden closed the door to Chalaine's apartment behind him, then just stood there for a moment rubbing his eyes. When he'd first arrived he'd been all ready for a fight, and that had left him totally unprepared for what he'd found instead. He'd all but shouted at the girl and had blamed her for everything that had happened—and all she'd done was agree with him. She'd even tried to take the responsibility for getting them—*him*—out of there again, and he was certain she hadn't made the offer without really meaning it.

And the pain! When he'd finally calmed down enough to notice, the pain and self-recrimination she all but radiated had almost knocked him over. She hadn't waited for *him* to blame her for what had happened, she'd already blamed herself and had accepted the responsibility. Just as if things might not have gone better if he hadn't been quite so patient with the bearded and arrogant Arnwell . . .

"And not once did she try to apologize for anything said between us," he muttered. That point bothered him most of all, and not because he thought it meant she had no regrets. Added to the fact that she hadn't once looked straight at him, he was convinced she thought what had passed between them was beyond apology. She'd often failed to look directly at him, but not with such complete misery . . .

Bariden sighed as he began to walk back to his own apartment. He hadn't known it at the time, but it looked like he'd made a bad mistake saying what he had to her. She acted as if she were always blamed for things, and had long since stopped arguing the accusations with a trace of truth, and simply accepted and believed them. He'd called her a snob, and one of *them*, and everything he'd felt toward those hateful people had spilled out over *her*. And all she'd done was be angry over his having forgotten her name—

"Damn," he muttered, the idea suddenly coming to him. Was it possible he wasn't the first to do that, or even the second or third? What would it do to a bright, attractive woman, to have people constantly telling her she wasn't important enough to be remembered? She was so quiet and withdrawn, lots of people must have found it impossible to do anything *but* overlook her. She was quiet because people ignored her, and people ignored her because she was quiet. Talk about reinforcing the bars of a prison . . .

Well, that tore it all the way. He'd misjudged everything about the girl, even the point of how badly he'd insulted her. He wondered how long it had taken her to come around to being *able* to feel insult over that sort of treatment. It had probably been years, and then he'd gone ahead and ruined it all by blaming her for doing it. He'd proven she was wrong about why he'd shown interest in her, and in her eyes that had made everything she'd done wrong.

Bariden reached his rooms in one of the blackest moods he'd ever experienced, and every bit of his anger was aimed at himself. He closed the door behind him quietly enough, but if he'd been anywhere else he would have slammed it off its hinges. He'd started out determined to court a girl he'd made a blunder with, and had somehow ended up doing little short of slapping her in the face. It was hard to understand how he could have been such a fool, such a clubfooted and club-mouthed idiot. He'd probably ruined any chance there had been of something developing between them, but it wasn't possible to simply shrug and forget it. His first concern had to be the matter of getting them both out of that place without starting a war, but his very next priority . . . right after finding the way home . . .

CHAPTER FIVE

I followed the servant along the hall, feeling only slightly better after the nap I'd had. I'd also had a bath and had produced some party clothes to wear, and one of the girl servants had even shown up to brush my hair. Nalkin hadn't had anyone wake me up to see the queen, because the queen had decided to give me a few private minutes before the feast. I was trying to work myself up to the point of feeling honored, but the best I could do was wish I was home again. All alone on my own world, with no one around to hurt or mess up . . .

"By the Diamond Realm, will you look at *you*," a voice came, one I unfortunately recognized immediately. "Chalaine, that must be one of the most beautiful gowns I've ever seen, and you look incredible in it. That electric blue does the most wonderful things to your hair."

By then he was standing in front of me, possibly still looking me over. From what I could see he'd called up his own finery, including a dark blue wide-sleeved silk tunic, cream-colored leather breeches and matching boots, a jeweled swordbelt, and a golden medallion to brighten up the dark silk tunic. I wore silver with my gown, earrings, necklace, and shoes, and not just because I like silver better than gold. Ever since I'd awakened, I'd had the strangest feeling about the things that were happening to us . . .

"Since we're both going to the same place, I insist on being a proper escort," he said, moving to my right to take my arm. He wrapped it around his own arm which put his sword between us, and then patted my hand. "We're ready to continue on now," he said to the two servants, the unfamiliar one obviously having been his. "Lead the way, and we're right behind you."

Our procession got under way again, but I was too uncomfortable to do more than notice that in passing. I had no idea what Bariden was doing, or why he was doing it. Couldn't he understand that the less contact we had before we parted, the happier I would be?

"Have I mentioned how wonderful your hair looks brushed out loose like that?" he murmured, fractionally tightening his hold on my hand. I'd tried to slide my arm free of his, but he didn't seem to want me to do that. "I've wondered how that auburn glory would look unbraided almost from the first moment we met, and now I finally know. The wait was worth it."

I held up the rather full skirt of my gown with my left hand, certain I could hear a really attractive grin in his voice. Under other circumstances I would have commented that it was getting kind of deep in that hall, but Bariden's purpose in saying what he had couldn't possibly be the usual one. It could be he was trying to show me what it might have been like if I hadn't ruined things, but that seemed a bit much. No, most likely he was trying to keep things going on a friendly basis until we got out of there, pretending we were still partners. Which, of course, we weren't.

"If there's dancing at the feast later, I claim the first one with you," he said next. "I haven't danced in a while, so I hope you'll forgive me if I'm rusty. I'm sure you'll be much better, and—you do dance, don't you?"

"Yes, I dance," I answered with a sigh. If friendly was what he wanted right then, that's what he'd get. "I wonder how long it will take to find a Sighted who knows where a gate is."

"It shouldn't be too long, so we'll have to be patient," he murmured back. "Just remember that the aim is to get both of us out of here, so don't be too quick to promise things. And if discussions are necessary, try to leave them to me. A good part of my education covered all the ways it's possible to say things without committing to anything at all."

"Diplomacy on the highest levels," I murmured back, deciding I needed to listen to something like that. I had no interest in learning how to do it, but knowing how it's done can help to keep it from being done to you.

Bariden made a sound of agreement, but didn't say anything else. We'd moved into an area of the palace that had more guardsmen stationed along the hall than any other part we'd seen, which probably meant we were getting close to the queen. Why she needed so many guardsmen I had no idea, especially since Bariden's father made do with a good deal fewer. She might have been in the middle of some sort of problem, and if so we'd probably be hearing about it in just a few minutes.

Our guides turned a corner, and when we followed we saw a set of ornate doors at the end of the relatively short hall. In addition to the guardsmen to either side of the hall, there were four more and a squad leader positioned directly in front of the doors. When the squad leader saw us coming he turned to speak to his men, and by the time we reached them they were out of the way. Our two guides each opened a door, then stood still to bow us past them.

A new guide was waiting just a few steps away to take over, but this time it was someone we knew. Nalkin was absolutely resplendent in plum-colored velvet kneepants and coat, lacy white silk shirt and white silk hose, gold-buckled, plum-colored leather shoes, and a heavy gold necklace. The room was L-shaped with the shorter leg nearest the doors we'd come in by, and once those doors had been closed behind us Nalkin gestured us forward.

"Her Majesty is waiting to meet you," he said softly when we reached him, glancing toward the part of the room we couldn't yet see. There was carpeting on the floor and silk drapes and a large mirror on the long left-hand wall, but aside from that and a few lamps, the entry area was unfurnished. "Do you need to be told the proper protocol when being presented to royalty?"

"If it's standard protocol, no," Bariden answered for us. "If Queen Lova requires something special, you'll have to tell us what it is."

"The queen isn't one for a lot of pomp and ceremony," Nalkin answered with a smile. "A simple bow and curtsy will do when you're presented, and if she wants anything else she'll tell you herself. But don't worry about being imposed upon. What Her Majesty wants is never an imposition. Follow me."

He turned and straightened his coat before walking slowly toward the place where the rest of the room would be visible, and Bariden and I exchanged glances behind his back. What he'd said about the queen raised more questions than it answered, most especially since Nalkin had looked only at Bariden when he'd made his comments. It didn't take a genius to figure out the most likely thing that Bariden would not find to be an imposition, but there was no sense in jumping to conclusions. Besides, Bariden was old enough to make his own decisions about things like that. Even if we *had* become friends, it would still have been none of my business.

"Your majesty, allow me to present the Lady Chalaine and the Lord Bariden," Nalkin announced from where he'd stopped to bow. "The lady defeated Arnwell the magician in today's competition, and the lord accompanies her. My lord and lady, step forward into the presence of Her Majesty Queen Lova II of Lovaire."

Bariden and I moved forward with that, and when we reached Nalkin's side we stopped to bow and curtsy. Bariden's courtly bow bent him all the way forward, so I was the first to get a good look at the queen. Since I like to tell the truth whenever possible, I'll have to admit it was all I could do not to stare.

Queen Lova sat in a fancy chair that wasn't quite a throne, which stood on a two-step platform that wasn't quite a dais. Her incredible gown was white silk and lace, and diamonds glittered at her ears and throat and on three of her fingers. Her hair was a bright, flaming red, worn long and loose and topped with a slender, stylized crown of diamonds. Her face—how do you describe a woman who turns every other woman no more than pretty by comparison? Radiantly lovely? Unbelievably beautiful? Inconsiderately unfair?

I knew it immediately when Bariden got his first good look at her. The arm under my hand stiffened, as though all of him was suddenly tightly braced against involuntary action. A glance at his face showed it expressionless, another dead giveaway. He stared at the queen as though she were nothing more than another living organism, but that had to be his high diplomatic training at work.

"We welcome you both to Our Court," Queen Lova said with a dazzling smile, her light and beautiful voice a perfect match to the rest of her. "We also offer Our congratulations to *you*, Lady Chalaine, for finding it possible to defeat Arnwell. He was our Court Magician, but considered the position more an excuse to take advantage of others than a responsibility or duty to the right. You have Our thanks for ridding Us of him."

A light pattering of applause came after that, showing there were other people in the room. Considering what the queen was like, it wasn't surprising they'd gone unnoticed till then.

"We have been considering means other than mere words to thank you for so valuable a service," the queen continued, still smiling at me. "That will require a private discussion between us, which we will certainly have in the very near future. For tonight we need concern ourselves with no more than feasting and merrymaking, which is just as it should be. Lady Chalaine, We ask that you allow Lord Wimail to escort you into the feasting hall, and now you may all retire."

There was a lot of bowing and curtsying as the queen stood up after dismissing everyone. Considering Nalkin's earlier hints I was surprised she hadn't said even a single word to Bariden, and I got the feeling he looked at it the same. The nonexpression on his face had turned peculiar, but then I forgot about it as we were joined by someone else.

"Lady Chalaine," the man said with a smile and a bow. "I'm Wimail, and I've been given the honor of escorting you to table. Allow me to offer my arm."

He was a fairly tall man with dark hair and gray eyes, a man who was handsome and knew it. He wore a green velvet vest, tight brocade trousers, green leather boots, and a frilly gray silk shirt. He also wore a sword, but it was hard to tell how much use the weapon had had behind all the gold and silver and jewels.

"And I'm Bariden," my former escort announced before I could take the offered arm of his replacement. "I know customs differ from place to place, but where I come from a man asks leave of a lady's companion before trying to walk her away from him. Even if he's been told to do so by his queen. That custom isn't observed here?"

"Only by the pitifully uninformed," Wimail responded coolly, looking Bariden up and down. "Since it's obvious no one has told you, allow me to do the honors. I'm the one who usually escorts the queen to table, which means you're expected to take my place even as I'm taking yours. While you stand here telling me about quaint customs in faraway places, Her Majesty stands unattended and unescorted. But perhaps that's another custom from wherever it is you come, the custom of ignoring queens."

"No, it's usually the ill-mannered we ignore," Bariden responded, but more to me than to a suddenly invisible-to-him Wimail. "Chalaine, I'll have to ask you to excuse me. I've just learned there's a duty I'm expected to perform, but I'll see you later. Think about what we discussed earlier."

He gave me a proper and unhurried bow before turning and walking away, heading toward a Queen Lova who wasn't quite as unattended as Wimail had suggested. Most of the men in the room were trying to get her attention, an effort completely beyond understanding. After all, why would a man want to be noticed by a woman who made other women look as attractive as tax collectors?

"What a relief," Wimail said from my right. "As long as he took to leave, you'd think he was being asked to attend someone's maiden aunt. As soon as he gets around to escorting the queen into the feasting hall, you and I will follow immediately. It's still my place to take the opposite end of the table from her, and you'll be seated to my right."

I couldn't help noticing that he hadn't glanced at me once while making that speech, which was actually a great relief. I wouldn't have enjoyed fending off the attentions of a man engaged in pouting over having been traded by the queen for someone else. He seemed to think the substitution wasn't likely to last long, and was therefore more annoyed than worried. For myself I was already getting bored, not to mention hungry. If we weren't given access to the food pretty soon, I'd have to supply my own snack.

With nothing else to do, I watched Bariden approach the queen. The men around her gave ground reluctantly, stepping back only because they had no choice. When he reached her he bowed and then said something, and she responded with a dazzling smile. I wondered what he'd said, which made me toy with the idea of speaking a spell that would let me hear their conversation, then decided against it. What they said to each other was none of my business, and I was supposed to be thinking about what he and I had discussed earlier. I wasn't sure if that was supposed to mean my not promising anything and letting him do all the talking, or what he'd said about how I looked. After all, it could have been either . . . Sure it could.

There was only another minute or so of small talk, and then the queen, on Bariden's arm, led the way toward the double doors that were to the right of where she'd been sitting. She was a tall, graceful woman who looked perfectly at home on the arm of a strong, handsome man, and I had a feeling Wimail was thinking the same. The second offer of his own arm was somewhat less than courtly, and then we were all but hurrying after the perfect couple in the lead. Servants opened the doors as they approached, and the feast was finally and officially under way.

The dining room we entered was enormous, and was already filled with what seemed like hundreds of people. One very long table, glitteringly set, stood empty in the middle of the room, but all the rest around it were filled. The others were smaller tables, each holding no more than twelve people, but were almost as richly set. When the queen entered everyone sitting down stood up, and those already standing turned. Along with the serving people they all bowed or curtsied, and I could feel Wimail eating it up and just about expanding. Obviously when he walked with or near the queen, he could pretend all that bowing and scraping was directed toward him.

A gigantic crystal chandelier hung over the middle of our table, its scores of candles making sure everything put in front of us would be well illuminated. Wimail seated me, then took his own place to my left at his end of the table.

Bariden had already seated the queen, of course, and other men were doing the same for other women before finding their own places. I'd always wondered why women were supposed to be incapable of sitting down all by themselves, and had never found anyone able to supply a definite reason. I might have asked Wimail, but he'd started a languid conversation with the woman to his left, who obviously admired him enormously, and it wouldn't have done to interrupt.

"Some people are endlessly fascinated by those who worship and adore them," a soft voice murmured on my right. "Trying to break into that fascination doesn't pay, not when you stop to realize what you'll have even if you happen to succeed."

I turned my head to look at the man, who had gotten himself seated without my noticing. His amused green eyes looked only at me, but there was no doubt he'd been talking about Wimail and the woman to his left. This man's hair was very dark, probably black, and it was hard to understand why the queen would have bothered with Wimail with him available. Handsome was too mild a word, and standing up he would have been Bariden's size.

"I, on the other hand," the man continued, "prefer to *exchange* worship and adoration. One-way worship ends up being boring no matter which side you're on, but I haven't yet found a proper partner. I'm Lord Naesery, by the way, and I already know you're the Lady Chalaine."

"Just Chalaine, without the lady," I told Naesery with a smile he seemed to deserve. "Where I come from, the single name has more significance than almost any title could add. Not that there's anything insignificant about a title. I mean—"

"No, no, it's quite all right," he said with a laugh when I began to trip over my own feet, the smile forgotten. "I know you were referring to yourself, not to me. But even if you *had* meant me, I wouldn't have been offended. The truth of the matter is, I did nothing at all to earn the title of lord. What fuss can you honestly make over a title that wasn't earned?"

It was amazing to discover that he felt the way I did, especially since he *had* the title. A servant came by to fill our wineglasses, offering a choice of yellow or white, which occupied us for the next couple of minutes. Once the servant moved on it was time for a subject change in our previous conversation, and I knew just the one I wanted to try.

"Tell me, Lord Naesery," I said as he leaned back toward me. "Why is it so many men indulge in this seating-of-women thing? Are we supposed to be helpless, or do men just want us to believe we are?"

"Dear girl, the proper answer is neither," he responded with a grin. "A man would be an idiot to consider a woman like *you*, for instance, helpless, but he still enjoys seating her. In general, it makes him feel good to do things for a woman he finds attractive, even so small a thing as that. It makes him feel like a man worthy of such a woman, rather than like a lout coming begging with hat in hand. Or like a thief, coming to steal what doesn't belong to him. It satisfies his sense of the proper, without any belittling reflection on the object of his solicitude. And I think I should add that my previous comments cover just about every man but Wimail."

"I take it you don't think much of him," I said with a laugh I couldn't hold back. "Would I be prying if I asked why?"

"To be truthful, it's mostly a personal and irrational dislike," he admitted with a shrug. "I have this old-fashioned and narrow-minded view of what a man's behavior should be like. If he decides to pair off with a woman, for instance, it ought to disturb him that she makes a regular habit of—entertaining—other men. He ought to have enough pride to bow politely and walk away, leaving her to her multitude of dalliances. To merely step aside each time and then go hurrying back when she's through—it makes one think of a lapdog, and distantly paints all men as shallow beasts without a trace of heart. Aside from that and the fact the man has no personality or intelligence, I have very little against him."

"Well, that's a relief," I said with a grin of my own. "For a minute there I thought you might not like him. Since I've started with intrusive questions, I might as well add another—which you certainly don't have to answer if you don't care to. Were you one of those that particular—woman—dallied with?"

"I was supposed to be," he answered with no self-consciousness or false modesty or even self-righteousness. For such a young and attractive man, he had the presence and ease of someone decades older. I might have suspected he was a sorcerer or wizard who had simply changed his appearance to one much younger than his chronological age, but Naesery wasn't Sighted. Since it's impossible for someone of power to hide it from someone else who's the same, I knew that as a fact.

"I was supposed to be, but I declined the honor," he said, the words going the least bit dry. "I've never been one to take a number and stand in line, not even for fame and riches. I suppose it's just a basic dislike of having my elbows jostled—or of command performances. Are you wondering if your—companion will share the dislike? But he hasn't been here long enough to learn about the lines, has he?"

"We had a small hint before we were presented," I said, realizing I couldn't refuse to answer a countering intrusive question. "But no, I wasn't wondering that about my—companion. What he does is his business, and none of mine. We barely know each other, and once we get home we'll be going our separate ways."

"But in the meantime you travel together," Naesery said, this time musingly, those strange green eyes considering me thoughtfully. "If I'd been asked to bet on it, I would have thought he was bright enough to see the riches under his nose. I'd love to ask what's wrong with him, but I'll ask instead how soon you expect you'll be free to leave. Unless I'm completely mistaken, the queen has plans that include your remaining here."

"It was highly unlikely that she wouldn't," I replied with a sigh, not very happy to have the possibility confirmed. "I'll just have to make her understand that I wasn't trying to win her competition, and I'm not free to give my time away as I please. Since the mistake was mine I was willing to stay here and try to fix it, but I can't consider that an option now. Bariden said he won't leave without me, and at least one of us has *got* to get back."

"Well, I'm glad to see the man has *some* sense," Naesery said, faintly put out. "Any man who would leave a woman behind is no man at all. Especially when the woman is one like you. But if getting home is so important, why aren't the two of you on the road there right now?"

"We would be, if we knew where the proper road was," I said, leaning back to let another servant put a small plate of cold fish and sauce in front of me. Once we were both served I added, "What we need is something called a gate, but to find it we'll also need someone like Arnwell, the former chief magician or whatever. Even his associate would do, if she happens to be familiar with the countryside. Without help, it could take us years to find one."

"Unfortunately, Arnwell isn't likely to be available for a while," he replied, picking up a fork with an even more thoughtful look. "He'll hide out somewhere to lick his wounds, and if his apprentice hasn't already found him, she certainly will shortly. Neither of them were particularly popular, so they're probably in a place no one knows about."

"If nothing else turns up, tomorrow I might have to try to track them," I said, lifting my own fork. "Assuming, of course, that the queen doesn't have any violent objections. If she does, well, it could get tricky."

We each gave our attention to the food then, and it was really quite tasty. There isn't much you can do with plain, cold fish other than supply a superior sauce, but in this case the sauce was only a little above average. I could have used magic to change it to something really worth eating, but that sort of thing is tacky when you're someone's guest. There wasn't so much that I couldn't finish it without trouble, so I forgot about superior sauces and did just that. When I finished I noticed that Naesery had done the same first, and was waiting to resume our conversation.

"You know, I'm fairly familiar with the countryside around here," he said as soon as I put the fork down. "If you'd like to describe this gate you're looking for, I might be able to tell you where it is."

"The gate we need looks like a brilliant slit in the middle of the air, at least from a distance," I responded with a smile. "If you're with someone Sighted, when you get closer the slit expands into a glowing curtain of light and that's your gate. If you're not with someone Sighted, the slit stays just as it is and you don't even know it's there. All you know is that you're uncomfortable in the area, and can't bear to hang around even a little while. I appreciate the offer of help, Naesery, but through no fault of your own you're not equipped to supply it."

"I appreciate the qualification, but the lack still smarts," he answered wryly. "I find I'd very much like to be of help to you, you see, even if that help takes you somewhere I can't follow. I enjoy the sight of your smile too much to want to see it disappear, so I'll do some checking around. If there's anyone capable of seeing that gate who *has* seen it, I'll let you know at once."

At that point we were interrupted again, by one servant taking away the remnants of the fish, and two others with a cart offering a choice of four soups. Naesery didn't seem disappointed that I wasn't able to thank him for his offer, and in fact didn't even appear to notice that I hadn't. Just as he hadn't yet put me in the position of needing to respond somehow to his compliments. He seemed to be the most open and easy-to-get-along-with man I'd ever met, even more attractive inside than he was on the surface.

But that didn't mean I was overlooking the possibility that the man had a purpose in offering help that he hadn't yet mentioned. His words seemed to indicate that he wasn't terribly fond of the queen or her favorite male partner, but disapproval hadn't kept him from attending the feast in a place at *their* table. The queen herself was seeing to giving Bariden reason to hang around for a while; what better way to handle *me* than to provide a very good-looking man who just happened to disapprove of that extremely beautiful woman? And one who also wanted to help me to get home. Wouldn't it be easier to depend on him rather than do any poking around of my own . . . ?

Thinking those thoughts didn't quite ruin the soup I'd chosen, but that was only because high-level politics wasn't as unknown to me as the queen probably assumed. I'd had my share of it from a couple of different sources, and had chosen to turn around and walk away before it all drove me mad. It had gotten to be a habit to suspect everyone I met of having ulterior motives no matter what they did, friendly or cold. If they were friendly they had to want something, and if they were cold they were trying to manipulate me or impress someone else . . .

I broke off a piece of fresh-baked honey bread and chewed with determination, trying to shake off most of those old feelings. It was hard to understand how anyone stayed sane when they played those games all the time, or even why anyone would want to play them. But so many people did, on almost every human-populated world, and not only played, but enjoyed the game. It seemed like such a waste of time, always maneuvering to gain or prove something, never satisfied with what you'd already gained or proved—

The sound of startled exclamations pulled me out of my thoughts, exclamations that were joined by a few screams of fright and shouts of distress. Looking down toward the other end of the table I saw what was causing the fuss—the sudden appearance of the magician Arnwell. He stood no more than five feet away from the queen, and the way he stood said he wasn't there to wish people a hearty appetite.

CHAPTER SIX

The robed and bearded Arnwell stood with folded arms very near the queen, but she didn't seem all that bothered. I spoke a quick spell to let me hear what was being said even if they whispered, and found I'd acted just in time.

"I don't see my place at your table, Your Majesty," Arnwell said in a voice that grated like metal but was nevertheless very soft. He'd dropped that pompous, overinvolved accent he'd been using, probably because no one was likely to be impressed any longer. "Tell one of these fools to get up and give me what's rightfully mine."

"My dear Arnwell, that's exactly the point," Queen Lova responded just as softly, satisfaction in her tone. "You no longer *have* a place here, not that you ever really did. Treating those around you like dirt is fine as long as no one is in a position to feel insulted. Once you slip from those heights, however, you find that your plight brings sympathy from an equal no one. You thought you were unbeatable and so acted as you pleased, but now you have to live with the consequences. You'll favor Us if you do that elsewhere."

With that she returned her attention to her meal, but the magician wasn't ready to be dismissed. Fury drew him up another inch at least, and he gestured with one hand. Rather than bringing a spell into play, though, the gesture proved to be a signal. At least a dozen of the servants standing closest to our table uncovered or unwrapped crossbows rather than food, and not one of them wavered with the least uncertainty.

"One of the consequences of doing as you please is the desire to continue doing it," Arnwell said as soon as the gasps of alarm and outrage had quieted. The queen had paled, but seemed determined not to shrink back or cower. "Magic may be able to counter magic, but it can't do anything at all against a dozen steel-tipped quarrels. Negotiations concerning my place at your court have been reopened, Your Majesty, and we'll get to the discussions as soon as I see to another small matter first."

The smirk on the man's face would have given one of the EverNameless the urge to hit him, and I didn't have quite their level of patient self-control. But I *was* curious about what Arnwell would do next, and since I'd already taken care of the crossbows, there was no reason not to indulge myself. As soon as the weapons had been uncovered I'd spoken a spell to freeze every weapon in the room, and had felt a similar spell locking itself into mine. Bariden's glance and very small nod said he'd done the same and was also aware of my effort, which meant we could both sit back and wait to see what cropped up.

"There's someone here I've been looking forward to seeing again," Arnwell said, stepping back to get a clear view of me without coming closer. "Give a woman a few lessons and a way to protect herself against magical attack, and she begins to imagine she's almost as good as a man. I was given public humiliation today by someone who isn't even fit to lick my boots, but that will change. By tomorrow she *will* be fit to lick my boots, and will do so as publicly as she gave humiliation, or she will be dead. Stand up and give me your decision *now*, you tart."

Since he'd raised his voice in order to speak to me, no one but those around the edges of the room had missed his speech. The silence surrounding us was frightened and unsure, the people producing it as motionless as the queen's guardsmen at their posts. Rushing forward probably would have gotten the queen hurt or killed, so they stayed in place and chafed at being helpless. Once again I wondered why everyone knew so little about magic, but that wasn't the time to consider the point.

"Most people consider me more dry than tart," I responded after a moment. "Of course, you couldn't be expected to know that, so you'll have to be forgiven. As for standing up, I don't see any need. I can give you my decision from right here, which is: grow up. Only children think they know it all, and children tend to get hurt when, in their ignorance, they try to do what's beyond them. And get rid of that stupid beard. Facial hair has never yet been able to increase someone's ability to do magic."

Needless to say, Arnwell didn't like any part of my answer. His rage grew so high his eyes nearly left their sockets, and the stirring and sounds from the people all around only added to it. They weren't *quite* laughing at him out loud, but they might as well have been. The spoiled brat Arnwell thought he was much too good to be laughed at, and patience wasn't his strong suit.

"Kill her," he snarled, talking to his crossbowmen without looking at them. "Three of you shoot her, and three more stand ready to shoot anyone else I point to! Every one of them will be on their knees to me, that I swear by the Highest Power! *Shoot her now!*"

"Don't get mad, they *are* trying," I said as reasonably as possible. "Their biggest problem is that I'm not letting the weapons work, and their second biggest is the compulsion you have them under. Doing that to people isn't very nice, but I seriously doubt if the point bothers you. But if you don't release them, I *can* make it bother you."

With that I called up a needle with a very sharp point, and let it tap at his hand. He howled and jumped back, gesturing frantically to banish an illusion, but the needle was no illusion. Those at magician level aren't yet able to produce the real thing, so they rely a good deal on making people believe whatever-it-is really is there. Banishing one of those illusions is possible once you know what it is, but banishing the real thing is a lot harder.

"You're not releasing them," I mentioned, this time tapping at the hand he'd gestured with. "If I have to say it again, that point will be made somewhere other than your hand. You have the right to be as stupid as you like, but you don't have the right to force others to join you."

"You can't do this to me!" he screamed, face livid and mouth almost foaming. "I am *Arnwell*, and in five years no one has even been able to *approach* me! I was born to be great, destined to reach heights that lesser minds can't even dream of! You *can't* keep me from my destiny, no one can!"

Then he screamed again, this time wordlessly. Since I hadn't done anything I wondered why, but a glance at Bariden answered the question. Very surreptitiously he was using one finger to direct something, probably a needle like the one *I'd* called up. From the way Arnwell choked and hopped around I wasn't sure I wanted to know where Bariden was sticking him, but it seemed to do the trick. Suddenly all those with crossbows jumped and looked wildly around, and then began to throw the weapons to the floor.

Which, in turn, caused even more confusion. The guardsmen who had been standing helplessly by tried to jump forward at once, but they were all holding spears. With the weapons-spell still in effect the spears were as good as bolted to the floor where the guards had rested them, and the guardsmen were yanked back when they tried to run forward. In the middle of all that bedlam Arnwell tried to slip away again, but this time I was watching. He got all of two and a half steps before I froze him in place, something he'd probably thought I couldn't do. He'd clearly been trying to stay out of what he considered my range, which only said something about his own.

"Okay, everybody quiet down!" I said after speaking a spell to amplify my voice. "Everything's under control, so there's no need for hysterics. I think you guardsmen ought to stand Arnwell up again, then take the quarrels out of those crossbows. I can't release the spell on your spears and swords until that's done, not when some of the crossbows will go off when the spell is gone. That's right, he isn't going anywhere."

Some of the guardsmen had abandoned their spears to rush to the magician, but when they tried to pull him out of the room he just tipped over. It took a moment for them to understand that he was frozen, and couldn't escape even if he wanted to. Two of them still stayed near him while the others went to the crossbows. Then someone who must have been an officer started to point to the servants who had produced the weapons, and it was time to interfere again.

"No, don't arrest those servants," I said in my still-amplified voice. "Arnwell had them all under a compulsion, and they had no choice about obeying him. I checked each of them before I spoke to Arnwell, and you can take my word for the fact that none of them was here voluntarily."

The officer paused to look to the queen, and she smiled and nodded her confirmation of the order. Then her smile came to me and warmed, and I suddenly wondered if I'd put my foot in it again. It was hard to see what could have been done differently, but when people are very pleased with you there's usually a reason. Although not necessarily one that you'll like ... And there was also the question of why Bariden was hiding his own magical ability. He would have been able to handle things personally a lot more easily if the queen knew she could get what she wanted from him as well ...

"Allow me to be the first to say how I admire your style of managing things," Naesery told me with a grin as soon as I leaned back. "You're clearly a good deal more talented than the unfortunate Arnwell, not to mention the possessor of a—sharper—sense of humor. And it was thoughtful of you to catch him for the guard. They probably would have found stopping him a bit more difficult."

"I think you know I didn't do it just for the guard," I replied after canceling the amplified-voice spell. "I need to question him before he's locked away in a dungeon somewhere, and that thought brings up a problem. He may only be magician level, but an ordinary cell isn't likely to hold him for long. If nothing else, he can put the nearest guard or jailer under a compulsion to release him."

"The queen probably expects *your* help with that," Naesery said, studying me with a faint smile. "Whether or not you give it will be your choice, but I suspect you'll end up doing whatever's right. I couldn't help noticing that your first concern was for those innocent servants Arnwell used as dupes. Those with power seldom worry about the helpless and unimportant, and that's a trait you share with the queen. Whatever other faults she may have, her people are always her first concern."

He reached for his wineglass then, leaving me to wonder if that made things better or worse. It was somehow easier to think of the queen as a self-indulgent parasite, not a dedicated ruler who loved the people of her country. I toyed with my own wineglass until things settled down, and once all the crossbows were secured and most of the guardsmen had returned to their spears, I removed the weapons-spell. One spear still hit the floor with a crash, but none of the swords went flying out of their scabbards. That meant no one had tried to draw one, which kept the confusion from starting again.

The two guardsmen stayed near Arnwell, but even though servants were bringing out food again, no one tried to move the magician. I had the feeling Queen Lova was keeping him there as a sort of object lesson, like hanging the severed head of an enemy from your city gates. Whatever, the unending stream of food and drink distracted most of those at the feast from paying much attention. Naesery supplied pleasant, meaningless conversation while we ate, making the meal even more enjoyable.

Right after various desserts had begun circulating, the unintrusive background music being played by the small orchestra changed to obvious dance music. People at other tables stirred, as if they'd been waiting for that, but no one got up or even looked like they were going to. And then the queen rose, bringing all the men at our table to their feet, and headed out to the clear area only a few steps away. Following her was Bariden, who took her in his arms when she turned, and then the two of them began to dance.

"They make a striking couple," Naesery commented as I called up a cup of coffee. That was the only thing not offered by the servants, and I tend to go into withdrawal when I have to do without. "As soon as the queen and her escort finish the first dance, everyone else will be free to indulge. Will you do me the honor of joining me on the floor? Only a very brave woman can qualify as my partner, which is, of course, the only reason I chose you."

"Oh, of course," I agreed, matching his grin with a smile. "I'll be glad to consider your proposal, but I'll need a few minutes to make a decision. I hope you don't mind."

"Not at all," he said with one brow high. "Please take as much time as you need."

He looked as though he wanted to ask questions, but we were no longer exchanging intrusions. Which was a damned good thing, since I couldn't think of an unembarrassing way to explain what I was waiting for. I supposedly had a previous request for the first dance, even though I hadn't in any way agreed to it . . . it had probably just been a silly comment, forgotten as soon as it was spoken, but still . . .

The orchestra finished the song it was playing, and the two dancers stopped to applaud the musicians while everyone else applauded *them*. Then the music began again, and while people rose to go out onto the floor, the queen and her partner began to dance again. I took another sip of my coffee before putting the cup aside, then smiled at Naesery.

"I've made my decision," I told him. "I'd love to join you on the floor."

"The delights of dealing with a brave woman," he said with a smile, standing to offer me his hand. "You can always count on her to come through for you. I promise I'll try to make this as painless as possible."

"As long as you don't ask me for the same promise," I murmured, which made him laugh as he guided me toward the dancing area. He put his arms around me and we began to move to the music, which proved we'd both been exaggerating our lack of ability. He was one of the best partners I'd ever had, making me seem more graceful than I'd ever before felt. I followed him easily through the steps of a dance I'd never done, learning it quickly and pleasantly without once appearing awkward. I was enjoying myself thoroughly, which made Nalkin's sudden appearance beside us more than simply surprising.

"I hope you'll excuse the intrusion, Lady Chalaine," he said with a bow. "The queen has asked me to request your presence at a private audience. I'm instructed to assure you that it won't take long, and you'll be free to return to the feast in just a little while. If you'll follow me, I'll take you to where Her Majesty is waiting."

"If you weren't offering to lead the way, I'd suspect you of wanting to get rid of me," I said, not terribly thrilled to hear that my "private audience" had been moved up. "To take my place dancing with Lord Naesery, I mean.

Why has the queen decided to see me tonight rather than tomorrow?"

"I'm afraid I wasn't told that," Nalkin answered with an apologetic shrug. "It may, however, have something to do with Arnwell and his disposition. She's already had the body removed to the audience chamber."

I turned to see that the magician and his guards were indeed gone, which meant the audience wasn't something I could refuse even if I'd been given that option. If I had to I could follow to wherever they'd taken him, but there was no sense in making unnecessary trouble. Besides, when you really need to question someone, you're better off doing it as soon as possible.

"Then we'd better get going ourselves," I said, then turned to Naesery. "I'd like to thank you for a wonderful time. I don't know if I'll be able to get back, and if I can't I wanted you to know that."

"If you aren't able to get back, then I'll see you at breakfast," he answered with a bow that didn't take those eyes from my face. "When you're ready just send a servant for me and I'll come to your apartment."

Well, at least he wasn't inviting himself in for a nightcap before that breakfast, I thought as I followed Nalkin across the feasting hall. Naesery didn't seem prepared to let himself be avoided, but he also wasn't trying to corner me. Or at least not very tightly. I wondered if he would turn out to be another problem, then dismissed the question as stupid. What else *was* there in those places but problems?

We left the feasting hall by a side door, and followed a short corridor to the audience chamber. Its door was decorated with two guardsmen to show that that was the place, and Nalkin knocked softly before opening the door and bowing me in. When he closed the door again he was still on the outside, which made Queen Lova and me the only ones in the room. Not counting Arnwell, of course, who stood frozen in midstep in the center of the small, cozy room.

"He used to hate it if I used this place as an audience chamber for him," the Queen said suddenly, her stare still on the magician. "He considered it an insult, you see, that I wasn't receiving him in a place as grand as his exalted status demanded. To tell the truth, I began to fear my people and I would never be free of him. Once he gained the place of Court magician, there was no dislodging him from it. And I think after this year's contest, he planned to depose me and declare himself king."

"A small amount of power is usually worse than a lot," I commented, walking to a large, soft chair covered in the same flower pattern as the couch the queen sat on. "Do you mind if I sit?" When she shook her head I made use of the chair, then continued, "If he wanted to be king, why didn't he just put you under a compulsion to marry him? Then the whole thing would have become your idea."

"A man who marries me can never become anything more than the Queen's Consort," she answered with a faint smile. "That's the law, and even I can't change it. Besides, I'd made it quite clear to everyone in my Court that I disliked the man intensely, and always would. If I suddenly changed my mind and announced that I was marrying him, everyone would have known his magic was responsible. And he wouldn't have wanted me there, as a constant reminder that he'd stolen what he had. He wanted to believe his brilliance earned him whatever he got."

"There's a big difference between inborn ability and brilliance," I said, joining her in looking at the man with the long white beard. Now that I took the trouble to notice, it was clear he wasn't old enough to be naturally white-haired. He must have used his appearance as window dressing, then, or because he thought that was what he *ought* to look like . . . "It's never a matter of how much you have, just what you end up doing with it. I need to speak to the man, Your Majesty, before you put him wherever it is you're going to. He may very well have a piece of information my companion and I need badly."

"I know," she said, again with that faint smile. "Nalkin told me about it earlier, and your companion danced all around the subject during the feast. That's one of the reasons I asked you in here now, so that you might speak to him before he's taken away."

"That was really very thoughtful of you," I said, meaning the words exactly as spoken. "A lot of people in your place wouldn't have bothered—or would have conveniently 'forgotten.' What are the other reasons you asked me in here?"

"I wondered how quickly you would notice I said that," she returned with a wider smile, finally moving her gaze from Arnwell to me. "The speed with which you did delights me, as I'd like to discuss that first. Do you mind?"

"I suppose my questions for him can wait a little while longer," I responded with a shrug, disturbed over her own question. It wasn't like a queen, to ask if people minded things . . .

"Good," she said, leaning back on the couch. "Would you like something to eat or drink before we begin? No? That's too bad. I've been trying to work up the nerve to say what I have to, and could have used a little more time."

Now her smile was on the weak and nervous side, but I didn't cooperate by commenting aloud. I didn't expect to like what she was about to say, but I still had to listen.

"All right, then the time has come," she said, visibly drawing herself up on the inside. "I think I'd better start by explaining what you've undoubtedly heard about my— bed habits. Before you make any judgments, you ought to know that my physicians have told me there's no more than a small chance I'll ever become pregnant. I've been trying to utilize that one chance by—trying as many men as possible, in the hopes that one of them will be virile enough to—overcome my handicap. So far it hasn't happened."

Her beautiful face was a shade or two less than perfectly calm and serene, but there was nothing of self-pity showing. She'd been trying to do something about a personal tragedy, but her efforts hadn't worked. I seriously doubted if anyone other than her physicians knew what she'd just told me, and that raised the question of why an exception had been made.

"You don't have to ask," she said, that faint smile back again. "You want to know why I've told you this, and I'll answer that in a moment. First I'd like your opinion of Wimail, the man I've chosen for my permanent escort. I deliberately let him escort *you* tonight, just so you could meet him."

"Well, I was honored, of course," I temporized, wondering just how far it would be possible to go toward the truth, but she waved her hand with a small laugh.

"No need to be diplomatic," she assured me. "I know just what Wimail is like, and that's the point. He's in love with the idea of being my usual escort, and nothing else bothers him as long as that continues. Another man in his place would be hurt by what I've found it necessary to do, and that's *why* there isn't another man in his place. It wouldn't be fair."

I suppose the abrupt understanding was very clear in my expression; she nodded with satisfaction, and then continued.

"Now for the question of why I told you what I have, and its equally simple answer. I need an heir, someone who will care as much about my people as I do, but I no longer believe I'll be able to produce one. You already care about people in general, and you have the strength to protect yourself in ways that I don't. I want you to stay here and be my heir, and let my people become yours."

Her smile had grown warm and welcoming, something I concentrated on to keep the stunned look off my face. After knowing me slightly for a matter of hours, the woman wanted me for her heir? And, at the same time, was offering me a home? If I could have doubted her I would have, but it just wasn't possible. Instead I thought frantically for a moment, and came up with something else to mention.

"This need for protection," I said, for once *letting* myself think the way those who play politics do. "A ruler who cares for her people shouldn't have to worry about protecting herself, not when everyone ought to love her for it. Is that why you have so many guardsmen around, because not all of your people understand how deeply you care?"

"If only my own people were involved, the guard would be totally unnecessary," she answered at once. "It isn't them my advisers want to protect me from, it's one or two of my neighboring rulers. They aren't quite as popular with their own people, so they have to find ways to distract them. Like looking around for other realms to conquer, after that realm's ruler has been—taken care of. If you wanted to ride around and talk to people before making a decision, I'd have no objection."

The clearly serious offer left me with nothing to say, and what came before it explained why the queen had gotten involved with a Court Magician to begin with. When powerful people are after your head, you do what you must to counter their plans. I could see that, all right, but still couldn't quite see myself settling down there. I had responsibilities, after all . . .

"Please stop looking so upset," the queen said with another of those warming smiles. "I wasn't expecting an immediate answer, not from someone who's so very much like *me*. You'd be faced with the need to spend many years here, learning what to do before you took the throne when I died or abdicated. Only then would your own rule start, and then you'd have many more years of work before you handed things over to your own heir. You'll have to think about it first, and while you're thinking, you might as well ask Arnwell those questions you have."

Yes, there was still that. I took a deep breath to steady myself, then spoke a spell that would unfreeze the magician but still keep him under my control. One syllable of the spell also required him to speak nothing but the truth, which would save me some trouble. The man shuddered and straightened, glanced at the queen, then turned to look directly at me.

"The queen believes you meant to depose her and make yourself king," I began, as good a place as any to start. "Is that true?"

"Certainly," Arnwell answered immediately and unemotionally. "I was born to be great, and what greater thing is there than to make yourself a king?"

"I'd say to make yourself useful," I couldn't help countering. "If you need a title to impress people, it's only because you can't *do* anything that would accomplish the same end. And while we're discussing it, how do you *know* you were born to be great?"

"My mother told me," he responded. "Even before she found out I'd be able to do magic, she *knew* I was destined for greatness. She made sure I knew it too, and naturally never denied me anything. You *don't* deny people who are going to be great, you know."

Queen Lova and I exchanged glances, both of us probably thinking the same thing. Arnwell *was* a spoiled brat, which would simply have ruined him if he hadn't been born Sighted. As it was, things had been made a good deal worse . . .

"Arnwell, my companion and I are looking for the nearest gate," I said, dropping a subject it was much too late to do anything about. "Even if there isn't one all that near, I still want its location."

"The nearest gate, as far as I know, is in the west wall of the palace," the magician replied immediately. "It leads to the west road out of the city, and should be just a little nearer to this room than the north gate."

"That's not the kind of gate I'm talking about," I said, wishing those under a truth spell weren't so prone to taking certain questions so literally. "I mean a gate that leads to other worlds, the glowing vertical line that spreads out into a glowing curtain when you get near it. If you grew up in this area you surely must have Seen one or at the very least heard about one from someone who was also—a magician."

"That doesn't sound familiar at all," Arnwell replied, no trace left of that very involved way of speaking. "I don't understand what you mean."

"I'm talking about places that would be in the country-side," I elaborated, trying to ignore the uneasy feeling I suddenly had. "No one would go to those places unless they *could* See the gates, because they would be very uncomfortable without knowing why. If you don't know much about the countryside, give me the name of someone with your gift who knows it better."

"I grew up in a small village about ten miles from the city," Arnwell said with a vague frown. "Since my mother worked to keep us fed, I was free to explore the woods in all directions before I started my lessons with the old woman who taught me magic. I can't think of anyone who knows the area better than I do, and no one has ever mentioned anything like what you're asking about. And the old crone who taught me told me everything she knew."

"What's wrong?" Queen Lova asked as I just sat there staring at the magician. "This gate is obviously important to you, but I don't understand why. Where is it supposed to lead?"

I shook my head without answering, more than simply upset. It was hard to imagine a world allowing magic having *no* gates at all, but that didn't have to be true. Its gates could be in remote, inaccessible spots, places no Sighted had been, which would make them completely unknown. That would explain the low level of magic users; without a regular influx of Sighted from other worlds, the natives would be working blind. With enough power a trained Sighted can do just about anything, but first you have to know how to get enough power to handle whatever your project is. If you try it without the proper strength and control, its not working might convince you it wasn't possible . . .

"I—need to do some thinking," I said at last, the understatement of the century. If that world didn't allow the creation of entries—which it didn't seem to—and its gates were inaccessible, then—then—"Do you mind if we speak again at another time, Your Majesty? I really need to be alone for a while."

"No, of course I don't mind," she answered with another of those smiles. "You take all the time you need, and then send word to me. Whatever your decision is, I promise I won't try to talk you out of it. And I hope you've asked Arnwell everything you need to. I'm afraid this is the last time he'll be available for questioning."

"Why?" I couldn't help asking. "Where is he supposed to be going?"

"He's going on that journey no one ever returns from," she said, weariness and strain suddenly appearing in her expression. "He's a menace to everyone around him, and right now the only thing holding him harmless is your power. If he should somehow escape from that—For the sake of my people, not to mention my own peace of mind, he'll be executed as soon as we're finished here. He was ready to hurt or kill anyone who opposed him, and I can't take the chance that he might somehow get loose again."

My first urge was to argue that decision, but then I closed my mouth without speaking. I'd been about to say that Arnwell *couldn't* escape my spell, but that was true only if I stayed in that world. If I somehow managed to find a way to a gate and through, the spell would disappear as soon as I was gone. That would free the man to go back to his original plans, which in turn would create all sorts of havoc and hurt. No, if I couldn't cure him of being the product of a damaged upbringing—and I couldn't—there was only one other possible choice.

"There's nothing else I need to ask him," I said, then returned him to the frozen state. "He won't be aware of what's done to him, but that's for my sake rather than his. He might have turned out all right if he hadn't been twisted, but then again he might not. I'll—send word when I've made a decision."

She smiled and nodded without saying anything else, then rang for a servant to take me back to my apartment. Three guardsmen waited for me to step out of the room before they went in, but I preferred not to think about their reason for being there. I had enough with the rest of what I needed to think about, and barely even heard the music when we went past the feasting hall. Party time was over for me, at least until I could straighten out my thoughts.

Once I was back at my apartment I dismissed the servant, changed my clothes, then sat down in a chair with a cup of coffee. I couldn't remember ever being that confused and uncertain, and the offer of a throne had very little to do with it. Anyone who reaches my level of skill can find a world somewhere and *take* a throne, whether or not the natives care for the idea. As long as there's no one around who's better at magic, and there are plenty of places like that, the throne is yours.

No, being a queen wasn't that big a deal, but what went with it—that's what I was having trouble with. Queen Lova *wanted* me—wanted *me*—and was willing to trust me with the well-being of the people she loved. No one had ever done that for me, offered me something that personally important. She would name me her daughter, and I had no doubt she would also treat me like one. A beloved daughter, someone to be proud of, someone to show off to her friends and associates . . .

I shifted around to pull my booted feet up into the chair, automatically holding the coffee still to keep it from spilling. What I needed was an impersonal point of view, but it wasn't likely I'd be the one to supply it. I'd been very young when my parents were accidently killed, but not so young that I was unaware of my loss. And then being taken in by my mother's cousin and her husband, supposedly because they wanted to raise me. What they'd wanted was control of my very large inheritance, to add to their own considerable wealth. When they discovered they'd have access to it only when *I* was old enough to have access to it, they'd taken out their disappointment on me. Nothing I'd ever done was right, or worth their paying attention to, and certainly nothing to compliment. If I hadn't had memories of my parents and the way it *should* have been done . . .

But memories hadn't stopped the time with them from being a sentence served in a torture pit. It had made things worse that neither they nor their children were Sighted, especially when one of them began to treat me like a cripple. The rest picked it up immediately, excusing me from things at the drop of a hat because I wasn't—quite—as I should be . . . others had picked up the habit from them, until I actually did feel almost incompetent. But I'd learned not to argue with them past a certain point, which usually took away their looks of smug satisfaction. Declaring yourself the winner of a battle doesn't mean much if the other side simply shrugs and walks away.

But now I was being offered the chance to get back what I'd lost, to be with someone who wanted me in a place where I was needed. And it looked like I might not even have a choice about staying. It could take years to find a gate—assuming finding one was possible in the first place—and by then whatever had happened in Bariden's world would be long over. Our going back then would be just about pointless, or at least my going back would be . . .

A knock came at the door then, pulling me away from inner argument. Rather than getting up I gestured the door open—and blinked in surprise.

"I hope I'm not intruding," Naesery said, stepping inside and walking slowly toward my chair. "I arranged to be told when your audience with the queen was over, but when it was you didn't come back. I wasn't going to bother you, but—Are you all right? Is there anything wrong?"

He stood not five feet away, the second handsomest man I'd ever seen, true concern in those gorgeous green eyes. If I stayed *he* would be there too, a man who had been immediately attracted to me. And wasn't I forgetting that it wasn't a question of 'if'? What real choice did I have?

"I'm fine," I answered with as much of a smile as I could produce. "As a matter of fact something very *not* wrong has happened, and I'm in the middle of thinking about it. Queen Lova has asked me to—stay here."

"Marvelous!" he exclaimed, breaking into a wide grin. "I was hoping she would, but sometimes queens end up acting politically rather than intelligently. Is there anything I can do to induce you to accept?"

By then he was crouching in front of me, his right hand having come to take possession of my left. As he waited for my answer he raised my hand to his lips—and that was when another voice broke in.

"I'd apologize for intruding if this door hadn't been left open," Bariden said, the words even but very soft. I turned my head to see that he looked straight at Naesery, and seemed to be speaking only to him. "I'm Bariden, and I don't believe we've been introduced."

"I'm Lord Naesery," my first visitor answered evenly as he straightened, proving he *was* Bariden's size. "Am I mistaken, or aren't you supposed to be attending the queen?"

"I was the queen's escort into the feast," Bariden answered, coming forward a few steps before stopping again. "When she left my duty to her was over, and now I'm here. If you don't mind, Lord Naesery, I'd like to speak to Chalaine for a few minutes. Alone."

By the words themselves you would have thought Bariden was asking permission, but his tone killed that idea completely. The steel-hard near growl was an order, and Naesery acknowledged that with a faint smile and almost nonexistent bow.

"A gentleman always accedes to the polite request of others," he said, for some reason distantly amused. "I do indeed mind leaving, but shall do so anyway. Lady Chalaine, please send a servant for me when your—visitor—has gone on his way."

My bow was more than the token Bariden had gotten, and then Naesery was striding past him and out of the apartment. Bariden followed to close the door that was left open for the second time, and then came back to crouch where Naesery had been.

"I can't believe you'd let a smooth article like that come anywhere near you," he said then, those light blue eyes pinning me where I sat. "What happened to the practical deductive sorceress I started this trip with?"

"Lord Naesery has been nothing but a gentleman," I muttered in answer, giving a lot of attention to my coffee. That gaze looked more disappointed than accusing, a reaction that made me very uncomfortable. "But there's something I have to tell you, and it isn't good news."

"Go ahead," he said after the briefest hesitation. "I also have news, but it can wait another minute or two."

"The queen let me question Arnwell before they—permanently settled the problem he presented," I told him. What I didn't mention was that I'd felt it when they executed him, a—loosening and freeing of the spell I'd placed. Restraining the dead isn't necessary, and would take a different kind of spell even if it were . . . "He told me he didn't know about gates, and no one he knew had ever mentioned coming across one. That would explain why they don't know more magic than they do. No easy access to routine crossovers."

"I can see you've decided most gates are out of casual reach," he said with a nod. "That would be a logical assumption. Is that it?"

"Not quite," I answered, wondering how he could take such upsetting news so calmly. "The queen—wants me to stay here. She can't have children, so she wants to adopt me as her heir."

"You haven't agreed to that yet, have you?" he asked at once, and *now* he was looking upset. "Chalaine, tell me you haven't given your word."

"I told her I'd have to think about it," I said, leaning back from his intensity just a little. "Why are you so bothered about *that* part of it? If we're going to be trapped in this world, there are worse things that could happen. Or were you picturing us taking off in search of a gate across the entire face of this world?"

"I'm picturing us checking out something I just heard about that's in this very palace," he said, relief letting him relax again. "The queen insisted that I stay with her for the first couple of minutes of the second dance, and after that she thanked me and left. As soon as she did I went looking for *you*, but you were already dancing with someone else. It didn't take more than a minute to decide I would cut in, but just before I started off to do it, one of a pair of servants spilled something. The man who did the spilling was just about horrified, and the two of them said something that made me forget about dancing."

"What could they possibly have said?" I asked when he paused, firmly refusing to think about dancing. Of course he'd started looking for me as soon as the queen was gone. He didn't yet know any other women here.

"What the girl with him said was, 'Now you've done it. If you aren't sent to the Shunned Room again, no one else ever will be.' And he came back with, 'I'll leave the job first, I swear I will! The last time I thought I'd die before I got out! I can't go back there again, and I won't!' He'd turned pale and his hands were trembling, and that turned *me* curious. I suddenly *had* to know what the Shunned Room was."

"You can't mean you thought it might be a gate," I said, trying to decide whether or not I believed the same. "No one would build so much as a shack around one, let alone a palace. And what about anyone coming through it? Wouldn't these people have figured out what it was when Sighted began to appear in the room?"

"I eventually ran through all those arguments myself," he agreed with one hand up. "I know just what you're saying, but I couldn't make myself walk away and forget about it. I had to find out what I could without making my interest too obvious, so I used a minor glamour and took a walk through the kitchens. That way I didn't have to bother with invisibility, but people still didn't notice me. What I found out was that there's a stairway at the back of the kitchens leading down to where the Shunned Room is. It's the only way to get to it."

"Why do I have the feeling you haven't yet used those stairs?" I asked with something close to suspicion. "And why did you need a glamour? Has anyone here said you can't go anywhere you care to? You're making it sound like they're our enemies, when most of them couldn't be nicer. These people here *care*, Bariden—"

"Chalaine, please," he interrupted, taking my hand. "I'm not saying they don't, or that they're not decent or fair.

What you have to remember is how we got here, and that it wasn't by accident. We *can't* assume getting out again is simply a matter of finding that gate and going through. If there's someone—or something—watching the area, I didn't want to warn them by going to look at it alone. I've already told you—if we don't leave together, neither one of us goes. Will you use those stairs with me while we both have a look?"

The light blue gaze that refused to leave my face was an underlining of his question, a request that wasn't quite that easy to agree to. I'd been offered something very special in that place, something I was reluctant to simply walk away from, but I did still have our original problem to consider . . . and the people who waited, neither alive nor dead, for someone to help . . .

"All right, I'll go and take a look with you," I agreed, but reluctant was too pale a word for the way I felt. I couldn't—quite—wish there would be nothing at the bottom of those stairs, but—"What will you do if we don't find anything? Take your horse and head for the nearest mountains?"

"I thought you understood that I wasn't going anywhere alone," he said, straightening as I banished my coffee cup and rose. "If we don't find anything and I can't talk you into heading for the mountains with me, I'll have to stay here with *you*. If you're going to be the queen some day, you'll need the right consort."

"You're volunteering to help me find a man?" I asked, feeling my brows go up. "Or do you just intend to turn thumbs down on anyone I find attractive? Really, Bariden, that kind of help I don't—"

"Wait a minute," he said, his hand on my arm stopping me halfway to the door. "I wasn't volunteering for anything but *being* the man. Am I wrong in thinking you weren't even considering that?"

"Well, of course I wasn't considering that," I said, for once looking straight at him. "I know you have no real interest in me, so why would I put you in an awkward position? I usually try not to embarrass people on purpose."

"I feel as if I've missed a large chunk of this conversation," he said, shaking his head with what seemed like confusion. Personally, I was delighted it was finally out in the open. "What do you mean, you know I have no real interest in you? How can you know something like that when it isn't true?"

"Hey, I wasn't trying to say I didn't think you cared about me," I told him quickly, finally realizing I must have hurt his feelings. "Since we're in this together I know you feel a responsibility toward me, but that's only because you're a decent man. It doesn't necessarily have to go beyond that, and in this case it certainly doesn't. But it's all right, I don't mind at all. If anyone understands how you feel, I'm the one."

"How do you think I feel?" he asked, glancing down at the hand I'd put to his arm before bringing those eyes back to my face. "And is that why this is the first time you've touched me in any way at all? Because you believe I don't want you to?"

"Bariden, think about everything that's happened between us from the first moment we met," I said with a sigh as I took back a hand that must have had a mind of its own. "I'd have to be crazy to believe there could be any interest on your part after all that, and I haven't quite reached the crazy stage yet. If you disagree—or think you do—it's perfectly understandable: that Spell of Affinity has you confused. Take my word for it, you don't want to have anything to do with me. If—*when* we get back, you'll see I'm right."

The deepening confusion in his eyes was beginning to disturb me, so I smiled a reassuring smile and headed for the door again. I suppose it would have been really nice if a man like Bariden *had* found me of interest, but that wasn't likely to happen. I hadn't "caused" much lately, but the calm could hardly last much longer and once it was gone . . . No, I was much better off not even thinking about it, and so was he . . .

The corridor outside my room was deserted, but Bariden cast a glamour to cover the two of us anyway. Explaining why we were wandering the halls could have been awkward, and there was no need for us to make ourselves look foolish. Bariden had gotten rid of his fancy party clothes just the way I had, and there was, of course, nothing we had to take with us. The horses we'd left in the palace stables weren't horses. If we did find a gate and stepped through, the horses would go back to the nothingness they'd come from.

Servants were still hurrying back and forth between the kitchens and the feasting hall, unbelievably with even more trays of food. I'd thought the meal was over, but it looked like some people were starting all over again. Any servants going by were careful to avoid us, but they also didn't notice us as we made our way to the back of the kitchens. In one corner to the left was a narrow set of stairs leading down, and most of those in the kitchens avoided that area as well.

"Hope as hard as you can," Bariden said as he led the way to the stairs. Those were the first words he'd said since we'd left my apartment, and I still wasn't sure if I agreed with the sentiment. Of course, I could always find my way back there someday . . .

The stairs were made of stone, as though someone had chopped them into the bedrock the palace rested on. They didn't look terribly new, but they also weren't as worn as they could have been. The wooden hole they went down through looked as though it had been built like that rather than added after the rest of the structure, and that was odd. If the room had been built *around* the hole and stairs, then people had known it was there. Why would anyone build over something that no one who wasn't Sighted could stand to be near for long? And why leave an easy way to reach that something? Things just didn't make sense . . .

I followed Bariden down the relatively narrow stairs, noticing that he was moving slowly enough to let me keep up with him easily. The steps ended about twenty feet down, and we didn't have to make our own light. A torch flickered on the stone wall to the left about fifteen feet ahead of us, dimly illuminating the narrow corridor. Two people could have walked abreast if they'd really had to, but not comfortably. Bariden continued to lead and I followed, senses sharp and defenses ready.

We couldn't have gone more than ten feet past the torch when we came to an opening in the rock to the right. I say opening rather than doorway because there was nothing of a door, just a round-topped opening that was only just high enough for Bariden to pass under. Rather than do that he glanced inside, then turned to me looking very relieved.

"Once again the power of hope does the job," he said with a grin. "Wizards will swear there's nothing to the idea, but I've seen it work too often to doubt. As specified, my lady, one gate ready to go."

By then I was standing next to him, and didn't need the sweep of his arm to See the gate. It hung in the exact center of the large stone chamber surrounding it, the back parts a definite semicircle against the flat wall with the opening. Rough stone benches were carved into the rounded parts of the walls, and faint torchlight flickered against the bright glow of the unopened slit. I stood there staring at it, one small part of me completely unsurprised that it was there, and Bariden's hand came to my left arm.

"Do you See that?" he asked very softly, head up as though trying to get a scent from a breeze. "There's some sort of spell on that room, but I can't tell what it is. Rather than being hidden it's very plain, but I don't recognize it. Have *you* ever Seen anything like it?"

"Now that you mention it, yes," I answered, suddenly Seeing exactly what he was talking about. "The feel of the thing says it's a Spell of Volition, and unless I'm mistaken it's aimed only at Sighted. And it isn't in the room, but around the gate. Unless you really want to use that gate, the spell won't let you activate it. Now isn't that strange . . ."

I let the words trail off as I tried to remember where I'd Seen a Spell of Volition before, but the memory wasn't cooperating. It refused to come within reach of my thought-fingers, no matter how far I spread them. And then I noticed that Bariden was staring at me rather than at the gate with its spell, his expression shadowed with worry.

"That means I can't simply drag you through the gate behind me, doesn't it?" he said, those light eyes showing the agitation he felt. "Damn it, I *knew* this would be a problem, I just knew it. Now what do we do?"

I didn't have to ask what he meant, not with all the times he'd insisted he would never leave without me. I was about to suggest it again anyway, but a sudden thought made me change my mind.

"Has it occurred to you that the way things stand *you* might not be able to go through either?" I asked instead, frowning at the idea. "I mean, even if you agreed to go alone, your heart certainly wouldn't be in it. Unless I'm mistaken, that would be enough to keep the gate from opening for you."

"And would incidentally explain why the Sighted of this world have never used it," he said in surprise. "If you didn't know what it was and what it would do, wouldn't there be at least a small amount of reluctance about using it? Someone like Arnwell might have been egotistical enough to try, but what are the chances an Arnwell would ever listen to the problems of servants or casually visit the kitchens? He may have spent five years in the palace, but he never found out this place was here."

"A punishment place for servants who mess up," I muttered, wishing more background thoughts would come clear. There was something about that entire arrangement that refused to make sense, but my analytical ability seemed to be out to lunch. I knew *something* was going on, and not knowing what had apparently helped me make up my mind.

"I don't like the idea of being shown a gate neither of us can use," I said after the pause to think about it. "That's a rotten trick to play on people, especially when they're in a place they're not supposed to be. I'm really beginning to want to get my hands on whoever is responsible, but I can't do that if we don't get through the gate. That means we *will* get through, and right this minute."

I brushed past Bariden and entered the gate chamber, holding my anger up in front of me like a shield. The Spell of Volition flickered as I moved closer, threatening to exclude me, and that got me even angrier. I was *not* about to let someone use my own feelings against me, not now and not ever. I marched up to the gate thinking about nothing but anger and outrage, Bariden close behind me, and suddenly the gate flared into a glowing rainbow curtain . . . Had to move fast . . . get to it and through . . . hold to the anger . . . forget about what was being left behind . . . Mother, it's been so many years, but I still miss you so terribly . . . if only I could have stayed *here* . . .

CHAPTER SEVEN

Bariden was all but standing in Chalaine's footprints when the gate flared wide. Without wasting an instant, he picked her up with an arm around her waist and stepped into the gate, making sure if it closed it would be *behind* them. He'd felt a flicker in the Spell of Volition, what had to be a reaction to the girl's feelings. No matter what she'd said, she really wanted to stay . . .

And then he forgot about that as Chalaine gasped, a reaction he wasn't far from himself. The gate—on the inside there were supposed to be a large number of choices about where to go, the gleam of many worlds vying to take the traveler's attention. This gate, though, was empty of all choice but two, the world they'd come from and one other. The two of them stood there in the star-rush as long as possible, trying to find a third choice, but there wasn't any. They had to move forward or go back, or else they could be swept away into oblivion.

The girl struggled in his grip, obviously wanting to be put down, and that settled the matter. If she decided to go back, he'd probably never get her through again—or himself, either. Forward was the only way they could go, something he knew without knowing why . . . One step would take care of it, one step and then they could talk as much as they had to . . .

He took that step, causing the gate ahead of them to flare, and then they were through into the world that held it. The darkness of night spread all around, concealing the details of their surroundings, but not the fact that they were outdoors. A few stars shone in the sky overhead and crickets chirped contentedly, but there was no moon to show them more.

"Put me down!" the girl snapped, kicking at his leg in an effort to be released. "You had no right to do that!"

"What I had was no choice," he answered, finally releasing her. "I could feel that spell about to push us out of the gate. And I think we now know why the gate we came from doesn't have a constant stream of arrivals from elsewhere. The only elsewhere travelers could come from is here."

"And that's something I've never seen before," she said with a hand to her hair, turning to look at the gate. "I've never even *heard* of a gate operating only between two individual worlds. What in Hellfire have we been tossed into?"

"I wish I knew," he assured her, also turning to look at the gate. "It *looks* like your average, ordinary gate—"

And then he stopped, because what he'd said wasn't true. He was no more than a long step past the gate, but it just hung there like a glittering vertical line in the dark. With him that close—not to mention Chalaine's also being there—the gate should have already spread into a multicolored curtain. That it hadn't meant—

"It won't open from this side," the girl said, completing his thought aloud. "From the other side you have to really want to go through, and from this side all the wanting in the worlds doesn't matter. Now I'm *really* getting mad."

A glance at her face in the limited glow of the closed gate confirmed that, showing her tight-jawed and hard-eyed. Bariden wondered if real anger would make her even more attractive than she was normally, then dismissed the thought. Getting mad when you might have to protect your back at any time wasn't smart, and they would be making enough mistakes by accident. No sense adding to that on purpose . . .

"I'm going to put up a shelter for us to spend the night in," he said, moving away from the gate. "In the morning we can look around and see what we've got this time, and then decide what to do."

"If we get a choice about it," she muttered, obviously not in the mood to be soothed. "Which I doubt we will. The only time we get what we consider a choice is when we're about to step into something where we won't be allowed to change our minds. If I knew what this game was about, I'd also know the best way to play it."

Bariden paused a moment to construct his spell, then raised both arms and spoke it. A small house appeared in the darkness, cheery light spilling out of its windows. He hadn't let himself wonder whether or not his spell would work, and now he didn't have to. Magic was possible for them in this new world, and once that was proven he was able to turn back to Chalaine.

"What did you mean, if you knew what game this was you'd also know how to play it?" he asked. "We *do* know what this is about, and it's no game."

"Then why do we have to be constantly alert to make just the right move?" she countered, glancing at him before heading toward the house. "The one who started us on this trip is the enemy we were trying to uncover, but wouldn't it have been simpler to kill us? If that first entry had led to a plane where we would have been immediately devoured, wouldn't he have been rid of us *without* all this nonsense? How much good will this clever game do him if we find an exit *off* this one-way road?"

"You're assuming there *is* an exit," he returned, moving along with her as a nasty thought occurred to him. "What if this 'game' you're talking about is fixed, and there's no possible way we can win? The enemy can be sitting somewhere with his feet up, watching us struggle and laughing his head off."

"That's possible, but not very likely," she disagreed with a headshake. "As long as we keep finding ourselves in places where magic is allowed, there's always the chance we'll also find a way to break out. We're not amateurs, after all, and even the most powerful wizard alive can accidently overlook something we See right away. No, someone is definitely playing a game, and we're apparently expected to pick up the rules as we go along."

"Rules," he muttered, gesturing the door to the house open to let them step inside. You tend to lose a lot of points when you learn a game by playing it, that and gold and sometimes even blood. Maybe it would be possible to get a look at the rule book some time, even if it were only one quick glimpse . . .

"This is very nice," the girl said, stopping in the middle of the front room to look around. "Not quite what one would call homey, but still very nice."

"Thank you," Bariden answered, having no need to do his own looking around. He'd put extreme luxury in the little house, including very thick carpeting, wonderfully comfortable and oversized chairs and couches, silk and jewels for decoration, diamonds for the lamps—he'd even made two bedroom suites behind the sitting room, just to keep the girl from feeling pressured.

"Only one thing seems to be missing," she said, using a simple word and gesture to summon a cup of coffee. "There, that takes care of it. And now if you'll excuse me, I'm feeling really worn out."

"Chalaine, wait," Bariden said quickly, stopping her from going toward the suite door on the right. "There's something I'd like to talk to you about before you go to bed."

"Sure," she answered with a small shrug, actually looking straight at him with those dark and lovely eyes. It was the second time she'd done that, maybe the third. Bariden didn't know why she'd stopped avoiding his gaze, but he didn't actually care. He preferred to think of it as a step in the right direction, and use it as the encouragement he wasn't getting in any *other* way.

"Why don't we sit down while we talk," he said, gesturing to a couch while he shut the door. "I almost feel as if I'm making a pest of myself about this, but I've never liked misunderstandings. You said something that isn't true, and I want you to know it."

"What did I say?" she asked with brows high, sitting to one side of the middle of the couch. Bariden knew women well enough to know what *that* meant, and he had no choice but to accept the boundary. The middle of the couch was the point he wasn't supposed to move past, a no-man's-land if ever there was one.

"You said I had no real interest in you," he explained after sitting on his couch-half and calling up his own cup of coffee. "You said I only think I'm interested because of the Spell of Affinity, and I'd be much better off without you. I don't happen to agree with any of that, and I want you to know I intend to prove the truth."

"Really?" she said with brows raised again, and then she smiled. "I'd love to know how you expect to do that—without using black magic."

"You're really convinced you're right," he said with all the disturbance—and annoyance—he felt. "You think I'm kidding myself, and you're just waiting for me to wake up and realize that. What will you do if I never wake up, and it suddenly turns out that you're wrong? Refuse to change your mind and simply walk away, or act like a grown-up and start listening to me?"

"But I'm not wrong," she said, so calmly and gently for what was actually stubborn arrogance. "I happen to be right, which you'll eventually have to admit. When that time comes, don't worry that I'll be upset or blame you for anything. I know how compelling ongoing spells can be, even if they aren't supposed to behave like that. When this is all over, I promise that we'll still be friends."

Even if I give in to temptation and strangle you? he wanted to ask that patient, superior smile she showed. Then it came to him that she might be acting like that on purpose, to "help" him get over his delusions faster. Instead of groaning he swallowed down some coffee, which gave her the chance to add something else.

"About my acting like a grown-up," she said, this time looking at him with veiled amusement. "I think I already am, but don't feel that you have to agree with me. Consider me a child as much as you like, I don't mind."

Bariden studied her over his coffee cup, frustration jabbing at him from all sides. Unless he was mistaken she'd just confirmed his guess, and was definitely "helping" him to get over his illusions. He'd never known a woman who wasn't immediately ready to take all the advantage she could, and now that he'd met one who thought about *him* as well as herself—she was convinced his interest couldn't possibly be real. If he managed to get out of that mess sane as well as in one piece, it would only be because the EverNameless decided to take a hand . . .

"You're not going to talk me into your version of the truth," he said at last, forcing his tone to be as calm and easy as hers had been. "I *will* find a way to prove I'm right, and when I do I expect an apology from you. A sincere apology."

"What happens if you prove the opposite?" she asked after a sip of coffee. "Will *I* get an apology, or will it just be one of those things people never talk about? Well, maybe we shouldn't talk about it."

The last of that was mumbled before she hid most of her face with the cup again, back to looking anywhere but at him. For a moment Bariden was confused, and then sudden insight gave him the probable answer.

"I'm going to put this badly, but I still have to say it," he told her, groping for words that would not make things worse. "I know you didn't want to leave that last world, but you did it to keep *me* from being trapped. We won't know if leaving was the right thing to do until this is all over, but I still want you to know how much your doing that means to me. Whatever happens, I won't ever forget; if it makes you feel better to blame me for forcing you through the gate, go ahead and do it. I *did* force you, and you're entitled to at least that."

Her answer was a nod of sorts, something that said she'd heard him but wasn't prepared to discuss the subject. And she still wasn't looking at him, which goaded him into saying something else he'd been wanting to.

"And you can stop being anything but yourself," he told her a bit more harshly than he'd intended. "All that clinical patience and understanding, watching your every word, never feeling or showing anything real—For a very little while in the last world I got a glimpse of the real you, and I liked what I saw. It's not likely to kill either one of us if you start showing it all the time."

Now it was her turn to be confused, but at least she was looking at him again. And then the confusion disappeared, to be replaced with something else.

"So you want me to be myself all the time," she said, surprisingly looking pleased with the idea. "All things considered, that could be the best suggestion either of us might have made. You *did* get a look at the real me, but you must have forgotten about it. Okay, you'll get what you asked for, but don't forget you *did* ask."

"Why do I feel as though I'm facing a master swordsman while armed with nothing but a practice weapon?" Bariden asked, very suspicious of her sudden good humor. "That must be the expression predators wear just before they start gobbling down their meal. What are you up to?"

"Me?" she asked, dark eyes wide with one hand to her chest. "Whatever could *I* be up to that wasn't the specific request of someone who ought to learn to think before he speaks? You asked for the real me, so you're going to get her. Unless you use this very last chance to be smart and change your mind. You won't get another."

Once again she looked straight at him, and Bariden suddenly *knew* this was one of the reasons she usually refrained from doing it. A quick look into her eyes made you believe she was soft and small and helpless; this steady stare was a different matter entirely, one most people would find themselves backing down from. Realizing that, Bariden felt more satisfied than surprised, and he gave her a faint grin.

"I appreciate the offer, but my image would suffer if people began to think of me as smart," he drawled. "That means my request is *not* withdrawn, so you keep doing whatever comes naturally. And this is fair warning: soon I'll be expecting us to be doing those natural things together."

"Of course you will," she answered dryly, then sipped at her coffee without looking away. "It's too bad it will probably happen a lot sooner than you—expect. Was there anything else you wanted to talk about? I'm looking forward to soaking in that bath for a bit before I go to bed."

So she'd listened to his spell and knew he'd put a tub filled with hot water in her suite. He'd half-expected to surprise her with that, then realized she'd deliberately let him know *she* knew. Part of what her real self was was Sighted, and she'd decided to rub his nose in it. Bariden was tempted to be annoyed, but there was no sense in going ahead with his plans if he would be that easy to get to.

"No, that's all the conversation I had in mind for tonight," he said, this time giving her a smile. "You go ahead and do your soaking, but if you need someone to scrub your back, give me a call. I guarantee you won't be waking me."

This time it was his turn to use an unwavering gaze, but she broke it in the only way it can be done without admitting defeat. If you aren't aware of someone's Significant Look and fail to acknowledge its existence, there's no contest to be defeated *at*. She took a long swallow of coffee, banished the cup before rising, then gave him a vague nod and smile before strolling off to her suite. No becoming flustered at overly friendly suggestions, no rush to escape an uncomfortable situation—Bariden had never seen anything to match it, not even the smoothness of certain ladies at his father's court.

"You're going to make this as hard as possible for me, aren't you," he murmured, now staring at the door she'd closed between them. "Instead of being soft and pretty and too quiet, you're going to be hard as blade steel, brutally direct, and as unimpressible as an eighty-year-old dowager empress. *That's* supposed to be your real self? I wonder who you think you're kidding."

But maybe that was one of the problems. If *she* saw herself like that, she'd expect him to do the same. Even if she was just exaggerating what she considered flaws, she'd still believe she was being nothing but honest. Getting around *that* ought to be fun, at least as much as being used as the target at quarterstaff practice . . .

"Damn," he muttered even more softly, banishing his cup before standing. By rights he ought to be thinking about how many other girls there were in the worlds, girls who would be more than happy to listen to reason. Instead, he could feel his determination increasing, accompanied by a wish that there was only a single bedroom. But it wasn't just a physical attraction he felt, a regrettable truth that intended to prove itself by not letting him quit. It was all of Chalaine that he wanted, and in order to get her he was willing to fight.

If he was allowed the *time* to fight. Their enemy was obviously herding them toward *something*, and Bariden had picked up the conviction that they would have to win against the something or lose a lot more than a game. It hadn't been too bad so far, but that was only so far and only for him. Chalaine would *not* be likely to agree, which led him to wonder what tomorrow would be like . . .

Rather than follow that line of thought, Bariden dropped it and went to soak in his own tub. And if he turned the water really cold, maybe he'd even be able to sleep . . .

They had no trouble getting an early start the next day, and that after a good breakfast. Once again an entry spell had refused to register, as though no such thing was possible rather than that someone stronger was disallowing it. They both felt that meant something, but neither of them could figure out what.

Bariden rode his horse-construct quietly next to Chalaine's, trying to talk himself out of being annoyed. The girl had used breakfast to tease him, and he'd been too distracted with thoughts of what lay ahead to do more than get caught.

"No, *I'll* make our food." she'd told him when he offered to produce whatever she felt like eating. "Men are never any good at doing things like that."

She'd been so offhand about it that he'd simply shrugged and let her call up whatever she pleased. He was halfway through the incredibly tasty meal before he realized that every single dish had originally been made by one of Bena's chefs—her *male* chefs. At that point he also realized he was being surreptitiously but carefully watched; although he wasn't being laughed at on the outside, inside was another matter entirely.

I should have done more than just glare at her, he told himself sourly as he watched the uninteresting countryside go by. She'd played a practical joke on him, probably as part of showing the "real" her, and he'd responded as if he were half asleep. But what really annoyed him was the fact that he didn't know how he *should* have responded, how she'd been expecting him to respond. Talk about feeling as if you were being tested and graded . . .

"I wonder if it's a coincidence that all these worlds are so ordinary," the girl said suddenly. She'd been looking around at the wood the road wound through, just as he had. "It probably isn't, but I can't think of any sinister purpose for something like that. Can you?"

"No, and I've been trying," he admitted. "We can't accept anything as a coincidence in a place where we've been deliberately sent, but unless our enemy is trying to bore us to death, I'm missing the point."

"Maybe the point is to throw us off guard," she suggested. "You know, let us think there's nothing dangerous around, and then hit us without warning. If that's it, it doesn't look like it's going to happen here, but maybe up ahead, where the cleared land starts . . ."

She let the thought trail off, but he didn't add anything as he studied the area they were approaching. The road left the woods only a short distance ahead, and the cleared land was obviously growing crops. That should mean there were also people up ahead, like in that village he could just see beyond the nearest stretch of farmland. Communal fields rather than individual farms could be good or bad, depending on how close the nearest city was. They'd just have to wait and see . . .

Their mounts were moving at a brisk pace, which meant it wasn't long before the wood and even most of the fields were behind them. The village was a good deal closer, an ordinary village that looked mostly lived-in. Nothing seemed too new or too clean, and nothing that was too old or badly kept. Ordinary, everyday, usual—except for the fact that no one was around the part of it they could see.

"It certainly isn't deserted," the girl said, obviously sharing his thoughts. "The people aren't out in the fields we just passed, but maybe there are other fields. Or maybe something's happening that's taking everyone's attention."

Bariden saw it too, then, the small amount of dust that seemed to be coming from the other side of the village. And sounds, as if people were talking—or shouting . . .

"Let's take a careful look," he told the girl, getting ready to move a little faster. "And this time try not to start anything."

She glanced at him over that but didn't say anything, and he chose to consider her silence as agreement. Urging his mount to a slightly faster pace he pulled out ahead of her, moving along the village street toward the dust and muted noise. At least it was muted until the street curved around to the left, past what looked like a smithy. Beyond it the open area was filled with what must have been most of the villagers—and two groups that didn't belong in a village.

Bariden came to a halt at the back of the crowd and dismounted, then began to make his way through the people who were watching some sort of confrontation. One of the groups that didn't belong was larger than the other, as well as being all male. The smaller group was apparently being led by a woman who was in the middle of speaking to her opponents even as Bariden drew closer from behind.

" . . . can't keep taking people to be his servants and slaves!" she said heatedly, hands closed to fists at her sides. "These people don't *want* to serve a sorcerer, and neither do any other villagers in this kingdom! If my father wasn't dying, *he'd* take care of Halvin—! And why would a sorcerer need servants anyway? If he's all that powerful, he should be able to see to his needs himself."

"I don't think there's any question about how powerful Halvin is," one of the woman's opponents answered with amusement that grated. "The king couldn't have matched him even on his best day, so what difference does it make whether or not he's dying? My lord doesn't owe you any answers, but if you must know, he *doesn't* need servants. He just happens to want them, to save himself the trouble of having to see to those needs you mentioned. You—"

The man's words broke off as one of his own people touched his arm, and he moved his head to the side to listen to the hastily whispered message. He and his group numbered at least fifteen, and Bariden could see them around the leftmost member of the woman's group. By the colors they wore only seven men stood behind the woman, and, incidentally, between the villagers and the more numerous intruders.

"I've just been given a message that concerns *you*," the man continued, smiling offensively at the woman Bariden hadn't yet seen. "My Lord Halvin says you have one minute to get yourself and your escort out of the way of his men, otherwise we're to add *you* to the number of young girls we're to get. That way you can find out firsthand what sort of serving he likes—when he decides to get around to you. It's his habit to make use of the prettier ones first."

The men behind him laughed out loud at that, a threat and an insult rolled into one. The woman's escort stiffened in outrage, but the way they were outnumbered left them very few options. All they could do was stand there and seethe, their own silence underscoring the woman's, and then the man spoke again.

"That minute is just about up," he said, now looking around at the woman's escort as he loosened his sword in its scabbard. "If you don't intend to move aside, my men and I have some bladework to do. Which, by the way, we mean to enjoy. It's been too long since the last time anyone was stupid enough to try to stop us."

He licked his lips with anticipated enjoyment, and his eyes told Bariden the man wasn't bluffing. He really was the sort who enjoyed killing, the sort who loved to make people crawl and scream before he ended them. Well, this was one time he was due to be disappointed, and if Bariden had his way there would never be any other times. Softly he spoke a freezing spell aimed at the fighters behind the man, and when—surprisingly—it worked, he stepped out and moved to face the spokesman.

"Stupid would be *not* trying to stop you," he said, making no effort to look at the woman. There would be time for amenities after the threat was taken care of. "Lowlifes like you never stop on your own, you lack the necessary intelligence. And if you want someone to use that sword on, you now have me."

"Well, what do you know, somebody who thinks he can play hero," the man growled, his skin darkening with the anger of insult. "I really like that idea, since my favorite hobby is making *dead* heroes. Come on, boys, we'll start with this one."

He unsheathed his sword, sneering when Bariden did the same, but the sneer didn't last long. He'd been expecting to hear the sound of other swords being drawn by his cronies behind him, and when he didn't he realized it immediately. He threw a quick look over his shoulder, paling when he saw everyone frozen in place, then looked back at the newcomer in shock.

"That's right, the—boys—aren't included in this," Bariden told him with a lot of satisfaction. "It's just you and me, so why don't you come ahead and make me a dead hero."

The man's fist closed convulsively tighter on his sword at the same time that he swallowed hard, a typical reaction of a longtime bully suddenly on his own. He looked as if he'd be happiest just turning around and walking away, but the way he licked his lips said he was thinking about something that would not allow that. Then he forced himself straighter, and made an effort to renew his previous sneer.

"Just because you're holding that thing doesn't mean you know how to use it," he said, obviously trying to convince *himself*. "In fact, it isn't likely you can, not when you had to be the one to do that to my men. You've got to be running a bluff, so I'm going to call you on it."

By then the sneer was real, and Bariden would have enjoyed shaking his head at the man's stupidity. He'd managed to make himself believe Bariden couldn't use a sword because he *could* use magic, and therefore would be vulnerable to someone with even a small amount of sword skill. Even if that were true, wouldn't Bariden then use *magic* to protect himself? The blind spots of people who didn't know how to think . . .

And then there was no time for thinking, only for reacting. The man charged forward with a yell, swinging his sword, obviously trying to drive his opponent back. Bariden stood his ground and simply blocked the swing with his own sword, the strength he put into the block also cutting short the charge. The man started hacking at him then, a clenched-teeth attempt to use his own strength, no technique evident in any of his moves. Bariden blocked the first three swings, ignored the following feint, then blocked the first backhand swing before beginning to reply.

And that was when the man gave it up. Twice he just managed to block Bariden's attacks, each time coming close to losing a body part, and then he hurled his sword like a block of wood and ran. The thrown sword was easy to knock aside; harder was not separating the man's backbone before he'd gone a full two steps. If Bariden had believed in slaughter he *would* have done it, but what was the point? Taking a coward in the back only started you on picking up *his* bad habits . . .

But three steps was still as far as the man got. A red aura suddenly enveloped him and then he burst into flame, his hair, his clothing, and even his flesh. The sounds of terrified horror from the people behind Bariden were drowned out by the burning man's screams, and all the big man could do was stand there and watch his former opponent die horribly. The flames were on the inside of a shell-like warding, and even if Bariden had been able to break through, it wouldn't have done the burning man any good. Even a wizard-level healer would have had trouble with the results of that much burning . . .

The screams from inside the shell lasted both too long and not really long at all, and when they and the flames disappeared there was nothing left. Bariden heard the whimpering of fear behind him, adding to the fury he'd begun to feel. What sort of twisted animal *did* things like that, and for what conceivable reason?

"He lost, so he deserved to be punished," a light, unconcerned voice came from the left, almost in answer to Bariden's thoughts. "If I allow someone the honor of serving me, losing is not permitted, nor is surviving the loss. Most men tend to fight to the death to avoid my little punishments, but every now and again there's a fool who lets his cowardice make him forget. At least this one won't forget again."

The man chuckled at his little joke as he inspected Bariden casually, as though the much bigger man was of minimal interest. He, himself, was very interesting, but only indirectly because of what he looked like. Slightly below average in height, dull brown hair and eyes, slender to the point of skinniness—even the silks and jewels he wore did nothing to disguise his complete lack of musculature and clumsy movements. His facial features were beyond ordinary to the point of boredom, and even his nose wasn't *too* large. Larger than average, yes, but only by a little. Slightly wider forehead than average, slightly weaker chin, slightly narrow-lipped mouth—all so ordinary no one would look twice—except for the expression in those flat brown eyes.

"I can't believe the fool was actually running toward *me*," the man continued with what sounded like annoyance. "He and I grew up together, and he made my life unbearable until I was old enough to begin studying magic. When I reached my current level of strength and began to gather servants, I gave him the choice of groveling at my feet and doing as I ordered, or dying slowly then and there. Even if he hadn't broken one of my most basic rules, I certainly wouldn't have protected him. Who are you, and what are you doing trespassing on my territory?"

"Right now I'm standing here trying to figure you out," Bariden answered, resheathing his sword before folding his arms. "Many Sighted go through the phase of wanting to be an absolute ruler, but it's so easy to do once you reach a certain level it also quickly becomes boring. After that they either go back to studying magic, or go out among the worlds to find something that's *really* fun. Why are you still wasting your time playing child games around *here*?"

Quick hatred flashed in the man's eyes, immediately joined by other, less easily read emotions. That reaction *really* made Bariden wonder, but before he could start guessing with the clues he had, part of the answer was given to him.

"That just goes to show how much *you* know!" the man shrilled, having lost the phony languidness he'd been speaking with. "I'm *Halvin*, and being stronger than everyone else means I don't *have* to go back to studying! And if being an absolute ruler is so easy, why doesn't everyone do it? Because it *isn't* easy, that's why, not even for the big and handsome ones like *you*! You're jealous that I can do it and you can't, so you're making up stories about other places to make me feel bad. Well, it isn't going to work because I *know* better. There *aren't* any other places, so I have to find my fun right here. Like this!"

He spoke a quick spell and launched something dark green at Bariden, something with a lot of teeth that came at him already chewing away. He was caught enough by surprise that the thing would have reached him before he could react, either with a counterspell or by throwing himself out of the way. Bariden took half a step back, braced for pain—but it didn't happen. The thing struck the warding Chalaine had forgotten to remove, and that was as close as it could come.

But that didn't stop it entirely. Bariden looked down at the small monster that clung to his warding at chest height, needing to watch it chew for a moment before he understood what it was trying to do. If he'd been unwarded it would have already chewed through him, that was easy enough to see. The point that took some thought was that the thing was now chewing at his warding, as if it expected to be able to break through. Briefly Bariden thought that interpretation must be wrong, and then it, with all the rest, gave him the answer.

"You're no stronger than sorcerer-apprentice, are you?" he said to Halvin, *knowing* he was right. "You're standing there expecting this thing to chew through my warding, because it *would* be able to chew through yours. And that's also why you haven't changed your appearance to something more heroic, which I'll bet you think you deserve. You're not yet good enough to change yourself without making things worse, so you have to settle for nothing but fancy clothes and maybe the occasional illusion. All of which also tells me why you haven't tried to unfreeze your thugs. You haven't yet learned how to counter anything more complex than basic spells."

"Stop trying to sound as if you're better!" Halvin screamed, so furious he was almost foaming at the mouth. "I'm the strongest around here so you *can't* be better, do you hear me, you *can't*! If I have to prove it, then I will!"

He began to speak spells then, one of which sent more green things with teeth, one that produced yellow and orange lightning bolts which tried to skewer Bariden. The rest were too imprecisely spoken to become anything more than a string of gibberish, but that didn't make the situation any less dangerous. The people behind Halvin's target were stumbling back with screams and shouts, certain that some of the lightning bolts would attack them instead, and someone could be hurt because of the panic alone.

Which told Bariden he was wasting time and maybe lives just standing there. He banished the toothy things and the lightning bolts with a single gesture, then spoke the spell ReSayne had taught him not long ago. It seemed there was a young wizard with a talent for unSeen magic who was coming up with some interesting new spells, simple, elegant phrases that accomplished what hadn't been possible until then. ReSayne had taught him the spell, but since the fiend wasn't Sighted it hadn't been able to invoke the power of it.

Bariden, however, *was* Sighted, and fairly powerful for his level. The spell, which produced a shimmering magic-resistant sphere around the person it was aimed at, worked at once, cutting Halvin's ranting short. He looked around wildly at the transparent bubble and tried to banish it, but he wasn't strong enough to affect it. His next try was to break it with a fist, and when he couldn't bring even one of *his* ineffectual blows into contact, his frustration and hatred took over completely. Before Bariden could explain exactly what the sphere was, Halvin spat out a spell and, unfortunately for him, it was very precisely done. Blue-white flames flared inside the sphere, contained and concentrated, and the sorcerer-apprentice didn't even scream long. In a matter of moments the flames disappeared, no longer sustained by the pile of ash that had shortly before been a man.

"Stupid to the end," Bariden muttered as he banished the sphere with a gesture, turning loose a brief stench of scorched flesh. "Someone should have told him that when you play games with fire, you have to expect to get burned. But even if someone *had* told him, he probably would have refused to listen."

"You're right," a soft voice said from behind his right shoulder. "His sort never do listen, they have to learn the hard way. I'd like to thank you for risking yourself to protect people who are strangers to you. It's the sort of noble thing my father always did when he was young."

By then Bariden had turned and was looking down at her, the woman who had been trying to protect the villagers when he'd arrived. She was a little taller than average, and seemed to be slender but roundly built under her plain but richly made white gown. She had bright red hair and green eyes, but rather than making her beautiful, the combination gave her a pixielike quality of quiet good humor and calm intelligence. And most startling of all, her glow was as bright as the one he'd seen from Chalaine!

"I'm Tenillis, daughter of King Graff," she continued without the least sign of boasting, her smile warm with the thanks she'd mentioned. "On behalf of my father I'd like to welcome you to our kingdom, and invite you to join us at the palace for however long you'll be here. If we don't owe you all the hospitality we can provide at the very least, we don't owe you anything."

"I'm Bariden, and you *don't* owe me anything," he replied, responding to her smile with one of his own. "If someone is causing trouble and you're capable of stopping it, it's your duty to do so. If you can and don't, you're directly responsible for whatever harm is caused after that. I don't mind being responsible for the things I do, but I don't like being blamed for the doings of others. And speaking of doing, what would you like done with *that* lot?"

Bariden nodded toward the heavies who were still frozen in place, and the girl Tenillis turned her head to consider them.

"I think I'd like them to be released two or three at a time so my guardsmen can disarm them and put them under arrest," she said, needing very little time to decide that. "Having Halvin's protection let them do anything they cared to, and now it's time for them to answer for it. One of the magistrates holding court in the municipal section of the palace will take care of that, and all we have to do is bring them in."

"Sounds fair to me," Bariden agreed, then waited while the guardsmen stationed themselves around the first of the heavies. When they were in place he released the surrounded men, waited until they were disarmed and bound, then did the same with the next few. It wasn't long before the job was done and Tenillis and her men were ready to leave, which meant it was time to find out where Chalaine was. He hadn't seen her since he'd taken the lead when they'd first entered the village, but the dispersing crowd of villagers parted to give him the answer.

She stood alone holding their two horses, silently watching people chattering happily in relief as they headed for their homes. The faint smile she wore said she was glad the villagers no longer had to fear for their lives and safety, and it didn't matter that she hadn't had a hand in seeing to that. The end result was what counted, not who would be taking the credit for it, an attitude that surprised Bariden very little. As he walked toward her, he realized he'd somehow known she would feel that way . . .

"Very entertaining show you put on," she said to him when he got close enough, her expression downright bland. "Is that the definition I'm supposed to use when you talk about staying out of trouble?"

"If you think back, you'll remember I said I wanted *you* to stay out of trouble," Bariden countered, holding his reaction down to no more than faint amusement. "I never said a word about me, so excuses are something I don't have to look for. We've been invited to a palace again, but this time without any promises of help. I would have asked, except that the late Halvin answered the question in a way I have to believe. You heard?"

"When he accused you of lying about other worlds?" she asked with a sigh. "I wish I hadn't, but unfortunately I did. Maybe there's a gate hidden in this palace, too."

Now that was a thought, one that made Bariden pause. What if there was . . . ?

CHAPTER EIGHT

"If there is a gate in this palace too, I don't know if I'll trust it enough to use it," Bariden said to Chalaine after a moment, taking his reins while he frowned. "It's fairly obvious we're being herded, but without the end being in sight I'm getting more and more nervous about blindly stepping forward. There's no telling when the next step just won't be there, and we'll—"

"Bariden, excuse me," Tenillis's voice came, and then she was standing there with them. "We're ready to leave for the palace now. Is this someone I should be introduced to?"

"As a matter of fact it is," Bariden answered, watching the two women inspect each other. The process was one most men preferred to stay out of, considering that it often looked like a wordless challenge. Like right then, for instance . . . "Tenillis, daughter of King Graff, allow me to present Chalaine, my partner and traveling companion."

"Be welcome in our kingdom, companion of Bariden," Tenillis said with a smile and a nod. "He's earned enough welcome for ten companions."

"So I saw," Chalaine commented, her own expression on the neutrally cool side. "I can tell you're Sighted, but it feels as if you're totally untrained. Is there any particular reason why that would be?"

"Just the best of reasons," Tenillis replied with one brow raised. "No true lady will involve herself with magic, not and expect to stay a lady. It simply can't be done."

"Oh, I know some who have managed, but basically you're right," Chalaine returned, and now there was a faint smile curving her lips. "The study of magic requires a woman rather than a lady, one who understands that it's *worth* occasionally getting your hands dirty. Few—ladies—are capable of understanding that sort of truth."

"For which we praise all the Powers that be," Tenillis replied with the same calm smile. "Once you reach a certain level of intelligence, you know there are some things you don't *want* to understand. Like that old saying goes, 'Only a fool seeks knowledge he's better off without.' "

"Personally, I think it's the fool who lets other people decide what he is and isn't better off without," Chalaine countered with even more amusement in her smile. "But that's undoubtedly because I'm a woman rather than a lady, and usually make it a point to test idiotic sayings like that. I haven't found one yet that wasn't meant to sway the shortSighted into taking a dead-end road."

"Now, ladies," Bariden interrupted before the conversation turned into a fistfight, then flinched when he realized what he'd said. Chalaine still wore that infuriating smile, but Tenillis was beginning to look rather upset. "Why don't we save this discussion for another time?" he quickly tried instead. "Since we have all those men waiting to be delivered to justice, we ought to get them taken care of first."

"You're right, of course," Tenillis said with a quick and grateful smile for him, one that warmed for no reason other than being there. "I'd almost forgotten my father is also waiting, not to mention anxiously hoping we were able to sway Halvin. He didn't want me to go, but there was no one else to see to his duty for him. Please follow us . . ."

She let the request trail off after emphasizing the word "please," then turned and hurried back to her escort. As if she thought he might *not* follow, and was begging him to change his mind. He turned his head to look at the most likely reason she thought he'd be going elsewhere, and once again Chalaine met his stare directly.

"What can I say?" she asked with a shrug, looking not in the least embarrassed or guilty. "That's the lamest excuse there ever was for not studying magic, not to mention that it has to be someone else's idea. People who let others decide what's best for them usually end up regretting it."

"But not always," Bariden felt compelled to point out, his annoyance rising again. "And aren't you doing the same by telling her she's wrong not to see things *your* way? If the way she's living her life satisfies her, what right do *you* have to tell her it shouldn't?"

"I wasn't telling her to change her life, I was arguing against an idea I don't agree with," Chalaine answered quietly, all amusement, real or pretended, now gone. "If you don't see it like that, there's nothing I can say to change your mind."

She turned away from him, ending the discussion by paying full attention to mounting up. Bariden hesitated a moment before doing the same, choking down a flare of anger. He *hated* the way she handed over the victory in an argument, which invariably turned it into a loss that couldn't be challenged. It also left him stuck with a position that he didn't necessarily subscribe to, which was *her* interpretation of *his* opinion. It was time for another talk about that infuriating habit of hers, but not there and then. He wanted privacy for that, and time enough to take as long as necessary . . .

Tenillis and her escort, each of them leading some of the horses Halvin's ex-henchmen were tied to, were already on the road leading out of the village. The procession didn't move very fast even when Bariden and Chalaine finally joined them, but they didn't have all that far to go. Less than five miles down the road was the palace they'd been told about, definitely impressive but even more surprising.

Rather than being high and crowned with battlements, it was no more than three stories tall in the center. To either side, however, it stretched on and on and on, a single building rather than a number of buildings standing close together. Bariden had never seen anything like it, especially the absence of a defensive wall. The place seemed to be open to anyone who wanted to enter, and quite a number of people were doing just that. And here, closer to the palace, the fields were full of people working.

They were less than half a mile away from the city-palace, when a mounted troop appeared from some lower part of the building to the left of what looked like a main entrance. The troop was more than large enough to help the guardsmen with the prisoners, and in a few minutes all but two of their escorts plus prisoners were on the way back to where the troop had come from. With most of the crowd gone, Tenillis backed her horse to the place on Bariden's left.

"Father must have seen us approaching, and sent extra guardsmen to help," she said, glowing happily like a small girl. "I'm glad he already knows things went well."

"If there were that many men available, why did you ride out with only seven?" Bariden asked, bothered as well as annoyed. "You could have been badly hurt, not to mention captured or killed. With more men—"

"Bariden, that was something *I* insisted on," she interrupted gently. "Even the presence of every man in my father's guard would not have kept Halvin from doing as he pleased, and the more there, the more who could die. I took only volunteers, and none of them expected to return. If father had been stronger, he would have looked at it *your* way. But now that he *is* feeling strong enough, we can go straight to him—Oh, Bariden, I hope you like him. I *know* he's going to like *you.*"

Her smile drew him forward with her as she began to move again, but not even a glance went to Chalaine, who rode to his right. Bariden expected his—companion—to comment about that, but all Chalaine did was urge her mount along just in their wake. Silence probably wasn't a good sign, but there was nothing Bariden could do about it. He'd have a talk with both women later, pointing out there was no reason they couldn't be friends . . . Sure, no reason beyond an instant mutual dislike . . .

Trying not to think about being caught in the middle of a female free-for-all distracted Bariden, so much so that the next thing he knew they were at the foot of the steps in front of the palace. Tenillis was being helped off her horse by one of the guardsmen, and only then did Bariden notice that she rode sidesaddle. Like a real lady, and unlike Chalaine, who was dismounting all by herself. That would be yet another point of discord between them, he realized, seeing to his own dismounting. As if it mattered what a woman wore and how she rode . . .

The horses were led away by the guardsmen, and Tenillis herself led the way up the stairs toward the doors that were standing wide. Two guardsmen stood beside these doors, and a glance around showed Bariden that the people entering and leaving the palace were doing it through other doors. This entrance must be reserved for the royal family and their guests, and needed nothing more than a couple of duty guards to keep it private.

That and a mild exclusion spell. Bariden could feel it as he passed through the doorway, a suggestion that anyone who didn't belong should find another way into the palace. It didn't have enough strength behind it to affect anyone with more power than the one who had cast it, but a fleeting look of disappointment on Tenillis's face said she'd been hoping Chalaine would have trouble. The words they'd exchanged must have really upset her.

A servant appeared and bowed to his princess, listened for a moment, then led the way toward a wide set of stairs leading upward. At the top the servant switched his bow to Chalaine and asked her to follow him, which she did after a hesitation so short it could have been imagination. But she didn't even glance at Bariden before walking away, not to mention saying anything to him. He was about to do his own bit to change that, when Tenillis took his left arm in both hands and briefly leaned against him.

"Father doesn't have the strength to meet more than one new person at a time," she said with a sad smile. "If two were presented, he'd try to be gracious to them both even if it harmed him, which it would. Tonight we'll have a private dinner of celebration, just my family and a few close friends. Father isn't allowed to attend things like that, so your companion will be able to rejoin you then. Right now she's being taken to a suite where she can rest and refresh herself."

"Tenillis, Chalaine isn't your enemy any more than I am," he said, trying to make her believe him. "I know you two got off on the wrong foot, but it doesn't have to continue like that. Holding a grudge would be foolish . . ."

"Oh, I'm not very good at holding a grudge," Tenillis said ruefully when his words trailed off. He'd been thinking about Chalaine's ability when it came to holding grudges . . . "I'm sure she and I will work out our differences in no time, for your sake if for no other reason. My father's apartment is this way."

Her smile of encouragement urged him to walking again, and this time she kept possession of his arm. Bariden had thought about telling her that Chalaine wasn't likely to be that easily convinced about differences, then decided to keep the comment to himself. It would be nothing but borrowing trouble, which he had no need whatsoever to do.

King Graff's apartment was as splendid and large as a monarch's private quarters ought to be, and seemed even more tastefully decorated than Bariden's father's. But it was also quieter, and those who moved through the outer rooms took pains to make no unnecessary noise. There might as well have been a sign reading "sick room," right above a pointing arrow; when Tenillis pasted a pleasant smile on her face as they approached a set of closed doors, Bariden knew which way the arrow would be pointing. As they reached the doors one of them was opened from inside, and Tenillis passed through first and moved straight ahead.

"Father, did you see?" she asked gently but happily as she approached an oversized four-poster. "The problem is solved, and our people are safe again."

"Yes, my dear, I certainly did see," a weak but steady voice answered from the bed. "Bring the young man closer and present him to me."

At Tenillis's gesture Bariden moved forward, and once he reached her side he was able to see the man in the bed. The king had obviously been a big man, but some wasting disease had taken the flesh from his bones and the strength from his arms. The bright red hair around his sunken face made it look even more pale than it was, but there was still life left in the sharp blue eyes. King Graff lay propped up on pillows with a silken cover in blue reaching to his chest, but something about him still said he was far from beaten.

"Your Majesty, allow me to present Bariden, a most welcome visitor to your realm," Tenillis said with a smile. "Through his efforts alone the sorcerer Halvin was defeated, and the land made safe once again for your people."

"You are indeed most welcome to Our realm, Bariden," the king's weak voice said with true warmth, his smile matching that of his daughter. "It's been much too long since a hero walked these halls, and it pleases Us to see another before Our death. Tenillis, wait for the young man in the next room. We would have words in private with him."

"Yes, Father," the girl said with a curtsy, then left with a parting smile for Bariden. She also left without any attempt to argue or even to hesitate, which raised Bariden's brows somewhat. Even his sisters didn't obey *that* wholeheartedly . . .

"And now, Bariden, we can speak man to man," Graff said once a silent servant had closed the door behind Tenillis. "Because I was worried about my daughter, I watched everything that happened through a vision sphere. If it had become necessary, I would have used the sphere to send all my remaining strength against Halvin in an attempt to end him. Whether or not it would have worked is another question."

Bariden nodded, understanding the problem. Attacking someone through a sphere meant for viewing is possible, but the attempt invariably drains the attacker completely. If that attacker started out strong and healthy he might survive, but it would still be quite a while before he got his strength back. And if the person being attacked was too much stronger, the attacker could conceivably give up his life and still do less than lethal damage.

"So I think you can imagine my delight when *you* stepped forward," the king continued, grinning weakly. "And then when you proved to be stronger than that emotional cripple—I *was* watching carefully, you know, and I saw you step out in front of the helpless without waiting to find that out. That you were stronger, I mean. You would have fought Halvin even if *he* proved the stronger."

"I don't like to see people being taken advantage of," Bariden answered with a shrug, faintly embarrassed. "And it's been my experience that there are times when strength isn't the most important factor. No competent sorcerer with imagination needs a flock of bullyboys to push ordinary people around; there are ways to do that with magic that are a lot more effective. If this Halvin *was* using them, either he wasn't all that competent or he had no imagination. In either case, I had no real doubts about being able to take him."

"You do a good job of rationalizing an act of pure bravery and courage," the king said with a chuckle. "If you're more comfortable like that, just keep on doing it. I, however, prefer to look at it differently, which brings us to the real reason I wanted to speak to you. As you can see, I'm dying."

"If you like, I'll be glad to see if there's something I can do," Bariden offered at once. "I don't have anything like a talent for healing, but maybe I can—"

"No, no, that's not what I meant," the king interrupted with surprised pleasure. "It's to your credit that you would make the offer, but even someone with your strength could do very little to help me. This disease has weakened my body on the inside, and the damage was already beyond repairing by the time I first noticed that something was wrong. My healers have been able to keep me free of pain, but that's the best anyone can do."

"Anyone *here*," Bariden muttered, disturbed that this brave monarch had no way to reach a wizard-strength healer. The ravages of disease *could* be repaired, but only by someone who had the strength *and* the skill . . .

"No, what I wanted to speak to you about is something quite different," King Graff went on, obviously having missed Bariden's muttered comment. "As I said, I'm dying, but that won't be the greatest tragedy of my life. What was infinitely worse was when my two sons were killed."

The man's face turned really bleak, and this time there was nothing to say. Bariden *had* no children, and therefore could only imagine what losing two would be like.

"It was a stupid accident that should never have happened," King Graff continued. "But it *did* happen, and it took both of them. Shortly after that this disease made itself known, and that was the end of all chance to produce another heir or two. Tenillis is very dear to me, but she's still a girl. What this kingdom needs is a man as heir."

"You can't be serious," Bariden protested in shock. "I'm nothing but a passing stranger, someone you don't know at all. And what about the people of this land? How would *they* feel, having a sorcerer for a king? It's not—"

"So you noticed that you'd said something foolish," King Graff observed with a faint chuckle when Bariden's words broke off. "They already know what it's like to have a magic user for a king, and they love the idea. If a king is capable of getting what he wants by magic, he tends to leave his people alone to build satisfactory lives of their own. It's been generations since someone of my line *hasn't* been able to do magic."

Hearing that made Bariden stop and think. He'd never had any designs on his father's throne, but that hadn't stopped the spread of rumors. Because he was better than most with weapons, a lot of people were expecting him to challenge his oldest brother for the throne once their father was gone. And the belief that he would win had made even more people very uneasy. After all, he was a highly competent sorcerer that they would then be stuck with as king. Who knew what he might decide to do to them . . .

"Woman or not, Tenillis is still your only remaining heir," Bariden said then. "It would be very unfair to exclude her, especially after what she tried to do earlier. And especially in favor of a complete stranger you know nothing about. I could have done what I did just to get you to make this very offer, to legitimize my takeover. If nothing else, I *do* have more imagination than the late Halvin."

"Even most trees have more imagination than he did," the king countered dryly. "The only intelligent thing he ever did was wait until I was too sick to stop him before starting his game of domination, and even that was more cowardice than intelligence. But that point alone disproves your contention. If Halvin was able to do as he pleased, you certainly could. A man's rule is legitimized if he takes over and no one is able to stop him. Who around here do you imagine is able to stop you?"

That was a question Bariden couldn't answer, but the king gave him a moment to do so anyway. When the moment was over, King Graff smiled gently.

"So, as you can see, your objections are groundless— with the possible exception of the one concerning Tenillis. I admit you have a point there, but the matter could be rectified rather easily if you made Tenillis your queen.

Or don't you consider her as attractive as she obviously considers you?"

"On the contrary, I find her very attractive," Bariden muttered, remembering the flash he'd gotten from her when they first met. The Spell of Affinity said they would do very well together, and the way she *asked* for things rather than demanding them seemed to support that. But still . . .

"Why don't you take some time to think about what I've said," the king suggested gently. "Even if a man is capable of making snap decisions, he shouldn't have to do it with the most important matters of his life. Get some rest, take a slow look around, and tomorrow we can talk again."

Bariden nodded, grateful for the reprieve. He did need some uninterrupted thinking time, especially in view of what Halvin had said before he died. If that *was* the last world he and Chalaine would be able to reach . . .

Tenillis wasn't waiting outside the sickroom as Bariden had thought she would be. She'd left a servant there with her apologies and the promise that she would see him later, along with instructions to show Bariden to his apartment. The big man followed the servant without comment, and once he was alone he sat wearily in a chair. The apartment was gorgeous, what he could see of it even better than what he had in his father's palace, but his mind was too agitated to appreciate it.

King Graff really *wanted* him as his heir, without any sense of reluctance whatsoever. That was what disturbed Bariden so deeply, that one major difference between the king and his own father. King Agilar was a large, pleasant man who enjoyed his children and loved them, but he wasn't Sighted. He had never made any obvious difference among his three sons, but Bariden had always had the feeling he was the one the king worried about most. As if there were something wrong with Bariden, something that couldn't be cured.

Or as if he couldn't be completely trusted. His father had never said that in so many words, but Bariden had gotten that feeling more than once. King Graff, on the other hand, obviously trusted Bariden without question, or he wouldn't have offered him his people and his daughter. It was so tempting to think about staying in a place where you were not only needed but wanted, really and truly wanted. A place that could become more of a home than you'd ever known . . .

He *would* think about that for a while, just a little while . . .

The apartment the servant showed me to was pleasant, but nothing like what I'd been given in Queen Lova's palace. I thought about that as I looked around briefly, then shrugged it off. This time it was Bariden's turn to play hero, mine to simply tag along and get in the way. Most especially get in the way. That girl Tenillis . . .

I called a cup of coffee into being, but rather than sit down with it I went back out into the hall. There were no guardsmen posted at my door with orders to keep me inside, and even the servant who'd guided me there was gone. That meant I could go for the stroll I wanted without creating any scenes or confrontations, a pleasant change I took immediate advantage of. I had some thinking to do, but also had the definite urge to take a good look around.

The hall I strolled through was made of marble, into which nicely carved doors were set to give the apartments privacy. But I'd already noticed that my apartment wasn't all that lavishly decorated, and now saw that the marble wasn't top quality either. There was no doubt that sweet, ladylike Tenillis had told the servant where to put me, and it wasn't likely to be anywhere near Bariden's apartment. That little sweetheart had staked him out as her own from the first minute she saw him, and had no intentions of letting *me* get in her way.

Which was something of a laugh. I paused to sip at my coffee before turning left at a cross-corridor, wondering if Bariden had told her yet that he and I were just friends. Our last conversational exchange had seemed to indicate he was ready to do just that, exactly as I'd said he would. It had been easy to see he found the girl attractive, and she was a princess, which matched his own station in life. The fact that *I* didn't like her at all meant nothing, not as far as he was concerned. I wasn't the one she was trying to catch.

A female servant came out of a room and hurried past me, intent on whatever her errand was. Her glance was very brief, only long enough to show her I wasn't someone she had to be concerned about, and a moment later even her footsteps were gone. There didn't seem to be very many people in that part of the palace, which might or might not mean something. I had been moving from corridor to corridor almost at random, letting my vague urge to explore choose the direction. If and when it led me to a dead end, I'd have no trouble finding my way back.

And then I turned one corner to see, about a hundred feet ahead, what looked like a breezeway or a small, enclosed bridge. Rather than there being rooms to either side of the corridor, there seemed to be large open windows. Walking down there confirmed that, but neither view looked out at the front of the palace. This was somewhere in back, then, and the stretch *was* a bridge of sorts. It connected the palace proper with a small building straight ahead, something that did *not* look like a simple extension of the palace. A flare of curiosity sent me on, just to find out what it *was*.

About twenty feet beyond the bridge stood a door, but a very plain door without carving of any sort. It was also unlocked, but I could detect a faint exclusion spell, one that would certainly keep out any unSighted who came calling. Someone who was Sighted, though . . . even the most untrained novice would be able to pass with no trouble at all . . .

Which meant I was all but being invited. I sighed as I banished my coffee cup, wondering just how credulous I was supposed to be. I'm not one of those who flatly refuse to admit there's such a thing as coincidence, but there *are* limits beyond which I stop swallowing. I just *happened* to get the urge to explore, and then, by pure luck, just happen to come across this door? Sure, of course, no problem. Any day of the week.

Rather than touch the doorknob I gestured the door open, ready for anything to jump out in attack, but not really expecting that anything. My suspicious mind had come up with a different idea, and when, after a moment, I stepped through, my suspicions were confirmed. Behind the door was a railed walkway, something like a balcony that gave an observer a clear view of a shrine. The building containing it was a simple, three-storied structure without separated floors or rooms, spotlessly clean but also undecorated. The idea of that, I suppose, was to keep anything from competing with the glory of the only thing it contained.

Which was, of course, a gate. It hung in the middle of the air, almost directly opposite the balcony I stood on, and the building had obviously been constructed around it. I could have created a bridge from the balcony that would have let me walk directly up to it, but what was the point? As close as I was the gate still hadn't flared open, and once again I could detect a Spell of Volition. If someone didn't *really* want to use that gate, they never would.

And that meant I now had even more thinking to do. Not to mention hunting Bariden down to give him the news. We were still being played with, and I didn't like it even a little. But we also had a decision to make, and that would be the hard part—for more than one of us . . .

Bariden stood with a cup of wine in his hands, glancing around the reception room. For the moment he was alone again, but certainly not ignored. Tenillis's ladies were in a cluster about twenty-five feet away, all but staring at him as they whispered and giggled among themselves. They'd been nervous about being presented to him, but none of them had let the opportunity pass.

But they hadn't been the only ones he'd been introduced to, nor the most important. When Tenillis had come to his apartment to tell him about the reception being held before dinner, she'd begged him to dress for the occasion. Her idea had been to have some of her father's clothes fitted to him, and she'd been delighted when he proved he didn't need anyone else's finery. The same outfit he'd created for Queen Lova's feast did the job, and Tenillis had been glowing when she'd entered the reception room on his arm.

And as soon as they entered, he'd been presented to the queen. Tenillis's mother was a strong, slender woman who obviously had her own opinions about things, but she'd greeted him with such warmth and approval that Bariden still hadn't gotten over it. And she'd compared him to her late sons, saying he was so much like them that it was almost like having one of them back again. After that, the introductions to members of the court had gone by in a blur.

"You seem to be enjoying yourself," a gentle voice said from his right. "If you are, I'm glad."

"It would be hard for someone *not* to enjoy himself in this beautiful room," Bariden answered, turning to a smiling Tenillis. "The only problem is, I don't yet see Chalaine. You did send someone to tell her about the reception, didn't you?"

"Of course I did," Tenillis answered at once, her green eyes making no effort to avoid his. "She should be here any minute, and will even have enough time for a drink before dinner."

"That's good," Bariden said, hoping she was telling the truth. He hadn't tried to see Chalaine earlier, mainly because he couldn't think of what to say to her. Or *how* to say what was necessary. After her, of course, it would be Tenillis he would have to speak with, and after them the king . . .

"See?" Tenillis said, sounding very pleased. "I knew I was right. Here she is now."

Bariden looked up to see the figure coming through the doors, tangentially realizing he wasn't the only one watching the entrance. Everyone in the room seemed to be staring, but not because the new arrival was that beautifully gowned. She wasn't gowned at all, but still wore the clothes they'd reached that world in. As the only female in the room in pants—and travel-worn pants at that—the growing murmurs of comment weren't ones of admiration.

"Oh, dear, she must have disliked the gown I sent her," Tenillis said, now sounding embarrassed. "I'm sorry, Bariden, I suppose I should have sent a selection and let *her* choose. This is all my fault."

"I don't think so," Bariden answered, trying to keep the growl out of his voice. "What you sent has nothing to do with what she has on. If she wanted to, she could have—"

"Tenillis, this is quite intolerable," the queen said suddenly, coming up on Bariden's left. "I realize that person is a companion of Lord Bariden's, but there *is* such a thing as propriety. If someone can't be bothered to dress properly for an occasion, they really can't expect to be welcomed.

I would very much appreciate it if someone did something about this."

"I'm sure Lord Bariden will speak to her, Mother," Tenillis said in a soothing way; immediately picking up and using the title for him that her mother had supplied. "I'd do it myself, but for some reason she doesn't seem to like me—Oh, here she comes."

Chalaine had been looking around, almost hesitating, Bariden thought. But as soon as she spotted him the hesitation disappeared, and she headed straight for him. Next to everyone else in the room she looked shabby and out of place, and strangely enough that calmed Bariden's anger. If you're simply trying to be difficult about something, why would you do it in a way that made you look almost pathetic . . . ?

"Bariden, we have to talk," she said as soon as she was in speaking distance, ignoring Tenillis completely. "I'm sure your new friends won't mind if—"

"Chalaine, Lord Bariden would also like to speak to *you*," Tenillis interrupted smoothly, her smile gentle and understanding. "It has to do with the standards of polite society, and lying won't do you any good. He already knows the truth."

"Really," Chalaine said, a flash of quickly suppressed anger in the eyes she turned on the other girl. "And what truth is it that *Lord* Bariden already knows?"

"He knows you refused the gown I sent for your use," Tenillis answered sweetly. "I've already admitted I should have sent a selection rather than just one, but under the circumstances it was rude of you to refuse the offer. Not to mention uncaring about simple civility. Very obviously, you have no interest in fitting into this sort of life."

"Well, at least I can't argue with your conclusion," Chalaine said, then turned those eyes on *him*. "But I'd like to know what Prince Bariden thinks about the rest of what you said. Especially since no one came to me with *any* sort of gown. Or even told me the occasion was formal. I was back in my apartment long enough for both."

"No, no, my dear, that's *Lord* Bariden," Tenillis corrected, her smile having turned pitying. "I realize you probably don't know one title from another, and thinking up that story you just told has helped to confuse you, but—"

"No, my dear, it's *Prince* Bariden," Chalaine corrected in turn, but without the smile. "With all the truths you've exchanged with him, I can't imagine how that one was overlooked. And I'm still waiting to hear what he thinks about whose story is made up."

Once again her stare had come back to him, but Bariden didn't mind. He knew exactly what he wanted to say, but waited just an instant too long. Before he got the first word out, Tenillis's mother took her turn.

"Tenillis, we should have known this man was a prince rather than a commoner," the queen announced, sounding more pleased than ever. "It was our mistake that we judged him by—other things. This exchange has been disgraceful as well as extremely distasteful, but at least it's almost over. I know your brothers would have done the right thing, just as Prince Bariden will. He may have—enjoyed—this person's—company—in the past, but now he no longer needs someone of her sort. After all, he now has—"

"And just what *sort* is that supposed to be?" Chalaine demanded, now making no effort to cover her anger. "Is it someone as mannerless as you, who doesn't even have the decency to insult people directly? I'm standing right here in front of you. If you have something to say to me, show a minimal amount of good breeding and do it to my face."

"How *dare* you!" the queen gasped in outrage while Bariden flinched. Luck had been with him in his life until then, and he'd never been smack in the middle of a potential catfight. Everyone knew a man in that spot had no guarantee of survival, especially if he was foolish enough to try interrupting. But something did have to be done to restore peace and quiet, so he'd have to—

"How *dare* you speak to me like that, you little slut!" the queen thundered, instantly beyond outrage. "You march in here like the intruder you are, call my daughter a liar, and then insult *me*. Just who do you think you are?"

"I don't just think, I *know* who I am," Chalaine countered, apparently having regained some control of herself. "What I am is someone who has *earned* what she has, not someone who was given a magnificent title in exchange for letting a man bed her. When I want to have fun, I never accept payment. Keeps my amateur standing intact, you understand."

Horrified gasps sounded all over the room as the queen went white, proving they were playing to a larger audience than four. In spite of himself Bariden was tempted to let it go on, just to find out if anyone could top that last statement. Had the situation been less serious he might have, but that was no time to indulge a morbid curiosity.

"All right, I think that's enough from everyone concerned," he announced, speaking loud enough to override anyone else. "You all started out looking for *my* opinion and thoughts, but none of you has let me get a word in edgewise. If you've changed your mind about wanting to hear from me, just say so."

"Certainly not, Prince Bariden," Tenillis assured him at once, her mother making no effort to disagree. "I, for one, would love to hear what you have to say."

Her smile of encouragement was really warm, and she seemed to be diplomatically keeping herself from taking his arm. A glance showed that Chalaine was also waiting to hear what he had to say, only not quite as happily. This was going to start even more trouble, but there was no possible way to avoid it.

"Tenillis, there's something about Chalaine you seem to be forgetting, and that one fact changes everything," Bariden said, making no attempt to soften his words. "She's a fully trained sorceress with the same abilities that I have, which means she has no more need of someone else's clothes than I do. And beyond that, if she'd decided to show contempt for everyone around her, I think she would have dressed in something really offensive, like a beggar's rags. Simply wearing her original clothes would mean nothing."

"Bariden, what are you saying?" Tenillis whispered, a hint of tears in her wide green eyes. "You can't believe I would deliberately lie to you? Not when knowing you has come to mean so much? I can see now that she knows you so much better than I do, so well that she knew what you would think. I should never have risked telling you the truth, but I wanted nothing of lies to stand between us. Oh, Bariden . . . !"

With that she turned away from him, ostensibly to hide her tears of pain. The queen's expression had changed to one of pure sympathy, and Chalaine wasn't showing anything but slightly raised brows. Bariden was willing to give credit for an excellent performance, but beyond that he was rapidly losing patience.

"Tenillis, your second mistake is forgetting that I really am a prince," Bariden said with exasperation. "At my father's court I grew up watching things like this, and always wondered why grown men seemed to equate tears with the truth. More often than not the tears covered something else entirely, like a determined attempt at manipulation."

"Are you saying you'd rather take *her* word over mine?" Tenillis demanded with a sniff after turning back to him. "I've *never* had anyone doubt me, especially not someone I cared about so much. Maybe you'd just rather not hurt her feelings, and if that's it, then I understand. You're not a man who would want to hurt *anyone's* feelings, but I really can stand it more easily than other women. As long as I know what the real truth is . . ."

The look in her eyes begged him while her tone went wistful, but apparently she'd forgotten Bariden wasn't the only one listening to her.

"If it's the real truth we all want, how about a truth spell?" Chalaine suggested innocently. "That way *no* one's word has to be taken, and nothing could be easier. You know how to do one, don't you, Bariden?"

"That's *enough*!" Tenillis shouted, turning to glare at Chalaine. "I've seen trollops like you before who think they know everything, but all you're doing is wasting your time! You'll *never* be as good as a true lady, no matter how long or hard you try! You're common dirt who simply doesn't belong here, but you don't even have the decency to leave! Why do you insist on staying where no one wants you?"

"As a rule, I don't," Chalaine answered with a faint smile, looking only at Tenillis. "And if you're an example of a true lady, I thank the EverNameless for whatever help they might have given in making me something else. I hope you get exactly what you think you want."

And with that she turned and walked away, neither hurrying nor dragging her feet. She was heading for the door out, Bariden knew, but before he could take a single step after her Tenillis was suddenly wrapped around his arm.

"Don't embarrass her any more, Bariden, please don't," Tenillis begged, wide green eyes filled with compassion. "We both know she doesn't belong, so just let her leave quietly. I promise you everything will work out much more smoothly that way."

"Work out for whom?" Bariden asked flatly as he deliberately unwound her from his arm. "I'm sorry, Tenillis, but if Chalaine doesn't belong here, I don't either. I would have said that a lot sooner if you'd waited to stage your production, and then all that acting wouldn't have been necessary. But you *are* one of the best I've ever seen, so do accept my congratulations on a fine performance."

And with that he walked off, leaving a furiously indignant Tenillis to begin sputtering in outrage. Whatever she had to say *might* have been interesting, but Bariden was more concerned with catching up to Chalaine. There was something she'd wanted to tell him, and with any luck at all her news would save him from having to make a very painful decision . . .

By hurrying just a little, Bariden reached Chalaine before Chalaine reached the first turn in the corridor. When he stopped her with a hand to her arm she turned blazingly furious eyes on him, so he quickly held up both hands in surrender.

"Don't attack *me*, I'm not a lady either," he pointed out, then grinned when she immediately looked startled. "But you'll have to admit she certainly is persistent. Someone else would have dropped the act fifteen or twenty minutes ago."

"Are you trying to say you didn't believe her at all?" Chalaine demanded, sounding half-disbelieving and half-hopeful. "When I first walked up to you . . ."

"I was already suspicious," he assured her, knowing she was mentally reviewing his expression from that time. "I'll admit her story was good, but it made sense only if it involved an ordinary woman. Using it against a full sorceress canceled most of it out, but she didn't understand that. And she kept thinking she could make me believe her, even when I specifically pointed out where she'd made her mistakes."

"A lot of men *would* have believed her," Chalaine said, almost grudgingly. "It's that air of sweet loving-kindness she projects. Most men would find it hard to accept that someone like her would lie and manipulate—and I had the impression you were very attracted to her. Unless I'm mistaken, you have a thing for redheads."

"You're very observant," Bariden admitted, starting them walking again. "I do prefer redheads, and I did find Tenillis very attractive. Especially when her father offered to make me his heir, and said I could marry her to legitimize the succession."

"And you really wanted to accept his offer," Chalaine said, staring at him so closely that Bariden felt uncomfortable. "There's something about this world that appeals to you more strongly than any other place you've ever been. But you weren't expected to make a decision on the spot, so you didn't."

"You're not guessing," Bariden observed, suddenly seeing the point. "Is that the way it went with you on the previous world?"

"Almost exactly," she agreed with a nod. "The only difference I can find is that last time you happened to overhear a conversation that led you to find the gate. This time I had the urge to take a walk and explore, and surprise, surprise. Guess what was at the end of my random stroll."

"I don't like the sound of that, and obviously you don't either," Bariden said with a frown. "This is the second time we've been brought to a world, told there was no way to leave again, then shown almost at once that there *is* a way. What kind of reason can there possibly be for this insanity?"

"A complicated one," Chalaine said, her pretty face troubled. "I spent some time thinking about this, and after a while I discovered I had a theory. On the last world, thinking there would be no way to leave it, I almost let myself accept what I'd been offered. It was all so perfect, so much what I would have chosen if I'd had the chance.

Not just a place, but a place where I was needed and wanted by very special people."

"Just like here for me," Bariden agreed, hearing an exact echo of his feelings in her words. "Not the place, but the people."

"And then, with the shock of rude awakening, you announced you had found a gate," Chalaine continued. "My first reaction was, well of course he's happy he found a gate. He doesn't *belong* here, not the way I do. There's no reason he can't use that gate alone, and I can stay here and make a happy life for myself."

"But there was a reason," Bariden pointed out. "I refused to leave without you. Was that the way it was supposed to go, do you think, or did I accidently mess up our enemy's plans?"

"I'd say most eventualities were planned for," she responded with a sigh. "Neither of us could have used that gate unless we were absolutely certain we wanted to, so we both could have been stuck. Or I could have refused to go, and you eventually got sick and tired of hanging around and used it alone. If you had, you would have found this world waiting for you without my being here to ruffle the feathers of the lovely heroine. Under those circumstances, how long would it have taken you to accept the offer you were made?"

"Probably about a minute and a half," Bariden agreed. "But you believed me when I said I'd never leave that world without you, and you were able to get around that Spell of Volition long enough for us to use the gate. That means you were still with me when we got here."

"And, I think, I was supposed to be in the middle of blaming you for making me leave the place of my dreams," Chalaine said, leading the way left up a cross-corridor. Bariden wasn't certain about where they were going, but he could guess. "If I *had* been blaming you, sweet Tenillis would have looked like a breath of free air after a week of being locked in a closet. You would have found her irresistible, and would also have believed everything she said. If I managed to get to tell you I'd found a gate, you'd probably decide I was trying to get even for your having taken away *my* dream world by taking away yours. In case you haven't yet guessed, there's a Spell of Volition on this gate, too."

"I had a feeling there would be," Bariden said with a sigh, then reached over to touch her arm. "Are you sure you *don't* blame me for having made you leave your 'dream' world? I know you didn't really want to go, and if I hadn't insisted—"

"If you hadn't insisted, I would have eventually gotten around to doing it myself," she interrupted, paying no attention to the hand on her arm. "Dream worlds are fine to live in, as long as you don't have friends left behind who badly need your help to regain their lives. I might be able to talk myself into forgetting about strangers in need, but friends are something else entirely. You weren't really the one who made me leave that world, so why would I blame you?"

"A lot of people I know would have done it anyway," Bariden muttered, wishing she'd said something about wanting to be with *him* more than staying in a dream. And she'd left the reception room without looking at him even once, probably because she'd expected him to support Tenillis. She still didn't believe he had any real interest in her, something that made him want to put a fist into a wall in frustration.

"And now, with most of the possible outcomes behind us, we have to consider what's ahead of us," Chalaine said, apparently unaware of what he was feeling. "That gate I just happened to find by pure luck and accident—do we use it as we're obviously supposed to if we don't stay, or do we try to find a gate a little more to our liking? That's assuming there *is* such a gate, and we can find it in less than two lifetimes, neither of which may be possible."

"I'm really tempted to lose my temper and start destroying things," Bariden said, glancing at the doors and walls they passed as his left hand tightened on his sword hilt. "No matter what we do we're still being manipulated, and the thought of that is making me furious. If we use the gate so thoughtfully provided for us, we're doing exactly what our enemy wants us to do."

"And if we don't use it we could be stuck here, which is another thing the enemy obviously wants." Chalaine's voice was filled with as much annoyance as his had been, telling Bariden she was ready to do some destroying of her own. "All this anger and frustration and indecision we feel can't possibly be a coincidence, not when there's a Spell of Volition on the gate. I'd say we're *supposed* to be in a turmoil, and possibly even disagreeing about what to do. If we were, it would be more effective than locking us up."

"So we have to agree on what to do, and then go ahead and do it," Bariden summed up. "We'll still be cooperating with the enemy, but at least we'll be in agreement about it. Would you like to toss a coin, or should we have some sort of contest where the winner gets to decide?"

"I think what we need to do first is cool off," Chalaine muttered, glancing at the anger she could certainly see on his face. "If we're supposed to be angry, then I for one don't want to be. We can stop to have something to eat, talk the situation over, then do whatever we decide to. And maybe you can talk me out of really *wanting* to go through that gate."

"You have to have a reason for what you just said," Bariden observed, actually finding himself distracted somewhat from the anger. "I'd like to hear what it is."

"My reason is as follows," Chalaine said, stopping just short of a breezeway area to look straight at him. "The more I think about this trap we've been forced into, the more I want to find a way out of it the enemy hasn't anticipated. The only way I can do that is to keep going straight through the way I'm supposed to, while at the same time keeping my eyes open. If there's the least little thing that hasn't been covered, I'm willing to bet I can find it."

"What's wrong with that?" Bariden was honestly puzzled. "I think it's a damned good way of looking at this mess, and a lot better than simply getting angry."

"But that's the whole point," she insisted, looking up at him with those big, dark eyes. "It's something someone of my temperament would be sure to think of, so how do I know I'm not being manipulated into the feeling? The enemy knows me well enough to have given me my dream world; doesn't that mean he knows me well enough to encourage feeling like this?"

"It's possible," Bariden allowed after a moment's thought. "In fact it's very possible, but it isn't something I would worry about. The enemy may have known you well enough to give you your dream world, but his effort wasn't *quite* good enough to do the job. If he really knew you, you wouldn't have been able to bring yourself to leave."

"I hadn't thought of that," she answered with a frown, her stare now directed inward. "He knows me somewhat well, but not well enough to really hook me. And that should mean he's underestimating me, which in turn should mean I have a better than good chance to find his mistake. How does that sound to *you*?"

"Not like a rationalization, if that's what you were asking," Bariden replied. "As a matter of fact, I was wondering why I wasn't *more* tempted by this place than I actually was. One answer could be that he doesn't know *me* that well either, and is therefore underestimating the both of us. Or mistaking what will really touch us. In either case, our chances of winning free look better now than they did five minutes ago."

"Even with that Spell of Volition in place," Chalaine agreed. "Since the gate is just beyond that door up ahead, why don't we stop here to have our meal? Or did you want to go straight through and stop once we're in the next place?"

"I think we'd better stop now," Bariden decided, eyeing the door at the far end of the hall. "If we just keep going we might find ourselves in another version of that first world, snow all around, no shelter, and no magic."

"Good point," she agreed, then turned away from him, thought for a moment, then raised one hand and spoke her spell. A table and two chairs appeared in the middle of the breezeway, the table covered with a large number of dishes. The chairs looked extremely comfortable, and when Bariden made sure to seat her before taking his own place, he saw an amused smile on Chalaine's face.

"Is something funny?" he asked as he sat. "If there is, I could use hearing about it."

"It's nothing, really," she answered with a shake of her head. "Just something I discussed with Lord Naesery on the last world. It's pure silliness, but I have something that isn't. Your comment about what we might find beyond the gate has given me pause."

"Given you paws?" he asked, immediately looking at her hands. Then it came to him what she'd meant, and he started to laugh. When she looked at him questioningly he explained the misinterpretation, which let her join him in the laughter. Bariden found it a beautifully close moment, but Chalaine must have been born without a romantic bone in her body. As soon as she stopped laughing, she was right back to the original topic.

"So far, we've been through one world without magic and two worlds with it," she said, holding up three fingers. "In the first world I was warded and you weren't, and that worked out to *your* benefit. In the second world you also weren't warded, but it turned out you needed to be. Here, in the third world, the warding I gave you turned out to be absolutely essential. Any guesses on how it will stand on the other side of *this* gate?"

"Sure," he answered, reaching for the pitcher filled with a cold soft drink. "Either I won't be able to survive without warding, having it will give me trouble, or I won't need it at all. Drink?"

"Yes, thank you," she responded absently as she nodded. "And you're right. The next world will most likely be one of those three choices, but we won't know which until we get there and then it might be too late. I think we should do something about it before we go through."

"Like what?" Bariden asked, replacing the pitcher and raising his now-filled cup. "How can we know in advance what we'll—wait a minute. I just had an idea, but you could be way ahead of me. Were you trying to say you already know about variable warding?"

"I've never heard of it," she answered with a frown. "What's variable warding?"

"It's something I heard about from a friend," Bariden told her, seeing no reason to mention that ReSayne was a fiend. "My friend is in touch with a demon who spends its time with a young wizard, and the wizard's specialty is unSeen magic. But the wizard also works with adapting ordinary spells, and she came up with warding that does more than simply vary in strength of response. Her spell for warding is like not having any warding at all, unless you happen to need it. Then you get only as much warding as you need, adapting and varying according to circumstance, and it's also voluntary. If you don't want your defenses set off, they won't *go* off."

"There when you need it, not there when you don't, and not there at all if you don't want it to be," Chalaine summed up with brows high. "That sounds like quite an improvement over automatic, preset responses, but why would your friend tell *you* about it? You don't *use* ordinary warding."

"That's why my friend told me about it," Bariden said with a smile. "My friend thinks I *should* be warded, and doesn't understand why I usually don't agree. But this sounds like the perfect time to try that spell, and I'd like *you* to use it, too."

"Why?" she asked, her big dark eyes showing faint puzzlement. "What do you think is wrong with my normal warding? I do have it keyed to intent, after all—"

"Which didn't help at all in the first world," Bariden reminded her. "It brought you something instead of protecting you from that something, and I don't want that happening again. Unless, of course, you *like* the idea of it happening again . . ."

"All right, point taken," she said, holding both hands up as she made a face at him. "I doubt if I'd get that composite again, but the way things have been going the next one would be worse. How does that spell go?"

Bariden produced a piece of paper and a stylus, then wrote out the spell while Chalaine removed her warding from him. He spoke the spell while she studied what he'd written, felt *something* settling around him, then watched *her* speak the spell. He wasn't able to detect anything after she was through, but most warding wasn't visible to the naked eye anyway.

"How do we find out if the spell worked the way it was supposed to?" Chalaine asked, obviously thinking along the same lines he was. "If I pick up this cup of mousse and throw it at you, my lack of intent to do serious harm might leave the warding unactivated."

"If you throw that cup of mousse at me and it hits, we'll then be able to test *your* warding," Bariden responded darkly. "And you won't have to worry about any lack of intent, that I promise you. If you insist on thinking about mousse, forget about testing."

"Whatever you say," she responded with a heavy, theatrical sigh that didn't quite hide the glint of devilment in her eyes. "Warding isn't supposed to work against the nonmagical anyway, but if the spell turns out not to work against magic either, don't forget who refused to talk about testing."

Bariden muttered a wordless response before joining her in helping himself to the food, but he wasn't really annoyed. As a matter of fact it was all he could do not to grin, but he didn't dare encourage her. He was absolutely certain the new warding would *not* stop mousse thrown in fun, and he didn't need to confirm it the hard way. The close, warm feeling between them had come back, and this time Chalaine wasn't chasing it away. He'd kick himself later if *he* did the chasing because of a faceful of sticky pudding.

The meal was delicious and the company silent but pleasant, but eventually it had to end. Bariden wondered briefly why they hadn't been disturbed by anyone in the palace, but wasn't in the mood to go back and find out. If he ran into King Graff and was told he could stay even if it was Chalaine he married rather than Tenillis . . . No, he was much better off not being faced with that sort of temptation.

When they both stood, Chalaine banished the table and chairs. Right after that she spoke a spell, and when Bariden heard it he realized immediately that it was an excellent idea. She'd turned her clothing variable, directing that it be heavier in cold weather and lighter in warm, an idea she must have gotten from the new warding spell. He realized then that he was still in his reception finery, so he replaced it with his usual breeches and boots, altered to fit the same spell.

It wasn't far to the door that hid sight of the gate, and it wasn't hard to construct a bridge from the balcony *to* the gate. As he followed Chalaine along the bridge, Bariden concentrated hard on what he expected the next world to bring. A way for them to break loose, of course, but also an opportunity to get even closer to Chalaine. He needed a chance to take her in his arms, and show her just what being near her did to him. He visualized that as he moved forward, promising himself that it *would* happen—and then the gate flared wide and let them enter.

This time neither of them hesitated going through and, unsurprisingly, once again there was just a single point for them to exit from. They stepped through the new gate, Bariden, at least, expecting the same sort of countryside they'd found until then—

But this time they were in a city, specifically in a back alley, and not far away someone was screaming.

CHAPTER NINE

Wherever that alley was it stank, the smell so bad it even seemed to dirty the darkness around us. And the air was cool enough to make my clothes thicken in response, just the way they were supposed to do. But that scream made me wonder if my new warding would be equally as effective, not to mention making me aware of the heavy feel of magic in the air. Somebody *strong* had been working in that city, and not just in one or two places . . .

"It's coming from that way," Bariden said, and I suppose he gestured in the direction he meant. It was too dark to see more than a thickened shadow of him, and that despite the closed gate hanging in the air behind us. Under normal circumstances I wouldn't have expected to find even a closed gate in the middle of a city, but "normal circumstances" said it all.

I saw Bariden's shadow form begin to move toward the end of the alley, and followed along with an unvoiced sigh. He was going looking for the source of that scream, but would never consider it also looking for trouble. I should have resented the fact that he seemed to believe it was all right for *him* to do the things he didn't want *me* doing, but for some reason I couldn't get angry. He was so—honest and open about his opinions and prejudices . . . and he'd actually taken *my* side against that Tenillis female. I still didn't quite know what to think about *that* . . .

"Over there, past that narrow intersection," he said, and this time when he pointed I could see the gesture. The buildings around us were on a narrow back street and were mostly of old wood, but a couple of them had torches in sconces not far from their doors. What I could see of the signs above the torches said the places were taverns, definitely of the sleazier sort. I toyed with the idea of creating enough light to let us see what was going on, but after a moment decided against it. If we were going to tell the world we were there, we'd certainly find a better time later on.

Bariden headed straight for where the screams were coming from, and I was right with him. As we got closer we could see five or six people standing around watching something on the ground, and once we reached the group the something turned out to be a man. He was screaming and rolling around as though in a lot of pain, but even the dimness couldn't mask the fact that there didn't seem to be anything wrong with him. His clothes looked to be a shade better than average for that neighborhood, his brown hair didn't reach much below his shoulders, and at some time that day he'd been clean-shaven. But he was still screaming in pain, and the next minute we found out why.

"Hey, Dal, what's happening?" a female voice asked, and then two women came up to the man apparently named Dal. The women were wearing low-cut gowns with slits in the skirts as well as too much face makeup, and the man was a hefty sort almost as tall as Bariden. He also wore a truncheon tucked into his belt between leather trousers and a light cotton shirt, and he shrugged at the woman's question.

"What's happening is that fool opened his mouth one time too many," he said, sounding more disgusted than upset. "He came into the place about an hour ago, and as soon as he had a drink in his hand he started to ask questions. How long has the king been a wizard? How many high-level sorcerers does he have under him? Does he guard the palace only with magic, or does he also have men stationed in some places? The only thing he *didn't* ask about was the last time somebody came by to challenge the king with magic."

"Or what spells the king has set up to let him know when new challengers show up," the woman added, also in disgust. "But even though he didn't ask it, he got part of an answer anyway. I bet he thought he was too well warded for anything like that to happen, and was real surprised as soon as he stepped outside."

"These down-country fools are all alike," the man Dal said, shaking his head. "As soon as they reach high-level sorcerer, they head for the nearest city to challenge the king. They never understand how big a step it is from where they are to wizard level. Or that those of us who live here don't use nothing but permitted magic because that's the way *we* want it. Maybe after spending the night screaming in pain he'll start to understand."

"Isn't there anything anyone can do for him?" Bariden asked, drawing the man's bored attention. "I'm new here myself, and I've never seen something like this. Can't anyone help him?"

"Only if they want to share what *he's* getting," Dal answered with a glance for me. "Touch him and you join him, and that means with hands *or* magic. He's learning a lesson now that could save his life, and the king doesn't want that lesson cut short. Without it the country kid might just go ahead with his challenge, and then the king will have to smear him. The king doesn't like smearing anybody he doesn't absolutely have to. It's a waste of his valuable time."

"I see," Bariden answered, and I, at least, could tell he didn't see at all. Giving someone extreme pain simply for asking a few questions—the man on the ground could have been thinking about *working* for the king rather than challenging him, and he would have asked the same things. If Bariden decided to try helping the man anyway, I knew I would back him up without the least hesitation. But rather than do that he took my arm, and we joined most of the other watchers in slowly drifting away.

"We may have been too hasty in simply stepping through that gate," he murmured after a moment, the people we'd walked away with having taken off in their own directions. "This place isn't going to be easy to accomplish things in."

"Or pleasant while we're trying," I murmured back, still able to hear the screaming. It also seemed that certain of the stinks were following us, as though delighted to have found places they hadn't spread to yet. "Are you sure you don't want to try to do something for that man? Maybe if the two of us work together—"

"Then the two of us could get caught," he interrupted with a headshake. "If not by *that* little trap, then maybe by another. I think you know me well enough to believe I *want* to help that man, but fighting blind against an unknown wizard's spell isn't the best way to do it."

Seeing the strained look on his face and getting a glimpse of the anger in his eyes told me something else as well. Walking away from someone who needed help was one of the hardest things Bariden had ever done, and also probably the most painful. It was another couple of points to chalk up against our enemy—as if we needed more things to blame him for.

"So what do we do now?" I asked, looking around at the narrow street that was taking us toward a wider one. "Leave the city, or stay here and hope we can figure out where to go next without breaking a law? I have no idea which would be the better move."

"Neither do I, but since we're already here we should look around before leaving," he said. "We also don't know what it takes to get in and out of a city in this world, and if we leave we may not be able to get back in. Or, for that matter, they might not let us leave without trouble in the first place. What we need is a room at an inn, preferably an inn with a talkative landlord."

Now that sounded like a good idea, at least as far as getting information on that world went. I had my own ideas about where the next gate was, and also about whether or not an entry spell would work. Those were two things we really needed to talk about, but not out there on the street.

The wider street we reached was the start of a better neighborhood, and more people were out and walking around. Most of the women wore long dresses or skirts, but every now and then there was one in breeches. The men wore simple shirts and pants and coats, and quite a few had swords. Those who were armed seemed better dressed than those who weren't, and they didn't hurry quite as much. But no one stopped to socialize with anyone else, and a general mood of lightheartedness was conspicuously absent.

Bariden spotted a place called The Horseman's Inn and headed us toward it, but I happened to look down the block and across the street. The establishment there was called The Travelers' Hostel, but I hesitated a long moment before pointing it out.

"I'm glad you saw that," Bariden said when I did. "It's potentially exactly what we're looking for, a place that will be used to strangers and their questions. But—why are you looking so uncertain?"

"Because we can't trust coincidence in this trap, and that's all we're running into," I explained, wishing I could take an end of my hair to chew. "As soon as we got to this world, we happened to find a man who was being punished for breaking a law. We wouldn't have known that that's what was happening, except that someone standing around happened to explain the situation to someone he knew. Now we're looking for a place it might be safe to ask questions, and I happen to see an establishment called The Travelers' Hostel. What do you want to bet we'll find out everything we need to in there?"

"You mean everything we're supposed to," he answered in disgust. "That isn't quite the same thing, and you're absolutely right. We're being herded in a specific direction, and as long as we keep following that direction we don't have a prayer of breaking loose. Let's bolt to the right instead, and see what happens then."

"They can solve that problem easily by not having any rooms available," I said, stopping his first step toward The Horseman's Inn. "In fact, we might not be able to get a room anywhere but where we're supposed to be. Why don't we try something that's not quite as straightforward as trying to get a room."

"I don't know if I trust that look in your eyes, but I can't see any way out of asking," he told me warily. "What have you got in mind?"

"It has nothing to do with mousse, so you can relax," I reassured him with a grin. "What you ought to remember is that we just saw something very upsetting, and I'm a poor little female who's having trouble handling it. After all, we haven't been in the city long and therefore don't understand its ways, which means I really need some place to sit down, and probably could use a fairly strong drink . . ."

"You know, I *hadn't* remembered that," he said with a delighted grin, then suddenly grew very concerned. "You poor little thing, you must be absolutely torn up over having seen that awful sight. I think we have to find you some place to sit down so you can pull yourself together, and maybe even get you a bracing drink."

By then his arm was around me to help hold me up, and I was so deeply touched by what I'd seen that I really did have to lean on him. I also had a hand to my mouth, but I couldn't quite manage to turn pale. It looked like I'd have to settle for acting pale, and hope that did the job.

Bariden coaxed and urged me through the front door of the three-story inn, and I clung to him in perfect poor-little-thing fashion. The innkeep, a tall, thin man, appeared almost magically in our path, and understood the situation immediately. He led the way to the left of the door into his common room, fussed in concern while Bariden got me seated, then sent a serving girl for a pot of tea and some cups.

There were at least a dozen other people in the common room, and four of the men and one woman came over to see if they could help. Considering the atmosphere of the city that was really nice of them, and Bariden handled it all beautifully. When the innkeep asked what was wrong, he sighed and patted my shoulder.

"We saw something pretty terrible," he admitted, sounding open and honest and a lot younger than usual. "I have to tell you, if she hadn't broken down first, I might have done it myself. We've been dreaming about coming to the city for years, maybe even being good enough to earn a place with the king, but now that we're here—our first day, and we have to see something like *that*."

I moaned a little to help him out, privately pleased that he'd spotted the people in the room who were Sighted. There seemed to be quite a few Sighted in that world, and every one of them would have known us to be the same. Mentioning that we'd hoped to take service with the king was a nice touch, and might even encourage someone to tell us why it was or wasn't possible.

"You still haven't said what *that* was," the innkeep pointed out, his rather high voice working to be soothing. "It couldn't have been a crime and wouldn't have been an execution, so maybe it was an accident."

"No, it *was* a crime," Bariden hastened to assure the man, running a hand through his long blond hair. "A man was rolling around on the ground and screaming, and we came up to the crowd watching him in time to hear something about his wanting to challenge the king. He was being punished for that, but all he did was ask some questions. *I* was going to ask some questions, but now I don't think I dare. All I want to do is take service with the king, but what if someone thinks I mean to challenge him? What would happen to me is bad enough, but what would become of my woman? She and I mean to marry as soon as I've found a decent position, and we were hoping she might be accepted too . . ."

He let it trail off, wisely not suggesting we were *certain* I'd also be accepted into service. Two young people from the country might be naive enough to think a woman had as good a chance as a man, but that might not be so in the big city. If the king was narrow-minded and old-fashioned, the only sorcerers he would take into service would be male.

"You really are newcomers, aren't you?" the innkeep said with an indulgent chuckle. "And you have to be from the real boondocks if you don't already know—Well, suppose I start from the beginning, eh?"

Bariden and I both nodded eagerly, encouraging his feeling of indulgent superiority. When people feel they're better than you are, they don't often hold things back. Everything they tell you shows how good they are, and people who react that way want to look *very* good.

"To begin with, you don't have to worry about the king's spell," he said, looking back and forth between Bariden and me. "I'm not a magic user so I don't know *exactly* how it works, but it always knows the truth. If all you want is information, you can ask a million questions and nothing will happen. If you're really after a challenge, one question is all it takes."

"Intent!" Bariden exclaimed in revelation, pointing at the innkeep. "I'll bet *that's* what it is, *intent*. If all you want is information, your intent is innocent. But if you've got something else in mind . . ."

He let the words trail off with a Significant Look on his face, letting the innkeep know he really did understand. The thin man smiled like a proud and indulgent father, and all but patted Bariden on the head.

"That sounds just right," he told him in approval. "So you see, you and the little girl have nothing to worry about on that score. Now, as far as taking service with the king goes, you happen to be in luck there. Once a week the king holds a competition for newly arrived magic users, and the winners of the competition get to face one of the king's sorcerers. If you win against the king's man, you automatically get to take his place. But if you lose, you don't necessarily have to go back where you came from. If you lose well enough, you'll be taken in as a Sorcerer's Apprentice. Your luck shows in that tomorrow is the day the competition is being held."

"That *is* lucky," Bariden agreed, duly impressed. "But there must be an awful lot of magic users coming to the city if they hold a competition every *week*."

"There are usually a fair number," the man said, this time looking to the others standing around for nods of confirmation, which he got. "Not so many that you'll be trampled in the crowd, but enough to make a contest of it. But how many show up isn't the reason for holding the competitions weekly. It costs a lot more to live here in the city than it does out in the country, and the king doesn't want a bunch of flat-broke magic users hanging around for a *monthly* competition. Something like that would be bound to cause trouble, so the king doesn't let it happen."

"The king sounds so *smart*," I ventured timidly, but definitely in awe. "Now I *really* hope I can take service with him. I'll be able to join the competition tomorrow too, won't I?"

"You could if you *wanted* to, little girl, but in your place I would think it over," he told me, and now he was being paternally serious. "If a man tries and loses, the worst thing that can happen is that he gets sent home in disgrace. For a girl, though, and especially a pretty girl like you—if you're defeated by a man who wants you, you *have* to stay with him and do whatever he says. Even if it's something that won't let you call yourself a good girl any more. Do you really want to risk *that*?"

The emphasis he put on the word—not to mention his very ominous tone—almost made me blink. But at least I didn't have to worry about answering. Bariden did it for me, and in no uncertain terms.

"No, she does *not* want to risk something like that," he announced, glancing at me sternly. "She *is* a good girl, and that's the way she's going to stay. But I don't understand. Why would men be allowed to leave, but not women?"

"Come on, boy, think about it," the innkeep urged. "When a man enters a competition he's serious about it, and if he doesn't really qualify he won't enter. Girls, though . . . we know they don't *mean* to waste people's time by trying for something they're not qualified to do, they just tend to be prone to wishful thinking. This way you won't find many of them entering as a lark, not when they're held to that requirement if they lose. And you're a man, so you know how men hate to do anything rough to pretty girls. This way they usually don't have to."

It was all I could do not to add that men also tend to hate *losing* to a girl, but I did manage to keep my mouth shut. Bariden nodded with enlightened understanding and agreement, though, then stood and put out his hand.

"I want to thank you for helping me out this way, sir," he said with sincere gravity. "No, for helping *us* out. They told us back home that city people would never give us the time of day, but I'm happy to say you proved them wrong. How much do I owe you for this tea?"

The serving girl had finally brought out a pot and two cups, just in time for me to wish we'd asked for something stronger. The innkeep, after accepting Bariden's hand, smiled and shook his head.

"No charge for the tea, boy, not when you'll be competing tomorrow," he said. "You and the little girl drink as much as you like, and then you can head back to wherever you're staying."

"As a matter of fact, sir, we're not staying anywhere yet," Bariden took the opportunity to say. "Since you've been so nice, the least we can do is take a couple of *your* rooms."

"You could if I had any left, boy," the thin man said as he turned away. "Since I don't, you can't. You and the girl enjoy that tea."

By that time he was heading back to his counter near the door, and the other people who had been listening had returned to their tables. Bariden sat back down slowly, and his expression was carefully neutral.

"I'll bet there are rooms at the other place," I murmured as I reached for the teapot. "And it looks like we'll be able to check on that in a very short while. If there are more than two cups of tea in this pot, I'll eat the table."

"Since we're not paying for it, we can't very well complain," he countered in a mutter. "I'm just wondering what else we'll find in that other place. Another helpful conversation between strangers, do you think, or someone willing to tell us what to do as a favor?"

"Whichever it is, the thing we'll have to watch out for is whether we're directed to or away from the palace," I said, pouring tea for both of us. "I'd be willing to bet it's to, but only if the rules haven't changed."

"You mean you think the next gate is there, the way it's been in the last two worlds," he said, taking his cup but looking only at me. "The chances of that are excellent, as long as the rules *haven't* changed. And in the next place, we'll have to ask about gates in general. If we don't, someone might notice."

I nodded my agreement with that, and we drank our tea in silence. It didn't take very long to finish it, but on our way to the door Bariden stopped near the innkeep.

"I just wanted to thank you again, sir, and wish you a good night," he said, then turned back as though he'd suddenly remembered something. "By the way, sir, I meant to ask this earlier. If—I mean *when*—I get accepted into the king's service, I *will* be able to keep my woman with me, won't I? I mean, I can't just march off somewhere and leave her all alone. They won't ask me to do that, will they?"

"I really don't know, boy," the man admitted, scratching at his cheek as he thought about it. "Those accepted into service live and train in the palace, but—I just don't know. You'll have to ask when you go to sign up."

Bariden thanked him for the tenth or eleventh time, and then we were finally able to leave. I wondered what he'd been after with his question, but when we reached the street I saw he was deep in thought. Rather than disturb a process that might come up with an idea to get us back to where we belonged, I decided to wait. I could always ask him about it later, and he'd probably only been trying to strengthen his assumed character anyway.

Walking down the block and across the street brought us to The Travelers' Hostel, and by then Bariden was back from the land of thought and paying attention. We walked inside to find a fairly plain entrance area in yellow-brown wood, with a counter to the back and a door in each wall to either side. Just beyond the door to the right was a staircase leading upward, and a heavyset redheaded woman in long skirts was just coming down. Her dress was a dark yellow that might have been meant to match the paneling, and when she saw us she smiled.

"What perfect timing," she said, heading directly for an opening in the counter. "I was hoping no one would have to wait while I was busy upstairs. May I help you young people?"

"We need rooms," Bariden said, closing the door before leading the way to the counter. "We're new in the city, and thought we should find a place to stay before we did anything else."

"That was a very wise decision," she said, reaching for a guest register. "With all the people in town to watch the competition tomorrow—you *do* know about the competition, don't you?"

"Whatever it is, I'm sure we'll have time to find out about it tomorrow," Bariden answered, sounding totally uninterested. "What we really need right now are rooms."

"Well, I have to say I thought you were already registered for the competition when you walked in here," she said, pausing in her checking of the guest register to get really friendly and chummy. "You *are* a magic user, after all, and magic users your age rarely come to the city for any other reason. You see—"

"How do you know he's a magic user?" I interrupted, not about to just let that pass. "Are you Sighted yourself, and that's why you can tell?"

Since I knew she *wasn't* Sighted, the question was far from idle. She hesitated a very brief moment, and then she smiled winningly again.

"No, dear, I'm not one of the lucky ones," she answered, then shifted her gaze back to Bariden. "But I've come to know the look of them, and this young man certainly has it. And I associate with so many of them, I've learned more about magic and those who use it than most. That's why I was saying—"

"If you know so much about magic, then maybe you can answer a question for us," Bariden said, taking his turn at interrupting the woman. "Has anyone ever mentioned how close the nearest gate is? And I don't mean city gates. What I'm interested in are gates having to do with magic."

"I've never heard anyone mention anything like that," she answered at once, all eagerness again. "If there *was* such a thing, the best ones to ask would be the sorcerers at the palace. And if you happen to be going there anyway—"

"Excuse me," Bariden interrupted again. "I know it's rude to keep cutting you off, but the lady and I are really tired and would appreciate those rooms. Tomorrow, after we've had a good night's sleep, we can all sit down together and talk."

"Tomorrow at breakfast, then," she grudged after a moment, trying not to look too disappointed, then returned her attention to the register. She looked through it, checked it a second time, then made a sound of annoyance. "Bother! I didn't realize it, but I'm afraid there's a problem. The afternoon clerk rented out more rooms than I'd thought."

"You're out of rooms?" Bariden asked, exchanging a surprised look with me. Personally I was more than surprised, since that wasn't the way we'd expected the game to go.

"Not completely," the woman answered with a headshake. "There's still one room left, and it happens to be a double. If you and the young lady know each other well enough to travel together, maybe you won't mind sharing a room for a night?"

The way she looked at Bariden was mild and very bland, but it was perfectly clear the next move was up to us. He glanced at me for the second time and I raised my brows to show I didn't understand either, but that seemed to help him make up his mind.

"If that's the only choice we have, we'll take it," he said to the woman. "How much do I owe you?"

"A silver piece," the woman answered, still playing bland. "That covers the room and either supper and breakfast, or breakfast and lunch tomorrow. Prices are always higher the night before a competition."

The woman really was persistent, but Bariden ignored the dangling hook and reached into an inside pocket of his swordbelt. The silver piece he produced was a trade coin, blank except for the stamp of a tiny scale exactly in the center of the obverse. That was supposed to tell anyone it was offered to that it should be checked for full weight before being accepted, but the woman didn't seem to know that. Or simply didn't care. The coin disappeared after she'd given it no more than a glance, and in its place she offered a key.

"Top floor, second door straight ahead on your right," she said, this time with a smile. "Rest well."

"Thank you," Bariden answered as he took the key, his arm around my shoulders then guiding me toward the stairs. We kept silent as we climbed to the third floor and found our room, and a moment later we were inside. After Bariden snapped his fingers to light a lamp, we could see that the room *was* slightly larger than average, with a big double bed, a settle, and an armchair. The bed was to the right of the door, and since it was a corner room, there were windows both opposite the door and to its left. Beyond the bed on the right wall was another door, possibly leading to a bathing room that would be shared with the room next to ours. The dark yellow drapes and carpeting weren't exactly shabby, the curtains and bed linen were almost white, and the quilts, armchair, and settle were just short of a rich brown. Not exactly luxury, but it could have been worse.

"So now we know they do want us to go to the palace," Bariden said after shutting the door and glancing around. "And they don't want us in separate rooms. Do you have any idea why that would be?"

"No more than about why they also want you in the competition," I said, walking over to the left to sit on the settle. "Unless you want to count the expression that woman was trying to cover. When she said, 'rest well,' it was almost as though what she really meant was, 'have fun.' I find it very difficult to believe that our enemy is trying to matchmake. Maybe there's a law against unmarried people sharing a room."

"And the woman just forgot to mention it to us," Bariden said with a nod as he removed his swordbelt, put it on a nearby table, and sat on the other end of the settle. "But that doesn't make much sense. If some official in this city decided to arrest us, who would bother to ask if we'd really done something? And not just bother, but have the nerve to?"

"And if they really do want you in the competition, why make it impossible by having you arrested?" I contributed. "For that matter, we could have been taken as soon as we stepped through the gate, even though that might have proven difficult. We *are* both strong magic users, after all, so maybe they were just being cautious. Or maybe it's something else entirely, and we can't see it because we really don't know what's going on."

The whole situation was annoying, and it needed a lot more than casual guesswork. It was time for some serious analytical thinking, and I do that best with a cup of coffee in my hand. As I'd done so often lately, I spoke the spell to create one, wrapped my fingers around the handle when it appeared—and then screamed with the pain shooting through my hand. It was terrible, as though I'd picked up a small ingot of metal hot from a forge, and it was all I could do to fling the cup away. It hit just beyond one edge of the dark yellow carpeting and shattered, splashing coffee in all directions.

"What happened?" Bariden demanded, suddenly right next to me and reaching for my hand. "Let me see that, Chalaine. Cradling it against your middle won't do any good."

Cradling the hand might not be doing any good, but that was all I was up to just then. Intense pain radiated out of it in waves, so strong it was making me sick to my stomach. Tears had formed in my eyes, my throat seemed capable of producing no more than moans and whimpers, and I couldn't stop rocking back and forth. From the way the hand felt I really didn't want to look at it, but Bariden refused to understand that.

"I said, let me see it," he insisted, his tone harder than it had been. "I can't do anything to help if I don't know what the problem is."

"The cup," I whispered, struggling to be coherent through continuing agony. "Hotter than Hellfire . . . must have burned . . . all the way in . . . going to be sick . . ."

"Chalaine, I'm not a true healer," he said, right hand now against my forehead. "I need a visual scan in order to do anything, so you *have* to let me look at it. I promise to be as careful as possible, and you can close your eyes. That's probably the best idea, so you go ahead and close them. I'll do the looking for both of us."

At another time I might have complained about being babied, but having a hand that feels seared down to the bone can change your mind about a lot of things. Rather than argue any more I did close my eyes, then let *him* move the hand. He did it gently with his grip above my wrist, and then he was silent for a moment.

"You're not going to believe this," he said after the moment. "I thought your spell might have been just enough off to cause too much heat, and since I wasn't listening, it was perfectly possible. Now, though . . . Chalaine, there's nothing wrong with your hand. It isn't burned at all."

He was right about my not believing him, and before I stopped to think about it I'd opened my eyes. From the way my hand felt it should have been ruined, charred black all the way down through the red of exposed flesh and the white of bone. Instead it looked just the way it always had, except for the curl of fingers into a claw because of the pain . . .

"That . . . isn't possible," I whispered, fighting to clear my mind enough to think. "The pain . . . it's still there!"

The look in the light eyes staring at me was pure confusion, liberally laced with frustration and helplessness. There was nothing wrong with my hand but I was still in agony, and there didn't seem to be a way to stop it. Then Bariden's expression changed, and he turned his head fast to look past me at the cup I'd dropped.

"Maybe—maybe *that's* it," he muttered, and then he raised his own hand in a banishing gesture. The broken cup and every drop of coffee disappeared, and then—so did the pain! Oh, I still felt an aching through my hand and arm, but that was just an echo of abused nerve endings. As soon as they settled down . . .

"What is going *on* here?" I demanded weakly. "The pain has stopped, but I don't understand what you did."

"What I did was make a lucky guess," he said, urging me to rest my head against him until I got some strength back. Strong pain can be exhausting, and he seemed to know that. "Everyone keeps saying how many magic users there are in this city, but business is still going on as usual. That combination *wouldn't* be usual, unless there are some very special circumstances. Do you remember what that man said, the one who knew about the questions the screaming man had asked? It was something about *permitted* magic."

"Yes, I do remember now," I said with a frown, forcing myself to lean away from him. There *is* such a thing as being *too* comfortable . . . "He also said something about it not being the decision of the people in this city to use nothing *but* that. There has to be a spell prohibiting everything not authorized."

"And creating your own food and drink has to be high on the list of forbidden things," he agreed, letting me go with what seemed to be reluctance. "The unSighted here have to be able to make a living, and if the Sighted provide for themselves in most things, that won't happen. Are you sure you're feeling strong enough to sit alone?"

"In another minute or so I'll be fine," I assured him, already gently flexing my fingers. The muscles hurt from bracing so hard against the pain, but that would be gone soon, too. "So when I called up that cup of coffee, I was breaking the law. How did you know that banishing what I'd created would also end the prescribed automatic punishment?"

"As I said, I didn't know, I was only hoping." His smile was more relieved than satisfied, and his hand came to smooth my hair. "We were told intent makes the difference here, and it wasn't your intention to do this hostel out of its rightful income. You simply made a mistake, and correcting that mistake showed you'd learned your lesson. It might not be as easy to get out of trouble a second time, but apparently first mistakes are dealt with rather leniently."

"That wasn't *my* idea of lenient," I assured him, feeling the urge to shudder at memory of what I'd gone through. "But now I think I understand why that woman who registered us didn't bother to check the silver you gave her. If the coin wasn't up to full weight *you* would have known it, and knowing it would have made your intention one to defraud. If you didn't immediately fall down rolling and screaming, you were obviously honest."

"I just thought of something else," he said, even as he nodded his agreement. "The warding we've got protecting us—either passive spells don't set it off, or we're not as well protected as we expected to be. Right now I'd rather not guess which."

"It's possible I'll be warded against a passive spell *next* time, but I'd rather not test the theory this second," I said, leaning my head back on the settle. "I've never been in a place where magic users aren't free to do whatever their skill level allows, and I don't like it. I also feel as if I'm not considered trustworthy enough to abide by whatever rules this place has without coercion, and that I *certainly* don't like. If someone had bothered to say something, I would have ordered that coffee from the kitchen rather than calling it up."

"But not everyone has your sense of right and wrong," he told me, leaning just a little closer. "Magic users are just as good or bad as anyone else, and a certain number of them would still do as they pleased no matter what the rules were. And you forget we're supposed to *know* the rules, even though we don't. You're not being considered untrustworthy, Chalaine, no one alive would think of you as that."

The last of his words had come out in a murmur, and the next moment his lips touched mine in a gentle kiss. By rights I should have stopped things there and at the very least pushed him away, but I suddenly discovered I couldn't do it. I *wanted* him to kiss me, as much as I wanted to kiss him back, and as soon as I did, his arms were around me. He pulled me close and held me tight as we tasted each other thoroughly, but after a pair of moments he pulled his head back to frown at me.

"I'm suddenly hoping very hard that there *are* no laws against people who aren't married sharing a room," he said. "What we discussed earlier about being arrested— it's occurred to me that arresting people is unnecessary, when breaking the law brings immediate punishment. I don't know if I have the right to ask you to try."

"But we're already sharing a room and nothing's happened," I pointed out, trying to tease away the worry in those very light eyes. "Are you saying you don't consider me worth taking a risk for?"

"I never said anything like that and you know it," he countered, now looking at me with a sternness that was trying to slip into a grin. "If that's what I was worried about, I'd make you sleep in the hall. Which I may have to do anyway. At this point I'm fairly certain I'll never be able to trust myself."

The urge to grin had left him, just as if he were the only one involved. And he'd also let me go, which was doubly annoying.

"Hasn't anyone ever told you the facts of life?" I asked, sitting straighter on the settle. "Making up a girl's mind for her is rude, whether you do it by attacking her or by bowing out gracefully. Since I'd supposedly be a full participant in whatever you originally had in mind, I'm entitled to a say in whether or not we try it. Or am I just making foolish assumptions, because your plans were based on solitary actions?"

"Why are you angry?" he asked in turn, part of my annoyance touching him as well. "Of course you were a part of my plans, but that's just the point. They were *my* plans, and I have no right to put you in jeopardy because of them. And I thought women *liked* a man who considered them before himself. You're making my concern sound like a crime."

"There's a big difference between concern and unilaterally deciding what's best," I returned, then realized I was wasting my time. "I know you're probably used to being in charge of what goes on around you, but you should have noticed by now that I've gotten used to the same thing. I think we'd better call it a night and get some sleep. With the competition being held tomorrow, it's bound to be a big day."

"All right," he agreed, settling on that after starting to say something else and changing his mind. "I suppose this isn't the best of times to argue opposing philosophies. But we do have something that needs to be discussed before we turn in. We'll head for the palace right after breakfast tomorrow, and see if it's possible to get in without becoming involved in the competition. Somehow, I doubt it."

"I have the same feeling," I agreed reluctantly, moving to the edge of the settle but not standing. "If everything happening is aimed toward that competition, they'd hardly leave so big a loophole."

"And that means we have to come up with a plan that will keep us together," he said, leaning forward to stare down at his folded hands. "I intend besting whoever I have to face even if that isn't part of *their* plan, which means *I'll* end up being admitted to the palace. What will we do if they try to say I can't bring my woman in with me?"

"So that's why you asked that innkeep the question," I said, finally understanding. "You were anticipating a possible problem. But don't you see, that shouldn't be a problem at all. I also intend besting whoever I come up against, so I'll have my own invitation into the palace."

"What do you mean, whoever *you* come up against?" he asked, raising those eyes to look directly at me. "Since you aren't entering the competition, you won't be coming up against anyone."

"Of course I'm entering," I said with a small laugh. "I didn't press the point with that provincial innkeep, but I'm not about to let childish threats keep me from doing what I have to. For all I care, they can threaten to sauté me with onions if I lose. I don't intend to lose."

"Neither of us intended to get trapped in a circuit of strange worlds, but it happened anyway," he countered, his tone and stare a good deal sharper. "What happens if you *do* lose, and you're forced to pay the price? I think it's safe to say you won't be able to overcome the spell that's designed to uphold that law, so what will you do?"

"What do you think?" I asked with a snort. "If I can't get out of that stupid penalty, I'll have to pay it. Since I'm not an innocent child it's hardly likely to kill me, even if it turns out to be distasteful in the extreme. But maybe it won't be distasteful, maybe I'll like it. At least I won't have a partner who's worried about breaking the law."

He stiffened at that, but I wasn't sorry I'd said it. For a man who was supposedly so interested in me, Bariden was awfully easy to discourage. It looked very much as though he *thought* he should be interested, so that was the way he acted even if he actually felt differently. He was doing a good job fooling himself, but not quite as good fooling me.

"You also would not have a partner who cared about you," he said very flatly after a moment. "No matter how easy you try to make it sound, letting a strange man use your body can't be a lark for any woman. But you won't have to worry about it, because it's not going to happen. I'll be the only one of us entering the competition, and we'll find another way to get you into the palace."

"Really," I said, getting slowly to my feet to look down at him. "And how do you expect to stop me from entering? If I needed anyone's permission the innkeep would have said so, and he didn't. Are you in the mood to test out my warding after all?"

Rather than answering immediately he also stood, which then made it necessary for me to look up. Because of that he might have been expecting a lessening of the belligerence I'd been showing, but if so he was disappointed. I've never backed down from someone bigger than me in an argument or fight, and I never will. Just to make sure he understood that, I also put my fists on my hips.

"Do you have any idea how tempting you make the thought of cold-blooded murder?" he asked then, his voice nearly a growl. "No matter what I say to you, you consider it a personal insult or a flat-footed challenge. Or a comment that can be ignored because you're convinced I don't really mean it. How am I supposed to make you understand that I don't want you to do certain things because I care about you? I'm not trying to run your life, I'm trying to save it!"

"Is that because lifesaving is a hobby of yours, or because you don't believe I'm capable of doing the job myself?" I countered at once. "Of all the lame excuses there are, 'I'm doing it for your own good' is the worst. Why don't you do us both a favor, and find someone else to protect. I'm not the kind who appreciates that sort of thing."

I turned my back on his frown of confusion and walked away, too upset to let that conversation continue. Every time he tried to make it sound as if I really meant something to him, all he proved was that he was doing his duty to someone smaller and more helpless. If he'd really felt anything for me he wouldn't have found it so easy to pull back after that kiss, using me as an excuse for his worry. It was himself he was worried about, which he wouldn't have been if things were the way he claimed . . .

I headed for the door that should lead to the bathing chamber, silently cursing the attraction *I* felt. If I didn't pay attention to what was happening we might never get out of that trap, but all I could think about right then was light blue eyes, blond hair, broad shoulders, muscled arms, a wide chest—Thoughts going in that direction would never lead to escape, and I suddenly understood why only one room had been available. Too bad they hadn't realized what they were dealing with where Bariden was concerned . . .

I snapped my fingers to light a lamp in the bathing chamber, then closed the door firmly behind me. If—no, *when* I got out of there and found the one who had done that to me, not even the possibility of his being a wizard would save him. Or her. Or it. I sat down on the tile floor and closed my eyes, intending to wait until Bariden was asleep before coming out. It would be better if I stayed away from arguing with *him*, but I pitied whoever I'd face in the competition tomorrow. With the enemy out of reach I needed a substitute to practice on, to show just how I felt about what was happening. And I *would* show it, no matter how skeptical my gallant traveling companion continued to be . . .

Bariden stood staring until Chalaine slammed the door to the bathing chamber, then he closed his eyes and rubbed them with the fingers of one hand. He had no idea what had just happened between them, except that it hadn't been an example of the closeness he'd been hoping for. One minute they'd been a step away from making love, and the next—

"I just don't *understand* her," he muttered, sitting back down to let out a long, slow breath. "How can it be a crime to care what happens to her?"

Nothing in the way of answers came in a blinding flash, which left Bariden exactly where he'd been: floundering in confusion. If he'd ever refused to touch Miralia because he was worried about her, she would have been delighted. Chalaine had come down insulted instead, and had all but drawn a line on the carpeting and dared him to step over it. For such a pretty little thing, she could be incredibly belligerent . . .

And it was obvious she still didn't believe his feelings for her were real. Or was back to disbelieving it. For a while things had gotten so much better, and then they'd come through to *that* world. He'd sometimes wondered what it would be like if most people were Sighted rather than not, but hadn't managed to picture what it would have to be like. Laws against unauthorized use of magic, laws to protect the unSighted and their businesses, all of it brought about by wizard-strength spells. And the wizard, who was also king, needing to protect himself from constant challenges for his position . . .

That had to be why there were also constant competitions, he told himself as he stretched out his legs. Take the best coming forward and assimilate them, put them in a position where they can either learn loyalty to the present ruler, or be watched closely if loyalty was beyond them. It wasn't a life he himself would have enjoyed, especially if he were the king. The need to decide what could and couldn't be done, what should and shouldn't be allowed . . . and who would or wouldn't be admitted into service . . .

"What reason could he possibly have for making that rule about women?" Bariden muttered, his gaze drifting to the door Chalaine had closed between them. The innkeep's reason, that women didn't take competition as seriously as men, was ridiculous. If anything, women who competed took things *more* seriously, and any man who didn't understand that usually ended up getting plowed under. Bariden could remember a few he'd taken weapons training with; most of the women had worked harder and had gotten to be better than most of the men they'd started with. If it wasn't the same with magic, there wouldn't be as many female wizards as there were.

No, there had to be something else involved, and Chalaine was about to walk into it with both eyes shut tight. She'd been told, in effect, to be a good little girl and mind her own business, so naturally she'd immediately decided to prove just how good a little girl she really was. She'd done the same thing two worlds back against that magician, but here the stakes were so much higher . . .

And there was nothing Bariden could do to stop her, even if what he wanted to do was knock her down, sit on her, and make her listen to reason. They were dealing with someone who knew them, so her reaction might not only be expected but actually planned for. He'd have to mention that tomorrow, and hope she'd be calmed down enough to listen. Otherwise . . .

Otherwise she could end up having no choice about giving her body to some stranger. Bariden knew he'd never be able to stand by and just let that happen, not even if it meant killing the other man to prevent it. No matter what she claimed, the Chalaine he was coming to know would be hurt by needing to do something like that, and he refused to let anyone hurt her. And that was probably the reaction they were expecting from *him*, which closed the circle nicely. And most likely into a noose, which would then be around both their necks.

Bariden spent a few minutes cursing softly, but it didn't do any more good than he'd expected. They were headed ever more deeply into the trap, with nothing in sight that could possibly be a way out. And he still hadn't managed to convince one small girl that he really cared about her.

He was covering himself with more glory every time he turned around, but he didn't know how to stop it or change it. How *did* you make a girl believe you were serious about her? Present her with a sworn statement to that effect? Write bad poetry for her?

Bariden sighed as he stretched out on the settle, leaving the bed for Chalaine to use. The settle wasn't long enough for him, but he'd manage to make do. He'd need as much sleep as he could get if he'd be competing tomorrow, and there wasn't much doubt about *that*. He and Chalaine both . . . even if he would have to kill someone if she lost . . . when all he wanted was *her*, smiling at him and telling him she loved having his arms around her . . . she was so different, so special . . . why, of all the women in the worlds, was *she* able to resist him so easily . . . ? Maybe tomorrow he'd ask . . .

CHAPTER TEN

The next morning had only one thing in its favor: by having breakfast brought up to their room, they avoided the conversation they were supposed to have had with the redheaded woman. Bariden felt stiff from having slept on the settle, and although Chalaine had been in the bed when he'd awakened, she didn't look as though she'd had a much better night. They took turns bathing before getting back into their magically freshened clothes—a preset spell they'd both had the foreSight to use—and for the time they washed and ate, not a single word was exchanged. While they were still at the table Bariden decided to change that and began to speak, only to find Chalaine doing the same thing at the same time.

"I'm sorry," Bariden added at once to the confused silence they'd also begun to share. "I didn't know you wanted to say something. Please go ahead."

"I think there's a law that requires me to insist that *you* go first," she told him with a faint, wry smile. "In spite of that, though, I'm going to accept your offer. What I have to say *should* be said first."

He nodded to encourage her, but she paused to sip at her coffee before bringing her gaze back to him.

"About last night," she said, sounding as though she were forcing the words out. "I've been thinking, and I've come to the conclusion that I owe you an apology. If I'd been the one who didn't want to have sex and *you'd* made comments about the decision, I would have been up in arms with outrage. The plain truth is, it doesn't matter why you refused. I should have accepted—and respected—the fact that you did, rather than give you a hard time over it. I apologize, and promise not to let it happen again."

"I don't believe you said that," Bariden stated, feeling the next thing to stunned. "There's not a woman anywhere who would look at it like that—! Chalaine, this time you have to listen to *me*. Not taking you to bed was one of the hardest things I've ever done, and if the choice had been mine it never would have happened. If not for this stupid world and the fact that we *have* to find a way out of it, there would have been nothing for us to argue about. Or at least I hope there would have been nothing."

He grinned in an effort to lighten the heavy unhappiness he could see in her, but the smile she responded with was still on the faint side.

"There probably wouldn't have been arguing as far as the sex was concerned," she answered, toying with a crumb on the table. "I think we find each other physically attractive enough that we'd be satisfied. But that's not to say we'd have nothing to argue about. I'm still entering the competition today, and that's something I *won't* be changing my mind about."

"Woman, you have to be the stubbornest being in the entire universe," Bariden growled, instantly filled with insult and outrage. "And you get me so crazy, I don't even know which idea of yours to argue first. If you did so much thinking, you should have spent some of it on our situation."

"What's *that* supposed to mean?" she began, obviously getting ready to bristle up, but Bariden didn't care to be interrupted.

"To start with," he plowed on, "I haven't taken a woman to bed for *sex* since I was a boy. What I expected to do was make love, and with a woman who means something to me. If all I wanted was sex, there are more than enough women around willing to give it to me. I'm scarcely so hard up that I have to take advantage of the woman I happen to be trapped with."

She parted her lips to interrupt, but Bariden still wasn't ready to let it happen.

"In the second place, you seem to have forgotten the discussion we had about the enemy knowing us," he ground out. "We decided he doesn't know us as well as he thinks he does, but how well does that have to be to know how you get when you feel talked down to? If you're not *expected* to enter the competition no matter what anyone says, there's nothing in these worlds you *are* expected to do. Go ahead and argue *that*."

She hesitated a moment, apparently considering what he'd said, then shook her head.

"Your idea is an interesting one, but it doesn't hold water," she counterstated. "Most of the time when people challenge me, either I ignore it or else I agree with whatever they're using to start the argument. That usually stops the disagreement on *my* terms, and leaves them with a win that's as far from satisfying as you can get. Would you like to tell me how *that* fits into what you said? It's not quite the same point of view."

Bariden took his turn at thinking for a moment, but what she'd said was true. Getting belligerent *wasn't* her usual way of responding to things, which left him with even more of a problem.

"Now I really don't understand," he admitted, leaning back to frown at her. "I'm as sure as I can be that your entering the competition is a trap, but it *doesn't* fit in with the way you usually act. Even Bena mentioned your habit of winning arguments by refusing to argue, so what's all this supposed to mean? Could the enemy have been watching us, and set this up in response to the new way you've been acting?"

"That would be giving the enemy more credit than I believe he deserves," Chalaine answered with a headshake, sipping at the last of her coffee. "Personally I think I'm supposed to play it safe and *not* enter, and only afterward would we discover that I wasn't allowed to enter the palace with you. That would give us a good-sized problem, and one we might not be able to think our way out of."

"Especially if they have it set up that anyone accepted either goes along with them on the spot or not at all," Bariden grudged. "That would really set the icing, but it doesn't explain my feeling. If the trap lies in your *not* entering, why do I still feel so strongly that that's the last thing you *should* do?"

"Maybe because it's the last thing you *want* me to do," she told him gently and almost with pity. "Bariden, I'm sure you do care about me as a companion in this mess, but you're trying to make yourself believe your feelings go beyond that. You've told yourself you're a man who's deeply interested in a woman, and what man in that position *wouldn't* worry about the woman's safety? You seem to believe that the more worried you are, the deeper your feelings have to be. Isn't it possible that *that's* where any personal trap lies, in *your* reactions rather than mine? Don't most people know how you prefer to think and act with the women you become involved with?"

Her dark satin eyes refused to let his go, at least until he answered her questions. Bariden toyed with the idea of getting up, walking out, and finding someone to get into a serious fight with, but that wasn't the time to indulge in basic pleasures.

"All right, so maybe people *do* know how I like to think about and act with women," he allowed with no grace whatsoever. "That has nothing to do with the fact that I'm *not* telling myself all sorts of fairy tales. I *do* know how I feel about you, and all the gentle disagreement in this world or any other won't talk me out of it. Without that main point *your* theory falls apart, so where does that leave us?"

"Still chasing our tails," she answered with a sigh as she stood. "Why don't we take a break from it by asking some of the questions we need answers to. If any of the answers don't turn out as expected, we may find that loophole we've been looking for. And the next time using personal magic *isn't* against the law, remind me to call up a hairbrush. This braid has already put permanent knots in my hair, and it can only get worse."

She threw the braid in question over her shoulder, then headed for the door. Bariden, about to offer to buy her a hairbrush, abruptly understood that she'd surely refuse to allow that. They only had a limited amount of money with them, and if they spent it on nonessentials and then couldn't leave that world, they'd have no opportunity to make more.

When you're forbidden to call up a cup of coffee, you're certainly not going to be allowed to produce gold or silver. Bariden cursed that world under his breath—not to mention what was proving to be a pitiful lack of foreSight on *their* part—and then followed her out.

They were able to leave the hostel without running into the redheaded woman who was probably the hostler, and once they were out in the streets the crowds quickly swallowed them up. Even at that early hour it seemed as if the entire city was awake and on the move, but the moving part didn't work very well. Bariden's questions about the location of the palace got him directions, but he and Chalaine had to fight their way through the throngs to use them.

Once they got close enough to their destination, the crowds started to thin. Only a handful of people seemed to have business at the palace, and none of them were Sighted. Bariden and Chalaine stood and watched for a few moments, taking the time to study the square and blocky building. Most palaces were like Bariden's father's, light and beautiful or dark and beautiful, but at the very least beautiful. This palace, though . . .

"It looks like it's made up of nothing but dungeons," Chalaine remarked, almost reading his mind. "Those five steps leading up to the central doors may stretch all the way across the front, but they look more like a barrier than a means of ingress. It's all so—gray."

"And a medium gray at that," Bariden agreed in a murmur. "Maybe it's meant to discourage people, to lead them to believe there's nothing inside that anyone could possibly want. Magic users are as vulnerable to suggestion as anyone else, so the effort would serve a double purpose."

"Yeah, to keep out all undesirables, magic users as well as thieves," Chalaine muttered back. "I'm not welcome in there, and the feeling isn't my imagination."

"No, it must be another spell," Bariden agreed, still studying the large gray edifice. "I feel the same thing, and there's no doubt to the impression. I wonder if we'll be able to make it over to talk to one of those guards."

Chalaine inspected the four or five guardsmen visible from where they stood, as though measuring the distances between them. The guardsmen were positioned just in front of those barrier steps, about thirty feet separating one from the next. Far enough apart to keep them from having conversations, close enough for each of them to support any of the others.

"We'll know if we can make it over to them once we try," she answered, then turned a little to take Bariden's hand. "You be the big, brave contest entrant, and I'll be the poor little girl just tagging along to keep you company."

"There's a chance they might suspect something if we do it the other way around," Bariden murmured as he got ready to lead the way. "For some reason most people refuse to think of me as a poor little girl."

The glance she sent him said he wasn't amusing, but in full truth Bariden hadn't been trying to be. He wasn't the one who had made the laws in that city, but every now and then Chalaine treated him as if the entire situation was his fault. He might have done the same if the situation were reversed, but that didn't make unearned blame any easier to live with. Bariden felt abused, and that wasn't something he enjoyed having to deal with.

There was a wide stone approach between the last of the shops and buildings and the place where the guardsmen stood, and Bariden led Chalaine across it slowly. The spell telling them they were unwelcome grew gradually stronger, so by the time they reached the guardsman Bariden had chosen, they were both sweating with effort. The easiest thing would have been to turn around and go back, but then they would have had to do without their answers. Chalaine's hand tightened its grip on his before they were halfway there, but even when they reached the guardsman she still hadn't said a word.

"Excuse me," Bariden said to the guardsman, fighting to act as if nothing was trying to tear him into small pieces. "I understand there's a competition that's going to be held today. Can you tell me where entrants sign up?"

"Entrants sign up right here, starting at two this afternoon," the guardsman answered lazily, all but drawling. The look in his dark eyes said he knew Bariden was suffering, an idea that was vastly amusing to him. "Competition starts at three on the dot, and any not here have to wait until next week."

"Three o'clock on the dot," Bariden echoed with a nod. "And those entrants who win the competition and are accepted into the king's service—they can bring their fiancées into the palace with them, can't they? I mean, if their fiancées have nowhere else to go?"

"Winners don't even get to bring in wives, not until after they get through the first of their training," the man answered after a short pause. He also looked Chalaine over in a way Bariden didn't care for, and then the man grinned. "If you win and don't have anywhere to leave her, come and see *me*. I'll take real good care of her for you."

"What about simply visiting the palace?" Chalaine asked before Bariden could stiffen all the way in insult. "Are there times when people are allowed in just to look around and see where the king lives?"

"It's none of anyone's business where the king lives, honey," the guardsman answered, his eyes moving over her as he spoke. "But even if people *were* allowed in, your boyfriend wouldn't be one of them. He'd have to get past the spell first, and it gets a lot worse before it gets better. If he really means to enter the competition, you'd better get him away from here now. If you don't, he won't be in any shape to so much as light a candle."

The man's expression under his round metal helmet was bland, but his eyes were still showing that enjoyment. He wore boiled leather armor with patches of ring mail, a sheathed sword and dagger, and leaned on a glaive. His attitude said Bariden's magic couldn't touch him, and Bariden's sword wasn't even to be considered. Bariden thought he was wrong on both counts, but before he could say so Chalaine tugged on his hand.

"Sweetheart, I'm sure the nice man knows what he's talking about," she said in a voice that proclaimed her to be young and not very bright. "If we want everybody to see what you can do, we'd better get you away from here now and to a place where you can rest. We've been enough trouble, so let's go."

Her hand squeezed his with the word "trouble," reminding him that they still didn't know all about how the law worked in that place. If he did the wrong thing he could trigger a protective spell, and that might be the end of his effort to get into the palace.

But he couldn't just turn tail and run away, not and still have any respect for himself. That guard had been laughing at him . . . Bariden straightened where he stood and locked eyes with the man. All knowledge of what the exclusion spell was doing to him was banished from his awareness, leaving nothing but the central core that made him what he was. He started at the guardsman, showing the man what sort of potential opponent he'd been toying with, and the guardsman suddenly lost his amusement. When the man swallowed hard, almost ready to retreat from the stare, Bariden was finally satisfied.

"Thank you for your help," he said softly with no inflection whatsoever, then turned and led Chalaine away. It was all he could do not to run back to where he'd be out of range of the exclusion spell, but he managed to keep himself to the same slow walk he'd used approaching. Rather than stop where they'd stood before, he continued on until they were around the corner and only then did he pause to slump against a wall.

"I'll say," Chalaine agreed, matching his slump with her back to the same wall. "They must change the range of that for the competition, otherwise I can't imagine there ever *being* a competition. And I hope you feel better now."

"Better about what?" he asked, resting most of his weight on his right shoulder, which in turn rested against the wall.

"Not better about, better than," she corrected, looking up at him with curiosity. "You and that guardsman both knew you couldn't make trouble, but he still let you back him down. You didn't like it when he teased you about looking after me, but after he backed down you seemed to feel better than you had. Considering how much trouble we could have been given, I also hope the effort was worth it."

"You're not by any chance scolding me, are you?" Bariden asked, suddenly very amused. "You must be forgetting I'm the one who *does* the scolding, just as I've always been. I never had to be scolded even as a child."

"A strange thing happens when you stop being a child," she returned dryly, folding her arms. "People change, only sometimes they're the last to notice it. The way you behaved just now was *not* like someone who's never even had a scolding. You just about threatened that guardsman, and you enjoyed doing it. Would you have enjoyed it as much if it had caused us to be stuck here?"

"You *are* scolding me," Bariden said with a laugh, suddenly realizing it wasn't for the first time. Back home he'd always had to be so careful not to do anything wrong, not even to do anything someone might possibly *consider* wrong. He was a prince of a well-respected house, but too capable a prince when you considered that he wasn't his father's heir. The rumors about him had always been filled with fear, so he'd had to go out of his way to be absolutely correct. It would never do to make people *really* afraid of him . . .

But that was just what he'd done with that guardsman, and he'd done it on purpose. He'd *demanded* respect and he'd gotten it, but the act of demanding had felt better than the respect. It was a freedom he'd never been allowed before, a freedom everyone else in the worlds seemed to take for granted. Never mind what other people think, just go ahead and do what's right. Rely on your own judgment and *trust* it . . .

"Would I have enjoyed it if I'd caused us to be stuck here?" Bariden echoed her last question with a smile. "No, I wouldn't have enjoyed that sort of an outcome, but since it didn't happen let's not worry about it. And I've decided you're absolutely right, you do have to enter the competition. I still don't like the idea and you'd better make damned sure you don't get hurt, but we've been given no choice. If we don't get into the palace—legitimately!—and find that gate, neither of us will stay out of trouble long enough to get an *eventual* chance. We move fast, or we won't find it possible to move at all."

"If you're saying that just to get out of a scolding, consider the effort a success," Chalaine told him with her brows high. "I'll admit I never expected you to change your mind, but I'm very glad you did. It's been clear from the start that we have to cooperate to get out of this, and cooperation between us hasn't been easy yet."

"I have a feeling it will soon become a *lot* easier," Bariden assured her, then pulled her to him for a quick kiss to which she didn't have time to react before he released her again. "And now you can take me back to the hostel for the rest I'm supposed to be getting, which you'll join me for. We have an appointment for this afternoon, and we don't want to be late."

He grinned as he held up his hand for her to take, and wasn't surprised when she ignored the hand and simply started back to their temporary quarters. Her beautiful dark eyes had gotten even wider than usual from the kiss he'd given her, and she didn't seem to know how to react to what he'd done. Well, that was all right. He'd gotten a very interesting idea, more of a theory, really, but if it turned out to be right she'd have a good deal more to be startled about. Yes, a good deal more, and she'd never be able to say she hadn't asked for it . . .

When we got back to the hostel we stopped in the dining room for coffee, Bariden's suggestion, which was more like an order. I didn't argue, and not only because I needed the coffee even more than usual. In less than an hour the man had somehow changed, and I was still trying to figure out in what way. And that kiss he'd given me—even the one we'd shared the night before had somehow been mild in comparison . . .

"We'd better spend some time thinking up individual strategy," Bariden said after the coffee had been put in front of us and the serving girl had left. "This time we'll be facing equals or superiors, so we'd better be prepared."

"They'd better not be much superior, or we'll be in trouble," I pointed out after sipping from my cup. Strangely enough the coffee in that world was at least as good as what I usually called up for myself, which was one small high spot among a forest of lows. It didn't help all that much to know I'd have what to drink if we ended up stuck there.

"I was once told by a wizard that where magic is concerned, attitude counts almost as much as skill," he answered, folding his arms on the table in front of him as he studied me. "If you believe you have no chance against your opponent you won't have, even if you happen to be better than him. Of

course, attitude won't win a confrontation against someone
with a *lot* more strength, but we won't be facing that except,
possibly, in the final encounter with the resident sorcerers.
But keep in mind that even there we have an edge. Some
people get lazy and sloppy when they consider their own
skill level in comparison to a novice. We're supposed to
be the novices here, so we'll be underestimated. Let's take
all the advantage of that we can."

I nodded to show I understood what he was talking about,
and in actual truth I wasn't all that worried about whoever
I would face. At Conclave you're sometimes given the
chance to measure yourself against the stronger wizards,
but not just for fun. At the end of the encounter the wizard
usually whaps you good, but you come away having learned
something. What I really had to guard against was being the
fool who stepped forward filled with *over*confidence . . .

"So *there* you are," a delighted female voice said, and
then the redheaded woman was at our table and sitting
down. "For a while I thought you might be avoiding me."

"After you've been so nice to us?" Bariden countered
with a smile, answering the coy charge that had been aimed
solely at him. "I'd never do anything like that, at least if I
could help it. The girl and I had to go out early this morning,
but now we're back and ready for that conversation."

"And just in time," the woman said with a smile as she
leaned toward him. "There's a competition being held this
afternoon that you *have* to enter, otherwise your visit to
this city will be over and they'll ask you to leave. At least
I'm assuming they'll ask you to leave. You *are* sorcerer
strength, aren't you?"

"Yes, it so happens I am," Bariden agreed with raised
brows. "But why would that be the cause of their asking
me to leave? Even if I miss the competition, I don't have
any plans to break the law."

"But that's just the point," she said with a certain amount
of anxiety. "If you stay past the time of the competition
without entering, you *will* be breaking the law. People of
sorcerer-level skill and higher aren't allowed to stay in the
city for more than a day and a night. If they stayed longer
they might make trouble, and the king doesn't like it when
people make trouble. Since you got here last evening, your

day and a night is up *this* evening. If you haven't entered the competition and won, you have to be gone by then."

Bariden exchanged a glance with me, probably thinking the same thing I was. The innkeep from the night before had said something about how expensive it was to live in the city for a week. He'd said that right after telling Bariden how good his luck was, because he'd arrived the day before a competition. *He* hadn't said anything about it being illegal for sorcerers to stay in the city, and when you came right down to it, who else would be entering the competition? Those with lesser skill would certainly lose, so why would they bother? And the woman also hadn't mentioned there would be another competition in a week . . .

"I hope you don't mind my asking this," Bariden said to her, "but why are you so concerned? You don't know us, so why would you care if we did get thrown out?"

"Now *that's* a question with an interesting answer," the woman replied with a sudden grin. "It also happens to be the reason I was able to buy this hostel. There will be a lot of betting during the competition, a lot of gold and silver changing hands. If you happen to know more about a particular contestant than everyone else, the gold and silver moves to *your* hand. The last time I felt this way about someone and bet on him, I won enough to buy this place. This time I could make enough to pay my taxes for a year *and* have this place redecorated. But I'll only win it if you compete, because I know *you'll* win. Will you believe me enough to take the chance?"

She was looking at him with such earnestness it was difficult to *dis*believe her, which was obviously the way it was supposed to go. If we hadn't known she was telling us only what she wanted us to learn . . .

"You know, all this talk about a competition for sorcerers has made me curious," I said, forcing her to shift her attention from Bariden. "What exactly will my friend get if he does win? If it's good enough, I might decide to enter myself."

"If you like wasting your time, go right ahead," the woman said with a shrug and a neutral smile. "What a man wins in the competition is a chance to be trained to work with the king, the best place there is *below* being king. A woman, though—the king doesn't think much of women, so if one of them happens to win, he rides her until she gets disgusted and leaves. Even if she doesn't leave, she isn't taught much and doesn't ever move up in rank. I've heard from one or two who tried it that a job as a chambermaid would be a better deal. So what do you say, good-looking? Are you going to make an effort to move into the palace?"

The last, of course, was addressed to Bariden, and he smiled faintly as he leaned back.

"I'll have to think about it for a while, but I'll probably go for it," he conceded. "What time is this thing, and how do you register for it?"

"The competition itself is at three o'clock, but you have to be there to register by two," she answered, now excited as well as delighted. "I am *so* glad you're being sensible, and just to prove it, I'll place a small wager for *you*. It won't hurt you to have a few extra coins in your pocket while you're training. You go upstairs now and get some rest, and I'll have you called in time to eat lunch before you leave. Come on, now, take that cup with you and go."

Bariden let her chase him out of the dining room, and I, naturally, went with him. The room was to the right of the front door as you enter, so we turned right again when we left and went up to our room. As soon as we were inside Bariden finished his coffee, put the cup aside, took off his swordbelt, then stretched out on the bed.

"After spending the night on that settle, I can use a couple of hours of comfort," he said, moving a little to maximize that comfort. "I'm also going to be thinking about attack strategy, and you might want to do the same. Unless you've changed your mind about entering."

His words weren't precisely a question, but I still shook my head.

"Not after hearing our friend with the red hair describe what a good deal it is," I said as I sat in a chair. "Her entire attitude was calculated to kill any interest I might have in competing, especially since I'm not the crusading type. If someone makes it clear I'm not wanted somewhere, I usually leave and don't go back. If we hadn't asked some questions before listening to her, I probably would have shrugged and sat back to wait for *you* to win."

"Which I probably *will* do," he said, tucking his hands behind his head. "I don't expect it to be easy, but if I show even moderate creativity I should have very little trouble. At that point we would be forced to separate, something they've been trying to accomplish all along. Want to bet that if I tried to refuse going into the palace alone, I'd permanently lose the chance to go in at all?"

"I never bet against a virtual sure thing," I said with a grimace. "Then we'd be left with the choice of plowing through that exclusion spell, or giving up and settling down here. I'm not too crazy about either option."

"If there wasn't important, unfinished business behind us, I doubt if I'd mind one of those choices," he murmured, but when I looked at him sharply his eyes were closed. "But why settle for just the cake when you can have *it* and the icing as well? Get some rest now, and try to do some thinking."

I didn't comment aloud on what he'd said, but one point came clear immediately: with what he'd given me to think about, I wasn't likely to get much rest.

I ended up stretching out on the settle for a while, but wasn't even nodding when the knock came at our door. I opened it to find a housemaid bringing the news that lunch was ready, and by that time Bariden was up and stretching. The housemaid went back down and in a few minutes we followed her, but lunch was very quiet. Bariden seemed lost in his thoughts, I tried to avoid mine, and the redheaded woman was nowhere to be seen.

As soon as we were through eating, we headed back to the palace. There were fractionally fewer people in the streets, so we were able to get through them with less trouble than that morning. I was also able to look around a little more, specifically at the buildings and shops. For the most part they were fairly well maintained, but it was obvious the maintaining was done with elbow grease rather than magic. Which was, after all, in keeping with the way things worked around there. Repairing your building or shop with magic would put manual laborers out of work, so magical repairs must be illegal. If a building fell because the repair wasn't done right, well, that was a small price to pay for not needing to find manual laborers a new line of work, wasn't it?

People were already beginning to line up along the approach in front of the palace steps, but they took care not to get in the way of anyone trying to sign up for the competition. Two tables had been brought out and arranged about ten feet away from each other, and two clerk-types sat behind each one. The table to the right had a man in front of it signing something, so Bariden led the way to the table on the left. The exclusion spell *had* been withdrawn from the approach, so we had no trouble getting over to it.

"I'd like to enter the competition," Bariden said to the man who looked up first. "What do I have to do?"

"Just give us your name and sign the release," the man answered with a faint, cold smile. "After that, whatever happens is up to you. Or to whoever you're matched against."

The other man, seated to that one's right, joined the first in smiling at the clever remark. The two looked very much alike, thin, brown hair and eyes, ascetic narrowness to their faces, long-fingered hands that were somehow more threatening than graceful. I had the feeling they were constructs rather than actual human beings, and that was perfectly possible. Constructs have no choice about how they'll act and react, and sometimes that's just what you want.

Bariden supplied his name for the second man's list, then leaned over to sign the piece of paper pushed forward by the first. I had an idea about the purpose of that release, but didn't say so. If I was right, I'd find out soon enough.

"I'm also here to enter," I informed them as soon as Bariden was through signing. "My name is Chalaine."

"A pretty name for a pretty girl," the first man said with nothing of the complimentary in his tone. "Entering the competition is your right, as long as you thoroughly understand what will happen if you lose. *Do* you understand?"

"If I lose, my opponent wins me," I answered with a shrug. "But that's something to consider only if I lose. And what happens if a woman loses to another woman? If the winner isn't interested, is the loser off the hook?"

The man I was talking to actually went blank for a moment, telling me he wasn't a man. He *was* a construct, and as such couldn't handle the silliness I'd thrown at him. Rather than handle it he ignored it, at the same time producing another wintry smile.

"If you understand what can happen, then you won't mind agreeing to it in writing," he said, sliding forward a fresh release form. "Once your signature is on this there's no backing out, so consider what you're doing very, very carefully."

"Can a man back out once he signs one of these things?" I asked, reaching for the stylus. "You didn't mention the point to Bariden."

"Men understand that they're committing themselves completely when they sign their name," was the haughty answer. "Women often have trouble with the concept, and that's why it's explained."

"Tell that one to someone who'll believe it," I answered with a snort, tossing back the stylus I'd finished using. "That release routine is being used to make people uncertain and unsure of themselves, to rattle them before the competition. It's a process of elimination that has nothing to do with magic, only with how much confidence you have. The men aren't told that because simply demanding a signature is enough to reach the nervous ones. Women *are* told, but right after emphasizing how much they have to lose. With them, it's *that* combination you use for rattling purposes."

The construct's face went blank again, then he picked up my signed release and gestured to our left.

"The waiting area for entrants is over there," he said in a voice that greasily anticipated disaster for both of us. "You're committed now, so all you have to do is wait for it to start."

Bariden took my arm and headed us toward the indicated area, then murmured, "If that last comment doesn't prove what you said, nothing will. I wonder how many kids they send back to the farm with that routine."

"Most of the ones who would do badly anyway, I would imagine," I answered in a matching murmur. "Probably most of the ones with the greatest amount of imagination as well. That last group is probably the one the king *wants* to chase away. Get rid of those who could come up with a good idea for taking over, and half your self-defense efforts see to themselves."

"You forgot to include the women on your list," he said. "Get rid of most of the women applicants, and you've gotten rid of the majority of your most determined competition. Determined and ruthless. Look at that. They seem to expect us to stand up for an hour."

I glanced at the large square that was marked off with metal standards at its four corners, and there *was* nothing else. Bariden had been right about our needing to stand, but that wasn't what I was thinking about. When he'd mentioned ruthless women, he'd sounded downright approving. Was that the sort of women he really liked, ones who were determined and ruthless?

If there was a more ridiculous question I could have wasted my time with, the following hour wasn't when I found it. Bariden and I were the first to step into the square with the man from the other table right behind us, but we didn't just stand there the way we were probably supposed to. With one hand on his sword to keep it out of the way, Bariden folded into a sitting position on the ground. I considered that the best idea I'd seen in a long time, so I promptly followed his example. The man who was our third hesitated for a moment, but then made it unanimous by joining us.

Our numbers slowly increased over the next hour, and those who made it to the square followed our example by sitting down. A guard officer came by to check his men at their posts, and for a moment I thought he would come over and yell at us for not standing. Then he must have realized who he was about to yell at—a large group of sorcerer-level magic users who were being given permission to use their skill freely—and abruptly thought better of the decision. The incident was faintly amusing, but that was as good as it got.

"I estimate about one out of every four changes his mind at the signing table," Bariden said abruptly, when the hour was almost up. "Since we have almost twenty entrants here, they certainly don't hold these competitions just for show. If the numbers today are typical, they must almost have to beat them off with sticks."

"If most of them aren't going to be allowed to *use* their magic, why let them be trained in the first place?" I wondered aloud. "Wouldn't it be easier to deal with untrained Sighted?"

"If you were a Sighted who wasn't legally allowed training, wouldn't you sneak around or even run away in order to get it?" he countered. "The Sighted have to be a very large part of the population, which means they're needed to keep the kingdom running. If most of them disappear in an effort to get what you've denied them, your kingdom becomes an untenanted wasteland. You have no choice but to let them be trained, set the strongest guard spells you can devise, then weed out the best of the lot to keep them from setting up shop on their own. Or from coming at you from a direction you're not watching. I wouldn't be king here for anything you could name. It's a bigger trap than the one *we're* in."

"I see what you mean," I said, and I certainly did. The king would have to spend all his time watching his back, and that after years of scheming to *get* the throne. Anyone who considered that living had to have something seriously wrong with them; to me it sounded like prison with no chance of escape.

Another few minutes went by with two more men joining our group, and then someone stepped out from between the two tables and walked toward us. He wore silken trousers and tunic in a silver and bronze, soft black ankle boots, had light eyes and hair, and was Sighted. He did no more than glance at the rather large crowd that had gathered, and stopped to speak to us as though they weren't there.

"Today's entrants number a round twenty," he announced in conversational tones, looking around at us as he spoke. "Twenty people who are sitting when they should be standing. Do you intend to go through the entire competition on your behinds?"

His voice sharpened with the question, and two or three people actually started to scramble to their feet. The rest were either smarter than those few, or somehow keyed in to Bariden and me. He and I—and the rest—didn't move, and the newcomer was amused.

"A promising group," he commented, looking around again at everyone but those who had stood. "A delightfully promising group. I'm Sarvallo, and we're ready to begin. Follow me."

When he turned and walked away we took our time standing, which means at least half the group was up and after him ahead of us. Bariden didn't seem any more worried about that than I was, even though the morning's sunshine had turned to clouds. If it started to rain before the competition got around to us, then we would have to compete soaking wet. Anyone who used an umbrella spell would most likely be wasting strength they'd need.

The man called Sarvallo took two sheets of paper from the nearer table, waited until everyone was gathered around him, then started calling off names. The people he called were directed to the right of the group, to positions marked by two of the constructs who had been registering entrants. As soon as a pair was in place facing each other, the constructs moved to the next position, which was invariably four feet away and ten feet apart. With twenty entrants there were ten pairs, and I was the only woman. I was called first to face a husky black-haired stranger who grinned, and a few moments later Bariden was called to face a big blond like himself. Obviously people hadn't been called in the order they'd registered, but whatever order *had* been used was totally obscure.

"And now you're all in position," Sarvallo said when the last pair was stationed, strolling to the middle of the ten-foot gap. "I think you already know how this competition works, but I'll cover the important points briefly. There can be only one winner from each pair of you. That one will go on to the next stage of the competition, and the other will go home. Those of you who lose are forbidden to enter another competition for a year, after which you may try again. The same rules do not apply to the lady among you, but she's already aware of that."

My opponent grinned even wider at that while others chuckled, which made me give in to a very nasty urge. Instead of ignoring the comment and the reactions it had brought, I looked at the black-haired man facing me and let a small smile curve my lips. As a matter of fact I locked eyes with him, letting him see how little the added threat bothered me, and his grin faded slowly away.

"All of you are ten feet distant from your opponent," Sarvallo went on. "This distance is more or less arbitrary, but the maintaining of it is not. Each of you will be allowed one step back from your present position, but a second step will be the equivalent of outright defeat. You won't be penalized for forward movement, at least not by us. By now you should know what happens if the person you're engaged with is stronger than you and you're too close to them."

What he meant was "splashing," a backlash of your own spell bouncing off the warding of your opponent, a nasty surprise for those who don't know about it. Your own warding *may* be up to protecting you from the product of your own magic, but a lot of people never think to include that in their warding spell. I knew exactly what Sarvallo was talking about, but an awful lot of the people around me looked blank and worried.

"When the signal to begin is given, you'll do well to begin at once," Sarvallo continued. "Your opponent will certainly be doing so, and there won't be stopping for any reason after that but winning or losing.

"Also, it's now necessary to point out something entrants occasionally miss. When you signed your name after entering this competition, you were specifically giving your sworn word to strive to the best of your ability to win. If any of you entered just to be able to say you competed, with no intentions of doing your utmost best, this is your chance to leave. If you don't you'll be bound by your sworn oath, and any attempt to break that oath will be harshly punished. After the punishment will come permanent expulsion from the city, but by then you probably won't care. Does anyone want to withdraw?"

There was a very small amount of foot-shuffling, but no one took the opportunity to leave. That meant we'd now given our sworn words, but with this group the gesture seemed unnecessary. If I'd ever seen a bunch of people more eager to get on with it . . .

Sarvallo nodded without saying anything, then turned and headed for the left side of the lines. That had to mean we were ready to start and, in spite of everything, I could feel my shoulder muscles tightening. Bariden and I *had* to win, or we could end up spending the rest of very long lives in a place we would quickly grow to hate even more than we already did. We *had* to get out, we just *had* to . . .

CHAPTER ELEVEN

Bariden watched Sarvallo walk past him, but in full truth he was watching his opponent more carefully. During his time in the last few worlds he'd noticed a tendency in himself to hesitate when it came to using magic in combat, a tendency he never showed with weapons. That had to be a result of the disapproval his ability in magic usually produced in the people around him, but the time for diplomatically soothing people's fears was over. If he didn't start using his skills in the right way, the mistake could end up being fatal.

And he also had to push away all worry about Chalaine. Hesitation had never been one of her problems, and she was as capable as anyone he had ever met. That in itself didn't stop him from worrying; only the admission that he *couldn't* help her worked the trick. Along with what would happen if *she* won and he didn't. He had an idea about what was ahead, and a suspicion that if he didn't do exactly right they would both be lost.

"Get ready," Sarvallo called as he reached the sidelines and turned again toward them. Some of the people near Bariden twitched, but no one actually attacked by mistake. Most of them were so keyed up, they'd expend every ounce of their strength in the first few minutes of the combat. After that they'd be vulnerable to anything including heavy breathing, and might even get knocked out of the competition by accidently coming in contact with something from the combat next to them. Weapons practice had taught

223

Bariden when to conserve his strength—and when not to. He'd play it as it came, for once trusting completely in his overall ability.

"Begin," Sarvallo suddenly announced, and more than half the entrants immediately did just that. Spells were muttered or shouted with or without gestures, lightning and thunder flew and crashed, and in one instance the ground even shook. Bariden, ignoring what was going on around him, noticed that his opponent was doing as he was and simply watching. The man seemed ready to defend against anything thrown at him, but wasn't attacking immediately himself. It could be worse than bad luck if Bariden's opponent had also thought out a plan beforehand . . .

But then the man's expression changed, and Bariden knew he'd hit good luck rather than bad. The man, like him, was big and blond but, unlike him, had seemed to be hoping his opponent would be one to waste his strength in immediate, all-out attack. When he realized Bariden wasn't going to be that foolish, his face twisted with fury, disappointment, and frustration, and he immediately launched his own first attack.

Which wasn't bad as that sort of thing went. A dozen daggers came flying at Bariden, living daggers with eyes which attacked by themselves. If they couldn't reach him they were supposed to drive him back, and the attempt might have worked with someone else. But Bariden's wizard-formulated warding was not about to let anything magical reach him, and it had been years since the last time he'd given ground when attacked with a weapon. He waited only long enough to be sure the warding was effective— with Chalaine's safety in mind rather than his own—and then it was his turn.

Bariden's opponent was already beginning to speak another spell when Bariden spoke his, a variation of the enclosing spell he'd defeated Halvin with on the previous world. Rather than being invisibly enclosed with his own magic, the man found himself trapped with a swarm of angry construct-bees and wasps. The enclosure was a lot like warding: almost impossible to banish or get through because its actual shape was hidden in invisibility.

The man yelled, swinging his arms as he tried to drive the insects away rather than banishing them, a reaction Bariden had been hoping for. It's easy enough to stay cool and in control when "magical" things come at you in a contest between sorcerers; you are, after all, braced against that sort of thing. But when it's everyday insects coming at you instead, habit overcomes training and you sometimes act without thinking. Bariden's opponent acted without thinking, and that was what lost him his place in the contest.

Still yelling and swinging his arms, the man did the only thing his unreasoning mind told him he could: he retreated from the stinging, buzzing onslaught, just as he would at any other time. When the retreat proved successful and the attack suddenly stopped, he was extremely relieved—until he realized *why* the attack had stopped. His retreat had taken him three paces back from his original position, which was more than enough to disqualify him. His opponent, Bariden, stood with folded arms, calm in his victory—at least on the outside.

Inside, the victorious Bariden was almost afraid to look to see how Chalaine had done. What if she hadn't won? What if she now belonged to a total, uncaring stranger? What if she hadn't *survived* to belong to anyone at all . . . ?

"Get ready," Sarvallo said from all the way to my left. As if anyone there *wasn't* ready. Another trick to rattle the entrants, and my black-haired opponent almost fell for it. He pulled himself back just in time, and even from ten feet away I could see his skin darken in embarrassment. I'd seen what he'd almost done, and the tightening of his jaw said he'd make me pay for having that knowledge. What had happened wasn't his fault or Sarvallo's, but mine, and what a new, unexpected reaction *that* was.

At another time I might have sighed over once again being blamed for something that wasn't my fault, but right then I was too angry to sigh. It had finally come to me that letting people blame you without cause made *you* responsible for the entire situation. Refusing to speak up in your own defense made you an idiot rather than a martyr, a coward rather than a brave but silent soul. And taking what people felt like dishing out wasn't good for *them* either. How were they supposed to grow up, if you didn't help to discourage them from childish ways?

"Begin," Sarvallo said at last, and brother, was I ready. My opponent opened his mouth and raised his right hand, but I was already speaking the spell I'd decided on. It was an idea I'd gotten from what had happened to Bariden two worlds back, with the magician Arnwell. My black-haired opponent suddenly found himself under attack by pink, hand-sized monsters that were almost all teeth, the nasty little things clinging to him the way Halvin's monsters had clung to Bariden's warding in the last world.

But some of *my* monsters were beginning to chew through my opponent's warding, something that shocked him away from offense and into defense. His banishing gesture got rid of less than a quarter of the things clinging to him, and two or three additional gestures didn't improve on that. The things stayed right where they were, a beautiful rosy pink conglomeration of teeth, voracious appetites, and nastiness, and millimeter by millimeter got closer to the man underneath the warding.

Which meant it wasn't long before the man panicked. He screamed as if imagining those teeth beginning to chew on his flesh, and began to jump around and brush at himself in an effort to get free. For a minute I was certain he would understand what I'd done and come back at me in attack, but it didn't happen. He jumped around, flapping and screaming, and then my monsters were gone and it was over. He'd moved beyond the two-step limit, and had been immediately disqualified.

But just then I didn't think he minded that. He took a moment to make sure all the monsters were gone before he wilted where he stood, still not understanding that he'd been in no danger whatsoever. Most of the monsters I'd sent at him had been illusions, along with a smattering of monster-constructs. He'd been able to banish the constructs, but just as Bariden hadn't been able to banish an illusion without knowing it for what it was, neither had he. Part of the illusion had been the monsters' seemingly eating their way through his warding, which made him believe I was enough stronger that my monsters could actually do something like that. It had never occurred to him that a sorceress would use illusion like a mere magician, and that was what had made the idea work like a charm.

With my own competition over I was able to look around, which showed me that more than half of the contests already had their winners. The majority of those had people stretched out on the ground, whether unconscious or dead, I had no idea. My first concern was Bariden, and even as I sorted him and his opponent out, the other man began to yell. He jumped around flapping his arms very much like my opponent had, and then he had flapped himself out of bounds. I hadn't had time to see what Bariden had done to him, but apparently we'd both gone for forced defeat rather than blood.

After Bariden's win, there were only two more contests that didn't yet have a winner. In one of them the two men were fighting for magical control of a giant, two-headed axe, each man standing in his place with fists clenched and sweat covering him. The axe hovered between the two, quivering as it inched first this way and then that, tilting a fraction forward, and then the same fraction back. As someone who had once been silly enough to try that sort of thing at Conclave, I knew it couldn't go on much longer. When you're up against someone of equal strength in a thing like that, it's no longer a matter of how much you can put into the effort, but how long you can sustain it.

The man on the far side of my line lost his concentration first, and then he lost the chance to ever try again. When no one is there to control whatever the two magic users are contesting over, the object goes flying toward the one who lets go first. I looked away just before the axe edge connected with the center of the man's face, pretended I didn't hear the chopped off scream, and didn't look back again.

By that time the last contest was over, with one of the two having been forced out of bounds by nothing but the other's strength. The loser had apparently wasted his own strength early on, and had run dry at the worst possible time. But at least he was still alive, which a number of other losers definitely were not.

"We'll now have a short intermission," Sarvallo announced from his place to the left, sounding as though we'd all been sitting through a concert. "If those of you who were victorious will wait over here, we'll soon have the area cleared for the competition's next round."

He gestured to a place on his right, the same place we'd waited for the competition to start, then walked off toward the constructs who had registered us. Rather than watching him any longer I made my way over to Bariden, who stood waiting for me rather than heading for the waiting area as the others were doing. "You have no idea how glad I am to see you still in one piece," he said as I reached him, his arm going around my shoulders. "Obviously your warding stood up all right."

"My warding didn't get a chance to stand up," I told him as we walked, trying to ignore that arm around me. "As soon as the word was given I jumped first, and my opponent wasn't able to get it together again. How about you?"

"My opponent managed to get the first spell spoken, but I've always preferred being best to being first." His amusement was real, and his light eyes twinkled as he looked down at me. "At least I can report that the warding worked just the way it was supposed to, which was the main point worrying me. After that first time, though, there was no longer a need for it."

"So now we've won the privilege of facing some of the higher-ups," I said, stopping with him in one corner of the waiting area. The day was slowly getting darker and darker, but so far there hadn't been any rain. "Obviously, we've reached the place where we have to change tactics. Our next opponents won't be ones we can play games with."

"I think you're more right than you know," he answered quietly, then gestured with his chin. "It looks like at least one someone kept close tabs on the contest."

Both of the things he'd said were strange, but when I turned I understood the second. Four of the men on the ground had someone bending over them, but the other three were simply being carried away. So three of the ten who were defeated had also died, proving those people weren't wrong for trying to discourage entrants. If Bariden and I had cared less about who we stomped over, it could have been five dead . . .

"At least if you survive, you get to be attended by a healer," Bariden murmured from behind me. "That's more than some places would allow you. I still can't say I like this world, but there are things about it that could be a lot worse."

"There's one thing that isn't worse," I said, turning back to him. "I haven't been able to try an entry spell, and now that I probably would not get zapped for trying, I can't afford to risk it. If the king happens to be watching, and he just might be, he could keep *us* from using the entry and simply use it himself. If he has anything really special arranged with his corps of sorcerers, he could do a lot of damage in trying to take over before he's stopped."

"I hadn't thought of that," Bariden said with a frown. "It must be hard to expand to other kingdoms on *this* world, where you would have to go up against another wizard and his group already ensconced and waiting. No, you're right, we can't afford to hand over an unsuspecting world, and that's assuming your spell would work. If it doesn't, it could still bring us a lot of unwelcome attention. We'll have to stick with the plan and find that gate."

"Assuming it *is* in the palace, and hasn't been moved to the top of a mountain or the bottom of an ocean," I muttered, but too low for him to hear. I was getting more bad feelings about that situation the longer it continued, but there wasn't any way to hurry it.

This time we stayed on our feet while they cleared the combat area, but no one in our small group said anything. The watching crowd took care of making any comments, and they seemed more in the middle of critical discussion than in simply watching a spectacle. I had the distinct feeling that even dying had to be properly done, otherwise the crowd would deduct points . . .

"All right, you may come forward again," Sarvallo announced when the last of the wounded was gone and the one patch of blood cleaned up. He was back to where he'd stood originally, and held a single piece of paper. "As you can see we had a rather large turnout today, and none of the contests produced two defeated rather than one, as sometimes happens. For that reason we're invoking the appropriate rule, and there will be one more contest between you entrants before you're permitted to face a palace sorcerer."

The only comments came from the watching crowd, and even they weren't surprised. If the other entrants weren't protesting, that meant the rule wasn't brand-new and just made up. But I still didn't like it, not when it meant even more of a delay, and I glanced at Bariden to share the feeling. Only then did I notice that he *wasn't* sharing the feeling, and in fact looked as though he'd just been proven right about something. I wanted to ask what that something could possibly be, but Sarvallo was continuing.

"We'll do this just the way we did before," he said, gesturing toward the two waiting constructs. "When you hear your name, go over and take the indicated place."

The first two names were the two men who had deliberately killed their opponents, and neither one looked very happy about the match. I had just enough time to decide the arrangement was very fitting, and then it was my name being called. I walked out to the second position on the same side I'd been before, facing the palace, and then came the really bad news I'd been half-anticipating all along.

"Bariden," Sarvallo called, sending my companion to the place opposite mine. My first urge was to demand someone else to face, but one look at Bariden's expression kept me quiet. Somehow he'd *known* we'd end up facing each other, and he didn't seem unprepared. As a matter of fact he looked downright calm, which got me even crazier.

"You stupid fool," I growled under my breath while others were called out to their places. "Don't you understand that if you lose to me, you can't come back for a *year*? And I can't simply stand here and let *you* win. I gave my word to try my best, and that would hold even if there *wasn't* a wizard-strength spell backing up the demand. How in hell can you stand there looking *satisfied*?"

He didn't answer me, of course, and not only because he hadn't heard me. Looking at him, I got the distinct feeling he wouldn't have said a word in explanation even if he could have. I couldn't understand that—until I happened to remember the special condition attaching to a loss of *mine*. But that was ridiculous. Bariden would never—I mean, even if he won, he would never—

"All right, get ready," Sarvallo said, heading for the sidelines to my left from the outside this time. No threats or theatrics, not with the children already eliminated, and not even a dig at me. Great. Equality at last, and just in time to let me flatten the one man I could least afford to do that to. Not that I had a choice. If I didn't do my best to reach him, everybody would know it. If I did do my best and beat him, he would be barred from trying again for a year. I couldn't even really hope that *he* would best *me*. Aside from the fact that I didn't want to *have* to serve him, what real chance could he have against someone who had spent all that time at Conclave, learning tricks he'd never heard of? The future looked bleak and downright hopeless—and it didn't help in the least that *he* looked totally confident.

"You may begin," Sarvallo said abruptly from his place to the left, and I had no choice but to do exactly that. Bariden had proven to be very one-track in his outlook, keeping physical doings with physical, and magical doings with magical. The best strategy against him would be a combination of the two, and one that would leave his warding unactivated. Magic and magical things would never get through, but things only *created* by magic . . .

I was surprised to see that he was already speaking a spell when I began mine, but jumping in first shouldn't help him. My spell was short and relatively simple, demanding the creation of a pit under his feet and a heavy stick to follow. Falling into the pit would throw him off balance, hopefully enough to let the stick knock him out before he knew it was coming. He'd wake up with a headache and possibly a twisted ankle, but with healers ready and waiting to help, it wouldn't—

I had just enough time to notice that he wasn't falling in the pit, and then everything went black.

Bariden watched Chalaine collapse to the ground with mixed feelings, the strongest of which was relief. His spell had made sure she wouldn't be hurt when she collapsed, so it was all over and neither of them had been hurt. Thanks to pure inspiration on his part, and a large chunk of luck.

Being careful where he put his feet, Bariden stepped off the invisible platform he'd created. One gesture banished the platform, the pit it had saved him from, and the stick that was undoubtedly supposed to have knocked him unconscious. The inspiration had come in when he'd remembered the wooden platform Chalaine had banished from under the magician Arnwell. Deciding she would do the same with the ground under his feet meant he was betting everything on a hunch, but the risk had paid off. He'd not only been able to protect himself, his own attack had been able to reach *her*.

He walked over to where she lay, deeply asleep and finally out of it. Their enemy had been trying to play cute again, but this time Bariden had been able to anticipate the major trap. It was certain Chalaine had more experience using magic against other magic users, and Bariden was well known to be reluctant when it came to attacking women, even in practice. With that oath binding her to try her hardest, she was the one who should have logically walked away with the victory. Bariden would then be barred from the palace for a year, but she would not have had the choice of joining him. Her last opponent would have been a palace sorcerer, without doubt a man who was considerably stronger. After that she would belong to *him*, and Bariden would have had to choose between walking away quietly or deliberately trying to break the law.

But now that problem was settled, and in a way that made him smile. He'd won the contest with her fairly, even though she might not think so. Half of his spell had gone to creating an invisible platform to protect him; the other half had created a very special vapor, literally under Chalaine's nose. There were times when healers had patients with serious wounds, and it was necessary to put those patients to sleep either before or after the healing. The vapor used was standard among healers, but very few others knew about it. Odorless and colorless, it did its job quickly, thoroughly, and without later side effects. Since it was only produced by magic, not magical itself, Chalaine's warding hadn't been able to stop it from appearing an inch in front of her face. Bariden had learned the spell the time he'd been seriously wounded in a fight, and he'd never forgotten it . . .

"Well, that makes the numbers more manageable," Sarvallo announced, and Bariden looked up to see that the other contests were also over. The two men to his left, who had been the first to be placed, were both down and could very well be dead. Bariden hadn't been paying much attention to them, but he had the impression they'd both developed a technique where most of their strength was momentarily concentrated into a pinpoint attack. The pinpoint was meant to thrust through an opponent's warding by sheer overload, and from there go on to thrusting through the opponent. Since Bariden's warding was designed to counter that sort of thing, he wasn't about to spend time worrying about it.

Of the three other pairs, only one of each two was still left standing. One of the three on the ground was only sitting, but he was a good four feet back from his original position. That meant there were four left who stood victorious, with one slightly more victorious than the others.

"Your win, my friend, seems a good deal sweeter than the others," Sarvallo said to Bariden with a suggestive grin. "I wonder why that is."

"I can't imagine," Bariden answered with the satisfaction showing only in his eyes. "But I'd prefer that no one tries to wake her until this is completely over. I'll wake her myself then, and she'll be fine."

"Oh, I'm sure," Sarvallo agreed dryly, then pointed to the table Bariden and Chalaine had signed up at. "You can put her there until this is all over. There's still one more contest, you realize."

"Yes, I'm very much aware of that," Bariden agreed just as dryly, then bent to lift Chalaine in his arms. Even unconscious she weighed so little, and that was the closest he'd ever held her. As soon as the nonsense was over, he'd have to change that.

The table was a good, safe place to put the girl, and Bariden stood beside her until the rest of the defeated were taken or helped from the area. By then four men had come out of the palace, men wearing silk outfits containing more silver than bronze. If that was an indication of rank, then they were higher—and presumably more skilled—than Sarvallo, who wore more bronze. They stopped at the bottom of the steps and waited, so unconcerned they almost looked bored.

"And now for the last of it," Sarvallo said to Bariden and his three fellow finalists. "In this segment you aren't expected to win, only to show how close you can come. If you *do* win you have immediate acceptance, but it would be foolish to count on that. Not only are these men more advanced in their training than you, but they haven't just been through two contests that drained at least part of their strength. Just do the best you can, and those who make the best showing will be accepted."

Bariden felt the urge to ask who would make the decision on that, but the answer was too obvious—not to mention inflammatory. As he listened to the names being called— the palace sorcerers going first, of course—he worried at the conclusions he'd come to. If the finalist in his place was supposed to be Chalaine, the sorcerer chosen to face her should be keyed to *her*. The flaw in that reasoning was the possibility that they'd anticipated her losing, and had sent someone designed to best *him* as well. If so, then the man would be easily able to cope with anything Bariden tried.

But if he dwelled on that possibility, Bariden might as well concede the match even before it started. All he could do was his best, and stick with the plan he'd already formulated. If it didn't work, he'd hopefully have time to think of something else. If not—well, no sense borrowing trouble.

Bariden was the third finalist called out, and the man he faced wasn't quite his size. But he was close as well as broad-shouldered and graceful, and the sorcerer reminded him very strongly of that Lord Naesery from two worlds back. Now that was strange—Suddenly Bariden was more angry than puzzled. It was Chalaine who was supposed to have stood in his place, and she'd been in the process of developing feelings for the man Naesery. Of all the low, underhanded things to do to ensure a win over somebody . . .

"Get ready," Sarvallo called, once again standing to the left of the lines, but the warning was wasted on Bariden. He was more than ready, and when the word "Begin" came sooner than it had before, he did just that.

The palace sorcerer wasted no time raising his right hand and speaking a spell, but Bariden was ahead of him. His first spell was something special, conceived from what he'd learned about the young female wizard's work. Since he was using her spell for warding, he'd decided a spell using his opponent's strength to bolster that warding would work very nicely. *Should* work nicely . . .

And it did! The sorcerer's first spell sent magical winds designed to blow him back from his place, *magical* winds rather than the real thing created by magic. It was likely the man hadn't used real winds because they would have caused harm among the spectators, but whatever the reason it still worked in Bariden's favor. Rather than blow him and his warding back, his warding absorbed the strength from the wind and used it to anchor him firmly and easily in place. It worked so well that even his hair wasn't ruffled.

The palace sorcerer frowned when his spell did nothing, obviously not understanding. Since the first stroke was supposed to be the last, it seemed he didn't have any follow-up spell ready and waiting. Bariden, however, did, and it was specially geared to an opponent with greater strength. As a matter of fact, it was based on his experience with hand-to-hand combat, something most magic users weren't familiar with.

Like the man he was now facing. He smiled when he saw Bariden speak a spell without anything happening, and then he raised his hand for the second time, spoke his own spell, and added a capping gesture. Now that was a mistake, Bariden thought as he felt his magical strength being drawn on sharply—just before the palace sorcerer was flung back a good five feet with a final flash causing him to lie motionless. The final flash was the capping gesture, of course, a mistake the sorcerer would pay for with a pounding headache when he awoke.

But Bariden was too gleefully pleased to spend time commiserating with his former opponent. His spell had worked perfectly, even though the sorcerer had thought it hadn't worked at all. He'd arranged it so that when the sorcerer attacked, his own attack was turned back against him with Bariden's strength added. That sort of thing wasn't hard to do, but with magic you generally didn't have the *time* to do it. Bariden had hoped that his presence rather than Chalaine's would throw off his opponent's timing enough to give him the opportunity, and that was just the way it had worked. Luck was really with him on that world, but only because he'd been able to anticipate the enemy. Their next move would have to be to leave that world as quickly as possible, otherwise . . .

"Well, I'm really impressed," Sarvallo said, and Bariden looked around to see that the ostensible director of the competition wasn't the only one who had been watching. The other three palace sorcerers and one of his fellow contestants were still in condition to pay attention. Of the final two, one was out cold or dead, and the second was down on one knee, retching hard with his arms wrapped around himself. Briefly, Bariden wondered if retching was considered a win or a loss.

"Today is definitely a day to remember," Sarvallo went on, his eyes glittering with something very like pleased possessiveness. "Three new sorcerers accepted, when I can't remember the last time there were as many as two. If we can keep *this* up, we'll have the Eastern kingdom outmatched in no time. As soon as the third of your number has been eased by a healer, Tinsin will show you to your quarters and familiarize you with the laws of the palace. There aren't many, so you should have no trouble remembering them. Again, my congratulations."

His bow was on the ironic side, and then he was gone up the steps as one of the three palace sorcerers came over to take his place. At the same time a healer went over to the man who was retching, but not to the one stretched out. That meant he was dead, and only had to be carted away. For something called a "competition," the contests were a very rough game.

"Who does *she* belong to?" the man Tinsin asked, gesturing toward Chalaine with his chin. "I'm hoping it was the entrant *I* defeated."

"Sorry, but she belongs to me," Bariden answered with a calm smile. "Does your comment mean that if I hadn't had a definite win against my opponent, he would have ended up with her? Even though I was the one who actually defeated her?"

"Of course," Tinsin agreed with a shrug and a grin. "If being in the king's service didn't give a man the best of it, why would he go through what you and these others just did in order to qualify? It looks like *you'll* enjoy being one of us right from the start."

Bariden was surprised by the man's friendliness, but a moment's thought gave him a possible reason for it. Aside from the fact that he and the other two were now members of the same elite group, they were also scheduled to begin advanced training. If simply studying magic eventually brought everyone to the level of wizard, there would be thousands and thousands of wizards rather than just a few hundred. No one knew what limited one man or woman to magician level while others climbed easily to sorcerer, but the limitation grew more stringent the higher you went. Only a very few would go on to become wizards, and Tinsin wasn't taking any chances. If Bariden or one of his fellow newcomers happened to reach wizard level while he didn't, he wanted no bad memories standing between them. Which, Bariden had to admit, was a rather wise move on his part.

In just a few moments, the third of their number was sufficiently healed to join them. Bariden picked up Chalaine again, and then Tinsin led them into the palace. It was the place they needed to go, but just getting inside was hardly likely to give them the rest. The first thing Bariden had to do was get Chalaine to some place safe, and then he would start searching for the gate . . .

CHAPTER TWELVE

" . . . wake up," the voice said softly and gently. "Everything's all right, so it's time for you to wake up. Come on, Chalaine, open your eyes and talk to me."

"Why can't I talk to you with my eyes closed?" I mumbled, curious about the point. "I don't talk with my eyes, so—"

"That's a good girl, that's right," the voice said patronizingly, beginning to get me angry. "You try to talk to me, and I'll help you to sit up."

That was when I became aware of the arm behind me, forcing me up from the nice, comfortable thing I'd been lying on. I really didn't care for that—any of it, in fact—and for some reason my warding wasn't working, so I spoke a spell to take care of it. Since I was feeling very vague for some reason, I spoke the spell slowly and carefully. I know I did it right, but all it accomplished was to cause the voice to chuckle.

"You don't really want to do that to me," it said, sounding amused. "And if you did, you'd have something of a problem. I was told to tell you your magic won't work in here, not with the king's spell actively set against you in particular. You lost the contest, so now you're mine to do with as I please."

I didn't like the sound of that at all, but the voice was beginning to seem familiar and memories were fighting to come within reach. I felt I had to do *something*, so I forced my eyes open.

What I saw then was a surprisingly comfortable-looking chamber, a lot larger than the last room I could almost remember being in. There was a good deal of darkwood paneling offset by wall hangings in bright red silk, two windows to the left with sheer gold curtains, and a heavy wooden door to the right that was beautifully carved. Straight ahead the wall was interrupted by a wide hearth of light-gray stone, where a small fire crackled pleasantly. At least four chairs of brown, red, and gold cloth, plushly upholstered, were scattered around the room, and a small table with two small, comfortable chairs stood to the left, between the hearth and the bed.

Bed. That's what I was sitting on, a big bed that felt incredibly comfortable, with a red silk cover under my folded legs. I had an impression of gold silk sheets and pillowcases without really seeing them, and the arm that held me up was attached to someone on my left. By then I knew who the someone was, but the rest insisted on staying hazy.

"What happened?" I asked Bariden, having a lot less trouble getting the words out. "Where are we?"

"Good, you're coming out of it," he said, no longer sounding amused. "If I'd let you sleep it off you wouldn't be feeling this confused, but I wanted you to be awake. Where we are is in my quarters in the palace, just where we hoped to be. I'm one of the three who were accepted."

"Three out of twenty," I muttered, putting a hand to the back of my head as the memories finally started to return. "That wouldn't be bad if all the rest of the seventeen had lived to try again. But you still haven't told me how we got here. The last thing I remember is—"

"Probably blacking out," he finished when I didn't. His arm was still around me, and when I tried to shift over and sit alone, his usual cooperation wasn't there. The arm stayed firmly around me, his big hand curved gently around my right bicep.

"I knew they were going to set us up against each other," he said, satisfaction heavy in his voice. "And they expected *you* to win, because you have more experience with confrontations even though they were only practice. I may not go to Conclave, but I still have some idea about what goes on there. If *you'd* won, they would have had us exactly where they wanted us."

"But instead we're where *we* wanted us," I said, twisting around to look at him. "And I lost, even though I was trying not to. Would you like to tell me how you accomplished *that*?"

"By being prepared," he answered, his grin too gleeful to be considered smug. "Just as I was prepared against the palace sorcerer who would have defeated you if you'd won against *me*. Aren't you going to thank me for saving you from a fate worse than death?"

"As soon as I'm sure I *have* been saved," I said, trying to dent his grating good humor. "For some reason, it doesn't quite feel like it."

"Can't imagine what would make you say that," he said, finally taking his arm back even though the grin had widened. "I have to leave soon for the tour they're going to give us of this part of the palace, so we'll have to continue our discussion later. Right now I want you to know there's a meal for you, and it's waiting on the table over there. Once you're feeling steady enough, you can get up and eat it. But don't try to leave this room. You're not allowed to walk around unescorted."

"Are they afraid I'll wander into a place that's sacred to men?" I asked as I watched him stand, more than a little annoyed. "And what if I don't *feel* like eating? Won't I get my gold star if I don't finish everything on my plate?"

"Chalaine, I'm the one who wants you to eat, and I'm the one who wants you to stay put." At another time he would have sighed as he told me that, but his sighing days seemed to be behind him. Right then the words were a statement rather than an admission, and he made no attempt to avoid my gaze. "I know you're not happy about the position you're in," he continued, "but that can't be helped. We'll be out of here as soon as possible, but until then you have to do as I say. I don't want you missing any meals, and I don't want you wandering around among sorcerers without magic of your own. And there's one more thing."

He walked over to the small table on the left, where I could now see dishes and things, then turned back to me with one of the things in his hand.

"Here's the hairbrush you wanted," he said, showing it to me before putting it back. It was a simple thing of yellow-brown wood and white bristles, almost looking handmade. "After you eat you can brush your hair, but don't braid it again. I've been looking forward to seeing it flow free again, the way it did at Queen Lova's feast. I'll be back as soon as the tour is over."

And he stared at me for a good half minute before going to the door and leaving, quietly pulling the beautiful carved wood shut behind him. I took my turn staring at the door, afraid to wonder what my expression was like. I'd known I wouldn't want to lose a contest in the competition to him, but I'd had no idea how hard I should have tried to avoid it. That wasn't the same Bariden I'd entered the trap with, and the new him was downright—daunting.

"He's the first man ever to get over worrying about how fragile I must be, and now he's going to make me pay up," I said out loud, telling the room some truths I had just noticed. "Even if it means putting off leaving, he's going to make me pay up on that loss. And something tells me it doesn't matter that I can't do magic right now. He would have made the same decision even if I were fully up to strength. Just as I was when he defeated me."

And that, of course, was the worst of it, along with his new attitude. It hadn't been hard keeping a distance between me and my temporary companion, but the same didn't hold true for this new version. He wasn't going to allow that distance, and the cold truth was I no longer wanted it either. Right from the start I'd found him handsome and attractive, but now . . .

Now he was no longer stiff and formal, or deliberately charming. He was sure of himself and comfortable in that certainty, and hadn't said a word about trying to make me believe his intentions. He'd let me know what those intentions were without words, and they were purely physical.

Which proved what I'd been saying all along. I blew a long, slow breath out as I pushed my hair back with both hands, then made the effort to get up. There wasn't even a hint of dizziness as I got to my feet, showing that whatever he'd done to me had worn off completely. I went to the door and tried it, but even though it wasn't locked it refused to open. He'd backed up his orders with magic, showing just how well he'd gotten to know me. But not as well as he *would* get to know me . . .

"Damn it, this isn't *fair*!" I muttered, hating the way his blind stubbornness was backing me into a corner. It was physical attraction he felt, after all, and once his curiosity was satisfied I'd certainly become just another name on his list. Back in the hostel I'd momentarily forgotten that, but his drawing away had reminded me. He was curious enough to want to try me, but not enough to risk getting zapped for it.

But now he was free to do as he pleased, and his new personality was strong enough to guarantee it. I'd never be able to refuse him because I didn't really want to, and that was the *most* annoying part. Of course, *my* interest wasn't pure lust, nothing but prurient curiosity, the way his was. Mine was based on a lot more than that . . .

I left the door and walked to the table, looking for and finding the cup of coffee I'd hoped would be there with the food. I sipped at it for a moment, feeling my thoughts squirming around, then had to admit there was no way out. I usually tried to be truthful with myself even if it hurt, and this was obviously going to be one of those times. Okay, Chalaine, say it straight out, and you can keep on pretending you're a real grown-up.

Right. I sat down in a chair and stared into the coffee, just to distract myself from how embarrassed I felt. Most of my very noble interest in Bariden *was* physical, just as his was in me. In its proper place there's nothing wrong with good, honest lust, as long as you can admit that's all it is. And as long as you don't try to take advantage of someone because of it. The way *I'd* tried taking advantage in the hostel room . . .

But since I was into being honest, I also had to admit that that incident still bothered me. The good thing about lust is that sometimes it leads to a deeper relationship, one based on more than simple physical attraction. That wasn't likely to happen with Bariden, not when the only thing we had in common was that Spell of Affinity, but where was the harm if I already knew that? Wouldn't it be perfectly all right to simply indulge myself a little . . . ?

This time I took a good swallow of the coffee, trying to drown self-disgust. Maybe *I* knew the truth of things, but there was a chance Bariden was still kidding himself. Even if it wasn't likely it was still possible, and ignoring it wouldn't be fair. Could I simply sit back and have some fun while he told himself he was beginning the greatest love story of the ages? Not if I ever wanted to be able to look at myself in a mirror again, not when it couldn't possibly become any sort of love story for *me*. Bariden and I came from two different worlds, and once we were out of that trap we'd go back to them . . .

Which meant it was up to me to say a good, firm no and stick to it. I leaned forward to rest my arms on the table, wondering how difficult Bariden's new personality would make that decision. I'd have the strength of knowing I was doing it for his own good, but would that be enough? If it wasn't I had reserves of stubbornness to call on, not to mention the question of how we would get out of there. And what precautions to take before stepping through any gate. Every new world we went to posed a different problem, and so far we'd just been reacting to them. Wasn't it time to try to anticipate what would happen next, and maybe get a jump on it? At that rate we'd never get out of the trap . . .

I spent some time thinking about what we'd gone through and what might be ahead, finally using the food to help me fight off depression. Every time we stepped through a gate things got worse instead of better, but we hadn't had a choice about stepping through. And we still didn't have a single clue about how to break free. At that rate the only thing we had to look forward to was a dead end, one where there would be no more gates and no other way out. If we didn't find our own road before then . . . I threw my fork aside and sat back, no longer interested in anything but the self-refilling coffee cup. Or maybe something a little stronger. Too bad there wasn't anything . . .

After a few minutes of silent brooding I noticed the hairbrush, which in turn brought memory of the order I'd been given. Even if I'd been in the mood to follow orders I wouldn't have followed that one, but my hair *was* badly in need of brushing. I'd use the brush to get rid of the knots, and then rebraid it. If Bariden wanted to see hair flowing free, he could look at his own.

It took some effort to get my hair brushed out, but I wouldn't have used magic to help even if I could have. I wore my hair long because I liked it that way, and didn't even mind how it picked up knots. Brushing it smooth and shining was a physical therapy for the mind, a time when all you have to concentrate on is repetitive movements of your arm. You can be as violent or as gentle as you have to be, and eventually you slip into a lake of calm and simply float there.

I finally found the lake and did some floating, but time was passing and I didn't know how much of it I had. Bariden could be back at any time, and I certainly didn't want him to think I was encouraging him. I put the brush aside with a sigh, reached to my hair and separated it into three long sections, then—

Then discovered that the three sections flatly refused to be twisted around each other. At first I thought I was just being clumsy and tried again, but after the third try there was no longer any doubt. That miserable son of a diseased she-dog had set a spell, just as he had with the door. Now that I'd unbraided and brushed my hair, it was impossible to braid it again.

I'm sure students of human nature find it fascinating how fast it's possible to go from easy calm to raging anger. For myself I noticed no time elapse at all, or maybe I was just too wild to notice. Whatever, I had just begun to stalk back and forth across the room when the door opened, and the fungus-rotted bastard himself walked in. A slow grin creased his face as soon as he saw me, and that was the absolute end. I headed straight for the table, snatched up the brush, then threw it at him as hard as I could.

When it comes to targets, I have a better than decent eye because I practice. Unfortunately, what I practice isn't throwing by hand, and Bariden is awfully fast for a man his size. He ducked before the brush could hit him smack in the face, and then he had swung the door shut and was charging at me. Refusing to be discouraged or intimidated, I reached for a serving bowl heavy enough to do some damage, but couldn't quite get it into position for the throw. I was only half turned back when Bariden reached me, and then he had one hand on the bowl and an arm around my waist. I kicked and struggled but still lost the bowl, and then he had both hands free to defend himself.

"I see you discovered at least one of the spells I used to anticipate problems," he grunted, having more trouble than he'd probably expected in holding me still. "You'd better stop struggling so hard, or you might set off my warding."

I told him what he could do with his warding—folded up square so that it was mostly corners—and then tried harder to kick him. I'd never used language like that in my life, which meant I'd had no idea how good it would feel. Somewhere in the back of my mind I expected Bariden to be furious at being spoken to like that, but when he finally managed to lift me off the floor he was laughing!

"I never believed a woman could be even more beautiful when she was angry," he chuckled, still trying to control my struggles as he carried me to a couch. The armless and backless piece of furniture let him plump me down easily, and then he was using his body as well as his hands to keep me down. "Don't you want to hear about what I saw on the tour?" he finally added.

"All I want to hear is that the gate is right outside and we'll be using it in the next five minutes," I growled back. "If that's not what you have to say, I'd rather fight."

"You've really changed, and I love it," he murmured, moving my wrists up above my head so that he could start to kiss my neck. "If you'd rather fight, then let's fight."

"*I'm* not the one who's changed," I ground out in desperation, finding it impossible to free myself. Those big hands of his were closed around my wrists, his leg was keeping both of mine still, and his lips—! "And this isn't my idea of fighting! Let go of me, you miserable coward."

"If it's cowardly to want to keep from getting mangled, then I'm a coward," he answered with a grin. "And are you sure this isn't fighting? I've always thought of fighting as fun, and I'm certainly finding *this* fun."

"You're not *funny*," I stated, no more than an inch away from blushing. "I don't want to be held down, and I don't want to be kissed—especially not by someone who's an overbearing dictator. If you like to give orders so much, go find someone who's willing to take them."

"But I have that someone right here in front of me," he said with one brow raised. "Aren't you the one who insisted on entering the competition, saying you would take the consequences if you lost? In case you missed the point you *did* lose, and to me. If nothing else, that gives me the right to hand you as many orders as I please."

"Then go ahead and do it," I answered with the best shrug I could manage. "I may have said I'd take the consequences, but I didn't say *how* I'd take them. If you're wondering what that means, you're in the middle of finding out."

"I don't think so," he came back, not a trace of anger or annoyance showing. "How *you* define things doesn't matter here, something I tried to explain to you yesterday. I was finally forced to agree that you *had* to enter, but that doesn't change the fact that you would have done it even if it wasn't necessary. I'd like to hear you admit you were wrong."

Once again I couldn't help noticing how calm and steady he was. And he hadn't let me go even if he *had* stopped the kissing. I squirmed around on the inside, having the usual trouble admitting I might be wrong. I'd had to be hard and certain for so very long, uncaring about the opinions of others to keep those opinions from cutting me open. Now . . .

"All right, I was wrong," I muttered, all but dragging the words out. "I was annoyed with the stupid system they have here—and with *you*—and never stopped to consider that it might be a more subtle trap than what I was anticipating. But I don't understand why I did that. What I should have done was ignore all of it, stand aloof and refuse to bite the dangling hook. Taking the hook with the intention of pulling the fisherman in isn't at all like me."

"You say that only because you can't see how much you've changed," he disagreed, finally releasing my wrists. "I remember thinking, when this first started, that I'd have to have words with you about the way you refused to discuss things. It was a habit of yours that really got to me, but we never had those words because you stopped doing it. What you started doing instead was challenging people who tried to put you down, demanding that they prove what they said or take it back. In my opinion that's a much healthier habit, but you let it take you too far. There are times when it *is* smarter to let things go by, especially when you don't know for certain what answering their challenge will bring."

He touched my face gently and then stood up to stretch, leaving me with something troubling to think about. I *hadn't* noticed myself changing, even though the time period covering the change was no more than a matter of days. During those days we'd both been affected, but why should that have happened? I sat up slowly, trying to decide what the revelation could possibly mean, but there were so many considerations and variables . . .

"Are you ready to hear what my tour was like?" Bariden asked, and I looked up to see him holding a glass of wine. "They also supplied us with a selection of polite snacks, afterward explaining we were responsible for providing our own meals and other requirements. A fully functioning sorcerer ought to be able to call up just about anything he can think of, and that was our primary gain: as long as we're in service with the king, we're exempt from most of the prohibitions the rest of the populace has to live with."

"That must help a lot in keeping the palace budget down," I said, getting to my feet. "Not to mention giving new recruits an incentive to behave themselves in order to keep what they've gained. What are the prohibitions you're *not* exempt from?"

"The first one is obvious," he answered, watching me move to the table to retrieve my coffee. There was a second glass of wine standing there, but I no longer wanted the something stronger I had earlier. "Any effort to plot against the king will get you bounced immediately. There's also a schedule where those here who do well in their studies can *legally* challenge the king. That, I think, is to keep groups from forming, where everyone supports a particular candidate. After all, why support someone else when you could easily have a chance of your own?"

I nodded as I sipped, reluctantly admitting the wizard-king seemed to know what he was doing. Giving your underlings permission to challenge you brought them at you one at a time, making them easier to handle than if they showed up in a group. And giving them something important to lose—full and free use of their abilities—also had to make any but a completely determined challenger think twice. Yes, the man did seem to know what he was doing.

"The second thing we can't do is produce our own gold and silver," Bariden continued. "If we get a vacation from our studies and want to spend part or all of it in the city, we have to ask for money to be issued to us. The king doesn't want a lot of extra coinage being spread around, driving up the prices of things, and if we break *that* rule we get burned the way *you* were over that cup of coffee. The third and last major rule is, no one harms anyone in the city. They're all under the king's protection, and he *will* protect them even from one of his own."

"Now that's interesting," I said, leaning back against the table as I considered the point. "A wizard doesn't need *anyone's* support to be king, let alone the people he rules, but this man is still careful of his subjects. I wonder why that is."

"I have the feeling that taking care of his people is something *he* needs," Bariden answered, gesturing with his wineglass. "Playing king feeds the need for power most people have, but usually the power need is matched by selfishness. Why would I care if the multitude is starving, as long as I have mine? Also, my *not* starving while they do proves how much better I am. But this king has the strength and ability of a wizard to take care of any power craving he might have, so he doesn't need the incidentals. That alone would give him people's fear, but what he seems to want is their respect and love. It seems to be part of human nature to want what you don't have, to struggle for what everyone says is impossible to get."

"Which would explain why he hasn't cast a general 'love-me' spell," I said with another nod. "The emotion would be false, and so would be the satisfaction. No struggle, no pleasure from achieving the impossible. Of course, he *could* just be playing fair and taking his job as king seriously. I don't like thinking he might be, but it *is* possible. What, if anything, did that tour show you?"

"This wing is where newcomers and the least powerful of the residents live," he said after finishing his wine, also coming over to put the glass on the table. "In the middle of it are chambers for practice and instruction, where those who are stronger than you help you to learn. There are also a couple of gathering rooms meant for relaxation, and every week the two sorcerers who have made the most progress in learning are each responsible for redecorating one of them. The one we got to glance into had diamond walls, ruby ceiling and floor, sapphire tables and sconces, and chairs made of solidified clouds. We were also told that that one was the less imaginative of the two."

"I should hope so, since even *I* could do better," I scoffed, then pulled myself up short. They used games to encourage people to learn, and I had no business responding to the lure of it. Not only didn't they want me to join in, I had no intention of staying around even if they suddenly changed their minds.

"One corridor leads to the next wing of the palace, where those of higher ability live," Bariden went on. "We weren't allowed to do more than look up the corridor from our end, and were warned not to try to go farther, either alone or with a friend or two. Anyone caught where he doesn't belong is taken care of by those who do belong in the invaded territory. We were told we would *not* be seriously or permanently hurt, we would only wish we *had* been. If we disbelieved that, we were invited to try it for ourselves and see."

"Which should do a better job of keeping you out than the most bloodcurdling of threats," I said. "And also make you work that much harder, so you can walk up that corridor because you've earned the right."

"That's the way my brother newcomers seemed to take it," Bariden agreed, folding his arms. "They looked at that corridor the way a beggar looks at a gold coin, and afterward didn't even seem to see the two guardsmen stationed in front of a door just past that corridor. The door they guarded was in *our* wing of the palace, but Tinsin, our guide, never said a word about it."

"If I didn't remember what happened in the last two worlds, I'd say it couldn't be that easy," I commented, trying to decide whether to feel relieved or suspicious. "Were the guardsmen Sighted, or did the door have any complex spells on it?"

"No to both, at least as far as I could tell," he said, looking no happier than I felt. "And, predictably, the set-up doesn't make any sense. Why have guardsmen in a palace filled with sorcerers? The weakest man here would have no trouble getting past them, so why not just spell the door and forget about guards? A wizard's spell could make it impossible for anyone to even see the door, let alone go through it. The only answer I can think of is the obvious one."

"That someone wants to make it easy for us to get through the gate that must be behind the door," I grumbled in agreement. "But even that doesn't make any sense. What if we'd done the wrong thing, and both of us weren't here in the palace? Did they expect one of us to go on through and leave the other behind?"

"That would depend on whether we were still together, wouldn't it?" he countered, those very light eyes thoughtful. "What if one of us had stayed on one of the previous worlds, and the other had gone on alone? Or what if one of us was killed in that competition? The survivor would *have* to go on alone, or else settle down here for life."

"But—the logic of that thought doesn't hold," I said, even more disturbed than I had been. "At least, not the way it should. If they were trying to trap me into belonging to someone else, why would they make it possible for me to get to the gate? And even with two alert guardsmen, it *would* be possible. I've been trying to figure out what they can be after, and this just makes the whole picture muddier."

"Tell me about it," he muttered, running an annoyed hand through his hair. "None of it makes any sense, and especially not running straight for that gate. People are still awake and moving around in this wing, so we'll give them enough time to settle down and fall asleep. In the meantime we'll get as much rest and nourishment as we can, and also see if we can come up with an alternative to using the gate the way we're obviously supposed to. If there's a way out of this trap, obediently following the bread crumb trail isn't it."

"But refusing to budge can't be the way either," I fretted, hating the idea of spending any more time in that place. "Why don't we get ourselves *to* the gate, and then we can argue about whether or not to go through? That way—"

"No," he denied quietly, dismissing the suggestion without a second thought. "Where guards are posted, guards are also relieved. If we're found there at the wrong time we'll *have* to go through, assuming no one alerts the king and he makes it impossible. We'll do our waiting here, where I can relax and enjoy it."

He turned then and raised his arms, but I heard nothing of whatever spell he spoke. Obviously I'd been cut off from magic completely, even to the point of not being able to hear it. That added even more to my annoyance, but then Bariden's spell manifested and I was distracted by the surprise.

A wall of gray mist had formed, with an archway standing open and inviting in the middle. Beyond the archway I could see lots of green forest around a pool being fed by a waterfall, soft green grass leading like a carpet from the archway to the pool. I was certain Bariden hadn't created an entry to another world, but what *had* he done . . . ?

"Part of that is illusion, but part isn't," he said, almost in answer to my unspoken question. "Let's go make use of it, and you can see if it's possible to tell which is which."

He put his hand out to me, those light eyes showing an expression I couldn't define, and that made me uneasy.

"Make use of it how?" I asked, staying right where I was. "And won't they come down on you for spreading out beyond the limits of your assigned quarters?"

"But I didn't spread out beyond my quarters," he answered, now looking amused as well as pleased. "That's one of the illusions. And what else would you do with a heated waterfall and pool but take a bath? Come *on*."

"I had a bath this morning," I began, suddenly *know-ing* I didn't want to join him, but that was as far as I got. Two steps brought him back to me, and then I was being pulled toward the arch by one hand. I tried to get loose—or even simply to hang back—but there was nothing to grab onto or to pry Bariden's hand open with, and then—

And then I was through the archway and stark naked. It didn't help that Bariden was just as naked, and in fact made things worse. If I'd had the choice—about anything at all—Damn it, this just wasn't *fair*!

"Give me my clothes back this instant!" I demanded, using both hands in an effort to stop the hulk who was pulling me toward the pool. The grass under my feet was like satin, something I had no desire at all to think about . . . "Damn it, Bariden, let me go and give me my clothes back!"

"It's too warm in here for clothes," he answered without turning, and also without slowing. "You'll get them back when we leave, and by then they'll have refreshed themselves. Let's swim a little, and then we can rest on the grass."

"I won't!" I insisted, for once in my life wishing I weighed more. "If you drag me in there I'll just climb right out again, so why waste the effort? Let me go now, and—"

"Chalaine," he said with a sigh, then turned back to look down at me. "Why are you going through these motions? I disappointed us both last night because I felt I had to, but those reasons don't hold any longer. You're trying to refuse because you're still upset with me, and I can't blame you for that. But once I begin to apologize properly, you'll change your mind. Let's just wait until then, and if you *don't* like it, *then* you can say something. Is it a deal?"

By that time my jaw was practically down to my toes, and I honestly couldn't decide what I most wanted to say first. Of all the incredible egotists I'd ever had the misfortune to associate with, Bariden took first prize without competition. My trying to refuse him was just going through the motions, and as soon as he made the effort I'd change my mind?

"Do you know what you can do with your deal?" I finally got out, glaring up at him with the beginnings of explosion. "You can—what in Hellfire are you grinning at?"

"You," he answered, reaching out one big hand to stroke my hair, his amusement increasing. "All I brought you in here for is to swim and relax, but you were so obviously expecting me to attack you—or do you a big favor—that it was painful. That's why I decided to put the big favor into words, just to get it out of the way. I'd *like* to apologize properly for disappointing you last night, but first you'll have to say you're ready to listen. Until that happens, let's go and get wet."

The hand that was still closed around mine pulled me after him again, but this time I couldn't think of anything to say. Part of me was very embarrassed over having misjudged him, but another part was wondering if I really had. Maybe that speech he'd made *had* been a deliberate attempt to get me angry enough to calm down, so to speak, but did that mean his intentions were nothing but honorable? At one point the answer would have been yes, but after the way he'd changed . . .

The pool of water began only a couple of inches below the bank, and the man who was beginning to make me paranoid didn't give me the chance to climb in alone. He took me by the waist and just about dropped me in, and while I was still squeaking in surprise he joined me. The surprise came from the fact that the water *was* warm, deliciously warm, even though it looked clear and cold. It was that perfect temperature for soaking, and was deep enough there to almost reach my shoulders.

"I liked the view better on the bank, but we've both earned a little pampering," Bariden said from behind me. "There are a couple of underwater ledges opposite the falls, so if we get tired of swimming but don't want to get out, we can stretch out there. Aren't you sorry now that you made such a fuss?"

"No, I'm not," I answered over my shoulder, bending my knees to let the water lap higher. "And while we're discussing the landscape, I'd like to know what made you come up with *this*. The last time you spoke a spell to produce accommodations, it turned out to be a modest little house with nothing in the least exotic. This, though . . ."

I let the words trail off as I looked at the falls, a misty cascade that fell from a good hundred feet up. The sound of it was only a whispering shush flowing through bright sunshine and the chirping of birds, making the whole thing a delight to every sense I had. An undertone of tinkling seemed to be calling me to play, and I had never felt so welcome in my entire life.

"When I called up that house, it was still the old me," Bariden answered in a murmur. "Magic was like a weapon or a tool, to be used only under strictly defined circumstances and only to the extent that was absolutely necessary. Since then I've learned that magic is like any other skill— wasted when limited by anything but common sense and honor. There's no shame in being what you were born to be; the shame is in failing to be that something because those around you can't be the same. Let's swim over to the falls and check on the temperature change I incorporated."

He moved through the water on my left, already swimming and glancing at me as he went past. I began to follow without comment, but not because I didn't know what to say. I kept getting the feeling I was completely out of control, and that had nothing to do with not being able to do magic. Bariden's entire attitude . . .

There was no gradual change in water temperature as I neared the falls. What I swam in was warm right up to the place the falls reached it, and only directly under the falls was it cold. The water was also deeper there and as far as I could tell the bottom was a long way down. Bariden glided up and splashed me with cold falls water, so after screeching I returned the favor. The splashing went on even after we moved away from the falls, and some time during that period the laughing started. Because of the laughter we both ended up swallowing a good deal of water, but after the first gulp I didn't mind at all. What I seemed to be swallowing was a light, sparkling white wine, definitely chilled, and the best vintage I'd ever tasted.

There came a time during the horseplay when Bariden surged through my water attacks to capture me. He tried a couple of times without being able to break through the barrage, and had to retreat with ringing laughter. The third time, though . . . Don't they always say, "Third time lucky?" It had never occurred to me to ask who the lucky one was supposed to be . . .

I was laughing when those massive arms closed around me, and he was grinning in triumph. That deliciously warm water lapped at our bodies, trying to coax us into tasting more of it, but I suddenly felt as if I'd already had more than I should have. Looking into those very blue eyes was making my head spin, and then he pulled me close and kissed me. His lips tasted of the wine, and small runnels flowed down both our faces from our hair, and his hard, naked body felt so good pressed up against mine, and—

"Bariden, stop," I mumbled as soon as I could, my hands spread out against his chest and arm. His lips didn't want to let the kiss end, and mine . . . "Bariden, this is nothing but lust we're feeling. It wouldn't be fair to—to—let it make us take advantage of each other."

"Why not?" he countered in a murmur, one of his hands in my hair, the other moving over my bottom. "If we're both *taking* advantage, we're also both getting it. What's wrong with that?"

"There's—everything wrong with it," I groped, trying to remember the very clear reasoning I'd used when I'd decided to stay away from him. "It just wouldn't be right, so we can't let this go any further."

"All right, then we won't," he agreed easily and comfortably, his lips and tongue moving to my neck. "We'll just go on with this and nothing else."

I gasped as he licked the water-wine from my skin, still being held in those arms, still pressed up against him. The water would have floated my body away from his if he'd let it, but he was holding me too tight for that. There was no bottom under my scrabbling toes, nothing but Bariden's legs and calves, but I had the feeling *he* was touching bottom. I also had the feeling I was about to drown, and being in water had nothing to do with it.

"You can't be serious," I finally managed to protest, my fingernails undoubtedly digging holes in him. "You can't just—keep on doing *this*! You have to let me go."

"I'll let you go if you can tell me you're not enjoying it," he murmured, his lips at my face and ear. "But you have to tell the truth, Chalaine, otherwise you won't be able to say it. Tell me truthfully that you want me to stop, and I'll let you go immediately."

I parted my lips to say what I had to, ignoring the way my eyes had closed in response to what he was doing— and the words wouldn't come. Part of me did want him to stop, but it was a very small part and had nothing to do with how I felt. I wasn't enjoying what he was doing, I was melting into a puddle of mush from it, and the mush had been forbidden to lie. He was in complete control of me, and all I wanted to do was relax and enjoy it.

"You bastard," I whispered, pulling him closer with my arms around his neck so that I could bite his ear. By rights I should have ripped it from his head, but all I *could* do was close my teeth with exquisite care. His cheek against mine was the smooth softness that came from being freshly shaven, and his groan of pleasure set the water around me to boiling.

"That's been suggested, but the contention can be positively disproved," he mumbled. "My being a bastard, I mean. Licking my ear like that won't do you any good. I promised not to go on to anything beyond this, and I won't break my word. If you want anything more, you'll have to release me from the promise."

I couldn't curse him out that minute, not when he immediately kissed me again. This time the kiss was more intense than I knew was possible, so much so that it took a while before I realized that at some point we'd stopped being vertical. I was still mostly underwater but had been put down on my back, with my head raised slightly as if on a cushion. Those ledges he'd mentioned when we'd first come through the arch, half a lifetime ago . . . Bariden's body pinned me to the soft, form-fitting surface, only part of his weight negated by the lift of the water.

And he was ready, as ready as I, but was still doing nothing but tormenting me. When his lips left mine to move to my right breast, I was finally able to say everything I'd wanted to. I cursed him roundly, expecting it to make me feel better, but I might as well have been pronouncing the alphabet. I didn't *want* to release him from his promise but he was forcing me to do it, in the most low, mean, underhanded way there was. No threats, no pain, just the most exquisite pleasure—how was I supposed to stand up against *that*?

I held out as long as I possibly could, but there's a limit to what any human being can take. Bariden must have paid attention to every woman he'd ever had sex with, noticing what reached them and what didn't, practicing the positive until he'd completely mastered it. The mush I'd melted into had no chance against him, and finally I had to admit it. I whispered my release against his promise, found it necessary to say it again to make it audible and at least partly grammatical, and then got a surprise.

"Thank you," he whispered back, those blue eyes holding to me with more than desire. "I was about to die from wanting you, and now you've saved my life. The only thing I can do in return is make sure you don't regret your decision, not now and not ever."

He kissed me again, but this time the kiss was a sharing unlike anything I'd ever experienced. I realized I kept thinking that, that almost everything I felt was a first, just as though there was more than lust between us. That was ridiculous, of course, but as my fingers slid through the long, soaken strands of his hair, I began to wish it wasn't. He moved me as no man ever had before, touched a part of me I hadn't even known was there. I knew he'd never belong to me permanently, but would it be so wrong to enjoy what he gave while I did have him? Wasn't a small slice of the pie better than no taste at all? Even if it left behind nothing but crumbs . . .

Another man would have been desperate to get on with it, but Bariden was still producing firsts. He stood on the ledge while lifting me into his arms, then carried me to the bank and a bed he produced with a snap of his fingers. We were both also instantly dry, showing that his original spell had been prepared for all eventualities. I was tempted to be annoyed over that, the proof of his certainty that he'd get me, but then he put me down on the bed, and all annoyance vanished. He was sharing another of those kisses, the kind I'd never get enough of even if I lived forever.

I think I half-expected the actual sharing of sex to be an anticlimax, so to speak, but once again I was wrong. If I thought I was mush to begin with, I learned what boneless really meant as soon as he entered me. I moaned and kissed him and tried to touch him everywhere, but his heavy stroking quickly drove me into a state of pure sensation. I knew nothing but that I didn't ever want it to stop, not even after I fell from the cliff twice in rapid succession. He had me completely, his to do with just as he pleased, and it pleased him to take me higher than

even the EverNameless could have gone. It was incredible, indescribable—and when it finally ended, we ended
it together.

He kissed me one last time before withdrawing, then lay
beside me to hold me in his arms. I needed very badly to
sleep right then, but even as I snuggled up against his chest
I reminded myself sternly about what I had to do. Keep
it light and unimportant, let him know it was fun but no
more than that. Head off all need for eventual embarrassing
good-byes, an effort that will be more than worth it. Once
you get back it will be completely over . . . don't forget
that . . . never forget . . . never . . .

CHAPTER THIRTEEN

Bariden awoke to find Chalaine still sleeping, and the way she snuggled against him brought a smile to his lips and the oddest feeling to his insides. He thought about that feeling for a moment, trying to define it, then silently laughed at himself. The feeling was one he'd never had with a woman before, not even those women he'd considered special. What he felt for Chalaine said he never again wanted to wake up without her being there, safely and lovingly beside him. He'd known from the first that she was different, and now he also knew he loved her.

And he would tell her that as soon as possible. This time she couldn't disbelieve him, not after what they'd just shared. He shifted more to the side so that he could put a hand to her back, needing to feel the softness of her skin again. That stubbornness of hers had almost kept them apart; if he hadn't counted on her feelings from last night to resurface . . .

"What are *you* looking so satisfied about?" a sleepy voice asked with a yawn. "Aside from the obvious, that is."

"I was just thinking how much I love your skin," he answered her with a smile. "And your hair. And your entire body. At this point, I might even be forced into admitting less than total dislike for your—singlemindedness. The wait was definitely worth it."

"Well, obviously sex *does* make some men expansive," she drawled, looking up at him with a teasing smile. "But it *was* fun, I'll give you that."

"Lovemaking, not sex," he corrected her without amusement. "I thought we got the difference between the two settled yesterday, but the point is worth repeating. When I take you in my arms it's to make love to you, not to have sex."

"If you insist," she capitulated with another yawn, not quite as convinced as Bariden wanted. "How much longer until we go for the gate? Or have you thought of something else we can do?"

"No, I haven't thought of something else, and not for lack of trying," he said, diverted from the previous topic. "I'm forced to admit that the trap is narrow at this point, making us go the way they want us to. If we try to stand still and look for another way out, the one ahead of us could be permanently closed off."

"I hadn't thought of that," she admitted with reddish brows high. "We're only assuming there's another way out, and that we'll find it if we look. At this point there might not *be* an alternative, and by refusing to move on we *could* be permanently trapped."

"Which, despite the position I've earned, I wouldn't care for," Bariden said, running a finger across her flat middle. "When the time comes for me to settle down somewhere, I want the location to be *my* choice, not someone else's. And to answer your earlier question, we still have a couple of hours before what I hope will be the best time to try for the gate. Let's rinse off, and then we can sit down to a meal."

"Why not?" she said with a shrug, stretching hard before sitting up. "The thing that still bothers me, though, is that we don't know *why* we're being put through this. I have a feeling that if we did know, we'd have the answer to a lot of other questions as well."

"Questions like what?" Bariden asked, watching the way her body moved as he got out of the bed. And that auburn hair, sliding around her arms to frame her in silken glory . . .

"We've already discussed some of them," she fretted, unaware of his appreciation as she followed him to standing. "Like, why *are* we here? If someone wanted to get rid of us to keep us from finding out what was done to the stricken people and by whom, it would have been easier to kill us. Why go to all this trouble instead, and gamble on our not finding a way out? But at least we know one thing for certain: this trap was prepared for both of us, not just you alone. Do you see that now?"

"At this point I'd have to be blind not to," Bariden answered with a nod. "We discussed this once before, but now there's no doubt. Most of what we've gone through *was* aimed at both of us, but I've just thought of something. What if the only reason we're in this trap is to prove we're *not* better than the enemy? I mean, what if he's unstable enough to want to prove his superiority in everything over everybody? That would be the reason we're still alive, even though, objectively speaking, it's such a bad idea."

"I don't know if I like the sound of that, or hate it," Chalaine returned, hugging herself as if against an inner chill. "On the one hand, those who are mentally unstable are prone to overlooking things that fall into one of their twisted blind spots. That would mean we had a better chance of breaking free, but only if the enemy has enough blind spots. If he doesn't, there could be something really horrible waiting for us at the end of this."

"Let's not start thinking that way," he cautioned, pulling her into his arms to hold her close. "If there's a Spell of Volition on this next gate the way there was on the previous ones, dreading what might be ahead of us could trap us here. I prefer to believe that we'll win against whatever's thrown at us, which is what has to be our enemy's major nightmare. If, deep down, he wasn't afraid we really were better, he'd never have set this up in the first place."

"Which should also mean that, given the chance, we'll be able to figure out who he is when we get back," she agreed, raising her head to look up at him. "With that in mind, let's get this show on the road. The sooner we get back, the sooner we'll have the chance to meet him face to face."

"Now *that's* what I call incentive," Bariden agreed, then joined her in heading for the pool. Five minutes would do for *his* part of the face-to-face encounter, five satisfying and really pleasant minutes . . .

They swam briefly to wash the sweat away, then got out and headed back to his actual chamber. As they passed under the arch of mist, his spell returned their clothes to them, fresh and sweet-smelling and better than new. He eyed Chalaine as he banished their unusual bathing room and got ready to call up a meal, and she eyed him right back.

"Why are you looking at me like that?" she asked, having already brushed at and straightened her clothes. "And if you don't mind, I'd like to braid my hair."

"But I do mind," he answered, looking at her with his head to one side. "And I was just wondering why you shouldn't be wearing skirts, at least for the meal we're about to share. The one time I saw you in a gown I loved it, but there hasn't been a chance for a repeat of that. What's wrong with right now?"

She parted her lips to say something in immediate answer, then paused to study his expression. She'd obviously noticed he hadn't done much pushing over the fact of her loss to him in the competition, nothing like what someone else would have done. All he'd really asked for so far was to see her hair unbraided, and now to have her in a dress. Considering the fact that they'd be leaving after their meal, there would hardly be the time for it to get any worse.

"What's the sense in arguing?" she asked at last with a defeated little sigh, looking away from him. "You're the boss here, and I'm just a worthless slave. Go ahead and do whatever you like, you know I can't stop you."

For an instant Bariden was shocked to learn what she really felt, but then he was brought up short by sudden suspicion. Chalaine hadn't even thought that way when she was still refusing to argue with people; now, with the change in her personality, it was completely out of place. And in a strange way it seemed familiar, almost as though she were conceding defeat with a definite purpose in mind . . .

Bariden made a soft sound of annoyance, aimed mostly at himself but not entirely. Of course what Chalaine was doing seemed familiar, it was a variation of her original tactics. Telling him to go ahead and do as he pleased was supposed to make him do the exact opposite, from shame if nothing else. He didn't want to be known as a bully, after all, and what else would taking advantage of a poor, helpless slave be considered? If he were a real man he would forget about pressing his unreasonable demands . . .

"You know, I really like the way that sounds," he told her after his momentary hesitation, letting enthusiasm flow in slowly but definitely. "Yes, I'm the boss and you're the slave, and I can do anything I please. I *do* like it, so let's make it a little more obvious."

His spell was only a few syllables long, and when he added the gesture all her clothes vanished. Despite the fact that they'd just spent a few hours being equally as naked, she squawked and immediately tried to cover herself with her hands. Bariden grinned, knowing there was a big difference between being naked *with* someone and being naked alone, and she looked up at him with embarrassment flushing hotly in her cheeks.

"Damn it, that wasn't funny!" she growled, a miniature fury looking daggers at him. "And this isn't the skirts you were talking about."

"So I liked your idea better," he answered with a shrug, his grin full as he inspected the loveliness she had no hope of hiding. "Drop your hands and turn around slowly, just to give me a *good* look at my slave."

"Bariden," she began with furious warning, then seemed to notice *all* of his expression. He was joking only up to a point; beyond that he was totally serious. She'd tried to force him to do things her way, tried to get out of paying anything at all against her loss. She'd been the one taking advantage, but Bariden was never going to be taken advantage of by a woman again.

"All right, you win," she conceded, not the words she'd originally intended to use. "I wasn't playing fair, and you caught me at it. I apologize sincerely, and won't ever do it again. Can I have my clothes back now?"

"In a minute," Bariden murmured, unable to take his eyes from her. "I love looking at you any time, but this time is better than most. Take your hands away and turn around slowly."

Her cheeks reddened again with the knowledge that a simple apology wasn't going to do it, and there was nothing she could base a protest on. He had the right to finish any game she started—if he could—and they both knew who had started that one. They also knew he was proving his ability to finish it, for him, at least, in the most pleasant way possible.

It took a moment before she was able to drop her hands, and strangely enough it didn't seem to be embarrassment any longer that was bothering her. She kept her eyes on him as long as possible before she turned, then quickly moved her head the other way to get him in sight again. That magnificent auburn hair swept around with the movement of her head, and the fact that she watched him while he looked at her was too much for Bariden. The two steps between them disappeared without notice, and then he had her in his arms.

"By the EverNameless, I've never loved so much about a woman," he breathed, burying his face in that hair. "I wish I were a poet rather than a prince. Then I would *have* all the words I'm only able to grope for. Chalaine, I—Do you know how much you mean to me?"

"I wish I didn't," she murmured in response, then immediately looked up at him to banish his confusion over so strange an answer. "What *I* would like to know, though, is if there's enough time for something besides a meal. I would really like you to—make love to me again."

That hadn't been a problem since the instant he'd banished her clothes, and he couldn't imagine when it *would* be a problem. He kissed her rather than answering in words, banished his own clothes, then joined her in bed. This second time was even better than the first, but at the end of it they weren't exhausted. It was more like exhilaration that Bariden felt, and the only thing he regretted was that they hadn't the time to swim again. He freshened them with magic instead, less satisfying but more thorough than bathing, then dressed them and called up a meal.

"I was hoping you'd forget about skirts, but after seeing this I'm glad you didn't," Chalaine said, examining herself in the full-length mirror standing in one corner of the chamber. "I've never worn anything in silver lace, most especially not anything as delicately lovely as this. If I spill something from the meal on it, I'll probably kill myself."

"I'm glad you like it, but there's no need to go *that* far," Bariden answered with a chuckle from beside the table. "Come and sit down and don't worry about it. If anything spills, I won't have any trouble cleaning it up."

"But right now I would, and that's made me think," she said, turning away from the mirror to walk slowly over to the table. "Except for that one brief time on the first world, I've never been in a position where I couldn't reach my ability at all. In fact, that time in the first world—and in this one before the competition—aren't the same at all. In both those instances I was constrained from using a skill I still had, but now I can't even hear it when *you* speak a spell. The experience is totally different."

"It has to be like losing your eyesight or your hearing," Bariden said with a frown as he seated her. "I should have realized sooner that you would be suffering, but at least it won't be for much longer. As soon as we're through eating, we'll be heading for the gate."

"That's not what I meant," she said, watching him take his own place at the table. "At first I was furious at being cut off so completely, but then it came to me that our ability with magic has been a handicap as well as a strength all along. Using magic keeps getting us into trouble even when that trouble looks like a benefit, and having the ability to use it has kept us from thinking. Aside from the new warding we're using and the variable spell I put on my clothes against unexpected weather extremes, when have we taken *any* precautions before stepping through a gate?"

"We haven't," Bariden agreed, sipping at his coffee as he considered that very excellent point. "We've been assuming we'd be able to handle anything that came at us, simply because we're magic users. I remember thinking back at the hostel that it had been stupid of me not to be sure we had a good supply of gold and silver coins before coming to *this* world, but I forgot all about it. If you hadn't said anything I would have stepped through the next gate, supremely confident that my magic *would* take care of anything that came up."

"So it behooves us to do some thinking *now*," she said, peeking under one plate cover to see what the dish was. "Silver and gold isn't the only thing we could have used on this world, and probably won't be what we need on the next. What we need to do is think for a while, and then make a list."

That was the most sensible suggestion he'd heard in a long while, so he joined her in thinking while they ate. He would have preferred a good wine with the meal rather than the coffee he'd provided, but they'd need clear heads for tackling the gate. And coffee *did* help when he needed to think, a fact that proved itself when they began to make their list. More than one good idea was put down, and when they were through he sat back to consider the results.

"Silver and gold in modest but adequate amounts, to form as soon as we step through the gate in order to avoid problems here," he read off to Chalaine. "A change of clothes for each of us. Food in concentrated form that will last a week, the same with water. A miniature tent that will grow to full-size when exposed to the air, fully insulated against heat and cold. Emergency medical items. Automatic healing spell, automatic strength-gathering spell—which may or may not work—and a spell that sends greater magical strength used against us back in the face of the one using it. Anything else you can think of?"

"Not at the moment," Chalaine said with a headshake, nevertheless looking bothered. "That should cover us whether we can use magic or not. But I have the feeling we're still overlooking something, even though I don't know what it can be. The magical ability of those around us has increased from world to world, you know. Next time we could be utterly and completely outclassed."

"Or we could be back to the beginning, where we outclass everyone else," Bariden pointed out. "There's no way of knowing until we see the place and ask a few questions, and anticipating anything in particular could be a mistake they're hoping we make. On the other hand—"

"On the other hand we could spend the next year coming up with guesswork," she said after taking a deep breath. "You're absolutely right, and worrying about it will only make us reluctant to use the gate. That is, it might make *you* reluctant. For my part, I can't wait to get out of here."

"And I certainly can't blame you," Bariden remarked, watching her take a final swallow of coffee before pushing the cup away. "If I were a slave the way you are, I'd be just as eager to be on my way."

"Aren't you ever going to let me forget that?" she asked, the color rising faintly to her cheeks again. "No, your grin says you aren't, so don't bother answering any other way. Maybe next time *I'll* get to be the boss, then you'll know for sure how a slave thinks."

She glanced at him from under those long, dark lashes, but there wasn't anything of a threat in her expression. She seemed to know that even if he *was* put into a position where he had to obey her, the results would never be the same as they were there. And Bariden would never have to be ordered to give her pleasure, not when that was all he wanted to do for the rest of both their lives. He'd never get tired of the incredibly wonderful feel of her in his arms . . .

"I think we'd better get to it," he said after clearing his throat and rising. "Another five minutes of conversation, and I *will* be reluctant to leave. Do you need anything right this minute?"

"Aside from my regular clothes and that hairbrush, no," she answered, running her hand over the silk lace of her gown for a final time. "I'll miss this, but once we get back I can always recreate it. Okay, go ahead."

Peripherally Bariden thought there was something odd about what she'd said, but most of his attention was on the spells he was ready to speak. First he changed their clothes, making his as variable as hers, and then he produced the physical part of their list. Last, and separately, he spoke the spells they were taking with them, spells he fervently hoped they wouldn't need. What they did need was to be out of that trap, but so far they hadn't spotted the necessary opening in their prison walls . . .

"Okay, I'm all set," Chalaine announced once she'd put her new hairbrush into the pack holding the rest of what they were taking. "And I'm also the one who gets to carry this pack. If we have to defend ourselves physically as soon as we step through the gate, you're the one we want to be unburdened."

Bariden was reluctant to agree to that, but he had no choice. If he played the gentleman and insisted on carrying the heavy pack, the gesture could end up producing disaster. He nodded as he watched Chalaine heft the thing, made sure it wasn't *too* heavy for her, then led the way out into the hall.

When he and the others had toured the area earlier, there had been a good number of men moving about the wing. Right now the corridors were as deserted as he'd hoped they'd be, with the only sounds of life coming from the nearest gathering room. The room, halfway down a cross-corridor on the left, was quickly behind them, and then they were moving through the soft whisper of empty silence.

It wasn't long before they found themselves approaching the room with two guardsmen in front of it. The guardsmen watched incuriously as Bariden moved closer, but they found Chalaine of enough interest to study her carefully. Not that it really mattered. As soon as Bariden was near enough to be certain the two weren't being guarded by magic, he froze them where they stood.

"Now we go in," Chalaine muttered, shifting the pack she carried in her arms. "And I think a couple of backstraps would be useful on this thing."

"Once we're inside," Bariden muttered back, moving between the two guardsmen to open the door. "You first."

Chalaine moved past him quickly and without comment, and Bariden followed the same way. Inside was a large, undecorated room of gray stone, not even windows breaking up the blankness. The only thing it held was the gate, the glowing slit clearly surrounded by a Spell of Volition. Big surprise, Bariden thought, turning to close the door, and then he saw what *was* a surprise.

"She looks like she's been waiting for a while," Chalaine remarked as he finished closing the door. "Aren't you going to introduce us?"

"Not until I get my own introduction," Bariden commented in return, studying the woman. She stood in the near corner to the left of the door as you entered, a position that had kept her out of sight until we were inside. A tall and slender blond, she stood with all the grace and confidence of a born warrior. She wore the sort of breeches, tunic, and boots that Chalaine favored, but hers were in very light colors, including the fawn boots. Her face was no more than pretty, but her gray eyes held depths that most eyes didn't.

"Since I have the advantage of you, I'll perform the introductions," the woman said with a faint smile as she took one step forward. "I'm Darmillanne, and you're Bariden and Chalaine. I've been looking forward to meeting you two."

"Since we've been in this city for just under a full day, that's interesting," Chalaine said, setting the pack on the floor at her feet. "Would you like to tell us *why* you consider us so fascinating?"

"I think I can answer that in part," Bariden said with sudden inspiration. "Darmillanne is Sighted, and I think what she forgot to mention is that she's also the king. Am I wrong, Your Majesty?"

"You know you're not wrong," Darmillanne said with amusement while Chalaine frowned. "And I liked the way you put that. Nothing about 'king' being the wrong title because I'm a woman. Most people would be too thickheaded to understand that as ruler of this place, I can call myself anything I damned well please."

"Not to mention that it's more politically expedient and saves you a lot of trouble," Chalaine added with a nod. "Men fight under the banner of a king, but they fight to *protect* a queen. The difference there is one of attitude, and lets them believe the queen would be helpless if they *didn't* fight for her. When it's a bunch of ambitious sorcerers you have under you rather than fighting men, letting them know you're a woman would have them challenging you every five minutes. Most men have this strange idea that they're better than a woman."

"So I noticed quite a while ago," Darmillanne answered with a soft laugh. "My predecessor had that kind of blindness, which suited me just fine, but it also gave me an idea that let me cut down on the worst competition I could face. It usually gives me a chuckle that no one yet has figured out my unreasonable attitude toward women—except for you, Bariden."

"I had occasion to think about the matter," Bariden replied with an easy shrug. "And now that I see the way you move and gesture, I find myself with another suspicion. Was that you disguised as a man named Sarvallo earlier today, directing the competition? I have the strongest conviction . . ."

"You *are* good," Darmillanne said, her nod accompanied by an approving smile. "Yes, that was me, sizing up potential competition even as I accepted them into service. And before you ask, I *don't* use what I learn to defeat them if and when they challenge me. Real challenges are what keep me on my mental toes, making me constantly work to improve my skill. Without them I'd get fat, lazy, and sloppy."

"But you don't allow challenges from just anyone," Chalaine said, deeply attentive to what they were being told. "When we first got here, we saw a man screaming and writhing on the ground . . ."

"One of *them*," Darmillanne said with scorn and a gesture of dismissal. "There are enough of that sort that it makes me tired. Whoever that Sighted was, he was more interested in stealing than in challenging. I don't blame people for wanting to be king—after all, once I was one of them. But there's a legitimate way of putting yourself into position to challenge, where you first qualify for service. Those who want something for nothing have no patience for doing things the right way, they just want the goodies without earning them. Without proving they *deserve* them. They'd take the privilege without doing the job."

"So that's what you teach those in your service," Bariden said, seeing more of the whole picture. "A sense of responsibility to go along with earned rights. If you're ever defeated in a challenge, you want it to be by someone who won't think of himself as an interloper. He'll know the place he won is his by right, and will therefore value it rather than strip it just to satisfy overwhelming greed. He'll take your place, but he'll also keep doing your job."

"Which takes a lot more work than most people seem to realize," she said, one hand moving up to rub at her neck. "More than *I* realized before *I* took over. Afterward, I spent some time wondering if my win hadn't been just a little too easy . . . He'd been king a long time, and he always looked so tired and bored . . . Well, none of that matters right now. What does matter is why I'm here, engaged in a pleasant conversation with two strangers who have been sneaking around my palace and freezing some of my guardsmen. Anyone care to make a guess about *that*?"

She looked back and forth between the two people standing in front of her, and Bariden exchanged a blank glance with Chalaine. The question she'd put was the one that had been bothering him since he'd first caught sight of the woman, and it looked like it was about to be answered.

"No guesses?" Darmillanne said after a moment, less of that too-bright friendliness in her expression. "Since there are also no time-wasting protestations of innocence and ignorance, you've earned a small reward. Have a seat, and help yourselves to the refreshments."

Her spell to produce chairs and cups of coffee was simple, clear, and spoken loudly enough for Bariden to hear every syllable. He considered that a generous gesture of reassurance from a wizard who had more strength than he did and knew it. As a matter of fact they both knew it, so he sat and lifted his cup as soon as the king and Chalaine were seated. Refusing a wizard's hospitality wasn't recommended for continuing good health.

"Now then, the reason I'm here," Darmillanne continued. "It goes back to the time I first became king. I developed the Sarvallo disguise to let me move around anonymously, telling people that Sarvallo was my most trusted servant. Since 'he' was heavily protected by magic even against physical assault, I could wander as I pleased. When I was offered bribes to tell people about the new king, I accepted the bribes, then made it up as I went along. Since I made no effort to keep the different stories straight, people soon noticed and disgustedly stopped wasting their silver and gold."

She grinned with real amusement at that, and Bariden couldn't help chuckling. Someone with a strict sense of duty would have steadfastly refused the bribes, but the woman had a sense of humor instead. And intelligence. Happily taking people's money and giving them nothing in return stopped the bribes faster than all the refusing in the universe would have done.

"At any rate, I wandered," she went on. "What I paid most attention to was the people and how they were taking the shift in power, and in the process I stumbled across

something very odd. In the newcomers' wing there was a
guarded door, and although I must have passed the place
a hundred times, I'd never before noticed either the door
or the guards. I considered going in and looking at whatever the room held, but first I went to visit my guard
commander.

"The man was incredibly officious, but I finally pried
loose the information he had. It seems that that room had
been under guard for years and years, longer even than the
commander had held his post. His orders were to *keep* the
door under guard, and never report the fact even to the king.
No one was allowed inside the room, but I had the feeling
the man had once taken a look out of sheer curiosity. When
I pushed him he admitted it, but said it really didn't matter.
The room was completely empty, and looked as if it always
had been."

She paused to take a sip of her coffee, and Bariden
suddenly guessed that she'd supplied it for *their* benefit.
The way she drank it said it wasn't her favorite bever-
age, but telling her story distracted her enough that she
didn't mind.

"After that I was even more curious, so I went back to
my apartment and started a methodical search of my predecessor's records. He kept a daily diary, bless his soul, and
that was when I discovered he'd been *chosen* to take over
for the ruler before him. Not that he wasn't powerful, you
understand. Thousands of men must have tried him in his
day, but none of them had even come close to victory.

"But because he'd been chosen, he'd also been giv-
en some information that a successful challenger would
have missed out on. He was told that once he became
king, he might come across a room he'd never noticed
before. If he did, he was to ignore it, not try to look
inside or do anything to change the situation as it stood.
The guards on the room were to be left where they were,
and under no circumstances were they to be replaced by a
sealing spell. His diary said he tried searching the palace
for the room, but apparently he never got to the newcomers'
wing or thought to check with the guard commander. After
a little while he forgot about it, and never mentioned it
again."

At that point Bariden exchanged a glance with Chalaine, and the king picked up on it immediately.

"You seem to have something to say," she observed, again looking back and forth between them. "Whatever it is, I want to hear it."

"I think Chalaine and I were reacting to what you said about the king being forbidden to replace the guards with a sealing spell," Bariden told her slowly. "She and I had been wondering about that, specifically because this wing is filled with sorcerers who couldn't be stopped by unSighted guards. Part of our question is answered if no one but the king can see the door or the guards, but the rest of it remains."

"Like why you two can see it," she said, resting her chin in her palm and her elbow on the chair arm. "I doubt if that's the part *you* meant, but it's the one *I'm* most interested in. But tell me first why you think the guards were there. That *is* part of what you know, isn't it?"

"It's more of a guess than knowledge," Bariden admitted with a sigh. The king was a damn sharp woman . . . "We think there are guards on the room because we'd have no trouble getting past guards, even without using magic. A sealing spell on the room would be another matter entirely."

"And wouldn't have been so easy to spot," Chalaine said suddenly, pointing at Bariden. "You might have dismissed a sealed room as a place someone wanted kept private, but guardsmen in the middle of sorcerers' quarters—You'd have to be dead to miss *that*."

"You're saying you two were *meant* to find this room, and without any trouble." Darmillanne saw the point at once, her tone now sharper. "Tell me why, and also who arranged this. Not to mention exactly what it is you're supposed to do in here. And stop looking at each other like that. If you believe I'll let you get away with telling me only what you think I ought to know, you've never dealt with a wizard before."

Bariden had to consciously keep himself from looking at Chalaine yet again, a gesture that would have been futile as well as stupid. She couldn't give him permission to speak any more than he could give it to her, and they both knew how important keeping the secret was. There was no way to judge how much damage they would do by telling the full truth, and—

"Wait a minute," Chalaine said, then looked directly at him. "Are you feeling what I am? That it would be disastrous to tell anyone what we're in the middle of? That grim look on your face says you are, so I have a question. *Why* would it be disastrous?"

"That's easy," Bariden answered with a snort. "It's because—well, it has to be because—I mean, it stands to reason—"

Only then did Bariden notice the blank wall, the empty place where a good, logical reason for keeping silent should have been. Up until then it had made sense not to announce to the world that they came from a *different* world; when people don't know about other worlds—as most of the ones they'd met didn't—they have a tendency to look at self-professed strangers oddly, to say the least. But this was a wizard now questioning them, and you don't try to keep secrets from a wizard, not if you enjoy life without pain . . .

"Damn it, somebody set a compulsion," he growled, feeling really stupid. "They took our natural sense of caution and intensified it, and we never noticed. Or at least I didn't."

"I don't think they expected us to be questioned by a wizard," Chalaine said, looking as annoyed as he felt, but also grimly satisfied. "And I also doubt if we were supposed to pick up the information we just did. This arrangement isn't new, it's been here for years and years and years. That probably means we aren't the first to take this trip, and won't be the last. Doesn't that tell us something?"

"It's time you told *me* something," Darmillanne interrupted, but with less impatience than a moment ago. "Start from the beginning, and don't leave anything out."

Bariden still felt an overwhelming reluctance to discuss the forbidden topic, but Chalaine seemed to be doing better against the compulsion. She began with the problem they'd been working on, described how they'd been pulled into the trap, then listed the various worlds and their problems. Once she'd gone through it to the end, she added,

"And I think I have my competition loss to thank for being able to shake off the compulsion against talking. My own strength is most likely supporting the compulsion, but being cut off from that strength has weakened the compulsion's grip. It's still there, but it doesn't have the original choke hold."

"Fascinating," Darmillanne breathed, now staring at the closed gate on her left and Bariden and Chalaine's right. "Other worlds, other kingdoms with different people and needs. And *your* world, where gates to other places are commonplace and plentiful. Absolutely fascinating."

"You haven't told us yet how you knew we would be here," Bariden mentioned in a casual way. It might help to know that, some time in the future.

"I set up a very simple spell in the corridor outside," the king answered without taking her eyes from the gate. "Everyone who came through here *ignored* the door and its guards, so none of them could be the ones meant to enter. My spell watched for someone who *noticed* the door and its guards, and when that someone appeared, I knew it immediately. I waited here for hours, but it was worth it. I now know what that beautiful thing is, and in general how it works. What you haven't told me yet is how you get around whatever spell is on it."

"Don't you want to know first if you *should* try to get around it?" Chalaine asked, the words very deliberate. "I have the feeling you've been waiting for years for someone to come looking for this gate, but since you didn't know what it was, you couldn't think the problem through in a rational way. Right now you're seeing *our* world, with all those plentiful gates, lying beyond this one. The fact of the matter is, it *isn't*, and going through may not even be a step in the right direction. It's the only step Bariden and I can take, but it could well turn out to be a dead end we're being herded to. Is that really what you want to leave all *this* for?"

Darmillanne's head turned back fast, and the look she gave Chalaine was narrow-eyed and suspicious. Chalaine returned the stare calmly, showing nothing remotely like guilt or embarrassment, and that annoyed Darmillanne even more.

"You're assuming I *have* decided to leave, which doesn't happen to be so," she said at last, her own words very neutral. "Just because I want to know *how* to do it, you can't assume I will. For one thing, I'd first have to decide whether to choose a replacement for myself, or just put someone in temporary charge until I got back. You did say that all the gates you passed through were two-way?"

"Absolutely," Chalaine lied without changing expression. "But wouldn't you *very* first have to find someone strong enough to maintain your spells here while you were gone? Once you step through a gate, any unmaintained spells you leave behind will immediately cancel themselves through lack of your talent to draw on. I've never had that problem myself, but I'm not a wizard. Those from our world who *are* wizards do have the problem, but don't often have trouble with it. There are enough of them that they can call on each other for help any time they need it."

A peculiar expression passed across Darmillanne's face, and Bariden had to fight to keep his own face straight. Chalaine was doing a very thorough job of ruining the king's unspoken but fairly obvious intentions, and all without arguing or refusing to tell the woman what she wanted to hear. She'd lied about the gates being two-way, but that was only commonsense self-protection. If the king had heard they were one-way, she would have been certain she was being lied to. Bariden would have bet gold that Darmillanne was seeing her sudden dreams of empire building crashing down, most especially after that comment about how many wizards there were and how well they cooperated.

"I think it's time Chalaine and I got moving," Bariden said then, putting aside his coffee cup. "Since we don't know what's waiting for us, we'd like to be as fresh as possible when we face it."

Darmillanne hesitated, then said, "Very well. I now know everything you do, except for the one question you still haven't answered. How do you get through the spell?"

"That's relatively easy," Bariden answered, standing as Chalaine did the same after retrieving the pack. "If you really want to go through the gate, it will open for you.

Here, you can watch us doing it, and then you'll know what to expect."

Darmillanne hesitated a second time, and Bariden didn't have to tell Chalaine to hurry in order to take advantage of it. Any minute the king could decide she didn't want them out of reach if she thought of any more questions, and they would end up settling down on that world whether they liked it or not. He and Chalaine moved toward the gate together, the sound of the king standing up coming clearly from behind them. She'd pushed her chair back; was she going to—

And then whatever words might have been spoken were turned into a gasp as the gate flared wide. Darmillanne couldn't have seen that sight before, and it gave Bariden and Chalaine the seconds they needed to move directly into the gate. An echo of sound followed, as though someone might be shouting behind them, but magic alone can't get past the barrier. The only visible gate was a single step away, and they took that step . . .

This time we were indoors, with what looked like a smallish and deserted hut enclosing the gate. Once we were out the gate closed, and a glance showed it seemed to be embedded in the back wall of the hut. I put down the pack I was lugging with a sigh of relief, and turned to look at Bariden.

"I don't think she'll be following right behind us," I told him as he watched the gate. "Even if she's angry enough to want to, the reasoning part of her mind will have enough doubts to keep the gate firmly closed. As a matter of fact, at her level of greed she may never get it to open again."

"I know she's ambitious, but greedy?" Bariden said, looking at me with one brow raised. "What makes you think that?"

"I thought it was obvious," I said with a shrug, wondering how he could have missed it. "Ambition may make you kill for what you want, but it doesn't make you want everything there is to have. Once she was king she also mingled as one of the boys, making sure there was nothing she didn't know about and therefore couldn't control. Overseeing the competition was part of that, and I'll bet gold she was there to eliminate anyone who looked like they might grow to real strength. Those entrants who put everything they had into attack—their efforts should have canceled each other out, but you said it killed them both. Using magic isn't like using physical weapons, and that shouldn't have happened."

"I hadn't realized that," he said, now looking disturbed. "I thought she was fairly decent, even though I didn't trust her not to stop us. Ambition would lead her to want to expand her kingdom, but—what about the personal challenges she answers, and all those laws that showed concern for the people?"

"Personal challenges," I echoed with a sound of disgust. "How hard is it to make someone believe he's ready when he really isn't? Especially when you're keeping tabs on him while disguised as someone else? All those freely allowed personal challenges were another way of eliminating competition before it turned into something she might not have been able to handle. She didn't use them to keep her on her toes, she used them to keep her on her throne."

"And the laws?" he asked, speaking calmly and quietly in the face of my anger. I'd been able to keep my voice down, but not my emotions.

"Those laws, except for one, weren't hers," I stated, knowing it beyond doubt. "They were established—or continued—by the king she eliminated, and were most likely being maintained by *her* strength without her knowing it. My best guess would be that she was being groomed to eventually take the throne, but decided that 'eventually' was taking too long in coming. Instead of waiting her turn, she ambushed her mentor and took everything on the spot."

"Was *that* why she looked so startled when you talked about maintaining other people's spells?" he asked with sudden surprise. "I thought—Well, I didn't think she was first finding out she was maintaining without knowing it. But she did mention that her predecessor had been chosen and trained by the king before *him*. Legal succession was the rule before her, but hers wasn't the same. How did you figure all that out?"

"The one law *she* put into effect told me," I said, now glancing around the hut. Packed dirt floor, rough wood walls, cut grass roof—architecture at its finest. "That rule about what's done with women who compete and lose is hers, a nastiness contrived through spite and fear. She said she wasn't underestimating other women the way *she'd* been underestimated, but the word she should have used was trust. She'd been trusted, and had used that to stab people in the back. She didn't trust other women not to do the same, so unless they were basically incompetent, she made sure they lost. The men were free to come back and try again—after all, *they* were manageable—but she didn't want her most feared competitors to do the same. I realized the law was hers when she didn't say a word about it to me. She knew I'd lost, but wasn't in the least concerned."

"If that's true, then we have her to thank for saving us some trouble," he said slowly, apparently considering what he'd been told. "We were certainly *supposed* to face each other in the competition, but under the old rules one of us would have ended up barred from the palace for a year. The only thing that saved us was that law, which let me bring you into the palace when you lost. Without it—I don't know what we would have done, but it wouldn't have been as easy as what we did do."

"Then—maybe we were meant to go in a different direction," I said, suddenly worried. "We saw nothing of the countryside at all, and didn't even ask someone besides the hostler any questions. What if we weren't supposed to get through *this* gate, but another one in a place we wouldn't find unless we left the city?"

"I'd say it's a little late to be worrying about that," he answered, taking a step back toward the gate we'd come through. "This gate is just like the others, and it isn't opening even with me right on top of it. What you said to the king about all the gates being two-way—it's too bad it wasn't true."

I stared at him and the unopening gate, a sinking fear twisting my insides, and that's when we heard the shouts and screams coming from outside . . .

CHAPTER FOURTEEN

Bariden ran out of the hut, and I was right behind him. Obviously there was a more immediate problem than whether or not we should be where we were, and stepping out of the hut showed it to us. The day was dark and cold, middle to late afternoon, the cutting wind saying a weather change was definitely on the way. It had been cold in the hut too, I realized, but we'd been too distracted to notice . . .

And those people who were screaming and shouting were far too busy to notice. There were quite a few of them, men, women and children, but their six male attackers were armed while they weren't. Some of the men were trying to defend themselves with sticks or hoes, but those don't do well against swords. The six attackers were laughing while they chopped down everyone around them including some of those trying to run, and acting as if they had nothing to worry about. Not five feet away from the hut we'd been in was the probable cause of that attitude. A man lay on the ground covered in his own blood, clearly dead or dying. Beside him was a compound bow and a quiver of arrows, the one arrow that had been in his string tangled up with the bow. The man seemed to have had the only weapon there, and the attackers had evidently taken care of him first.

"At least they're not in armor," Bariden muttered, and his sword was already in his hand. "You stay back out of it, Chalaine, and don't try using magic unless they come at you over my body. We still don't know the rules in this place."

He glanced at me with more—expression—than your usual glance contains, and then he was running toward the very uneven fight. Six to one is terrible odds, but he was probably hoping he was good enough to take a few of them out before they could make their numbers count. I itched to try a freezing spell—and would, if it looked like he was about to be bested; waiting until he was down was an absurdity only a man would think of. I would use magic as and if I had to but, happily, there was something else to try first.

The downed man's bow was spattered with his blood, but at least the string hadn't been cut. I stepped around him carefully but quickly, retrieved the quiver and then the bow, withdrew three arrows from the quiver, then renocked the arrow he hadn't had a chance to loose. No one else had gone for the weapon, of course, not when touching it would bring the six attackers down on the toucher with swords swinging. Terror tactics designed to minimize resistance . . .

But just then the six men were being distracted from their fun by Bariden's approach. Everyone including them wore what looked like homespun made by an amateur, and their swords had apparently seen better days. Bariden shouted something I couldn't hear as he ran, and those men with sticks and tools fell back away from the ones with swords. The attackers had stopped laughing as they looked at the newcomer, and one or two were snarling in outrage. The rest, though . . . did those expressions mean they already counted Bariden's clothes and weapon theirs . . . ?

"Guess again, you slime," I muttered as I drew the nock back to my ear. Three of the six were coming forward to meet Bariden straight on, but the other three, two to the left and one to the right, were circling around in an effort to get behind him. The wind whipped my hair around in gusts, the worst kind of wind where arrows are concerned, but I'd loosed under conditions like those before. The front one of the two on the left first . . .

Carefully timed between gusts, the arrow flew straight and true, right into the chest of the man I was aiming for. Hearing his scream and seeing his blood was more upsetting than I'd thought it would be, but I couldn't afford to let squeamishness distract me from helping Bariden. I nocked another arrow from the three I held with the fingers of my left hand, shifted aim, then took out the attacker sneaking around on Bariden's right. I was reaching for a third arrow when I suddenly noticed what was going on with the fight, and the sight stopped me still with my jaw hanging.

That problem I usually had with causing things to happen—I hadn't seen any evidence of it in quite a while, but now it was back with a vengeance. The first man I'd shafted had apparently stumbled backward, but not to simply fall down. He staggered into the man behind him, the other one on that side trying to flank Bariden, and the two had tangled up and gone down together. The one on the right, also with an arrow in his chest, had spun around rather than staggering or falling, and his sword had chopped into one of the three men facing Bariden. That one was clutching a bleeding middle and staring disbelievingly at the wounded man who had chopped him, and then he added the icing. With a vicious thrust he put his sword into the man who had accidently wounded him, and the two fell to the ground together.

Which left only two opponents for Bariden. I blinked at the way that had happened, wondering why the twisted talent was suddenly working *for* me rather than against. Not that I was complaining. We needed all the help we could get, and the thing couldn't have chosen a better time to appear.

The two men left were suddenly less eager to face Bariden, but he gave them no choice about it. He brought the fight to them with such speed that they had to try attacking in turn, and that became their final mistake. He slashed open the one on his left and caught the other with his backswing, and the two began to crumple to the ground together.

The last one of the six, the one to Bariden's far left who had gotten entangled with the first man I'd shafted, had made it back to his feet. He'd begun to run in with his sword raised high while the previously last two were still unhurt, but his timing was terrible. He reached Bariden seconds after he'd dealt with the two, just as Bariden turned to him with sword extended. He ran onto Bariden's blade as though he'd hit a brick wall, but the big man he'd tried to attack wasn't thrown off balance. The move had been carefully calculated to take out the last of the six, and when Bariden jerked his sword free, the fight was over.

It took a few seconds for the people huddling out of the way to begin moving naturally again, and when they did they went first to those of their own who had been hurt. Too many of the bodies on the ground were beyond help, but some would survive their wounds and recover. Here and there a man or woman cried quietly above someone who hadn't been so lucky, and the very quietness of their mourning sent a shiver through me.

"Hurting the helpless is a cowardice I've never been able to understand," Bariden muttered as he came up to me, his expression savage over the waste of innocent lives. He must have cleaned his sword without my noticing, since it was already back in its scabbard. "And considering this wind, that was incredibly good shooting. I had no idea you could use a bow so well."

"Archery is my nonmagical hobby," I said with a shrug, wondering if he'd noticed the rest of what had happened. "It takes a lot of practice to gain the proper grace of style, not to mention hit what you're aiming at, but it's worth the effort. But to tell the truth, it's never been worth *quite* as much as it was today."

"I'm just glad you made that effort," he said with a gentle smile, putting an arm around my shoulders. "I might not have survived this if you hadn't. And we'd better get you inside out of this cold and nasty weather. I can see how you're shivering—"

His words broke off as he looked down at me, but I was already with him on that. I *was* shivering because of the cold, but I shouldn't have been. The variable spell on my clothes should have kept me warm, but it didn't seem to be working. Bariden's expression said he was just realizing his own clothes weren't adjusting to the weather, but before either of us could say anything, a small group of people approached us.

"Please . . . we need to ask you . . ." one of the women said, all but trembling with fear. "Did you do that for yourselves . . . or for us?"

Bariden and I exchanged a glance, not quite sure how to answer. The woman who had spoken—thin to the point of gauntness, her ankle-length dress faded to a washed-out brown and white, she stood with two other women just like her. Behind them were others, and the men among them were trying to hide the presence of sticks and hoes.

"We did it for us and you both," Bariden answered carefully, looking around at them. "If people don't stand together when they're attacked, no one is safe. Who were those men, and what did they want here?"

"They were from the next village over," one of the men supplied while the women just hugged each other in relief. "They must have heard that we lost two of our fighters, and the other three were out trying to get the two taken swords back. What they wanted—why, what *would* they want, if not our food and blankets and prettier women? What else *is* there to want?"

There was no easy answer to that, not when you looked around at the village. A scattering of primitive huts, a dirt street, struggling fields beyond the farthest huts—for people who did nothing but scrabble to survive, what else *was* there?

"Will you—will you stay to protect us until our own fighters get back?" another man asked. He had brown hair and eyes, unlike the first man who was blond, but the two were as thin as the women. "We'll share with you the way we do with our fighters, and you can even have one of the empty huts. There are other villages around here besides the one those six come from . . ."

He let the words trail off as his eyes begged us, the same way the eyes of all of them begged. Even with the six swords they'd gained they were helpless, at least until some of them were trained to *use* the weapons. Beside me Bariden stirred, undoubtedly bothered by such naked need, but I couldn't wait any longer to ask the most important question.

"But how can you possibly need protection?" I blurted, more upset than I'd realized. "You're all Sighted, every one of you. Why can't you use magic to protect yourselves?"

"We're not from around here," Bariden added hastily as they all stared at me as though I were crazy. "We don't know anything about what's happening here, so you'll have to tell us. And don't worry, we *will* stay to protect you until your fighters get back, so please—tell us what's going on."

"Don't know how anybody could be that much of a stranger," the second man muttered while the first rubbed his face with a grimy hand. "It's the same for everybody . . . Well, I guess it doesn't matter, even though I hate saying it out loud. We're just as good as *them*, we all know that, but they got to their power first so we're out of luck. They say the truth is we can't do what they do, that we're just not up to it, but the truth *we* know is that they need somebody to look down on if they're going to feel special. That's why they force us to live like animals, scraping out an existence and accepting their handouts."

"Kam means we can't do magic because *they* won't let us," the first man said while the second fought to control his anger. "They claim they haven't done anything, but even if we get a spell and try it, it doesn't work. Whatever we do has to be done by hand, the slow, hard way, while they— they all live like kings. Can't you see it just by looking at their city?"

The man's gesture was as bitter as his words, and we turned to the right to see what he was talking about. Just beyond the hut we'd come out of there was a sparkling haze of sorts, something that suggested a kind of visible warding. We could see through it easily enough, but walking through was probably impossible.

But what there was to see! It was close enough that it seemed to stretch into forever, a city the likes of which I'd never even imagined. The buildings looked as if they were made of pastel crystal and precious jewels, and each was the size of a small palace. Lacy walkways extended between some of the buildings, and the land between them and us looked like exquisitely cared-for gardens. Even as I watched, a small party of people rode beautiful horses out from one of the palaces and turned left. I couldn't hear their laughter even though I could see it, and their clothes were magnificent creations in all the colors there are. They looked as though they were heading out for some exercise and maybe even a picnic, but I didn't have to wonder where their picnic basket was. When they got where they were going, they would create whatever they wanted.

"Twice a year, midwinter and midsummer, they give us handouts," the first man's voice came from behind us. "Blankets and cloth mostly, along with tools and seed for planting. And extra food, things *they* didn't have to grow or raise in order to have. They claim they can't give us everything, that we have to work to make lives of our own and anything else we might want, but why *should* we have to? *They* don't have to, so why should we?"

"Because watching us crawl and struggle makes them feel good," the second man said, answering what should have been a rhetorical question. "They keep us from what ought to be ours, and expect us to believe it isn't them doing it. Well, if it isn't them, who else *could* it be? We sure as hell aren't doing it to ourselves."

I turned away from the sight of magnificence that was totally beyond reach, and Bariden reluctantly turned with me. The small group of people near us were all agitated, some as furious as the two men who had spoken, the rest miserable to the point of tears. One man seemed to be crying from frustration, and I could understand exactly how he felt.

"Is it possible to get into that city?" Bariden asked, one hand rubbing at his neck. "Do they hire servants from any of the villages, or come out on any sort of a regular schedule?"

"Why would they need to dirty their city with servants like us?" the dark-haired Kam asked bitterly. "They have magic to do what has to be done, no lower life-forms needed or wanted. None of us ever go in, and they don't come out. When it's time for the handouts, the things just appear."

"Like magic," the blond man added, the words very flat. "We've got to go and bury our dead before the skies really open up, but first I'll get you some blankets and food. These three huts are empty, and you can have your choice among them. You keep that bow, girl. There isn't a man here who can use it half as well as you do."

The conversation was breaking up because it had started to rain, a light drizzle that might keep up for the rest of the day, or turn into a true downpour. The crystal city beyond the mist had been bathed in golden sunshine, something I'd seen but hadn't really noticed.

"Chalaine, go back to where we left the pack," Bariden said quietly. "I'll be with you in a minute."

I picked up the quiver of arrows before getting in out of the rain, then turned in the doorway to see what Bariden was up to. He had his dagger in his hand as he walked toward the six bodies we'd made, and when I saw him bending over the first of the men I'd shafted I was able to turn away. He was retrieving the arrows I'd probably need next time, and although I knew it was necessary, the very thought of it made me sick.

It didn't take long before he joined me in the hut, but by then I'd managed to get a fire going. The smoke hole in the center of the roof looked like it had been chopped through rather than planned for, but there *was* a wooden rain shield over it that kept out all but a fine mist. It was starting to rain harder, which meant I was glad a woman had already run in, dropped a pile of blankets and a small cloth package, and immediately run out again.

"I'm glad you knew how to do that," Bariden said, putting the two arrows he'd retrieved near the quiver before coming to stand near the fire. "I've never had occasion to do it by hand, and I was picturing us shivering in the damp."

"A Sighted friend of mine goes camping out as his hobby," I answered, carefully feeding a larger piece of wood into the fire. There was a pile of wood in one corner of the hut, and despite the musty smell it gave off, I was glad it was there. "He took me with him once, and insisted on teaching me how to do this. He said it couldn't hurt to have the knowledge, and one day might even come in handy. I haven't touched the pack."

He looked at me as I straightened, obviously feeling the same reluctance I did about checking on our "preparations." It was all we had, a representation of what we'd thought we'd learned, a last hope I couldn't bring myself to seek the truth about.

"The longer we put it off, the worse it will be when we do look," Bariden said after a very short hesitation. "And we already know the gold and silver is useless. When not having a blanket or food can mean your death, you don't give those things away for shiny but valueless pieces of metal. But there has to be *something* we can salvage."

He went to the pack and opened it, and it turned out he was right. The extra sets of clothes he'd provided were all right, and so was my hairbrush. The medical items still included bandages and a small jar of ordinary salve for cuts, but the cream to accelerate healing had disappeared, as had the lotion for pain. The bars of concentrated food were there, but Bariden took one small taste and spit it out. Without the flavor of a magnificent meal, the stuff had to taste like sodden paper. The small jug of water was just a jug of water, and would not be refilling itself. The miniature tent was nowhere to be seen, and certainly wouldn't have worked even if it had been there.

"Everything depending on magic is gone, but what was created by magic isn't," Bariden said where he crouched beside the pack, his expression thoughtful. "I wonder if that means anything."

"It means we've had it," I supplied, turning away to walk to the doorway and look out at the rain. It was falling really hard now, and the dark of the clouds had merged with the dark of approaching night. As a landscape it made me shiver with chill, but as a picture of what our future would be like, it was perfect.

"I don't know how you can stand there and watch mud being created," Bariden said, coming up behind my right shoulder. "You seem to have a thing for water—which reminds me of a question I kept meaning to ask you. That day we met for the first time—why *were* you carrying that giant ball of water?"

"I was in the middle of an experiment when the Summons came," I explained with a faint smile of memory. "It had occurred to me that in most places people put out a fire by throwing buckets of water on it, one at a time. Sometimes, if there are enough people and buckets it's two or three at a time, but that's still horribly inefficient. If they had *spheres* of water available instead, spheres that contained five to ten gallons of water each, everyone could grab a sphere and throw it . . . instead of running back and forth lugging buckets . . . or yelling for help from a Sighted . . ."

His left arm came around my shoulders when it was clear I couldn't go on, and then I was turned around and held tight to his chest with both arms. He made soothing, comforting noises as he patted my back, but if he thought I was crying he was wrong. I was feeling too desolate and defeated to cry, too much like someone at the dead end of a long and unpleasant road. I rested my cheek against his shirt without saying anything, only thinking about all the effort and planning we'd wasted.

"Look, I know how you feel because I feel that way, too," he said after a moment. "If there's a next gate out of this place, it ought to be in one of the palaces in that incredible city. Right now we can't get in there, but tomorrow we might suddenly *find* a way in. You're not going to give up when we might be only one more step from home?"

"Those might-be's should answer your question," I said, moving myself away from him and out of his arms. "We 'might be' only one step from home, but we might also be a thousand steps from it. Or too far away even to count the steps. I'm sick and tired of this game, and I don't want to play any more. Even looking at *that* is beginning to bother me."

He knew by *that* I meant the closed gate in the wall, and I wasn't joking. I was tired of being led from one world to the next, chasing the dangling carrot of eventual escape. We weren't *going* to escape, and it was time we admitted it.

"I don't happen to agree," he said, and I heard him closing the door and pulling in the latchstring. "That gate hanging there is sticking its tongue out at me, and I've never taken that from anyone. I'm good and sick of this game too, but I won't give up until I win. The only reason you're not seeing it the same is because you *are* tired, which means you need to get to bed early for a good night's sleep. Tomorrow you'll hate the sight of that gate as much as I do."

"If so, then I'll move to one of the other empty huts that man mentioned," I said, going back to the fire to put on another piece of wood. "Continuing to struggle is just what's expected of us, and I refuse to keep on doing the expected. If whoever-the-enemy-is doesn't like it, I have a suggestion about what he can do with himself."

"By the EverNameless, you're even stubborn when you're depressed," Bariden came back with exasperation. Then he was in front of me again, those blue eyes shadowed as he looked down at me with folded arms. "And what if *I* don't like it? Are you going to tell *me* what to do with myself?"

"Why not?" I countered reasonably, folding my own arms. "I know you've come down in life, but that's no reason for me to discriminate against you. And I think I'll move tomorrow even if Sight of the gate *doesn't* bother me. If you're going to be busy making plans, you won't want to be distracted by depression."

He studied me silently for a moment, then said, "We can discuss that tomorrow. Right now it's time to think about bed, but don't let your thinking dwell on details. It won't be pleasant for us here, or even particularly comfortable, but we *will* survive. And we'll win, Chalaine, we *will* win. Even if you doubt everything else in this world, don't doubt that."

He turned away from me then to walk to the side of the hut, bent down, then straightened with what looked like a long, lumpy sack in each hand. The thin sacks seemed to be about three feet wide, and when he got them back to the fire he shook them one at a time, apparently trying to distribute their contents evenly. When he had them side by side near the fire, he headed for the pile of blankets the woman had brought.

"The people of this village pay well for protection," he commented after picking up the blankets and looking at them. "One old and two relatively new for each of us. But after the deaths from that attack, they probably have blankets to spare. It's too bad we can't say the same about beds. I've never slept on a straw-filled pallet, but people do, so I'll manage. Now, let's see . . ."

He took the two old, frayed blankets, folded them in half, then placed one on each of the sacks. After that he spread out two of the newer blankets one on top of the other, then the final two as a sort of doubled, turned-down cover. I stood there silently and watched him, feeling more depressed by the minute. Pallets, those lumpy sacks were pallets, and we were expected to use them instead of beds.

"We can't afford to sleep in our clothes, not when the refreshing spell won't be working any more," he said, reaching to his swordbelt to remove it. "We'll let them air out overnight, and if it isn't raining tomorrow we'll find out where clothes washing is done. After that we'll have fresh clothes as often as we can wash the worn set."

He set his scabbarded sword down on the ground near where he would sleep, then sat to wrestle his boots off. I continued to stand where I was, totally opposed to cooperating with that particular inevitable in any way at all. Adapt and survive? For what reason? To give the enemy more fun as he watched our useless struggle?

"Chalaine, you aren't getting undressed," Bariden said, the reminder gentle. I looked up to see that he was standing again, his tunic off and draped over his boots. All he had on was his leather breeches, and suddenly a previously dismissed idea popped up again.

"Damn it, that fool *is* matchmaking," I growled, annoyance coming to join depression. "First there was only one room at the hostel, then I *had* to stay in your quarters in the palace, and now this. He must have been having a grand old time watching, but the show is over. I'll be damned if I perform for a fool."

"Hold it," Bariden said before I could turn away in anger. His tone was still calm, but not quite as gentle. "That statement doesn't fit the facts, and I think you know it. Didn't we agree that the results of your competition loss were due to the king's spell rather than anything done by the enemy? That single room at the hostel was probably meant to distract us from effective planning, after which we would have walked into the competition unprepared. Here—didn't you say yourself there are two other empty huts available? Where can deliberate manipulation possibly come in?"

"Just because it isn't easy to see, that doesn't mean it isn't there," I answered with almost no hesitation at all. "Everything else that's been happening is manipulation, so why shouldn't this be? If you enjoy doing everything the enemy wants you to, go ahead and do it. I don't enjoy it, so I won't."

This time I did turn away, and even walked to the hut wall behind me. I could hear the sounds of rain outside, but without windows I couldn't see it. It was chilly in the hut away from the fire, but it was also stuffy with the door closed. I hated that world, more than any of the others, more than anything I'd ever experienced—

"Chalaine, stop it." Bariden's voice came from directly behind me, gentle again but strong with certainty. "The way you're acting has nothing to do with the enemy, and not even with these primitive conditions. You know what's really bothering you, so why don't you say it?"

I looked down at hands that were shadowy blobs in the darkness, feeling how close he was. He must have gotten his feet filthy, walking shoeless on that dirt floor . . .

"Chalaine, say it," he repeated, those big hands coming to my upper arms. "Refusing to admit the truth doesn't stop it from *being* the truth. Say it out loud so we can both hear it."

"I don't want to belong to you," I stated in a very low voice, fighting to keep from trembling. "This world is made for that kind of an arrangement, and you're taking advantage of it without a second thought. You're too big for me to fight without magic, so you think you have it made. But I hate the whole idea, so I want you to *un*make it."

"I see," he said, the words at long last uneven, his hands dropping away from my arms. "You don't want to belong to me. I thought it was something else, but this isn't the first time I've been wrong. And I certainly didn't mean to make you feel that you were being taken advantage of. Since you hate the arrangements I've made, allow me to make different ones."

I heard him move back across the floor, there were sounds of activity, and finally there was silence. After a moment of that I looked over my shoulder, and the new arrangements he'd made were very obvious. His pallet and blankets were still in the same place, but mine had been moved to the near side of the fire. Bariden lay in his blankets with his back to the fire—and to me—and all conversation seemed over for the night.

Which was just as well, since I had nothing more to say. I went to my pallet and straightened it a little, then sat down to pull off my boots. The rest of my clothes would have to stay on, since I had no intentions of sitting up all night just to feed the fire. Once it went out the hut would be really chilly, and the blankets would never—

I put my face in my hands to be certain I made no sound, my back to the fire and to the man I'd offended. Deliberately offended, despite the kindness he'd been showing me. He'd been going to make me sleep beside him and once there would certainly have made love to me again. But I couldn't let him do it, not when one more time would have forced me to admit I was in love with him. He loved my hair and my skin and having me in his bed, but I loved *him*. The two things weren't at all the same, and the difference would have killed me.

Was killing me. I slid my hands down to my mouth, freeing my eyes to stare at fire shadows on the wall. Chances were excellent that we were trapped on that world for good, and once Bariden was able to admit that, he'd probably insist that we marry. But I didn't want him because he had no other real choice, because we shared knowledge of a far different life. He wouldn't have understood how I felt and would have insisted, and I wouldn't have been able to refuse. I *did* want to belong to him, but only where he chose me above all others, not where he settled for the only available choice.

So I'd ended everything before I said the wrong thing, choosing loneliness over reluctant acceptance as I had many times before. And it would turn out to be the right choice, especially if we stumbled over a way to get out of there. Once we got back, Bariden would be relieved not to have a blurted confession of love on his hands. He'd be able to go back to his old life with no complications blocking his path, and I'd be able to go back to mine . . .

Our pack lay on the floor not far from my pallet, so I stretched to it, slid the hairbrush free, then sat again to brush my hair. First thing in the morning I'd move to another hut, and then I'd sit down to do some serious thinking. There was something wrong about what had happened to us with this last gate, and if I could put my finger on the point it might work to get us out of there.

But just in case it didn't, I'd say nothing about it to Bariden. I'd loved the way he'd kept trying to make me feel better, the wonderful strength and determination he'd shown. It was all so much a part of the total him, the man I'd remember for the rest of my life. He deserved the best, and as much as I hated to admit it, that wasn't me.

I was even too stubborn to settle for something I wanted desperately, not unless it was on my own terms.

The brush I held slid through my hair, now that most of the tangles were gone. Its handle was smooth to my fingers and palm, and holding it that close almost let me taste Bariden's trace. He was the one who had made it, after all, so his trace would always be part of it. It was as much of him as I would ever have, and probably more than I deserved. What a fool, to fall in love with a man like that, and then refuse to settle . . .

I sat there until the fire died, brushing my hair while quiet tears streamed down my face, and then I went to sleep.

Bariden walked slowly through the village, pretending he was thinking, in reality trying not to think. Most of the men and women and older children were out in the fields, trying to get as much done as possible before it rained again. The older men and women still in the huts had their hands full with the very young children, half of whom apparently hated the mud, the other half wanting to play in it. They nodded to Bariden but otherwise ignored him, and that suited him perfectly.

And that was just about the only thing that did suit him. The sky was low and gray with the threat of more rain, the wind was colder than the day before, the ground was almost pure mud, and none of the huts he'd glanced into held more than the one that was currently his. Pallets with blankets, small piles of dirty clothes scattered around, a few pots and pans, the occasional tool . . . As if all those people had just moved in, rather than having been there long enough at the very least to have put in the crop that was almost ready for harvest.

And that magical city, beyond the shielding mist! Every time he caught sight of it he felt the urge to pick up a rock and throw, fueled by the fervent hope that he would somehow hit a crystal wall and shatter it. Beyond the mist it was sunny and looked warm, and the grass glistened with the drops left by a pleasant shower. No mud, no poverty and misery, just beauty and the wealth of luxury provided by a power denied to him and those around him . . .

Denied, lots of things were denied. Bariden stopped and stared at the thick forest beyond the edge of the poorly cultivated fields, remembering the most important thing that was being denied him. I don't want to belong to you, she'd said, sounding as if she were talking about slavery. It had been obvious something important was bothering her, and he'd been so *sure* he knew what it was. She was being forced to admit that she loved him, just as he'd already spoken of his own love. Once she said the words there would be nothing left to stand between them, and even *that* world would be beautiful . . .

But the words she'd said hadn't been the ones he'd expected, and when he heard them the world came crashing down instead. He'd been so hurt he'd fallen back on a refuge of childhood and had sought escape from life in sleep. He'd awakened that morning already searching for what he might say to her, but it turned out he didn't have the chance to say anything. She and her few possessions were already gone, moved to the empty hut two huts from his.

"Not even next door," he muttered to the distant forest and not-distant-enough clouds. "She wants to be as far away from me as she can get, even if it's only another twenty feet. And there's nothing I can do about it."

Which wasn't strictly true. As he turned and started back to his hut, he admitted silently that it was a matter of nothing he *would* do. As she herself had pointed out, he was big enough to carry her back to his hut over his shoulder. Neither she nor anyone else would be able to stop him, but the idea left something of a bad taste in his mouth. If the woman you held in your arms didn't want to be there, you were cheating yourself as well as her. Without the deep, intoxicating pleasure of mutual desire, you might as well use your hand. Only inexperienced little boys didn't know that . . .

And besides experience, Bariden had enough stiff-necked pride not to want anyone who didn't want him. He would feel like a beggar with hat in hand if he went after her, even if he *was* capable of dragging her back. He usually ignored people who didn't care to know him—even in his position there had been a few—and he would do the same now. The very same. Even if he *couldn't* stop loving her.

Time passed without notice while Bariden wandered around, but his attention kept coming back to the mistlike warding that blocked access to the magical city. In an effort to know what the warding was like, he tossed a few rocks and sticks at it. Everything thrown went into the mist cleanly, but didn't come out again on the other side. It would probably exclude living beings rather than absorb them, Bariden guessed, but both exclusion and absorption would be automatic. What he needed to do was get the attention of someone inside, someone who would bring him and the girl through the warding. Once they had access to the crystal palaces, finding the gate would be no harder than it had been up until then.

But, assuming he could get someone's attention, what could he possibly say to make them want to allow two intruders inside? He could tell the truth about their situation, but would that be enough to make those high-living Sighted cooperate? If it wasn't, what *would* be enough?

Bariden pulled his pallet to the door of the hut and sat on the end of it, looking outside at the mud and trying to think. His biggest problem was lack of sufficient detailed information, but he wasn't likely to get what he needed from the villagers. They were so involved with hating the people beyond the mist, they didn't *want* to know any details about them.

And while he thought about the villagers, he might as well consider what he could do for them. With their fighters away they were just about helpless, but there were now six swords in the village not being used. He could start to train the men in small groups when they came in from the fields, teaching them the feel of a real sword in their fists but training them with practice weapons. It would be hard for them to work all day and then practice, but he could keep the sessions relatively short and still give them the basics. Since it would work toward preserving their lives and the lives of their families, they would be more than willing.

An older woman came by with two cloth-wrapped packages, one of which she handed to him without comment. She took the second to a hut to his left, where Chalaine sat in her own doorway looking everywhere but at him. With the way the huts were set in a curve he could see her easily, but looking would have been a waste of time. He looked instead at the food that was wrapped up in the cloth, but in a way that was worse. The small chunk of unidentifiable meat was boiled, and so was the unpeeled potato. The cut of bread was almost as hard as the rocks he'd thrown to test the warding, and didn't even look as appetizing. He hadn't tasted what they'd been given the night before, but somehow he knew there would be nothing of seasoning or artistry used in the cooking. In order to stay alive he would have to eat the food, but the experience wasn't one he was looking forward to.

It took Bariden a while to get around to the food, and then it took effort to swallow it and keep it down. He distracted himself with thoughts of what he would teach the villagers first, and eventually became absorbed in setting up a schedule. The day dragged on and on, but at least it didn't rain again. Some older children drove a small flock of sheep past his hut, and then the villagers were back from the fields.

Bariden decided to give the men a few minutes to relax before he chose the first ones he would train. *He* felt bored and impatient from not having done anything all day, but it wasn't the same for them. While he waited he toyed with the idea of suggesting the men might be able to set up a rotation in the fields, giving him different groups of men to work with for short periods during the day. That would let all of them be trained in the fastest time possible, and—

He broke off the thought at sight of the men approaching, what looked to be almost every man in the village. Here and there two or three argued desultorily, an exchange of words rather than a prelude to physicality. The rest looked interested or satisfied or annoyed, but they weren't coming to speak with Bariden as he'd thought they were. Without even a glance in his direction they approached Chalaine's hut, and stopped about five feet from it.

"What can I do for you gentlemen?" Bariden heard Chalaine say as he got to his feet. Part of the crowd was blocking his view of what was going on, and he had the definite feeling he'd soon find that a problem.

"We heard you weren't with the fighter any more, so the untended men drew lots," the man named Kam answered.

He seemed to do a lot of the village's talking for it. "Riss here won the draw, so you'll go with him. The rest of us came along so you'd know the drawing was official. Go and get your things now, it's getting close to suppertime."

"That's no problem," Chalaine returned with a shrug, rising to her own feet. "Since I'm not going with him, it doesn't matter *what* time of day it is. Was there anything else?"

"Of course you're going," Kam said with a smile as most of the men with him chuckled. "Women aren't allowed to live alone, not as long as there's a man who wants them. You'll go to Riss's house as is proper, and you'll tend to him. If you don't, you won't eat."

"That's your idea of a threat?" Chalaine asked with a snort of ridicule. "After tasting what I was given earlier, it sounds more like a major favor. Why do you people live like this? There's not a stick of furniture in any of these shacks, those fields are planted so sloppily half the ground is wasted, and you keep grass-destroying sheep instead of cattle. To top it off you make no effort even when it comes to what you put in your bellies, so what *do* you do to make life better? Or don't you want it better?"

"How can it be better when we're denied what should be ours by right?" Kam demanded, he and the others no longer amused. "Those thieves in the city have stolen our rights, and all we have to call our own are our houses! How much sweetness is a life like this supposed to provide?"

"Life isn't supposed to provide the sweetness," Chalaine countered, looking around at all of them. "Life provides the opportunities, and it's your taking advantage of the chance that turns the trick. There's a big, thick forest less than a mile from here, with all the wood anyone could want. Why aren't you using it to make chairs and tables and beds, and maybe even *real* houses with windows? Just because you can't use magic, that doesn't mean you can't use sweat. Why—"

"Enough!" the man who had been pointed out as Riss shouted, one hand in the air and the other over an ear. "I don't want this woman any more, not when she shows the world how stupid she is. Taking her into my house—*house*, stupid woman, not shack—would be more trouble than any possible pleasure I might get. If anyone else wants her, it's fine with me."

Bariden watched the other men in the crowd mutter and shuffle, but none of them stepped forward to claim Chalaine. It wasn't necessary to guess to know why that was, and now that their business with her was finished, he had his own to discuss with them.

"Kam, I'd like a word with you," he called, and all the men seemed glad of the opportunity to walk away from a distasteful situation. Most of them just turned in his direction, but Kam and the blond man who had spoken the day before made their way through the others to stand in front of him.

"I've got an idea I think you'll like," Bariden said when he had everyone's attention. "Those six who came attacking your village yesterday weren't very good with their swords, and if they're typical of the fighters around here, your troubles are over. I can teach you men enough to be able to protect yourselves in a very short time, especially if you take turns working in the fields and working with me. I'm ready to start this afternoon, so who wants to be in the first group?"

Bariden looked around, intending to count the number of volunteers before deciding on class size, but there wasn't a hand in sight. And not only that, but they were all looking back at him as if he were out of his mind. The only explanation he could think of was that they hadn't understood him, but before he could rephrase what he'd said, Kam held up a hand.

"Two fools speaking out on the same day," Kam stated, his other hand over an ear. "No wonder they didn't stay in the village where they belonged. If they weren't fighters, we wouldn't want them *here* either."

"What's so foolish about learning to defend yourself?" Bariden demanded while the other men made sounds of agreement with Kam. "Do you like it better being helpless?"

"When our fighters are here, we *aren't* helpless," Kam said in a patiently-explaining tone. "They fight for us, and we're perfectly safe. That's what fighters do, you know, in return for not having to work in the fields. If we have to work in the fields anyway, why would we want to learn how to fight?"

"And if we did all learn to fight, who would be left to feed us by working in the fields?" the blond man put in, almost as patient. "The women can't do it alone, otherwise they would already *be* doing it. The oldsters can't, because then we'd have to cook and care for the brats ourselves. Do you understand now how foolish you were being?"

"That's not what I understand, but I still withdraw my suggestion," Bariden said, knowing when he was just wasting time. "And since it's starting to rain again, you'll probably want to get back to your—houses."

It wasn't just starting to rain it was beginning to pour, and that roused the villagers somewhat out of their slowness of movement. They still didn't hurry, though, and Bariden couldn't stand it. He stepped into his own house, kicked the pallet out of the way, and slammed the door.

"Of all the stupid, useless, closed-minded fools ever created—!" he fumed, then had to turn and open the door again. He still didn't know how to start a fire, and with the door closed it was too dark to see anything. Of course, with it open his floor would soon become a sea of mud, but what difference did *that* make? He was already floundering neck-deep, and in more than mud.

"We've got to get out of here," he muttered, staring out at the rain. "There *has* to be a way to reach the people in that city, some way to get their attention. Assuming they're willing to *give* their attention. What if the handouts they provide twice a year satisfy their sense of responsibility to those less fortunate? What if the only difference between them and these people is that they can do magic?"

The thought was downright sickening, and there were enough things in that world to turn Bariden's stomach. He turned away from the door to pace the room, remembering that Kam had said it was almost suppertime. Now that was a prime example of stomach-turning if ever there was one, and if he wanted to avoid it he'd better start thinking. So, how do you attract the attention of someone who has lots of experience ignoring unwanted overtures . . . ?

"Excuse me," a quiet voice said from behind his back. "Do you mind if I come in for a few minutes?"

Bariden turned to see Chalaine just outside the hut, standing in the pouring rain rather than stepping inside without permission. If any girl in the universe ever needed a keeper . . .And then he remembered how she felt about him.

"For a few minutes, no," he allowed, working to keep his tone cool and uninterested. "What can I do for you?"

"I was wondering if you were still as anxious to leave this place as you were yesterday," she said as she stepped inside, one hand pushing back her sodden hair. She hadn't rebraided it, and it hung in dark strands against her equally sodden tunic. "If you are, I think I know where the necessary gate is."

"So do I," Bariden answered. "In that unreachable city beyond the mist. And I'm not *as* anxious, I'm beyond climbing walls. Those people are—Go and light a fire before we get into this any more. If you just stand there and shiver, you'll end up with pneumonia."

Bariden all but growled the last two sentences, having had no intention of saying them but finding the words popping out anyway. Chalaine looked like a half-drowned cat, and one who couldn't quite meet his eyes. He couldn't stand seeing her like that, shivering from the cold and wet. He couldn't put his arms around her, and he couldn't build a fire . . . and he couldn't find their way out of that place . . .

Rather than let the list of couldn'ts build any higher, Bariden watched Chalaine build the fire. She went and did it without comment, using wood from the corner and some sort of small metal device that was near the wood. She opened the metal device, used it to make scraping noises, somehow produced a tiny flame in the bottom of the box, then transferred the flame to a slender stick before blowing it out in the box. Small branches had been put in the fire circle first, and setting the slender stick under them soon had *them* alight. As soon as the fire had definitely caught, Chalaine added a larger cut of wood, then went to replace the metal box beside the wood pile.

"Here, wrap this around you until the fire gets a little hotter," Bariden said, handing her a blanket before going to close the door. "Now, did you mean you know where in the city the gate is? That won't help us much if we can't find a way *into* the city."

"No, that wasn't what I meant," she answered, already wrapped in the blanket and sitting near the fire—and still not looking at him. "We have to start a little farther back, specifically with the last world. From what we learned, it was guaranteed that one of us would lose the competition and end up needing to leave the city. It wouldn't have been possible for the one who was accepted into service to sneak the other in secretly, not with wizard-strength magic to fight. Either one or both of us would have had to leave."

"Both of us," Bariden decided as he sat on the other side of the fire. "If we were still together, and we were, we wouldn't have let ourselves be separated. We both would have left the city and—what? Found another gate?"

"I think so," she agreed, fiddling with one corner of the blanket. "The gate we were supposed to find, one that would take us deeper into the maze. But we reached this one instead, and it led to what looks like a dead end. Those people out there will never have more than they do right now, because they flatly refuse to work for something that others get with magic. They'll spend lifetimes stealing from and killing each other, all the while staring hungrily through the mist at what will always be beyond their reach."

"And I have the feeling those inside the warding are no better," Bariden said, watching the hungry flames lick at the wood. "The least they could have done was make the barrier solid so no one *could* see through, and also stop feeding their vanity with twice-yearly handouts. If you want to help people you teach them how to help themselves, you don't make them dependent on you. But you said this *looks like* a dead end, and that means you don't think it is. If so, where do we go from here?"

"Not into that city," she said, reaching one hand out to warm it near the flames. "If we spent our time concentrating on a way to get in, we'd be no better than those people out there. I had no idea where we *would* go—until that conversation of a few minutes ago. Didn't anything about it strike you as odd?"

"Everything about it was odd," Bariden returned dryly. "Especially that gesture of refusing to listen to something by covering *one* ear. I'd love to know where they got that."

"Probably from the same place they get everything else, the Sighted in the city," she said. "But that wasn't what I meant. These huts they all live in—those people got me so annoyed I called them shacks, and the one named Riss went to great pains to correct me. To them it's a house they return to, even without windows, furniture, plumbing, or amenities. A house, not a hut or shack."

"And?" Bariden prompted. "I can see that means something to you, but I'm still drawing a blank. What do *you* think it means?"

"Well, actually, it's stretching a point," she admitted, glancing up at him and then quickly away. "If a place is a man's house, it's also usually his home. A lot of people use the two words interchangeably, and, well, have you ever heard that saying about what a man's home is supposed to be?"

"A man's home is his castle," Bariden said slowly with dawning understanding. "Or, to match our current needs, his palace. This hut was given to me when we got here, so it can be considered *my* palace. And my palace has a gate!"

"But one that won't open for us," Chalaine pointed out, dampening his excitement. "As I said, I think I found the gate we want, but we still don't know how to make it work. That's the next thing we have to think about, and I came here to tell you so we'd both be working in the proper direction. I appreciate the blanket and the fire, but now I ought to be getting back—"

"Don't move," Bariden interrupted, pointing a finger at her while his mind raced furiously. "Give me a minute to think."

She settled back looking puzzled, but that was all Bariden noticed. He was too busy putting certain clues and hints together, and when he was through his excitement had doubled.

"That's got to be it," he said with a laugh, raising his head to look at her again. "It was all right there, but I let myself be misdirected. If this doesn't teach me not to assume, nothing ever will."

"Assume what about what?" Chalaine asked, still looking puzzled. "You don't mean you have the answer?"

"At this point it's only a guess, but it's one I'm willing to bet on," he responded with a nod. "Now it's your turn to think back, to the time we got here. We discussed the king and her machinations, then heard the attack going on outside. We rushed out and ended the attack, learned that the villagers are all Sighted, then were told no one outside the warding mist is allowed to do magic. When we came back in here we also discovered that what had been produced by magic was still in our pack, but what depended on magic wasn't. We'd already noticed that the gate wasn't opening for us even though there was no spell of any sort on it, so we decided we knew what we were up against."

"Where does 'decided' come into it?" she asked, those dark eyes forgetting to avoid him. "We did know what we were up against, from matching it to what we saw and were told."

"And was that a truth we made any attempt to prove or disprove?" he countered. "These villagers are Sighted, so when they said magic was forbidden to them, we believed it. After all, there were a lot of Sighted in the previous world who were constrained from using most of their talent by a single wizard. There seem to be a lot of wizards here, so why shouldn't it be possible that *all* magic is forbidden?"

"Are you saying—" she began, frowning in confusion. "What *are* you saying?"

"I'm saying think about our major source of information," he told her, leaning forward a little. "Those people out there are hopeless cases, unwilling even to learn enough about weapons to protect their lives. They said they got a spell from the Sighted behind the mist and tried it, but it didn't work. Chalaine, does being Sighted guarantee that if you speak a spell it will work?"

"Of course not," she breathed, now a picture of revelation arrived. "If you try a complex spell without having first learned the basics, you can't put the necessary strength into it. Without strength and training the complexity will overcome simple inborn ability, and nothing will happen. And those people out there are too stupid and lazy to have bothered with the basics. They'd expect to be able to do magic just by waving their arms!"

"And we didn't try our own hands at it because of the situation in the last world," he agreed somewhat grimly. "You called up a cup of coffee without thinking, and paid for it with a lot of pain. That kind of thing tends to make you nervous, not to mention overly cautious. We were told we couldn't do magic here, so we simply took their word for it."

"Making those villagers absolutely right about one thing," she growled. "They called us fools, and we are. Or at least I am, but I'm willing to change and learn."

She sat up straighter and spoke a spell, and suddenly she was no longer huddling into wet clothes, soaked to the skin. All the rainwater had been banished, and a cup of hot coffee had appeared in her hand. Bariden spent no time watching her take the first, groaningly wonderful sip; he spoke his own spell, which brought him a turkey sandwich as well as a cup of coffee.

"So once again we tripped over our own natures," Chalaine said at last while Bariden was occupied with wolfing down the sandwich. "I didn't try a spell because of that episode with the coffee, and you didn't try one because in your position you're used to *not* using magic. What else are we doing to blindfold and hobble ourselves?"

"We're still assuming," Bariden supplied after he'd swallowed and had a sip of coffee. "It didn't help that my previously cast spells were canceled when we came through that gate, but maybe in the end it helped enormously. There's still one assumption tripping us up, I think, but this part of it is *my* guesswork. What did we do in other worlds that we didn't do here?"

"I don't know," she groped, making a vague gesture with one hand. "Get ourselves invited to a fancy meal?"

"Since we got the fanciest available here, I'd say no," he answered with a brief smile. "What we did on all previous worlds was ask about gates, and try to call up an entry. We passed on the entry part in the last world for a reason. If you hadn't been afraid the wizard-king might be listening, you wouldn't have decided against trying."

"And here I didn't try because I believed I couldn't do magic," she said with a nod. "Does that mean you think it might work? Even though it didn't work anywhere else?"

"One of the questions that occurred to me was *why* it didn't work," Bariden said. "If magic in general worked, and it did, why wouldn't an entry spell work? And how can there be gates linking only two worlds? Everything we know about gates insists that it's the points from *multiple* worlds that brings them into being. Two points alone might start the process, but other points would then be drawn in. How is it *we* keep finding nothing but what ought to be impossible? And as two final questions, why were the spells I prepared canceled as we came through this gate, and why won't it open for us? There's no question about our being able to do magic, so why won't it open?"

"Logic would say there's only one possible answer," she replied slowly, staring at the gate. "If it looks like a duck but doesn't walk, quack or swim like a duck, chances are it's something else. These aren't gates we've been using, they've only been made to look like gates. That means they're probably entries instead, but I still don't see it all. How does that help us?"

"It helps if my final guesswork tucks in," Bariden responded, almost heavily. "When you told me the way out has been under my nose all along—Well, I jumped to certain conclusions. The first was that these aren't gates, and that's why specific spells didn't come through with us the way they would with a real gate. We were supposed to believe our magic was useless here. Then came the part about why entry spells didn't work, when these were almost certainly entries. Could it be that entry spells *do* work, but only in a few, specific places?"

"Why, of course!" Chalaine exclaimed, her large, dark eyes even wider. "There are planes that are very hard to reach, where connecting up an entry takes hours or sometimes days. One reason for that is supposed to be the lack of—amenable entry sites, you could call it. Only certain points of those planes will accept the creation of an entry, so you have to wait until your spell connects up with one. If you were on the inside looking out instead, you could go through to any part of your own world, but only by using one of those limited points! Bariden, you've done it! You've found the loophole that will get us out!"

"I certainly hope so," Bariden muttered, all excitement and pleasure strangely gone. "Why don't you try an entry spell on the indicated point to let us know for sure?"

"In a minute," she answered, banishing her cup and jumping to her feet. "First I have to get something I left in my hut. I'll be right back."

He watched her race out into the rain without understanding, then dismissed it all with a shrug. As soon as she got whatever it was she wanted to take with her, they'd find out if his guess was right. It was stupid for part of him to wish he was wrong, something that would continue to keep them there together. He already knew how she felt about him, and that wasn't likely to change no matter how long they spent in that world. They'd both be better off at home, where distance would let him pretend to forget . . .

"Okay, all set," she announced as she came back in, needing to banish water damage again. "Keep your fingers crossed."

"Isn't that a gesture the unSighted believe will prevent magic from affecting them?" Bariden asked as he got to his feet. "What good do you expect it to do *us*?"

"As much good as it does them, which is to say, at least it supplies hope," she responded. "And we'll need every bit of help we can get, considering the strength of the one we're up against. Here goes."

She raised both hands and spoke her spell carefully, but it wasn't necessary for either of them to hold their breath. The false gate flared wide instantly, inviting them to step through, which they did. Side by side, partners in adventure, strangers in every other way . . .

"Well, it's about time!" an indignant voice announced, and then Bena was bustling up to them. Chalaine's entry had brought them to his father's palace, in the corridor outside the kitchens. "Do you two have any idea how frantic everyone's been? First you disappear into nothing without a word to anyone, and you stay away for an entire day. Now you come back out of nothing without the least warning, scaring a body—"

"An entire day?" Bariden protested. "I don't know what kind of clock *you* use, Bena, but for us it was a lot more than a day. Are you sure that's all it's been here?"

"It's probably a matter of different flows," Chalaine said before Bena could answer. "A day here can equal a tenth of what's experienced elsewhere. But that's not in the least important right now. We were in the middle of an investigation when we were forced off the scene, but now we're back. Let's get that cleared up first."

"Cleared up how?" Bariden demanded, suddenly feeling left behind. "When we were dragged out of here, we had no idea what was being done or who was doing it. What do you imagine has changed?"

"Only one thing," Chalaine said, turning to look straight at him. "I had an entire, uninterrupted day to think. Since I started from the very beginning, I now know who the enemy is."

CHAPTER FIFTEEN

The chamber wasn't very large, but there was still plenty of room for those of us who occupied it. It had taken a couple of hours to get the interested parties together, and I'd made sure to use the time wisely. Once the preparations were complete I'd gone out to the garden near the kitchens to wait, my feet propped up and a cup of coffee in my hands. Bena came by to offer me something to eat, but I had no interest in food. All I wanted was for that farce to be over, and then I'd be able to go home. Home . . .

At the moment there were eight of us sitting around a conference table, plus a group of guardsmen positioned around the chamber. Those last were there because of Bariden's father's presence, and King Agilar had brought four of his advisers. Along with me, Bariden, and Master Haddil, that made the primarily involved eight.

" . . . and that's how we managed to get back," Bariden was saying, the end of his report on what had happened to us. He'd been shocked to hear I knew who the enemy was, but the reaction had worn off by the time we gathered in his father's meeting chamber. He also hadn't pressed me for details, knowing he would hear all about it soon enough.

"Just the fact that you *are* back, and safely, would be enough for me, Bariden," King Agilar said warmly, his smile looking real. "I'd sooner lose my kingdom than one of my children."

The man was tall and slender with light brown hair and blue eyes, a good deal less imposing than you would expect a king to be. In point of fact he seemed more gentle than anything else, and it wasn't possible to doubt what he'd said.

"Thank you, Father," Bariden answered with a warm smile of his own. "Your support has always been my greatest source of strength. But getting back safely wasn't the only thing we accomplished. Chalaine says she knows who's behind the trouble here, and I'm certain she does. If she hadn't been sure, she wouldn't have said anything at all."

"An admirable quality, Lady Chalaine," King Agilar said with another smile, moving those mild blue eyes to me. "I'm sure everyone here is just as eager to hear your thoughts on the matter as I am."

"Not everyone, Your Majesty," I said with no amusement at all. I was also no longer looking at Bariden, who sat opposite me to his father's right. I was to the king's immediate left, and two of the advisers shared my side of the table. The other two were next to Bariden, leaving the end of the table opposite the king for Master Haddil.

"Not everyone wants this problem solved, Your Majesty, at least not yet," I said. "People are nervous about what's been going on, but they haven't gotten panicky yet. The best time to come up with a solution would be once the panic did set in, which would make the revelation more a miracle than simple good fortune. There are two other teams of sorcerers working on this. Does anyone know how *they're* doing?"

The king seemed surprised at the question, but he didn't ask why I wanted to know. Instead he looked in Master Haddil's direction, and that worthy cleared his throat.

"As far as I know, the other two teams haven't discovered anything at all," he said, speaking to everyone rather than just to me. "Of course, I haven't had any reports from them since yesterday, so that could have changed by now."

"Could it have changed far enough that they've *also* gone missing?" I asked next, immediately drawing his gaze. "What I mean is, do you know for certain that they haven't been snared the way Bariden and I were?"

"No, I don't know that for certain," he answered slowly, his stare thoughtful. "Do you?"

"Not for certain, but it's a good bet," I returned, then looked at the king again. "None of those four struck me as the brilliantly deductive kind, but even they could get lucky and trip over something obvious. But the main reason they would be gone would be as a blind, to cover the disappearance of Bariden and me. If only he and I were tossed into a trap, someone might start wondering why."

"But the why would be obvious," one of the advisers on the other side of the table protested. "You might have gotten too close to the truth, which is in fact what did happen. How else would it have come to you?"

"It so happens it came to me because I had an entire, boring day to sit through, and nothing else to do but think," I told him. "If I'd been left here—well, if I'd been left here I would have come to the same conclusion, but that's the point I'm trying to make. Prince Bariden and I were gotten rid of because we were both determined to get to the bottom of the mystery, because we were *capable* of doing it, and because we were investigating here, in the palace, where the answer happens to be."

"You're saying one of the people close to me is responsible," King Agilar said after a moment of silence from everyone. The statement surprised me, but it shouldn't have. A stupid man wouldn't have been capable of creating such a happy, prosperous kingdom.

"That's exactly what I'm saying, Your Majesty," I agreed, then turned to look at my former teacher. "Isn't that right, Master Haddil."

This time the silence was thick and shocked, since my inference couldn't have been any clearer. Master Haddil returned my stare without expression for a moment, and then he smiled.

"You can't possibly mean *I'm* responsible, child," he said, completely unworried. "Not only is the suggestion ridiculous, it makes no sense. Considering the damage the problem is doing to my reputation, I'm the one suffering most here after the victims. And if I were responsible, why would I be so foolish as to bring in others to investigate? Why run the risk that one of them would find me out?"

"Let's discuss the foolishness of bringing in others first," I said after sipping at my coffee. "Wouldn't someone who was making no headway on a problem, but who refused to ask for help, look even worse? It was something you *had* to do, so you went about making the necessity work for you. By inviting in your four best students first and turning them into victims, you accomplished two things. The first was, obviously, getting them out of the way before they could discover you were the guilty party. The second I was there to see for myself, and it did an incredibly efficient job."

"It discouraged others from getting involved," Bariden said suddenly, snapping his fingers. "Of course! I was there too, and when the people Summoned heard that the four best among them had fallen victim, most of them turned around and went home."

"After that performance showing how distraught their teacher was, how could they be expected to do anything else?" I agreed. "Only six of us were left to look into the matter, but four of the six didn't count. They were self-centered or ineffective nonentities, who would waste their time on dead-end leads without ever noticing they weren't getting anywhere. They'd be too busy feeling important, and trying to make themselves *look* important."

"And the last two?" Master Haddil prompted, apparently nothing more than interested. "If four of the six didn't count, presumably the last two did."

"The last two were the most dangerous," I obliged him, shifting in my comfortable chair. "One of the two was a prince of the kingdom, determined to catch the miscreant for his father's sake. The other was a very close friend to one of the sorcerer victims, a sorceress who was considerably more effective than most people believed. Those two would need special treatment, and they got it."

"By being thrown into a trap," Master Haddil said with a nod, but I shook my head.

"It started well before *that*," I said, and there were sounds of surprise around the table. "In point of fact it started a little while before I was Summoned through the entry. You located me and saw what I was doing, Master Haddil, and it gave you a really good idea. When your entry appeared in my workshop, there was a very subtle spell on it twined around the general Summoning. I was to come *at once*, but was specifically not supposed to drop everything first. In point of fact, I was compelled to bring what I was working on *with* me."

"Don't tell me!" Bariden blurted, and I nodded without looking at him.

"Yes, that whole episode with the sphere of water was a set-up," I confirmed. "I was compelled to bring it with me, tripped as I came out of the entry, and the sphere was knocked out of my hands. I remember thinking everything would be all right when Master Haddil's warding destroyed the sphere, but that didn't happen. Master Haddil's warding bounced it, straight at a sorcerer who wasn't warded and also didn't know what was in the thing. Believing it was nothing but a very large soap bubble, he let it hit him."

"Are you accusing me now of having so atrocious a sense of humor that I play practical jokes?" Master Haddil asked mildly. There was a hint of amusement behind the calm of his stare, but I didn't share the feeling.

"That was no joke," I told him, meaning the words in every possible way. "It was another plan with more than one purpose, basically meant to sabotage the investigation. I was made to look and feel like a self-conscious twit, Prince Bariden was made to look like an incompetent idiot, and the two of us got off on the worst possible foot. You knew from the start, you see, that he and I would be paired as partners for the investigation."

"He rigged the spell on the tiles," Bariden growled, coming to the obvious conclusion. "He said the spell would produce the *best* pairings possible, but he had the spell already prepared. He didn't speak it where we could hear it."

"Probably because the spell demanded the *worst* possible pairings," I agreed. "He had already given *you* a reason for disliking *me*, but he isn't the sort to leave things to chance. He also arranged for me to have a similar reason, and the spell must have been very simple. He just made sure you would *not* hear my name any of the times it was mentioned, and also gave you no opportunity to ask what it was."

"By the EverNameless!" Bariden roared as he glared at Master Haddil, a very appropriate choice of words. "No wonder I couldn't remember what it was. I never heard it! And I'll bet he also made sure you noticed."

"He didn't have to," I said grimly, sending my own glare toward the wizard. "He knew me well enough to *know* I'd notice, that's why he did it in the first place. He was hoping we'd spend our time arguing and accusing rather than being productive, but it didn't work out like that. He kept an eye on us, of course, and when he saw me find the clue that would eventually lead to his discovery, he hurriedly arranged that trap."

"So you think you have more than pure guesswork and imagination?" Master Haddil asked pleasantly. "If so, by all means, do continue. I can't show everyone how wrong you are until I hear everything you have to say."

"Oh, you'll hear it, all right," I told him dryly. "What I found was an odd residue in the bathtub of the guest bathing room of the first victim. Since the merchant hadn't been in the apartment long, I wondered why it was there. *He* had his own bathing chamber, and he hadn't yet had the opportunity to have guests. It couldn't have been left over from a previous guest, not when the queen's Chief Housekeeper is known to inspect empty apartments on a regular basis. If everything in the apartment isn't perfect, whoever is responsible for not having done his or her job is dismissed.

"So the residue meant something significant, but I was distracted before I could realize that consciously. The memory came back to me while I was doing all that thinking, and suddenly everything fell into place. Someone had tried to get rid of the substance down the drain of the bathtub rather than down the sink or commode, because the bathtub is emptied by pipes and the other two are emptied by magic."

"My goodness, that argument would convince everyone in the kingdom of my guilt," Master Haddil commented soberly. "I wonder if I should confess now, and save people the effort of actually accusing me."

"Jumping in before I can explain what I mean won't distract anyone, Master Haddil," I said as quickly as possible. "These people aren't so stupid as to let you divert them before they can hear all of it. If my accusation won't hold water, they'll know it once I've finished."

The wizard's expression was completely neutral, but he couldn't be very happy. Two or three of the king's advisers had been one breath away from supporting his ridicule, but what I'd said kept them silent. To interfere now would be to acknowledge oneself as stupid, and none of them cared to do that. It would be better to sit there and listen, and declare me wrong once I was through.

"So a drain was used that didn't depend on magic while two that did weren't," I continued. "The problem was to figure out why that was, and it took some skull sweat before I did. Finally, though, I realized that to dump a substance down a magic drain causes *all* of that substance in range of the spell to be disposed of. If you've got grease of some sort on your hands, for instance, and some of it dripped on your clothes, and got on the doorknob, and maybe even spilled on the floor both inside and outside of the bathing room—*all* of it, every bit, would be cleaned up by the spell as soon as you deliberately tried to clean up some of it. That's the reason for *having* a spell like that, rather than a plain, ordinary drain. And here in the palace, I'll bet the range of that spell is wider than it would be anywhere else."

"I still don't understand, Lady Chalaine," King Agilar said, looking disturbed. "If the substance was an important clue, wouldn't the person who left it *want* it cleaned up completely? Why try to get rid of it in the first place, if you don't want to be rid of it entirely?"

"You'd want to get rid of it in the first place because that's what was left after it had been used," I explained, trying to be as clear as possible. "You would *not* want all of it cleaned away, though, if there was a chance the person you used it on would be carried close enough past the bathing chamber that he was in range of the spell. *That* would cause the substance to also be cleaned out of *him*, and he would no longer be frozen in place by some sinister, unknown malady. Then all your plans would be ruined, and you would have wasted your time. And before anyone argues the point, the commode spell works differently from the sink spell, but works on *ingested* substances."

This time there was a commotion rather than silence, all four of the advisers trying to speak at once. Bariden seemed to understand completely, the king looked really disturbed, and Master Haddil raised his voice to drown out the advisers.

"I think—" he shouted over the gabble, then went on more quietly when the four gabblers settled down. "I think that sounds very clever, but it doesn't quite fit all the facts of the problem. When the healer was called, he couldn't find any trace of a drug that might have been given to the victim. He tried a general banishing of all noxious substances, and that didn't work either. How, then, could there have been *anything* given to the victim for the drain spell to clean away?"

"That's easy," I answered, and all the attention shifted back to me. "The drug was protected by a spell, to make sure it *wasn't* banished. The healer couldn't find it or get rid of it because it was protected by the strength of a wizard."

"But that's still no reason for me to use the bathtub," Master Haddil countered, and all eyes and heads swung to him. "If I called the stuff up and protected it, I could have banished the unused portion just as easily."

"Not in that apartment you couldn't," I disagreed, bringing the heads and eyes back. "You knew there would be people poking around in there, and one of those people would be me. I expect you learned about the forensic sorcery I'd been dabbling with, and knew that if you used magic *in* the apartment, I'd be able to tell. You also couldn't afford to take the unused portion with you. If even one grain of it spilled where it shouldn't, I might have been able to trace it to you with a general match and search spell. Those were two of the procedures I was going to use if the investigation hadn't been abruptly cut short. The only thing I *don't* understand is why you didn't include me in the first group of four. Or were some of *them* into forensic sorcery too?"

This time when the heads swiveled back there was no easy answer from him, not even a sneering denial. The silence lasted about six heartbeats, and then King Agilar stirred.

"But why would he do such a thing?" the king asked, almost plaintively. "He's lived and worked at my Court for so many years . . . This is all beyond belief and understanding!"

"Your Majesty, over the last year or so I've heard occasional rumors coming out of this kingdom," I told him gently. "As prosperous and peaceful as this place is, people have been wondering why you need such a powerful wizard as Master Haddil. He's never gone out of his way to be friendly with your townspeople—or anyone else—so many of them would be happier if he went elsewhere. After all, when a wizard isn't involved with protecting you, he's probably occupying his time plotting against you . . ."

King Agilar's expression showed brief impatience with so ridiculous an idea, but he didn't miss the reactions of his advisers. The two I could see easily and clearly flushed with embarrassment as they avoided looking at Master Haddil, showing they, at least, believed that sort of nonsense. Those to my left might have done the same thing, and if they did it would hardly be unexpected.

"In this instance the rumors were almost right," I continued. "Master Haddil is comfortable here, or for one reason or another doesn't care to leave. You've supported him up until now, but the day could very well come when you're persuaded to give your people peace of mind. Rather than wait for it to happen and then try to change your mind, he came up with a crisis that would demand his continued presence. The crisis would get worse and worse, other magic users would fail to find an answer or get taken themselves—and then he would finally crack the thing and revive the victims. The nefarious enemy would remain a mystery, and that would also require that *he* remain. After all, if he left, the evil genius could decide to strike again . . ."

By then everyone's attention was on Master Haddil, who studied me silently with a finger to his lips. His gray eyes appeared thoughtful, and then he sent me a faint but deliberate smile.

"You've changed, Chalaine," he commented, just as though we were in the middle of an ordinary conversation. "You used to avoid arguments and confrontations with the very first sign of disagreement. Now you continue on in your newfound aggressiveness, making things up to support your stance. Your need to show the universe that you're *somebody* has you creating fantasies—"

"They're not fantasies, and she isn't lying," Bariden interrupted with a growl, his light eyes cold. "She's a woman talented beyond the ordinary, but she doesn't believe in making herself look good at someone else's expense. You won't get out of this by casting doubts on your main accuser. If you're all that innocent, prove it by showing us where she made her mistake."

"I can show you one mistake rather easily," Master Haddil replied with that same smile, while I tried not to think about the way Bariden had defended me. A reaction left over from our time as travel companions, surely . . . "If I *were* guilty, as everyone at this table now seems to believe, I would be a guilty *wizard*. Two of you have sorcerer-level strength, but I'm sure you know that means very little. Don't you think it's a mistake of the first magnitude not to take *that* into consideration?"

Master Haddil's pleasant expression didn't change, but you couldn't tell that from the way the king's four advisers froze. They *were* in the midst of accusing a fairly powerful wizard of misconduct, and they suddenly knew they'd never do anything that stupid again. Not that they might not want to, but they'd never be *able* to . . .

"But I *did* take into consideration the person I was accusing," I said, speaking as calmly and quietly as he had. "That's why I went to Conclave while this meeting was being arranged, and explained my conclusions to *them*. They decided there was enough evidence to question you under a truth spell, which will settle matters without confusion or doubt. If you think I'm bluffing, try speaking a spell."

By then he was looking startled and unsure, as though he hadn't been expecting that particular move. Some people did tend to underestimate me, but I hadn't thought Master Haddil was one of them. Whatever, he suddenly got to his feet and spoke a freezing spell aimed at everyone in the room, but the final gesture did no more than the words. His ability was being restrained by wizards his strength or stronger, their channel into that world established earlier by me. I couldn't use the strength I'd arranged for, but it was more than clear they could.

When everyone understood Master Haddil *was* being restrained, they all jumped to their feet and began shouting. Most were demanding that the guards arrest him, and the king was trying to get everyone calmed down. I'm not all that fond of bedlams, so I left my own chair and slipped out of the room. Not only wasn't I needed any longer, I really didn't want to stay.

But as I walked down the corridor I had to push away impatience, stemming from the fact that I couldn't yet leave that world. I was the one maintaining the link for the Conclave wizards to reach through to Master Haddil, and if I left he would be free again to do as he pleased. The representatives from Conclave would be there as soon as they decided who should go, but until then I was stuck. Well, there was always that small garden as a place to wait, and I was already heading in the right direction. When they didn't need me any longer, they would let me know.

I was about halfway to my destination and had just turned a corner, when I saw a group of palace ladies approaching from the other direction. They were the usual sort of high-nosed females who thought they were worth something just because their fathers were, the kind whose male counterparts usually started a fight with someone who was guaranteed not to fight back. Normally I would have turned around and gone a different way just to make sure there would be no trouble, but right then I wasn't in the mood.

And, to cap my decision, one of the beautifully gowned young ladies of station had spotted me and was staring. To turn back then would have been to retreat, and I hadn't even retreated from facing down a wizard. Granted, it hadn't been a very satisfying time, nothing like what I'd been looking forward to. Master Haddil and I had never been close, but he had also never refused to teach me what I needed as quickly as I could handle it. Bena thought his criticism of me had been harsh, but in actual truth it had been only as hard as it needed to be. And there had never been a moment's pity or unnecessary condescension . . .

"You there, girl," I heard in commanding tones, which brought me back from the fringes of guilt. "I want a word with you, so stop where you are."

The young lady of station addressing me seemed to be the leader of the group, all six of them just enough older than me that they could play woman to my "girl." Their gowns were silk in various pastel colors, a very pale yellow for the one who was speaking. She also had red hair, green eyes, and a beautiful face, but not enough sense to see that I wasn't in the mood to take nonsense.

"But *I* don't want a word with *you*," I pointed out mildly as I continued to approach their group. "And even if I did, I don't make it a habit to talk to people from ten feet away. Not unless I think they might bite. Do you ladies bite?"

"Those who oppose us find that we do," the redhead answered, stepping directly into my path. "But in your case, we simply didn't care to be dirtied. Your sort never *has* known enough not to approach people you don't belong with, but this time you've really overstepped yourself. Why don't you save yourself the eventual embarrassment and go back to your own kind."

"My own kind," I echoed with brows high. "And overstepping myself. Do you have any real meaning hidden in that nonsense, or is this simply something you tell everyone you see? If it is, you must be *very* bored."

"Only those without breeding get bored," the redhead countered, her tone still even despite the flush beginning to color her cheeks. "And those who play stupid aren't always playing. I'm Lady Miralia, the betrothed of Prince Bariden. If you think you've made a laughingstock of me by disappearing with my fiancé for a day, you're very much mistaken. You're the one who's the laughingstock, for letting him take advantage of whatever tiny amount of virtue you might have. I'm the one he loves and the one he means to marry, and I want you away from him *now*. I don't mind if he dallies a bit until the wedding, but I *will* insist the woman be someone of quality. You, my girl, simply don't qualify."

Her five cohorts smirked from their places around and behind her, silently echoing everything she'd said. I'd felt a stab from what I'd been told about Bariden, but nothing like what it would have been if I'd let myself be stupid about him. It looked like everyone in the palace knew he and I had been gone together, but this specimen in front of me didn't care about the reasons for it. She probably considered the problem we'd been working on nothing more than a lame excuse for sneaking into bed. The Lady Miralia reminded me of that princess Tenillis, who had been so eager to clear me from her path to Bariden. The main difference here was that I had no interest any longer in arguing possession of his attention.

"Do you have any idea how embarrassing it is for me to stand here and watch you make a fool of yourself?" I asked, long practice letting me keep to the mildness. "Not only isn't there anything of consequence between Prince Bariden and myself, you've just announced you're not woman enough to satisfy the man you expect to marry. I hadn't known that sort of frankness was required from someone of your exalted station."

There was an immediate burst of snickering from Miralia's audience, and I didn't think it was aimed at me. The same thought must have occurred to the redhead; she flushed even brighter, and stiffened with humiliation.

"How dare you!" she hissed with great originality, the words venom-covered. "I know the point is probably beyond you to understand, but I am *not* a slut like you! When I marry I'll be dressed in white, and *that's* why I say nothing about my fiancé's dallying. Actions that are fit for a man are not fit for a woman, but obviously you've never been taught that."

"Different people learn different things," I observed with my own originality. "For instance, you seem to think virginity is something special, probably for the same stupid reason everyone else does, but you've missed a couple of points. Back in the days when savages sacrificed virgins to their gods, it wasn't just girls they used, but boys as well. That means if the idea is valid, it should go for men as well as women."

"That has nothing to do with—" she began impatiently, but I wasn't through yet.

"But the idea *isn't* valid," I plowed on. "You have to remember these are savages we're talking about, but they were only backward, not stupid. On ordinary occasions they sacrificed chickens and ducks, moved up to a lamb or sheep only when they had to, and used a young bullock only if the situation was dire. They didn't hand over their best right from the start, not when handing it over might jeopardize their survival. That's why, when they absolutely *had* to use humans, they usually offered virgins."

"But that proves that virgins are special," one of the other girls objected, obviously caught up. "The savages were giving purity and importance to their gods."

"The savages were giving unknown quantities to their gods, *pretending* they were important," I corrected. "They needed a lot of children if their tribes or clans were going to prosper, but they had no knowledge of medicine and certainly no trained healers. Babies died for many reasons back then; some were born dead, some died right after birth, and some were too sickly even to survive infancy. The most valuable possession those men had was a woman who bore strong, healthy babies, a woman who wasn't barren or weak. If they were seriously interested in giving their best, they would have given one of *those* women, not an untried child of about nine or ten."

"Now that's too much," another of the girls protested, highly indignant. "All the books show virgin sacrifices as young women, not little girls. And if children were so important to those people, why would they kill one?"

"Because, in their eyes, girls of that age *were* young women," I said, ignoring Miralia's attempts to break into the conversation. "A girl became a woman as soon as she passed through puberty, and shortly thereafter she was paired with a boy who had survived his manhood testing. If she didn't have her first child by the time she was twelve or thirteen, it was only because she came late to puberty. The male virgins were of the same sort, boys who hadn't yet changed and survived the rites of men. After all, why waste a warrior and hunter who had already proven himself?"

"None of that means anything at all!" Miralia finally got in, the opinion inflexibly firm. "*We* don't come from savages, and *our* families believe firmly in the purity of women. It's a tradition that's been carried on for centuries—"

"It's a joke that's been carried on for centuries," I interrupted again. "Specifically a man's joke. If a girl has no experience when she marries, her husband doesn't have to worry about whether or not he'll be as good as the others

she's tried. Rather than needing to develop an effective
technique, he can get away with minimal effort that still
satisfies *him*. Lazy is what they are, that and little boys
who think that size is what really matters . . ."

I was only half-serious about that particular part of it, but
Miralia picked up on the wrong half. Seeing my amusement
made her think I'd been pulling her—chain—the entire
time, and that got her mad.

"Thank you for explaining to us why you take to bed with
every man you meet," she pronounced, the look in her green
eyes malicious. "The practice must be utterly fascinating
to those who study the rutting of animals, but we find it
sickening. Just make sure that the next bed you crawl into
doesn't belong to Prince Bariden, and I'll never need to
lower myself by talking to you again. Is that clear?"

"What if it isn't?" I asked just to be difficult, my head to
one side. "You're a silly child who thinks she has the right
to tell other people what to do, but what if I decide to ignore
you? What do you imagine you could possibly do?"

Her immediate sneer said she was judging me by what
I looked like, and because of that believed I was helpless.
She wasn't able to see the stubborn hurt inside me that was
beginning to create a great anger, and probably wouldn't
have cared even if she could. How she had missed the fact
that I was a sorceress I didn't know, but it was beyond
doubt that she had. Her sneering red lips parted to speak
whatever threat she had ready, but someone else's words
beat her to it.

"Chalaine, hold on, I have to talk to you," we both heard,
and by the time I turned, Bariden was just about up to us.
It looked like he'd been moving fast, probably because he
had an unanswered question about Master Haddil.

"Bariden, have you been *running*?" Miralia demanded
with vast distaste from behind me. "Keeping low company
has obviously taught you low habits, but we'll break you of
them soon enough. You may kiss my cheek in greeting."

If I'd been Bariden I would have told her what she could
kiss of *mine*, but all he did was stop and frown at her.

"Miralia," he said, just as though he hadn't seen her
before she spoke. "What are you talking about? And what
are you doing here?"

"It so happens I was on my way to find you," she answered, smiling now as she moved past me to stand right in front of him. "Since we're going to be married, it's only right to greet you properly when you get back from a trip. I really did miss you, darling."

And then she put her arms around his neck and kissed him. I knew she was going to do that, so as soon as it started I turned away and strode off through the line of her followers. They were too busy sighing romantically to notice, and once I got past I spoke a spell to make sure I couldn't be followed by the use of magic. A brisk walk got me to the next cross-corridor quickly, and once I turned the corner I ran. Running isn't at all a low habit, not when it can get you away from someone you never want to see again for the rest of your life.

Bariden was so surprised by Miralia's kissing him, that for a moment he stood frozen. Then, realizing it was more shock than surprise, he tried to end it. Miralia had *never* kissed him like that, not in bed and certainly not in front of people, but the death grip she had around his neck was hard to break. It took some effort to pry himself loose without hurting her, and by then he was good and annoyed.

"Miralia, stop it!" he told her sharply, holding her by the arms to keep her back from him. "What in the worlds has gotten into you?"

"Nothing but love, darling," she answered with one of those pleased laughs that always meant she'd gotten her way about something. "Don't you think I have the right to kiss my fiancé?"

"Since when are we supposed to have gotten engaged?" he asked with a snort. "The last *I* heard, you didn't care to see me again until I apologized for something I hadn't done."

"Oh, that was just a silly little misunderstanding," Miralia laughed again. "You know you love me, and everyone else knows it too. That's why they were so delighted when your mother announced our engagement this morning. She's throwing a party for us tonight, and—"

"She announced *what*?" Bariden shouted, refusing to believe his ears. "My mother—! She had no right to do anything like that!"

"Of course she did, darling," Miralia cooed, now preening herself. "She *is* the queen, after all, and as a dutiful son you must obey her. I still haven't decided exactly *when* I want the ceremony to take place, but she and I will discuss it and decide together. Now . . ."

Suddenly, Bariden was looking around rather than listening. It wasn't Miralia he'd run through the halls trying to catch up to, and he cursed when he found Chalaine gone. It wasn't surprising that she'd walked away when Miralia began her nonsense, but—Abruptly Bariden was jolted by a horrible thought.

"Miralia, be quiet!" he growled, interrupting the silly girl in midbabble and putting instant insult on her face. "I want to hear that you didn't tell Chalaine this fairy tale about our being engaged. Let me hear you say you didn't tell her!"

He was gently shaking her by the arms, but from the way Miralia reacted, he might as well have been beating her with a stick. She gasped in horror and tore herself free from his grip, then glared long-bladed daggers at him.

"How *dare* you treat me as if I were one of your common playthings?" she hissed, so outraged her pale skin flushed crimson. "I have no idea who or what a Chalaine is, but if that's the name of the creature who was just here, you can be *certain* I told her the truth! You and I *are* engaged, Bariden, but that won't save you from having to pay for the way you just humiliated me. Oh, yes, you'll pay, all right. You'll . . ."

By then Bariden was running up the corridor, too sick inside to waste time worrying about Miralia's spite. He'd made up his mind to get it all out into the open with Chalaine, to ask her why sometimes it seemed she returned his love, but other times there was nothing from her. He'd promised himself not to drop the subject until he was satisfied he had all the answers, but when he'd turned around in the conference chamber once everyone had stopped yelling, it was to find her gone. He'd hurried after her, tracking her with magic as he had once before, and he'd finally caught up—

But not before Miralia had made everything a thousand times worse. Bariden was cursing under his breath as he reached the cross-corridor, but the words that usually acted as a release for his anger did nothing when Chalaine was nowhere in sight. It was as though she'd turned invisible—which was perfectly possible—or had disappeared in a puff of smoke—which *shouldn't* have been possible. He didn't even know which way she'd gone—

"Damn fool," he growled at himself, then spoke the tracking spell again. Finding her the first time had canceled it, so it just needed to be revived. Wildly impatient, he waited for her footprints to glow to life along the floor, waited . . . waited . . . then was forced to notice that the spell wasn't working. He spoke it again, just to be sure he hadn't made a mistake in his hurry, but there was no mistake. No mistake, no footprints, and no Chalaine. She must have done something to keep him from following her again . . .

From halfway up the corridor behind him, Bariden could hear Miralia shrilling something, probably demands. At one time he would have gone back and tried to calm her down, but right then he wouldn't have cared if she shrilled the palace into a pile of pebbles and rubble. Without even turning to look at her, he headed up the corridor toward a stairway that would take him to his apartment.

Once in his own apartment he threw himself into a chair and called up a cup of wine, and that was all he could think of to do. His mind raced around madly with the need for action, the need to win against opposition as he had in the trap, but there was nothing to get a grip on. What he wanted was to find Chalaine, but how in the name of the Diamond Realm was he supposed to do that? She'd used magic to keep herself from being tracked or traced, and if he tried to find her by ordinary searching it could take years. Even if she didn't move from wherever she currently was. In a palace the size of that one, someone determined to stay lost would never be seen again.

Even *with* the system of hall messengers. Chalaine didn't have to let herself be seen by any of them, and that would neutralize them completely. Bariden banished the wine and called up a brandy, then drank it down with a speed that would have horrified his old manners teacher. He needed the jolt the brandy would give him, something—anything!—to clear his thinking. He refused to give up on the idea of searching, but how in hell was he supposed to find her . . . ?

"Ah, Bariden, how delightful to see you again," a voice said, and then a very large white rose appeared, hovering just above the floor. The long-stemmed rose was fresh and beautiful, but it also had two green eyes that inspected Bariden with amusement.

"ReSayne, is that you?" he demanded, then shook his head. "No, forget that, of course it's you. Who else would come visiting as a flower."

"Well, I did say I would be back once my experiment was finished, and I also said I'd have another new look." ReSayne didn't raise its brows, but only because it didn't have brows. "Is something wrong? You seem even more agitated than the last time we spoke."

"A lot has happened since then," Bariden muttered in answer, running a hand through his hair. And then he stopped to stare at the fiend. "Now isn't that strange. I didn't think of it even once, and I should have. I wonder . . ."

"Do you mean a lot has happened with the problem you were working on?" ReSayne asked, its green eyes concerned. "I'm available to help with it if you still need me, and I'll wear this beautiful new form. It's so tiring when people run screaming at the sight of me, but no one runs screaming from a rose. That's one of the main reasons I chose it. Tell me what your problem involves."

"The problem's been solved," Bariden said, still faintly distracted. There was something that didn't fit, something strange . . . "Chalaine and I were forced into a trap to get us out of the way, but we managed to get free again and she figured out who was responsible. Master Haddil is in custody now, waiting for the arrival of wizards from Conclave to confirm his guilt. They'll also be able to cancel his spell on whatever drug he fed the victims, and then the healer will be able to banish it and restore them. Everyone is certain he visited the victims in person in order to drug them, and once they're able to speak they should confirm that."

"Then why are you acting so out-of-sorts?" ReSayne asked, hovering fractionally closer. "You said the name Chalaine—That isn't by any chance the female you were so interested in, the one who needed to be pursued? You can't possibly have failed with *her* when you were so successful with everything else."

"Why not?" Bariden asked sourly. "Between her and Miralia, I'm beginning to feel completely outnumbered. One refuses to believe I love her, and the other doesn't care if I do as long as everyone thinks I do. Love her, that is. It's past time that I put my foot down about a few things, but I have to start with Chalaine and I can't. She's hiding somewhere in this overdecorated pile of stone, and I can't find her."

"And if I recall correctly, you said she's a sorceress," ReSayne commented. "It's very difficult to find a sorceress who doesn't want to be found, but—Exactly how many sorceresses *are* there in the palace just now?"

"As far as I know, only Chalaine," Bariden responded, sitting up straight. "Do you think you can find her, ReSayne? For me it would take years, but for a fiend—! Just find her for me, and I'll do the rest."

"I'm pleased to see you now have the proper attitude toward personal problems," the ReSayne flower said with satisfaction. "Knowing you must handle things yourself is the first step toward success—"

"ReSayne, save the lectures and homilies for later!" Bariden said impatiently, now on his feet. "Can you or can you not find her?"

"It's not a question of can, but of have," ReSayne replied with a sniff. "I know how upset you are, Bariden, so I forgive your total lack of good manners—All right, all right! You needn't interrupt me again! You may or may not know that when I seek for a human, I follow their trace through—well, you have no word for that. Let's just say I follow their trace, and when I arrived here in the palace I was startled to seemingly find you in *two* places at once. Of course I realized immediately that the stronger trace was you, and the other simply something you'd produced. But I *was* curious, so I went to see what that something was."

"Something *I'd* produced?" Bariden echoed with puzzlement. "But that isn't possible. I always banish anything I happen to call up, so no one will find it and get upset. But what can this possibly have to do with Chalaine?"

"The item with your trace was a plain, uninteresting thing," ReSayne continued, almost as though it hadn't heard Bariden. "Made of yellow-brown, unpolished wood, it's what you humans call a hairbrush. The young female sorceress was sitting on a stone bench and using it on her hair, long, dark hair with red all through it. And she had dark, sad eyes . . ."

"Yes, that's Chalaine!" Bariden shouted, wishing he could grab the fiend and shake it hard. "Please, ReSayne, tell me where she is!"

"Locations in human terms are difficult for me," ReSayne responded soothingly. "I promise you, Bariden, I *am* trying. The female sat in a small garden, spatially close to that very large place of substance experimentation. You *must* know the one, where substances of different sorts are put together with many others, and then subjected to heat in one fashion or another? The results of the experiments are almost always taken away, to be disposed of ritually, I think, considering the intricate workmanship on the containers used. I've never understood why they produce such *large* samples with each experiment—"

"The kitchens!" Bariden pounced with a yell. "She's in a garden near the kitchens! ReSayne, I owe you!"

And then Bariden was racing out, incidently banishing the brandy in his system as he went. He'd need a clear head for what he intended, and now that he knew Chalaine was in one of two places . . .

The first garden he checked, beyond the far side of the kitchens, was empty. He'd pretty much expected that, since only he and the gardeners seemed to know it was there. It was the second garden his hopes were pinned on, but when he reached it he didn't hesitate out of fear that it might be empty. Needing desperately to know, he stepped out—and there she was. Just as ReSayne had said, sitting on a stone bench all the way to the left, Chalaine was brushing her hair with her back to the doorway. The movement of her arm was slow and automatic, as though her thoughts were on something else entirely. Bariden closed the distance between them quietly, then cleared his throat.

"That's right, it's me again," he said when she turned quickly and those big, beautiful eyes widened even more. "I did say I wanted to talk to you, but you disappeared. Do you mind if we have our talk *now*?"

"How did you find me?" she demanded as he moved around her to sit on the other end of the bench. "And if you have any questions about what happened with Master Haddil, just save them for later. Right now I'd rather be alone."

"Finding you wasn't hard," Bariden lied, "and what I want to talk about has nothing to do with Master Haddil. It has to do with us, and it won't wait until later. Chalaine, you and I have gone through a lot together, and I think I'm entitled to a frank answer. Can you sit there and say with complete truth that you don't have any deep feelings for me? You and I are more of a team than I'd ever dreamed would be possible with a woman, and I can't bear the thought of losing that. Actually, I can't bear the thought of losing *you*, but I know I'm about to. What can I do to keep it from happening?"

"I'd say everything possible has already been done," she answered, staring down at her hands and the brush they held. "You're back where you belong, and as soon as the wizards from Conclave get here I can go back to where *I* belong. I don't find teamwork with a married man very appealing, especially since the problem we teamed up for has been solved. And I don't have to guess how your new wife will feel about having me around. She doesn't approve of that sort of teamwork, and very frankly neither do I."

"Chalaine, I'm *not* engaged," Bariden said forcefully, ready for the point. "My mother and Miralia got together, and *they* decided they wanted an engagement. I was through with Miralia even before I met you, but she's determined to marry a prince. For my part I want a woman who doesn't care *what* I am, only *who* I am. A woman like you."

"I'm sure you can find lots of women like me if you start going to Conclave more often," she said, beginning to get to her feet. "The Sighted you met when you were young are jerks, but many Sighted aren't. If you give them a chance,

I'm sure you'll find that out for yourself. As for me, I'm too stubborn to settle for less than exactly what I want. I'm sorry, Bariden, but that doesn't happen to be you."

"*Why* isn't it me?" he demanded, also getting to his feet, hope crumbling to dust in his hands. "Chalaine, I love you more than life. *Why* isn't it me?"

"What did you say?" she asked as she looked directly at him, startlement widening her eyes again. "I thought I heard—No, it must have been my imagination—or wishful thinking."

The miserable female actually began to turn away from him again, but now he knew what the problem was. If he'd had the time he would have cursed himself for an idiot, but instead he took her arm and pulled her back to him.

"I said I love you more than life," he repeated, looking down into those big, beautiful eyes. "Didn't you hear me when I told you that before, or did you simply not believe it? Right now I want to know if you feel the same, but I warn you ahead of time: if I hear an answer I don't like, I'm damned well going to ask again after I speak a truth spell."

"Don't you have to *know* the truth before a truth spell can make you tell it?" she whispered, raising a hand to touch his cheek with gentle fingertips. "Isn't it possible that what we feel for each other is just physical attraction, nothing but plain ordinary lust? Think, Bariden, and then tell me how well we'd fit into each other's lives. I spend most of my time alone, studying and living on empty worlds, changing that only when I go to Conclave. You, on the other hand, are a prince, used to being at your father's Court. You'd want to stay here rather than come with me, but—can you imagine what everyone would think and say if they learned you were getting involved with someone like me? You'd feel defensive and embarrassed, and after a while—"

Bariden had just started to interrupt her, knowing what she said wasn't true, but he was interrupted in turn. Chalaine had undoubtedly avoided the hall messengers on her way to the garden, but he hadn't seen any reason to do the same. A really good reason had just come out, though, and was clearing its throat in a way that wasn't going to stop until its presence had been acknowledged.

"All right, Ordran, what is it?" Bariden snapped, knowing the older man never gave up until his message was delivered. "Say what you have to, and then go and make sure I'm not disturbed again."

"Forgive me, Your Highness, but part of that command isn't possible," Ordran answered, calmly pleased rather than upset. The man had never hidden his dislike for the third prince of his king's House, and although Bariden didn't know why he was disliked by the man, he now found he didn't care. His days of trying to be pleasant to obnoxious old messengers were over.

"Well, spit it out!" he growled, and had the satisfaction of seeing Ordran's smugness fade. "If you can remember the message, just deliver it. *I'll* decide what is and isn't possible."

"I beg your pardon, Your Highness, but it's the queen who decides," the messenger returned stiffly, apparently trying to work up the nerve to be nasty. "Her Majesty your mother commands your immediate appearance in her reception room, and I'm to escort you there. Without delay."

"And if I do delay, you'll make sure she knows about it," Bariden said, annoyance mounting quickly to anger. "Too bad, man, but you won't get the chance to tell on me. It so happens I want to see her as well, and now is as good a time as any. Come on, Chalaine, this involves you too."

He took the woman he loved by the hand, and led her past the startled messenger and back into the palace. He'd always gone out of his way to avoid confrontations and harsh words with his mother, but she'd finally pushed things too far. He'd force himself to say what she deserved to hear, and then he'd—he'd—

He didn't know what he would do, but that didn't matter. As long as he had Chalaine beside him, all the universe would be his for the taking. And he *would* have her beside him, no matter who tried to keep it from happening . . .

CHAPTER SIXTEEN

Everything was happening too fast, but I couldn't seem to make it slow down. First Bariden finds me when I would have sworn it was impossible, then he actually says he loves me, then he goes trotting out dragging me behind him . . . If I didn't know better, I'd think the EverNameless were into bad practical jokes . . .

I finally got the chance to catch my breath when we reached the queen's reception room, or at least its anteroom. No one ever just walked in on the queen, and there was a fussy official at a desk in the large anteroom to make sure of that. His face wore that expression common to all ascetics and most petty tyrants, the expression that says you're beneath their notice so don't even think about making a fuss. A large number of people were sitting on the elegant chairs the room contained, and they all looked up when the official at the desk did.

"Ah, Prince Bariden," the official said, grudging the acknowledgment. "I expected you much sooner than this. The queen commands that you await her pleasure out here, and she'll see you in your turn. You—Just a moment! Where do you think you're going?"

By that time we'd finished crossing the anteroom, and it was obvious where we were going. Bariden had no intention of waiting around for his "turn," a decision that delighted me. From what I'd seen in the last few minutes, if that was the way they treated a prince around there, he would have been better off being a commoner.

The double doors ahead of us were cream trimmed with gold, with matched footmen to either side of them looking confused. They weren't supposed to open the doors unless the fussy official gave his approval, but that was the queen's son heading for them. Not knowing what to do kept them rooted in place, so I made the decision *for* them. A flick of my finger opened the doors without their help, and the next moment we were through them.

It would have been nice to have had a minute or two to think about what I was getting into, but one glance around the queen's reception room said I wouldn't be getting it. There were a couple of dozen guests in the room and almost half a dozen servants, and all of them turned to stare at us as we passed. The smiling group around the queen in her thronelike chair stopped smiling at our abrupt appearance, as did the queen herself. Bariden's hand tightened a little around mine, but he didn't stop until we were right in front of them.

"Mother," he said with a bow, ignoring everyone else—including the redheaded Miralia, who stood to the queen's right. "I was told you wanted to see me."

"What I *wanted*, Bariden, was for you to wait like a gentleman until you were given permission to enter," the woman answered in frigid tones. Blond-haired and blue-eyed, most people would have considered her beautiful, especially with her gown and jewels. Outer beauty has never impressed me much, though, which meant the king's pleasant and friendly homeliness was much more attractive to me than she could ever be.

"Sorry, Mother, but I haven't the time to waste sitting around in your anteroom," Bariden answered, sounding bored already. "If you think there aren't enough people out there, find someone who has nothing better to do. If that was all—"

"No, that was *not* all!" the queen snapped, thrown off-balance by his answer, but not about to let him walk out again. "I don't know what's gotten into you, but you *will* watch your tone with me. And it so happens you *do* have something to do with your time, and that's preparing for your upcoming wedding. Your bride and I will see to the most important details, but there are any number of things perfect for your attention since they can't possibly be ruined. Knowing your memory, I've had a list prepared and written down."

"You expect me to be absentminded about my own wedding?" Bariden asked with a light, ridiculing laugh while I seethed. If that stupid woman insulted him one more time . . . "No, Mother, my wedding day is something I'm really looking forward to, since that's the day my beloved and I will become one. And wasn't that generous of my mother to volunteer to help with the details, Chalaine? She's so good at this sort of thing, you'll have nothing to do."

He put an arm around my shoulders and hugged me warmly, pretending he didn't hear the concerted gasp from everyone watching. The queen went pale while a flushed Miralia lost her smirk, but the battle wasn't over. Bariden had dropped his hornet's nest, but no one had really been stung yet.

"What can you possibly be talking about?" the queen said at last, scrabbling inside herself for firmer footing. "You know very well the woman you'll be marrying is Miralia, so why ever would you mention another name? Really, Bariden, someone with so miniscule a sense of humor as you, should know better than to joke in public. It's always taken the wrong way. Since I announced your betrothal myself this morning, I should know who your bride is."

"You should, Mother, but apparently you don't," Bariden said, sounding more aristocratic than the biggest snob I'd ever met. "Miralia and I parted company days ago, an action recommended by the healer I consulted. He said the nights I spent in her bed were putting me in danger of frostbite."

Miralia's mortified "Oh!" was drowned out by the laughter from our audience, and this time it was the queen's turn to flush. She was losing ground rapidly, so she grabbed for the first point in sight to stop the slide.

"For shame, Bariden!" she cried, leaning forward with both hands on the arms of her chair. "You find it amusing to admit to taking a maiden's virtue before turning your back on her forever? No son of mine has ever been such a cad, nor will one ever be! You will honor your unspoken obligation to a lady in proper marriage, and I'll hear no more on the subject!"

"But surely you'll tell me who this maiden is that you mention," Bariden immediately pounced, giving her no chance to follow through on her dismissal. "Such lofty sentiments should never be wasted, most especially not on a woman who *wasn't* a maiden. If she had been, I wouldn't have touched her."

Miralia was beet red, obviously wishing she could fall through the floor, and trying hard not to look in *my* direction. Considering the conversation we'd had, I didn't wonder why. Those who make the most noise about virtue are usually trying to hide the fact that they believe they have none of it, or wish they had none. I now knew which Miralia was, and in a little while so would everyone in the palace. But if I expected that to finish things, the queen had other ideas.

"And I say she *was* a maiden, and you *did* despoil her!" the woman stated, ice forming on every word. "Will you call me a liar, Bariden? I'm your mother and your queen. Will you shame yourself even further by disputing my word? I think not."

The woman was back to feeling triumph, since even without looking at him I could tell Bariden wasn't prepared to go *that* far. It must have cost him a lot to do as much as he had, and being basically honorable was proving a terrible handicap for him. He'd never be able to call his mother a liar no matter how rotten she was being to him— but he wasn't standing there alone.

"Honestly, Bariden, your family must live in the dark ages," I said with a laugh, immediately drawing the queen's glare. "Haven't they ever heard of a truth spell? Why bother wrangling over who's lying, when everyone can know for certain? It only takes a minute, after all . . ."

"Don't you dare!" the queen shrieked when I lifted my hand, the color coming and going in her face. "I should have known you were a freak, for like calls to like, doesn't it? You both make me sick, and I curse the day I ever gave life to someone so undeserving of it! You've been nothing but a shame and a disgrace to me, Bariden, and—"

"Bullshit!" I stated, cutting into her tirade with sudden insight. "For a high and mighty queen, you're a real fool. Don't you think everyone can see that it isn't shame but envy eating at you? Bariden was born with an ability you think *you* should have had, and all this time you've been blaming *him* for *your* lacks. You should be ashamed of yourself for putting your son through that kind of hell, but I don't think you're capable of it. You have to be sensitive and intelligent in order to feel shame."

"That's a lie!" the queen finally managed, one hand to her breast. Her face was still mottled, but her eyes showed the truth. "I am *not* envious, how could I be? Who would want to be a freak, when they could be a queen? And he's *my* son, so the ability must have come from *me*! That counts even more than—than—"

"Sorry, lady, but it doesn't work like that," I said, feeling no more pity for her than she'd felt for Bariden. "Wizards have studied the matter, and they tell us that if a woman carries the sleeping seed, *all* her children are born with it. If only one or two of the children show talent, it comes from the father. The only thing you gave your son is his hair and eye color. All the rest, including his goodness, comes from his father."

Bariden's arm tightened around me at that, but the queen didn't notice. She slumped back in her chair, and there was still nothing to show she felt ashamed. Bitterness now twisted that outwardly beautiful face, and I could see she'd never accept what I'd told her. She'd decide at last that I was lying, and would spend the rest of her life feeling cheated of what she considered her due.

"Get out of my sight," she muttered at last, looking at neither Bariden nor me. "It sickens me to have to see you, and I never want to do so again. Get out!"

"I feel really sorry for you, Mother," Bariden said quietly. "Now that I understand, I can finally feel sorry for you."

He took my hand again, and we walked out through absolute silence. To their credit, most of the men and women in the room looked sympathetic, but not for the queen's position. Miralia had stood frozen beside the woman she'd thought would make her a princess, and she hadn't looked

sorry for anyone but herself. Her plans had probably included goading Bariden into challenging his brother for the
throne once their father was gone, and now she would
never be a queen either. I usually approve of ambition
in people, but not at the cost of other people's lives and
happiness.

"What now?" I asked Bariden once we were out in the
hall. "You ought to tell your father about this, just so he
knows and can be prepared."

"I have the feeling my father already knows," Bariden
said, rubbing the back of his neck with one broad hand.
"It must be the reason he always gave me so much love
and understanding. He knew I would never get it from my
mother. I've always felt he knows a lot of things he doesn't
talk about, including the fact that this blowup had to come
sometime. The only part of it I regret is what I had to say
about Miralia. I shouldn't have had to humiliate her in order
to defend myself."

"You wouldn't have had to defend yourself if she hadn't
tried an ambush," I countered. "You can't jump out in
attack at people, and not expect the possibility of getting
whacked yourself. She has nothing to complain about, and
you're just being a sweet but softheaded idiot."

"Well, at least you added 'sweet,' " he said with a short
laugh. "If I have to be thought of as an idiot, that's the kind
I prefer."

"It was my pleasure," I said with a matching smile. "We
aim to please, but I do have to repeat: now what?"

"Now we get married," he answered, putting both arms
around me but not pulling me close. "You asked me a lot of
questions before we were interrupted by my mother's spite,
and now I'm going to answer them. Can it be a physical
attraction we feel for each other? Sure it can, because that
attraction is there, but you're not the first pretty girl I've
ever been involved with. Can you honestly say you've never
associated with a man who was considered handsome?"

I was forced to shake my head at that, since lying would
have been a waste of time. One look at Hannar—my former
lover and current friend who would soon be unfrozen—and
most women melt into a sizzling puddle. And Hannar hadn't
been the first—or the best.

"So that takes care of the physical," Bariden continued after my headshake. "You also asked how people would react if I announced I was getting involved with you, and I saw the answer to that just a few minutes ago. Most of the men in that room had naked envy on their faces, an expression that stayed there even when they learned you were Sighted."

"Then I'm glad I didn't look," I mumbled, beginning to feel very cornered. "Strange men and naked expressions . . ."

"Stop that," he scolded gently. "You wanted the truth, and you're getting it. The last objection you had was about where we would live, and the answer to that is, I don't give a damn as long as we're together. It probably won't be here, not after that scene with my mother, but we'll find a place to suit us both after the wedding."

"Bariden, stop saying that," I objected, one step away from squirming. "You still don't know what you're getting into with me, so we *can't* jump into marriage. We'll live together for a while, and then, if you manage to survive—"

"Chalaine, we *have* lived together for a while," he counterobjected, but without the squirming. "I refuse to spend years or decades waiting for some nebulous 'something' to happen to me. What in the worlds are you afraid of?"

"I'm not afraid, and it isn't nebulous," I insisted, finding it was possible to be even more uncomfortable than I'd been. "Hannar wasn't worried either, but if I hadn't thrown him out he wouldn't have lived long enough for us to be friends. I—have an effect on people I associate with, especially Sighted people, and they tend to have . . . accidents. Like you with that sphere of water, when we first met. And believe me, that's only the mildest of examples."

"That's not right," he said with a sudden frown. "Don't you remember, it—"

"Excuse me, Your Highness," a voice interrupted, but this time it was a respectful voice. "I regret the intrusion, but I have a message from the king."

Bariden turned his head to look at the second messenger to bother us in less than two hours, but his reaction wasn't the same as it had been with the first.

"That's all right, Stollen, I understand. What's the message?"

"His Majesty asks that you attend him in his private audience chamber," the man Stollen answered. "He also asks that it be as soon as you find convenient, since there's still one part of your joint problem remaining unresolved. He said you would know what he meant."

"I think I may know even more than that," Bariden murmured, his expression distracted. "Thank you, Stollen. Please tell my father that I'll be right there."

The messenger bowed and then took off, but Bariden stood where he was, obviously thinking. Since his arms were still around me I couldn't quite think of it as a waste of time, but I *was* suddenly curious.

"What could he mean by saying one part of the problem is unresolved?" I asked. "With Master Haddil caught and the mystery solved, what could be left? Maybe he's talking about a different problem, one you and he have privately."

"No, it's the same problem," he answered with a headshake that banished his distraction. "It must be time to clear up all those loose ends, the ones I've just begun noticing. I'm glad they didn't wait until I began tripping over them. Come on, Chalaine, let's go get our answers."

"What answers?" I demanded as he took my hand and led off again. "And who are 'they'? Bariden, answer me. Who are 'they'?"

He didn't answer, but after just a few minutes I no longer needed him to. A guardsman admitted us to a small, comfortable room done in leather and polished wood, obviously the private audience chamber we'd been told about. The king was there, sitting in an ordinary, high-backed chair upholstered in butter yellow leather, and one of those with him was Master Haddil.

Bariden felt Chalaine coming to an involuntary stop at sight of Master Haddil, but he'd been expecting the wizard to be there. He got Chalaine moving again, guided her to a deep leather chair and into it, then turned to bow to his father. King Agilar waved away the courtesy, and gestured to the chair next to Chalaine's.

"Just make yourself comfortable, Bariden," he said in his plain, warm way. "We've dispensed with formalities for the moment, so we can just get on with it. Between you and Chalaine, you should know everyone here."

"I know Tramfeor," Bariden said, nodding to the wizard as he sat. It had been years, but of course the man hadn't changed at all. Black hair, light eyes, a ready smile, and a tall, athletic body . . . "Chalaine, Tramfeor is a wizard I met a long time ago, when I was still a boy. Master Haddil was away from the kingdom then so he didn't stay long, but he did spend some time talking to me. He's also the one who gave me the Spell of Affinity."

Chalaine's startled glance told him she was already heading up the right path, only a short distance behind him. Master Haddil was looking comfortable and pleased, which was another thing he'd expected. The fourth man, a Sighted, was someone he didn't recognize, but evidently Chalaine did.

"And I know Addadain," she said, indicating the small, frail-looking Sighted who had light brown hair and gray eyes. "He's a wizard I met at Conclave years ago, who decided to unofficially adopt me. He let me test myself against his strength whenever I learned something new in the way of combat magic, and never took it easy on me or let me get sloppy. He would even listen to my troubles occasionally, and showed superhuman restraint by never telling me what to do about my problems."

"That wasn't restraint, that was cowardice," the small Addadain answered with a laugh, his voice hardier than his appearance. "Suggesting things to a woman isn't quite as dangerous as offending a demon or a fiend, but all too often the results become exactly the same."

"Speaking of fiends, aren't we missing someone from this group?" Bariden asked while the others chuckled. "ReSayne was a large part of this, so shouldn't it be here?"

"You seem to be catching up to us rather quickly, Bariden," Tramfeor said, his light eyes filled with approval. "Yes, ReSayne should be here, and it is. Would you like to join us more obviously, my friend?"

"I suppose I might as well," ReSayne's voice came with a sigh, and a section of the brown, yellow, and blue carpeting suddenly showed two leaf green eyes. "I had the feeling he was already beginning to understand when he ran out to find the female, but I might have been wrong. Since he showed no surprise at all when he walked in here, it's clear I wasn't."

"I met ReSayne a number of years ago," Bariden explained to Chalaine alone, no one else appearing surprised at the fiend's presence. "It told me I'd done it a favor, and was therefore beholden to me. I tried several times to find out what the favor could possibly have been, but never managed to get an answer. What I did get, though, was a way to call it if I had a problem or found myself in trouble. Hearing that, you should be asking the same question I asked myself when ReSayne popped up again right after we got back."

"The question being, why didn't you think to call it when we were trapped in that cycle of worlds," Chalaine supplied promptly with a nod. "Could the answer possibly be related to the reason you didn't know my name?"

"You mean something like a selective forget-spell?" Bariden replied with brows high and eyes wide. "So that even when I mentioned the special warding spell a—'friend'—had taught me, I couldn't remember I was able to contact that friend no matter where I was? Why, Chalaine, whoever could have done that to me?"

He noticed out of the corner of his eye that she joined him in looking silently toward the three wizards, but most of his attention was on them. Tramfeor shifted in his chair and cleared his throat, Addadain brushed at invisible lint on his blue trousers, and Master Haddil—*Master Haddil*—grinned then laughed out loud.

"These last few days have been more fun than I've had in ages," the wizard said without the least shame, casually smoothing at his yellow robe. "Once this is over, Your Majesty, I really will have to see about finding a temporary replacement for myself. The last decades made me dull and stiff without my realizing it, but now it's time to revive. When I return, I'll be the same fun-loving fellow I was in your father's day."

The king did nothing but nod agreement and try to hide his amusement, and that was beyond too much. With a growl, Bariden started to get out of his chair, but Tramfeor stood faster and waved him back.

"Now, now, let's not lose our tempers and start something we'll all regret," he said to Bariden, then turned to look at his brother wizard. "Please, Haddil, try to remember how *you* would feel if all you saw was what had been done. Until these young people are told *why* they were put through Hellfire, their anger is more than justified."

"If they had any idea how successful they've been, they would be stiff-necked with pride rather than anger," Haddil returned, then waved a hand. "But you're right, of course, Tramfeor, and I apologize for my outburst. Go ahead and tell them what we've been up to."

"For that I'll have to start some years back," Tramfeor agreed, turning again to Bariden and Chalaine. "In those days we had two problems, and since we didn't yet know the same solution would serve both, we handled them separately. Since I was the one involved with *you*, Bariden, I'll start with you."

Bariden watched wordlessly as the wizard went back to his chair, but his mind clanged with everything he had to say. He'd listen to their explanation, but if he wasn't fully satisfied afterward, their being wizards might not save them . . .

"The problem brought to *my* attention concerned a young Sighted prince in a predominantly untalented kingdom," Tramfeor went on once he'd gotten comfortable again in his chair. "If he'd been an ordinary boy we would have convinced his parents to allow fostering, and his foster parents would have been carefully chosen Sighted. As it was, the suggestion wasn't even made to his father. There was no Sighted king available, and the boy had a right to grow up as the prince he was.

"So a careful eye was kept on him by the Court wizard, who also helped to train his talent. He became altogether too good with mundane weapons, but that shouldn't have mattered. What mundane weapon, after all, could possibly equal the skilled use of magic? It struck me as nothing more than odd, and I stepped in personally only when I was told about the young man's attraction for the fairer sex. It would never do to have some ambitious young *untalented* lady claim his heart, and then use him and his gifts to gain advantage for herself. With that in mind I gave him the Spell of Affinity, expecting that he would begin to visit Conclave on a regular basis, and there discover that Sighted women had a much greater affinity for a man in his position.

"Unfortunately," and Tramfeor's sigh was heavy, "the young man developed a strong dislike for Conclave and didn't visit at all, not to mention on any regular basis. He also did almost no traveling, preferring to remain at his father's Court. His studies in magic progressed, however, and he was provided with a confidante he might discuss things with. His close association with humans was virtually nonexistent, and ReSayne proved to be perfect. The young man had little trouble being open with a fiend, and occasionally even took its advice.

"But by then our problem was growing critical rather than resolving itself." Tramfeor got to his feet and started pacing, his brow wrinkled in concentration. "The young man should have already been going out among the worlds, testing his strength as a magic user, deciding in what direction to follow life first. Instead he stayed resolutely at home, rarely used his considerable magic talent, and was unhappy in the extreme. To make matters worse there were rumors in the kingdom, whispered fears that he meant to challenge his eldest brother for their father's throne. In such a matter his brother would have to face him personally, and everyone knew the elder prince would have no chance even if magic *wasn't* used. There was that unimportant point about his ability with mundane weapons, you'll recall . . .

"And so there was a heated debate at Conclave, among those of us charged with protecting Sighted and unSighted alike." Tramfeor's sigh was lighter this time, and he stopped to gaze at Bariden. "Some members of our group insisted that you be removed immediately from this kingdom, told that you would *not* be permitted to take over, and then sent on your way. Those of us who thought we knew you best disagreed, insisting that you *had* no intention of taking over, and where in the worlds would you be sent on your way *to*? Another, smaller segment had a suggestion there, one that quieted us all and made us think. But before we came to any definite decisions, Addadain stepped forward with his own problem, and described how it impinged on ours. Addadain, would you be so good as to continue?"

The small, frail-looking sorcerer stirred in his chair, but made no attempt to get up as Tramfeor had. Bariden noticed that Chalaine also stirred, but he didn't reach out a hand to her as he wanted to. What Tramfeor had said about his being such a problem—he'd had absolutely no idea, and now that he did, he wasn't sure how he should feel . . .

"My part of the story starts years ago too," Addadain began, his mild gray gaze on Chalaine. "I was asked to make the acquaintance of a young visitor to Conclave, a girl who came on a regular basis but who rarely mingled. Before I approached her I was told a few things, and what I heard I didn't like. The girl had lost her parents at an early age, both of whom had been Sighted. But her mother had been the first in her line to *be* Sighted, and therefore had a large mundane fortune from her family. For that reason the mother's cousins claimed immediate custody of the girl, greasing their way through the courts with gold. They had their eye on increasing their fading wealth by taking control of the girl's fortune, the only way some unSighted find it possible to prosper. When the girl's father's people found out what had happened, they tried to make arrangements through Conclave to have the girl fostered with one of them. The cousins, however, visions of gold and property dazzling them, refused to even consider the idea."

"And they also never told me anyone had made the offer," Chalaine put in, anger in her voice. "Not even after they found out my mother had protected me from being robbed blind."

"Yes, a nasty, vindictive lot," Addadain agreed, his gray eyes sharing her anger. "And we, being bound by our own rules, were forbidden to interfere—at least overtly. Privately we made sure you had someone capable to begin your training in magic, but it wasn't possible to protect you from the venom of those who blamed *you* for *their* poor planning and jealousy. Isn't it too bad their nastiness produced a result that turned around and bit them."

Addadain grinned, enjoying the thought of whatever he referred to, but Chalaine stiffened in silence. She wasn't happy about whatever had happened, but Bariden could see that Addadain hadn't noticed.

"The result I'm talking about was the stimulation of a rare—offshoot talent, I suppose you could call it—in their victim," Addadain said to his audience with a measure of quiet satisfaction. "I think everyone here is familiar with the concept of an accident-prone, someone who falls into every accident and mishap that comes past. The young girl's offshoot talent was to bring out that condition in others, so that if someone slipped on a wet floor, say, they didn't simply recover their balance or fall down. In trying to recover their balance, their windmilling arms would knock down treasured vases or lamps, or send an expensive, carefully prepared meal to splatter on the floor, or ruin the balance of someone standing next to them. If they fell there was usually a cascade of things that went with them, and the fall itself was both painful and embarrassing. The girl's guardians took as much of that as they could, then agreed to let her go to Conclave just to get her out of range for a while.

"And that should have helped immensely, but it didn't," Addadain said, borrowing one of Tramfeor's sighs. "At Conclave the girl discovered that Sighted were even more susceptible to her talent than mundanes, and also that she had no real control over when the talent exercised itself. She even began to learn Hellfire combat, and there was never a problem. But just let someone pass a joking remark, and there was a good chance that someone would *not* make it away from Conclave undamaged. It didn't happen every time, mind you, but at least as often as not."

Now Chalaine was staring down at her hands, a slender, unmoving figure carved out of misery. So that was what she'd been worried about, Bariden realized, the terrible threat she'd been trying to warn him against. He reached out a hand to stroke her hair, forcing himself not to say anything. The wrong words could only make things worse, and he didn't yet know what the right ones were.

"And, of course, since gold attracts gold but problems attract complications, there was another dimension soon added to the trouble," Addadain continued. "The girl became a pretty young woman, and the young men at Conclave quickly noticed. The unfortunate part about *that* was the young lady's seeming air of helplessness and vulnerability, which made the young men react in one of two ways. Either they tried to take advantage of her innocence, or they immediately became concerned and protective. With two reactions one should have been better than the other, but in this case one was *as bad* as the other.

"To begin with, our young lady's background had left her neither innocent *nor* helpless. Those who tried to take advantage of her learned that rather quickly, and I don't think I have to go into details about what happened to most of them. But most of those who tried to be overly protective met a similar fate. Our young lady had developed a strong attitude of independence, and being smothered was something she couldn't accept. For a short while you wouldn't believe what a disaster area Conclave turned into . . ."

Addadain shook his head, not in the least amused, and Tramfeor apparently shared the feeling. They both must have been there to see it, Bariden thought, and that's why they know it wasn't something to laugh at.

"Well, the ripples in probability caused by the young lady's talent had to be allowed to settle down, so I arranged for her to study with Haddil," Addadain went on. "It was something she had already decided on for herself, having once met Haddil at Conclave. It was time for her to change teachers anyway, and the greatest benefit to the arrangement was that Haddil did his teaching here, in King Agilar's palace. The young lady would finally get away from the family she'd been forced to live with, and would also attend Conclave only when her study schedule permitted it. It seemed ideal, and Haddil jumped at the chance to take her on. Haddil, it's now your turn."

"Obviously," Master Haddil agreed, still comfortable. "When I heard about Chalaine's unusual talent I wanted to study it, and when I finally met her to talk to for longer than five minutes, I also wanted to teach her. She obviously had a large amount of potential, and was not only willing, but eager to train it. She was nervous when I interviewed her and just short of unsure of herself, and I decided on the spot to do nothing to calm her. I wanted to see her special talent come into play, you understand, and so couldn't afford to become friendly with her. That might have inhibited the talent, and I was confident I could protect myself from any overly serious consequences. After all, I *was* a wizard, and Addadain seemed to have no trouble coping . . ."

Master Haddil's expression had turned wry, causing Addadain and Tramfeor to chuckle. So it hadn't been as easy as he'd expected . . .

"No, Prince Bariden, it *wasn't* as easy as I expected it to be," Master Haddil confirmed, reading Bariden's expression. "I hadn't known, for instance, that Addadain had been chosen to comfort and companion the girl because he seemed to have a resistance to that sort of thing. And he and Chalaine had grown close, an added factor in the matter of his protection. I had neither of those two factors working for me, and I'll never forget the time I first encountered the talent I wanted to study—head-on. And if you laugh out loud, Chalaine, you have my solemn promise that I'll turn you into the ever-popular frog. An orange and purple frog."

"Oh, be a sport, Haddil," Tramfeor urged while Addadain laughed and Chalaine choked trying not to. "I never heard that story, and I'm certain Bariden hasn't either. How about you, Your Majesty? Did you hear anything about it?"

"I'm afraid I saw the results, and I'd really dislike being turned into a frog," King Agilar said as he fought not to grin. "It might be best if we dropped the subject and moved on."

"Just remember what curiosity did to the cat," Master Haddil warned Tramfeor, more than a little amused himself. "Oh, all right. It was the most unbelievable thing, and I was totally unprepared. We have a really great artist living in this kingdom, and she'd asked me to do her a favor. She'd come across paints on an artifact from a dead world, and was so taken by them that she was desperate to try them in her work. She promised to pay me with a painting of my own if I examined the composition of the paints and made some for her, so I gladly agreed. I already had one of her paintings and treasured it . . .

"Well, I'm sure you can guess what happened. I examined the paint and produced buckets of every shade I could See or extrapolate, completely forgetting that I'd scolded Chalaine that morning for being less than perfect in a lesson. The scolding had been deliberately severe and unjust because I hadn't seen hide nor hair of the talent I wanted to study, and I was growing impatient. Did I mention that the paints were indelible dyes of the consistency of glue, that while I was working I was brought the four large, very delicate feather pillows the queen wanted me to reinforce with magic, and that the messengers bringing the pillows didn't know they were opening my workroom door to Princess Efria's four cats who were being chased by Prince Trayden's two wolfhounds?"

"No, oh, no," Tramfeor begged, holding up both hands as he laughed so hard the tears flowed down his face. "Please, no more! I can't stand it!"

"I think I did hear something about that," Bariden remarked, privately delighted that Chalaine had gotten even for being treated unfairly in such an—interesting— way. "Everyone wondered why you didn't simply banish the mess, and so did I."

"Banishing isn't very easy when your mouth is full of feathers, your hands are glued to your worktable, and there's bedlam raging all around," Master Haddil answered dryly. "I was covered head to toe with paint and feathers, and the messengers were completely involved with trying to chase the dogs and cats out of my workroom. If King Agilar hadn't happened by, wondered what the uproar was about, then had the good sense to send for my most senior apprentice . . . Well, as I say, I'll never forget the time."

"Bariden happened to be away from the palace that day, attending some sort of mock battle the kingdom's troops were staging," Addadain put in, his eyes sparkling. "I remember we eventually checked up on that, just to be absolutely certain."

"Certain of what?" Bariden asked, feeling confused. "You didn't think I was involved in that? Not that it wouldn't have been a classic case of comeuppance . . ."

"Now, now, Your Highness, I paid for my mistake," Master Haddil scolded mildly. "The last thing I need is for you to feel *you* must avenge the injustice done your lady. And as for the thing we wanted to be certain of, that's a very important part of the story. You see, Chalaine's talent reached me a number of times over the years, and although only the first instance was so very spectacular, there was no doubt about the other times. I conferred with Addadain on a regular basis, and almost by accident we discovered the one thing those few but definite instances had in common: every time, for one reason or another, you were gone from the palace."

"What could that possibly have had to do with it?" Bariden asked, exchanging a confused glance with Chalaine. "We didn't even know each other at the time, so it has to be a case of incredible coincidence."

"It wasn't," Tramfeor stated. "They found out because I'd stopped by to speak with Haddil about you, and I had a list of your activities over the past year supplied by ReSayne. I wanted to be sure Haddil realized how infrequently you left the palace, but seeing the dates made him realize something else entirely. He kept complete records of his incidents with Chalaine's talent, and the two lists matched exactly. The only times he had trouble were those times you were away from the palace."

"But—that doesn't make any sense," Chalaine protested while Bariden simply stared. "Even Addadain was affected once or twice, and if he hadn't convinced me he firmly believed I wasn't responsible—Are you saying you think Bariden somehow—cancels out the effect I have on people?"

"There's no doubt about it," Addadain reassured her with a smile. "Haddil and I conducted a few experiments, and the point was proven conclusively. As long as Bariden is around, no one has to worry about accidents."

"Ha, you see?" Bariden told her, really delighted now. "I knew you were wrong when you used that sphere-of-water example to prove how dangerous it is for me to be around you. Don't you remember that you yourself said Master Haddil staged the incident? Since you can't have it both ways, and I happen to believe what you said about Master Haddil, they're telling us the truth. As long as I'm around, you don't have to worry about causing people problems."

"But that isn't entirely true," Chalaine said, frowning in disagreement. "I distinctly remember seeing that miserable talent work while we were still in the trap. It was in that last world, when I used a bow while you went after those six swordsmen by yourself. Or didn't you notice that two arrows knocked four of them out of play almost immediately?"

"Yes, I noticed, but I was too relieved to worry about it," Bariden admitted with his own frown. "You like to think something like that will happen if you're badly outnumbered, but it rarely does. When it not only happened but actually saved my life, I refused to ask the gift to open its mouth."

"Why didn't someone tell me that happened?" Master Haddil suddenly demanded of Tramfeor and Addadain. "That's absolutely marvelous! Don't you understand what it means? It means that instead of completely canceling out the ability, Prince Bariden may be holding it still long enough for Chalaine to begin to exert control over it! If that proves to be true, it will add enormously to their assets for what they'll attempt."

"Haddil, they haven't agreed to attempt anything yet," Tramfeor warned after no more than a glance at Bariden. "Let's finish the preliminaries, and then we can get on to the rest. Really, Bariden, we aren't doing it this way just to annoy you. You first have to understand what's involved before you can make decisions."

"That isn't entirely true," Bariden felt compelled to comment in what was almost a growl. "If I become convinced we're getting a runaround, I can decide I've heard enough and ask Chalaine to leave with me. After that you might compel us to stay, but you can bet we won't go along with whatever it is you have in mind."

"And yes, it's become obvious that you do have something in mind," Chalaine said, clearly backing him up. "But if you take much longer in getting to the point, we'll be too *old* to go along with you."

"No wonder they did so well," Master Haddil commented to his brother wizards. "They immediately present a united front to opposition—All right, all right, I'm getting on with it! Now where was I? Oh yes, the discovery. Well, once we were certain Bariden could keep the worlds safe from Chalaine, we took the obvious next step. We didn't know *why* Bariden was able to do what he did, but we wanted him to do it permanently from then on. So we arranged 'accidental' meetings between the two of you, in the hope that nature would then take its course."

"But we never met," Bariden protested, then looked at Chalaine. "At least I don't remember our ever meeting. Please don't tell me I just nodded in passing and then kept going."

"If you did, then I must have done the same," Chalaine assured him, then looked back to the wizards. "Unless the meeting was a disaster, and you made us forget it."

"No, there was no need to arrange for any forgetting," Master Haddil said, taking his turn at sighing. "Every single arrangement we made fell through, and you can't imagine how maddening it was. If *you* were available, Prince Bariden, something came up that kept Chalaine occupied. If *you* were available, Chalaine, Prince Bariden got caught up. At one point the two of you were a single room apart, and the combined efforts of three determined wizards were unable to bring you together. We tried again and again and again, and then Chalaine was through with her studies and left. Now that, my friends, is more than simple bad luck. Something was telling us it didn't want you two together."

"At that time," Tramfeor added hastily, undoubtedly noticing Bariden's expression. "We were so upset and confused that we went beyond Conclave to the Hidden Realm, and applied for a consultation appointment with one of the Elder Ones. We can discuss this here because the room is sealed, and King Agilar has allowed us to render him incapable of repeating anything he hears. I'm sure you two know who the Elder Ones are, even though no one ever speaks of them."

Bariden nodded as he exchanged a glance with Chalaine, seeing that she also showed agreement. All Sighted knew about the Elder Ones, but also refrained from ever discussing them. Most wizards lived a very long time and then died, but every once in a while there was a wizard who *didn't* die. He or she kept learning and learning, and one day they were admitted to the ranks of the Elder Ones. It was said quite clearly that you just had to be able to do one particular thing, and your admission was automatic. What that one thing was had never been mentioned to or by anyone, but once you reached a certain level it was supposed to be obvious.

And the Elder Ones didn't hide out, or indulge in esoteric pastimes for their inferiors to gasp at in awe. The joke of the Hidden Realm was that it was easily accessible to every Sighted, and if you wanted an appointment you put your name on a list. In a few days you were told, by messenger sphere, when to show up and at what time, and when you got there you spoke to one of the Elder Ones. It was said they looked like the most ordinary people except that they were nicer and more pleasant, but the power they must be able to wield . . . ! If the thought made a Sighted too nervous to want to consider it long, no one in the universe wanted the untalented to find out about them. Safer to start a rumor that the EverNameless were on a rampage . . .

"We were given an appointment with the Elder Ones, but we couldn't make ourselves stop fretting," Tramfeor went on. "We'd been so certain we had a solution to Chalaine's problem, even though we couldn't see how the arrangement would do Bariden any good—aside from the obvious, of course. We had to wait months, and the worst part was the message that came along with the appointment information. It said, 'Do nothing further,' and couldn't have referred to anything but the joint project we'd been working on. That meant the Elder Ones already knew all about it, and might even have their own interest in the matter."

"By the time the appointment rolled around, we were all but quivering wrecks," Addadain said with a grin, taking up the narrative. "It wasn't too farfetched to assume we'd been messing in something the Elder Ones had a finger in, and we had no idea how they would take it. The consultation room was pleasant but ordinary, and before we had a chance to sit at the table, a woman entered through another door. She was small and slender and quite lovely, and her smile put us immediately at ease."

"She wasn't *that* small," Tramfeor contributed, "but she

was definitely beautiful and very gracious."

"She wasn't small at all," Master Haddil added his own, "but she definitely had an air of artistic beauty."

"*At any rate*," Addadain recaptured the floor with the phrase, "we sat and presented our problem. We also apologized if we'd intruded in something she or one of the other Elder Ones had been involved with, but she laughed and brushed the apology aside.

" 'After all,' she said, 'how could you possibly have known? And if we can't make things go the way they should no matter *who* interferes, we don't deserve to be directing. And that's all we're doing, just directing certain scenes to make the action flow more smoothly, which will make the play a success.'

" 'Play?' I echoed. 'Are you saying we should consider life a play?'

" 'Not at all,' she returned with a smile. 'That's just a handy conceit some of us use, to make it easier to understand what we're doing. Nothing in life is inevitable, but some outcomes have a higher probability than others. And some outcomes are more beneficial to everyone, high probability or not. If you can trace an event far enough into the future, seeing its impact on everything involved with it, it's sometimes possible to know whether that event is generally good or generally bad. If you and all your confreres agree on one or the other, you might then want to make sure that event does or doesn't occur. But you never jump into the action, and you never take your eyes off the future. If something unexpected happens, and all too often it does, that can change everything.'

" 'I don't think I'd care to get involved with something that complex,' I told her, meaning every word. 'Is that what we were interfering with, a beneficial change of the future?'

" 'Oh, goodness, no,' she answered with a laugh. 'This is just a small segment of probability, a side trail that will affect only a small number of people. Ignoring the situation would move it into the mainstream and cause a few unpleasant occurrences, so we're directing the action into the best probable path. There are no guarantees of happy solutions on that path, but it does keep the major players out of mischief on the mainstream path.'

" 'How much of it are we permitted to know?' I asked, and she smiled again and told me. I think she smiled because of the way I put my question, assuming she had the right to know things I didn't. The truth of the matter, which I finally saw after thinking about the interview, is that she has the *ability* to see things I don't. If I were to develop the ability I could see them too, and 'right' doesn't enter into it anywhere."

"Which is fine for philosophical discussions, but not for explanations," Master Haddil said firmly, then looked at Bariden and Chalaine. "We were told you two may not be the best possible match for each other, but finding anything better would be harder than looking for that needle in its haystack. You'll be happy together for the rest of your lives, and so forth, but first the two of *you* needed proof about that. And you needed to show what you're made of, if you were going to have a chance at what the Elder Ones had to offer."

"And that's why we all dreamed up that little charade," Tramfeor took over. "If you two managed to get together after a start like *that*, even you would have to admit you were meant for each other. King Agilar's help was invaluable, of course, and he understands fully what's at stake. Haddil did all the dirty work, first providing victims and then scaring off most of the help he supposedly needed so desperately. You and Chalaine were guaranteed to stick with it, Bariden, so all we had to do next was toss you two into that trap."

"*Before* Chalaine discovered who the main culprit was," Master Haddil put in with a chuckle. "I went to incredible extremes in order to cover my tracks, but Chalaine *has* picked up more forensic sorcery than I've had the time for. I was very proud of you, my dear, when you reconstructed everything so neatly, then refused to let me make you feel unsure of your conclusions. The ability to figure out what's going on is all but useless without the courage to present your conclusions against opposition."

"And now we're up to that trap itself," Bariden said while Chalaine smiled wryly at Master Haddil's compliments. "If we were tossed in there to get to know each other rather than to keep us out of the way, why were all those worlds so—strange and complicated? And why more than one world to begin with? A single room with no way out and nothing to divert us would probably have gotten us together a lot sooner."

"Well, getting you together wasn't the only purpose of setting you on that circuit," Addadain admitted, smoothly picking up the next part of it. He'd called up a cup of something for himself, as had Tramfeor and Chalaine, but Master Haddil was sharing the wine that had been put in front of King Agilar by a servant before they'd started talking. Bariden considered joining Master Haddil and his father in sampling the wine, but mentally shook his head and called up coffee instead. That discussion was far from over, and something told him he couldn't afford to be anything less than completely alert.

"And we had nothing to do with creating or accessing those worlds," Addadain continued. "That part of it was arranged by the Elder Ones, for purposes we don't completely understand. The arrangement tested you in some way, tested each of you individually as well as together, and we had no way of judging good from better. All we could do was supply one of us to help out."

"And that one was ReSayne," Bariden said, then enjoyed seeing their surprise, including the fiend's. The green eyes in the section of carpeting had been following the narration closely, and now rose up into the air surrounded by gray-blue smoke.

"How in the worlds did you know that?" ReSayne demanded, one step short of outraged. "My performances were perfect, and even the Elder Ones said so!"

"Your performances and *transformations* were perfect," Bariden allowed, feeling only partial amusement. "It was your ego that stuck out like a bandaged thumb, both before, during, and after the fact. You couldn't tell me what you were doing but you still wanted me to know, so you waved a bunch of clues under my nose. I still don't understand why you did it."

"I did it because we're friends, and even though the deceptions were for your own good, I didn't feel right about lying to you." ReSayne spoke quietly and without affectation, something Bariden had never seen it do before. "I've gotten to know you better than most fiends do humans, and I couldn't bring myself to betray you completely. If what I did helped ease your mind at all . . . did you figure it out before or after you came back?"

"After," Bariden answered, wondering if the fiend was finally being honest, or simply manipulating him again. "The key to it was the lame way you gave me directions to where Chalaine was after I lost her trail. All that roundabout description of the kitchens, as though a fiend would have no idea what the area was or what it was used for. Was I supposed to have forgotten that the first thing you did when I summoned you at the start of this, was criticize my eating habits? If you know enough about food that you know what should or shouldn't go with duck à l'orange, how can you not know about kitchens?"

"And what were the clues that told you ReSayne was involved in the circuit?" Addadain asked while the fiend simply looked amused.

"That part of it was very subtle," Bariden said sourly. "The first time it showed up after my summons, it was surrounded by the gaudiest clash of colors I've ever been blinded by in my life. When I mentioned that, ReSayne gave in immediately and changed itself to a chair. At the end of the conversation it promised to think up something new for the next time we met, and sure enough, when I got back it showed up in the form of a giant rose.

"That was when I realized I hadn't remembered in the trap that I could call ReSayne, and that thought triggered another. All those things, the gaudy cloud, the chair, the rose—all of them had still had two bright green eyes. We'd come across a lot of redheads in the trap, supposedly because I have a liking for redheads, but there had also been a lot of people with odd green eyes. Male and female people, different worlds and different attitudes, but still that same green. It's probably the only thing ReSayne can't change about itself."

"Damn it, I just realized something," Chalaine said angrily, glaring at the fiend. "That Lord Naesery, who showed such interest in me—Naesery is an anagram for ReSayne! I was being ardently courted by a fiend in man's clothing!"

"Ardently courted, yes, but not won over," ReSayne pointed out quickly in a soothing tone. "As a man I found you immensely attractive, Chalaine, but it was perfectly clear you felt only a moderate amount of attraction in return. When it came to competing with Bariden, there was simply no contest. If Lord Naesery had been really important to you, you wouldn't have left him behind and continued on at another man's side. Truthfully, I was glad that you did. Bariden is important to me, and therefore so is the woman meant to be his."

"And then you became Princess Tenillis, and tried your hand with me," Bariden said when it was clear Chalaine couldn't argue the fiend's point. "The Elder Ones must have made you seem Sighted, somehow, just to fit the part. You were probably also the hostler in the next-to-last world, but I don't believe I spotted you in the last one."

"That's because I wasn't in the last one," ReSayne confirmed, pleased smugness back in its voice. "You two were supposed to have been forced to leave the city after Chalaine won against you, where you would have been directed to the 'gate' leading to the next world. There was a whole string more of next worlds, but you surprised us by winning and reached the 'gate' that led to a dead end."

"So that arrangement with the female king *was* something that threw off your plans," Chalaine said, leaning forward. "But if those worlds were supplied by the Elder Ones, how did an independent character manage to show up?"

"It isn't quite that simple," Addadain put in when ReSayne looked perplexed around the eyes. "Those worlds weren't created by the Elder Ones—quite—and they never claimed to have full control of them. They could slip ReSayne in where they wanted it, and for all we know it was taking the place of real people, but—the details weren't something they felt we should know."

"But one thing we do know is that you made it to the dead-end world sooner than you were supposed to," Tramfeor said, capturing Bariden's attention. "The circuit worlds are a test course the Elder Ones use for their own purposes, and I understand that only once before did anyone think their way out of the dead end with so little to go on. A number found their way out by accident, but all the rest eventually had to be rescued. The Elder Ones were very pleased."

"So what did it win us?" Chalaine asked in a very neutral tone. "A pat on the head and an 'attaboy,' or a prearranged honeymoon in the world of our choice? And while I'm asking, what gave them the right to test us in the first place?"

"Chalaine," Master Haddil began in a warning tone, but the girl wasn't listening. She was up on her feet and staring at Addadain, apparently addressing her comments to him.

"The Elder Ones aren't gods and we aren't their followers," she said, just as though she hadn't been interrupted. "They had no more right to test us than you three had the right to decide what man I should pair up with. If life was too difficult at Conclave with me there, you had the right to ask me not to come back. You had *no* right to consider me a problem to be solved, like your own private puzzle or mystery. I sat here and listened to everything you had to say, and now I don't care to hear any more. If Bariden and I won a gold star for escaping from that trap, take my half back to the Elder Ones and tell them where I'd like them to put it."

And then she turned and was heading for the door. Bariden swallowed a squawk and jumped after her, having no idea what the problem was but not about to let her disappear again. He reached her before she made good on her getaway and pulled her into his arms, but she stood there square and blocky, as if he were a stranger accosting her on the street.

"Chalaine, what's wrong?" he asked softly, stroking her beautiful, thick hair. "If you want to get out of here we'll leave together, the way we should. Walking out on me as well as them would be—"

"A setback for their plans?" she interrupted harshly, looking up at him. "You heard everything I did, Bariden. How can you stand there and ask me what's wrong—when you should see it as clearly as I do?"

"Are you saying you think I'm not being *allowed* to see something?" he asked, her disturbance immediately arousing his suspicions again. "Tell me what it is, and if it makes no sense when it should . . ."

"Prince Bariden, please!" Addadain called from his chair. "I think I know what she's talking about, but she's wrong. If you two will just come back to your seats—"

"Think about it, Bariden," Chalaine urged, those dark eyes staring up at him intently. "They wanted us to get together, because you have some ability that puts a damper on my erratic talent. *They* wanted it, remember, and now you can tell me the reason you first got interested in me."

"Why, it was because of that Spell of Affinity—" Bariden began, then stopped when her meaning hit him. "The Spell of Affinity that *Tramfeor* taught me, and Tramfeor is one of them. But that was years ago, and their nonsense doesn't stretch back that far. Not to mention the fact that I know how I feel about you."

"Do you?" she asked, much too coolly for his peace of mind. "Or do you know how they *want* you to feel? The pleasure of winning a woman you're blindly in love with could be what *you're* getting out of the bargain, just as I'd be getting stability in my life. How long ago that spell was first given to you doesn't matter, not when they can reach you through it and not with the Elder Ones involved. I don't know what any of them are after now, but whatever it is, I'm not interested. Whether or not you are is for you to decide."

She moved out of his arms and headed for the door again, and Bariden just stood there and watched her. Could she be right, and what he felt wasn't *really* what he felt? There had been so many games played with them that they'd known nothing about . . . how many more were there that they never *would* find out about . . . ?

"Chalaine, wait," he said, stopping her with her hand on the knob. "Maybe what you suspect is true, and maybe I'm just being a fool, but—I *can* remember every step of the way from attraction to love. You're everything I've always wanted in a woman, and you're even what I didn't know I *should* want. You're the perfect companion for trouble or fun, someone who can surprise and delight me, someone I miss terribly when she isn't there. If what I'm feeling isn't real, tell me what *is* real and how I *should* be feeling. After all the time we spent together, tell me what you think it should be."

Bariden didn't hold his breath as she stood on the verge of walking out of his life forever; if she left, the pain would be so great he'd no longer have a life. He'd studied magic long enough to know what could be done with it, and it simply wasn't possible for *any* spell to make him feel like that. His love for Chalaine was as real as anything could be, and he had to make her believe that.

"Chalaine, I can't do this alone," he said to her back, her slender form motionless with indecision. "I've gotten too used to having you there to do it with me, whatever the 'it' happens to be. I know by now that you love me, so you don't have to worry about saying it. What I do need to hear, though, is that you believe in *my* love. It isn't just lust, or someone else's suggestion, or even the Elder Ones using the Spell of Affinity to reach me with magic. It's a man's true love for a woman, but it won't be anything if you don't stop looking for reasons to doubt it. Without you it's a pile of cold ashes, but it's all I'll have left if—"

He broke off as she turned and raced back into his arms, hugging him so fiercely she actually almost knocked him over. He quickly folded his own arms around her, saying a silent thank-you for any help the EverNameless might have supplied. He'd intended talking for as long as she stood there, hoping to reach through to her, but he'd been running out of what to say. Another minute and he would have started babbling and repeating himself . . .

"It's nice to see at least one of them has good sense," ReSayne's voice came, dry as usual. "You'd think a man trying to convince a woman of his good intentions would remember something important about the spell that was supposedly making him want her."

"Like what?" Bariden immediately demanded, swinging around to face the fiend without releasing Chalaine. "I swear by the Edge of Chaos, ReSayne, if you make things worse again, I'll—"

"Now, now, you can't threaten a fiend, Bariden," ReSayne scolded him primly. "It's not only unheard of, it's silly. I was just going to remind you that your Spell of Affinity found 'Tenillis' at least as attractive as Chalaine, but that didn't stop you from leaving Tenillis snuggling up to thin air while you went chasing after Chalaine. One of the things the Elder Ones wanted to know was if you would do that, and you did."

"Why would they want to know that?" Chalaine demanded, also without letting Bariden go. "What difference would it make, when all they wanted was for him to neutralize me?"

"No!" Addadain said before the fiend could answer. "That—nonsense, as Bariden correctly called it, was *our* idea, Haddil's and Tramfeor's and mine. The Elder Ones want something else, but it can only be done if you two really want to be together. They were the ones who kept you from meeting earlier, when *we* tried to arrange it, because the time was wrong. Neither of you was ready to make a commitment, not to each other, and not to something worth dedicating your lives to."

"And you wouldn't have learned anything from the test situations," Tramfeor contributed, on his feet but still near his chair. "They were testing to see not only how you handled the challenges, but whether you were capable of learning to adapt. In a very short time you both changed significantly, but more through interaction with each other than from any other cause. You supported each other up the face of the mountain, and in that way both of you reached the top."

"And I've had personal proof of that," King Agilar said gently to Bariden, only the second time he'd spoken. "Haddil cast a spell that let me watch you with your mother, and rather than being overwhelmed by outrage and hate, you felt sorry for her. It's always been my most fervent wish that you would someday understand the sickness that twisted her so cruelly, the sickness of envying her own son. She'll pay for what she's done to you by spending a very lonely old age; I'm sure you know her sickness tainted her relationship with *all* her children, and now not one of you can even *force* yourself to feel close to her."

"She may have been trying to get around that with her effort to pair me with Miralia," Bariden said, pitying the woman who had never been a real mother to him. "Miralia is another one who wants what she's told she can't have, and she must have been hoping they would grow to be close. I doubt if she realized that one of the things Miralia probably wanted was to be queen."

"Which wouldn't have happened even if you manage to make yourself a king," Tramfeor said, much too casually. "*Your* queen will need to be a very special someone, a woman who'll be able to support you in every way."

"And what's *that* supposed to mean?" Bariden asked flatly, knowing better than to believe Tramfeor was talking about his father's realm. "I have no interest in being a king, and if Chalaine had wanted to be a queen she would have said so. We don't yet know what we'll do with ourselves, but we have plenty of time to decide."

"Maybe not as much as you think," Tramfeor returned, and this time there was no apology in his manner. "You two make a more formidable pair than you realize, and the time has come for you to hear about it. There isn't much more, but we'll appreciate it if you go back to your chairs to listen."

Chalaine looked up at Bariden with silent questioning, not quite sure if walking out would be the right move, but he wasn't any *more* sure. He thought about it for a moment, and then shrugged.

"Just because we listen doesn't mean we have to agree," he pointed out. "If there's anything you don't like, say the word and we'll both be gone."

She nodded her acceptance of the arrangement, and they walked together back to the chairs. While they did, the wizards exchanged looks among themselves. They'd all wanted Bariden and Chalaine together, but hadn't anticipated the sort of team they made. Now they were in the midst of finding out, and the team might not be as easily handled as they'd expected.

"What you two have the potential of doing together is another factor that made the Elder Ones keep you apart," Tramfeor said once they were seated. "They needed to know more about it before they made any decisions about you two, and apparently investigations of that sort take time. When they finally decided to set everything in motion, that potential was the first thing they tested. Do you remember the first world, and the house where other Sighted were already trapped?"

"Of course," Chalaine answered. "They weren't doing

anything but accepting the situation, and we changed that. Did they, at least, make it back to Conclave?"

"To Conclave, and from there to the Hidden Realm to report," Tramfeor said, surprising them both. "They watched the two of you very closely, and were impressed no end. To begin with, you each noticed how attractive the members of your opposite sex were, but there was no interest beyond that even when you were encouraged to find some. That was incidental, of course, to the main point, the presence of constructs to make your lives miserable. The first thing *you* did, Bariden, was refuse to let one approach you."

"That's ridiculous," Bariden scoffed. "I didn't even know the things were around until Chalaine told me, and then we decided I wasn't visited because I wasn't warded. How could I have refused to let one approach me when I didn't even know they were there?"

"That's what the observers couldn't figure out after they tried to send you one," Tramfeor countered, folding his arms. "Each of them tried in turn, but none of them could do it. And then there was Chalaine, who did nothing to stop the thing from appearing. All *she* did was change its composition to make it vulnerable to silver."

"I did not!" Chalaine yelped, looking as shaken as Bariden felt. "I *noticed* the thing was vulnerable to silver, and simply used the fact against it. It isn't possible for Bariden and me to have done what you claim. That world had an inhibiting field backed by someone with a lot of power, so we couldn't have used magic even if we'd wanted to."

"I think you're now beginning to understand why the observers were so impressed," Tramfeor said, looking back and forth between them. "Neither of you should have been able to do anything at all, but both of you did anyway. And then, when it came to escaping from the place, you joined together and forced an entry into existence."

"We *all* forced that entry," Bariden corrected, but Tramfeor simply shook his head.

"No, the others deliberately refrained from adding their strength," he said, and Bariden wished he could disbelieve him. "They wanted to be able to study the two of you longer, but when the entry appeared they couldn't refuse to use it. One of the Elder Ones was alerted by the presence of the entry and was able to shift the two of you into the circuit worlds, otherwise you would have escaped then and there."

"Tell them about the time in the next-to-last world," Addadain suggested, while Bariden and Chalaine looked at each other in confusion. "What they did when Chalaine's hand was being burned for calling up a cup of coffee."

"Oh, yes, I almost forgot about that one," Tramfeor said with a nod of thanks to Addadain. "The wizard king of that world was putting a lot of strength into her law spells, to make sure no Sighted got away with breaking one of them. The pain and sense of being burned to cinders was supposed to have lasted for at least an hour, but you, Bariden, refused to accept that. You—somehow—linked with Chalaine despite the pain that had destroyed her control, and—somehow—ran the spell to its end. Banishing the cup Chalaine had created should have done nothing and *did* do nothing. It was the combination that accomplished its purpose, but only by achieving the impossible."

"I don't understand what any of this means," Chalaine stated evenly, but still groped toward Bariden to clutch his hand. "What, if anything, are you trying to tell us?"

"We're trying to tell you that you're not ordinary magic users, either separately or together," Addadain said slowly, taking over in a very serious tone. "The Elder Ones have some theory about the repression you both grew up with, and how it affected your abilities in unexpected ways. Mixed in is something about the fact that both of you are from relatively new lines as far as being Sighted goes, and the new isn't completely like the old lines we're familiar with. We three don't understand it ourselves, but that's why the Elder Ones were watching you. They spotted the signs early, and watched to see where they would lead you."

"That somewhere turned out to be here, listening to what we have to say," Tramfeor resumed, giving Bariden the impression he and Addadain *needed* each other's support. "The fact is you two aren't the first to develop in this way, and two of your predecessors got together to accomplish something that shouldn't have been possible. By the time the Elder Ones noticed it was too late to stop them with anything less than direct intervention, and that's one thing they won't do unless the alternative is to let the universe blow up. Anything with lesser consequences *has* to be handled by us, the superior beings people call wizards."

"Only in this instance not so superior," Addadain said, for the first time sounding bitter. "The Elder Ones told us we would be out of our depth in this problem, but we had to lose one of our number before we believed it. The problem involved more than a question of strength, and strength is all we have. You two have the more, which is why you're being asked to take this on. Your performances in the circuit worlds led the Elder Ones to believe you have a good chance against those we don't, at the very least an even chance. If you win, you'll be king and queen of a realm that very badly needs the help only you can give."

"And if we lose, we'll no longer be a potential problem to anyone," Bariden said, just to show that the point hadn't gotten past him. But the rest of it—! "As far as that goes, you people can't afford to let us stay together if we refuse to try, can you? We'd be too much of a potential threat, but not as hard to stop and separate as our—'predecessors.' We haven't been together long enough to learn everything we can do, or how to accomplish it voluntarily. If we don't agree, we'll be forced to go our separate ways."

"Yes, but you won't *know* that it's being done," Tramfeor said, refusing to avoid Bariden's gaze. "It will be as if you two had never met, and you never will meet again. We won't let you suffer if you have to refuse, but we don't want to suffer either. We can't afford to let two people like you walk around uncommitted."

"Now I know why there are *three* wizards in this room," Chalaine muttered darkly. "Someone's afraid one or two won't be enough. Giving us the choice of risking our lives or living them alone is a really lousy thing to do."

"But that's not the choice you're being given," Addadain disagreed, finally rising to come and stand beside Tramfeor. "If we have to separate you, you'll be compensated by meeting people each of you will like well enough to spend your lives with. It won't be love, but neither of you will be unhappy or alone. So that choice you mentioned is this instead: stake your lives and ability in an effort to help people who really need it while you help yourselves, or accept a life of quiet, unexciting satisfaction with no remembered regrets. The choice really is yours, and whatever decision you make won't be argued with."

Bariden saw Chalaine turn to look at him, and his expression couldn't have been as neutral as he'd been trying to make it. Her own expression showed she knew exactly what he was thinking, which caused her to blow out a small breath of resignation.

"Okay, so I'm totally outnumbered," she said. "You've already made up your mind, and you want to go for it. But just like in the trap, either we both go or neither of us does."

"Which is the way it should be," Bariden said, stroking the hand that still held his. "We're a team, and a team always acts as one. Would you really want to live the quiet life, even if we were allowed to stay together? When there are people in trouble, people only we can help? We'd be fighting for a place to turn into home, and what better thing is there to fight for?"

"Shorter hours for more pay?" she offered, but her heart wasn't really in it. "Oh, all right, you've got me again. I had a taste of the quiet life, and even the addition of congenial company wouldn't do much to change my opinion of it. Where's the dotted line where we sign our lives away?"

"Not so fast," Bariden interrupted before the three wizards broke out into cheering. "Since everyone else has conditions, I've decided to put forward one of my own. If we lose against our opponents, Chalaine, you and I won't have anything more to worry about. But if we win we get to start our own dynasty, and I want to be prepared for that. A king and his queen need to be married, and I want to see to that first thing. Do you agree, Father?"

"Absolutely," the king of *that* realm said immediately, his delighted amusement visible only in his eyes. "If you give certain women the chance, Bariden, they'll hem and haw and drive you crazy with delays. Your Chalaine strikes me as one like that, so get it put into the general contract before she develops cold feet and backs out."

"You really *are* ganging up on me," Chalaine announced indignantly, but glancing around showed her five men chuckling without the least sign of sympathy. "Well, just remember it took five of you to make it work. And no, Bariden, you don't have to say it again. I agree too."

"I was hoping you would," Bariden said with a grin as he kissed the hand he held. "I can't expect to use any talent I have against the one who helps me to have it. So, gentlemen, what happens now?"

"First we attend a wedding, and then you two leave on a rather unusual honeymoon," Tramfeor said with his own grin. "We'll try to give you some appropriate wedding gifts before you go, but the Elder Ones sent a message that they feel will do you more good. The message is, 'Get to know your neighbors.'"

"What kind of a message is that?" Chalaine asked, her distraction saying she was already thinking about it. "Chances are any neighbors of our opponents are also under their heel . . . unless they've made an alliance for some reason . . ."

"Maybe the alliance they made is with puppets, people who don't belong where they are," Bariden mused, also drawn into the question. "If that's true, there may be others around who are trying to get back what was taken from them unfairly. That would give *us* allies, and even the slightest edge is better than none. Yes, that definitely has possibilities . . ."

"You know, I'm hungry," Chalaine announced. "If we're going to think about cryptic messages, I want something to eat first. And a bath, I definitely want a bath, but first I need something to eat."

"Allow me," Master Haddil said at once, coming to join his brother wizards where they stood. "The bath you'll have to see to for yourself, but I'm prepared to create us all an incredible meal. Does anyone have anything special they'd like included?"

"How about chocolate mousse?" Chalaine asked with a lazy grin for Bariden. "I understand it's traditional for cases of ganging-up-on . . . or ought to be . . ."

"Forget it," Bariden tried to say with a growl, but found himself laughing instead. Life with Chalaine was going to be incredible, and he couldn't wait for it to start. Maybe they ought to start it right after the meal, so *he* could take care of Chalaine's bath. And with that in mind . . .

"No mousse, but what about whipped cream instead?"

The others seemed to have no idea what he meant, but once again Chalaine knew exactly. Her laugh rang out along with his, and then she leaned close.

"We'll discuss it later," she promised, brushing his lips with her own. "In *my* version of a bathing room. I think you'll like it."

Think? Bariden laughed. There was no think about it.

As soon as we finished eating Bariden excused the two of us, then dragged me off through the halls. The King called after us that he intended to see to the wedding preparations personally, and would recruit Bena to help him. I sighed as I thought about all the teasing I'd get from Bena, especially after I'd given her a hard time for matchmaking between Bariden and me. That was one point I'd *never* live long enough to hear the end of . . .

"And here we are, finally at my apartment," Bariden announced, hustling me inside and closing the door behind us. Then he muttered a spell I didn't quite catch, and turned back to look at me with a grin. "*Now* let someone try to come in to interrupt us. If they do, I guarantee they won't just be *from* the you-know-who, they'll be one of them in the flesh."

He meant the Elder Ones, of course, which immediately brought to mind thoughts of the Hidden Realm. The past days had been chock-full of hidden realms—not to mention surprises—and we still had at least one hidden realm ahead. And our hidden talents, which made us even more different than we ever would have guessed. But this time we weren't different and alone, which made all the—difference—in the worlds. Wherever we went we'd be going together, and we'd do our damnedest to make the place ours. There had been a few comments during the meal about the kingdom we'd be heading for, but no one had even come close to mentioning where it was. I wondered if any of them knew . . .

"Are you regretting your decision already?" Bariden asked, and I looked up to see that he'd guided me into his bedchamber without my noticing. Talk about your subtle hints.

"I'm trying to make myself believe that I actually promised to marry you," I answered, for the first time *really* looking him over. Thick, longish blond hair, clear, light blue eyes, shoulders wide enough to strain the cloth of his tunic, trim waist, long legs, firmly muscled arms, incredibly handsome face . . . "You must have caught me in a weak moment, when I was thinking about what nicely rounded buns you have."

"Hey, that's supposed to be *my* line," he protested indignantly, but a grin shone from his eyes. "And I'm about to come down all insulted. Is my body the only thing you want me for?"

"Absolutely," I agreed, moving close to slip my arms under his and circle that body. "You'll be nothing but a sex object to me, kept only as long as you can satisfy my depraved lusts. In a little while, two or three hundred years at most, I'll probably toss you aside for a newer model."

"You'd better make sure first that your newer model is better than average with a sword and magic," he countered, and there was a hardness to the words despite his continuing amusement. "I like to think of myself as a generous man, but the one thing you won't ever find me sharing is my woman. The point is nonnegotiable, so you'd better think about whether or not you can accept it."

"Do you *really* want me to be your woman?" I asked, feeling the strangest tingle at the idea. "I know I'm far from worthless, Bariden, but you—"

"Hey, none of that!" he interrupted to scold, locking his hands together behind my back as those blue eyes looked down at me sternly. "It's enough that I feel that way about *you*. There isn't anything I can give you that you can't get for yourself or from another man, and that includes this muffling or neutralizing I do for your special talent. Master Haddil was careful not to say it in so many words, but I'm willing to bet he believes you're already on the way to controlling that talent by yourself. All you needed me for was to start the process, and that's been done."

"But that isn't true," I protested, seeing he was serious. "What I can or can't do for myself doesn't matter. What does matter is that you *are* the only man to consider, because you're the man I love. Granted, I know a lot of men who are better looking and have much better bodies, but—"

"Hey!" he said again in outrage, but the emotion wasn't real. The beautiful smile in his eyes *was*, and that was what counted. "Do you want me to take up wife beating even before you're my wife? A woman who's about to be married shouldn't consider *any* man better than her future husband, not in any way at all. That kind of talk is completely inappropriate, and I don't want to hear it again."

"Yes, Bariden," I agreed meekly, snuggling up to him to hide my grin. "I promise you won't hear that kind of talk again."

"And I don't want you thinking it, either," he added dryly as his arms tightened deliciously, proving he was really getting to know me. "You have more deviltry in you than ten fiends and demons put together, but don't think I'll let you get away with indulging it. You'll be a good girl with me, and you'll behave yourself."

"Yes, Bariden," I said again, just as meekly, then deliberately moved in his arms. "I think you'd better let me go now. If I'm going to be a good girl, I'd better find an apartment of my own. Proper behavior is a lot easier for me when you're not around."

"You little brat," he growled, then suddenly let me go but only to scoop me up in his arms. "For that you deserve to be ravished, and I'm here to see to it. You didn't know I'm the best ravisher in the kingdom, did you? You thought I was only fair-to-middling at it, so you took a chance in the hopes of getting away with it. Now what have you got to say for yourself?"

"Oh, please, sir, please don't ravish me," I wheedled, banishing my clothes with a gesture before sliding my arms slowly around his broad neck. "I'm a poor, helpless little girl creature, and I didn't realize who I was dealing with. If you don't ravish me, I'll never do this sort of thing again."

"Well, that settles *that*," he decided aloud while I kissed his face and ear and neck, then he headed directly for his bed. "For the sake of my future married life, your fate is sealed, poor little girl creature. Ravishment, here we come."

"That's, 'poor, *helpless* little girl creature,' " I murmured, taking a moment to get rid of *his* clothes. "And how cruel you are, to ignore my pitiful pleas . . . Say, how do people manage if they *aren't* magic users? I mean, this clothes thing. Do they really have to wait while they take things off piece by piece?"

"I'll show you how it's done next time," he promised in a murmur, putting me down on the bed and immediately joining me. "With some practice and imagination, it can be a lot of fun . . . but not as much fun as you, my beloved woman. Are you sure you really do want to go through with this?"

I knew he wasn't talking about making love, so I reached up with a smile to stroke the worry out of his face.

"Yes, my love, I really do want to go through with it," I assured him with full truth. "We both need a place that's *ours*, not to mention somewhere we can find out exactly what sort of—'new' people we are, and I have a feeling that won't be all there is to it. Those worlds that they call the circuit—they weren't just arranged at random, and we were supposed to have learned something from them. If we learned the lessons well enough, we should find them of value at some point."

"*If* we learned them well enough, and if we can figure out what they were," he agreed, then leaned down to kiss me briefly. "One thing I *did* learn, though. There's a time for thinking and planning, and a time for the more important things in life. Guess which time we're up to now?"

"I can't imagine," I answered, pulling him down on top of me. "How about a teeny little hint."

He gave me more than a hint, and believe me, it wasn't teeny. The hidden realm waiting for us would have to wait a little longer, *would* wait until we took care of the more important things in life. But after that . . .

SHARON GREEN grew up in Brooklyn and discovered science fiction at the age of twelve. A voracious reader, she qualified for the school library medal, but didn't get it because the librarian disapproved of sf. ("If you want to press the point," she writes, "you *could* say that Lucky Starr, Space Ranger, got me in trouble in junior high school. It would be the literal truth.") Later, she earned her B.A. at New York University, where she got rid of an unwanted admirer by convincing him that she was from another planet.

Currently Ms. Green lives in Nashville, Tennessee, with her cats and her Atari computer. A prolific writer, she is the author of over twenty books, including *The Far Side of Forever*, the Terrilian Warrior series, *Lady Blade, Lord Fighter*, the Jalav series, and *Dawn-Song* and *Silver Princess, Golden Knight*, which are currently available from Avon Books. When she's not at her computer, she is engaging in one of her diverse hobbies: Tae Kwon Do (in which she has a purple belt), knitting, horseback riding, fencing, and archery.

RETURN TO AMBER...

THE ONE *REAL* WORLD, OF WHICH ALL OTHERS, INCLUDING EARTH, ARE BUT SHADOWS

ROGER ZELAZNY

The Triumphant conclusion of the Amber novels

PRINCE OF CHAOS 75502-5/$4.99 US/$5.99 Can

The Classic Amber Series

NINE PRINCES IN AMBER 01430-0/$4.50 US/$5.50 Can
THE GUNS OF AVALON 00083-0/$4.99 US/$5.99 Can
SIGN OF THE UNICORN 00031-9/$4.99 US/$5.99 Can
THE HAND OF OBERON 01664-8/$4.99 US/$5.99 Can
THE COURTS OF CHAOS 47175-2/$4.50 US/$5.50 Can
BLOOD OF AMBER 89636-2/$3.95 US/$4.95 Can
TRUMPS OF DOOM 89635-4/$3.95 US/$4.95 Can
SIGN OF CHAOS 89637-0/$3.95 US/$4.95 Can
KNIGHT OF SHADOWS 75501-7/$3.95 US/$4.95 Can

Four Wondrous Stories
of Adventure and Courage by
B R I A N
J A C Q U E S

BESTSELLING AUTHOR OF
THE PENDRAGON CYCLE

STEPHEN R. LAWHEAD

In a dark and ancient world,
a hero will be born to fulfill
the lost and magnificent promise of . . .

THE DRAGON KING

Book One
IN THE HALL OF THE DRAGON KING
71629-1/ $4.99 US/ $5.99 Can

Book Two
THE WARLORDS OF NIN
71630-5/ $4.99 US/ $5.99 Can

Book Three
THE SWORD AND THE FLAME
71631-3/ $4.99 US/ $5.99 Can